## BOOKS BY KATE GOLDEN

*A Dawn of Onyx*
*A Promise of Peridot*

# A PROMISE OF PERIDOT

# A PROMISE OF PERIDOT

## OF

# PERIDOT

KATE GOLDEN

BERKLEY ROMANCE
NEW YORK

BERKLEY ROMANCE
Published by Berkley
An imprint of Penguin Random House LLC
penguinrandomhouse.com

Original map design by Jack Johnson

Library of Congress Cataloging-in-Publication Data

Names: Golden, Kate, author.
Title: A promise of Peridot / Kate Golden.
Description: First edition. | New York : Berkley Romance, 2024. | Series: The sacred stones
Identifiers: LCCN 2023035708 (print) | LCCN 2023035709 (ebook) |
ISBN 9780593641927 (trade paperback) | ISBN 9780593641934 (ebook)
Subjects: LCGFT: Fantasy fiction. | Romance fiction. | Novels.
Classification: LCC PS3607.O4523 P76 2024 (print) |
LCC PS3607.O4523 (ebook) | DDC 813/.6—dc23/eng/20230814
LC record available at https://lccn.loc.gov/2023035708
LC ebook record available at https://lccn.loc.gov/2023035709

First Edition: April 2024

Printed in the United States of America
1st Printing

Book design by Daniel Brount
Interior art: Flower background © sokolova_sv/Shutterstock.com

*For my readers.*
*They're really all for you.*
*Your passion changed my life. Thank you for everything.*

A world of lighte blessed across the Stones,
A king doomed to fall at the hands of his second son.
A city turned to ash and bones,
The fallen star will mean war has once again begun.
The final Fae of full blood born at last,
Will find the Blade of the Sun inside her heart.
Father and child will meet again in war a half century past,
And with the rise of the phoenix will the final battle start.
A king who can only meet his end at her hands,
A girl who knows what she must choose,
A sacrifice made to save both troubled lands,
Without it, an entire realm will lose.
A tragedy for both full Fae, as each shall fall,
Alas it is the price to pay to save them all.

LIGEIA, THE SEER OF LUMERA, 113 YEARS AGO

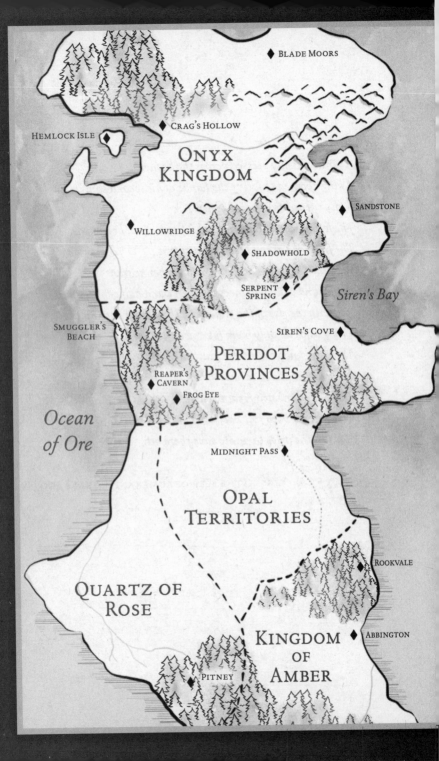

# 1

## ARWEN

I'M GOING TO BE SICK AGAIN," WARNED RYDER AS HE HUNG his head over the wet steel edge of the ship. Angry droplets of rain pelted us both as I rubbed soothing circles into the damp fabric clinging to my brother's back.

"I'm here," I said, trying to send lighte into his knotted stomach. I waited, and waited some more, until I couldn't help but tense my fingers against the void I felt where my lighte should have regenerated days ago.

Nothing.

Still nothing.

Ryder retched into the churning sea below us.

In the ten days since the battle of Siren's Bay, I had healed the entire ship of all their wounds without my power. The injuries inflicted by Lazarus's army, burns singed and gashes slashed by both lighte and Fae weapons, were more damaging to the Onyx and Peridot soldiers than any mortal steel. It had been the most taxing work I'd ever done.

And all the while, elbow-deep in bandages and sickly, fevered sweat, I tried to grieve.

We had held a small, makeshift funeral for her—the woman I had always thought was my mother. Against the rhythmic creaking of ropes and the quiet flapping of sails, the unscathed soldiers aboard had lowered her body into the sea beneath us. I said a few words, all of which felt flat and foreign in my mouth. Mari sang a hymn. Ryder cried. Leigh didn't look at any of us, and then slunk into our cabin belowdecks before we even finished.

It had been awful.

Kane had asked if he could join us. I believe his words were, *"I'd like to be there for you, if you'll let me."* As if his presence might have somehow made me feel better, instead of infinitely, *infinitely* worse. I hadn't wanted him anywhere near my family. Or what had been left of them.

Then, the storm came.

A thunderous assault of rain, with waves that sloshed against the ship like battering rams. It raged and raged throughout our entire journey. Those who sought even a minute's reprieve from stale cabin air were immediately soaked in a frigid deluge. Yesterday the captain had rationed the ship's coals, leaving us without hot water. I already couldn't stomach any more lukewarm porridge.

I looked down at my fingers on Ryder's back. They were eternally pruned, like little raisins. He heaved again, and down the bow a couple feet, a Peridot woman in a weather-beaten wool cloak followed suit.

Though I was lucky not to suffer from seasickness, the same couldn't be said for the rest of the passengers. The stomach-turning sounds of retching echoed at all hours of the day and night. I offered care to whomever I could, but without my lighte there wasn't much to do.

I hadn't offered any help to Kane, though.

I'd watched him climb a rickety set of stairs with ease a single day after being pierced through the chest by a spear of ice. He'd scaled them two at a time—nimble, strong, lively even.

And yet, he had needed me to heal him so critically that day in the Shadowhold infirmary?

All lies. More and more lies. My head swam with them.

I waited for the instinctual rush of fear to ripple through me when I thought of the fate he'd kept from me all those months. The prophecy that foretold my death at Kane's own father's hands. But I felt nothing.

I had felt nothing for days.

After a lifetime of too much fear and tears and worry—now I couldn't muster anything at all.

With one final dry heave, Ryder slumped down against the metal and sucked in a deep breath. "That has to be the last of it. There's nothing left in my stomach to vomit up."

I frowned. "A lovely mental image."

His answering smile was weak.

But in my mind a memory was unfurling. One of a slow autumn evening—silent save for the sounds of wind rustling among the weeds outside my home. I'd been sick after eating something moldy—Powell's *leave no scrap behind* mentality at work—and my mother had rubbed my back in steady sweeps, calming me as I purged. I could have healed myself then, but chose not to. I liked how it felt to have her comfort me. I liked her hand on my shoulder, her quieting words. Leigh had been born recently, and both Ryder and I missed being the sole objects of her affection.

It was such a selfish, childish thing to do. To retch for an hour rather than heal my own illness just to keep her by my side in the chilly evening air, away from her new baby, husband, and son.

But it felt so good to be cared for.

And now—

Now I fell asleep every night wondering who the woman even was.

Had she found me on the road one day?

Had someone forced her to raise me?

And if so, where in the world were my real parents? They were both full-blooded Fae, so most likely living in another realm. A melting one of parched earth and ash, governed by a tyrant—

"Feeling any better?"

My attention snapped to Mari, wandering over wrapped in a thick fur cloak. She'd raided the ship on our first night and somehow found the most fashionable pieces aboard. But even her elegant new pelt couldn't hide the way her copper hair clung in wet ringlets to her face or the icy drops that showered her nose and near-blue lips.

At the sight of her, Ryder straightened and folded his hands confidently across his chest. "Right as this rain. Barely even sick." He inclined his head toward the Peridot woman still heaving down the deck. "It's all these other folk I feel sorry for."

"He vomited the entire contents of his stomach out and then some," I said to Mari.

Ryder glared at me, and Mari gave him a compassionate frown. "Sorry to hear it. This storm is unrelenting."

"Yeah, well—" We sailed over another swell and Ryder turned pale, clutching at his stomach. "I . . . I am going to go talk to someone about that. Right now." He dashed for the other end of the ship and out of eyesight.

Mari lifted a brow at me. "Talk to someone . . . about the storm?"

I shook my head. "He's too proud."

"I think it's sweet that he's embarrassed. Here." She produced a small glass vial from her skirts. "Give him this. It's Steel of the Stomach."

"Isn't that potion used for undertakers?" After I'd read the book on flower species I got from the Peridot library twice, I had started working through Mari's grimoires out of sheer boredom. She didn't have much use for them anymore anyway. Not now that she had the amulet.

I didn't blame her. Mari never learned to wield her magic properly after her mother, the only living witch in her family, had died in childbirth. The necklace that we stole from Kane's study, the one that belonged to Briar Creighton, the supposed most powerful witch of all time, allowed her to harness her power—and quite a bit of it. Now she did magic whenever and however she pleased. And the amulet never left her neck.

Mari shrugged, pawing absently at the violet charm as it hung below her collarbone. "I figured it might help him. It was easy to brew."

The only issue was that she wasn't *actually* pulling any power from Briar or her lineage. I replayed the moment in which Kane told me the amulet was merely a trinket—that all the spells Mari cast with such ease these days were her own—and fished for guilt. I owed her the truth, but I only found a well of apathy where my ethics used to be. I didn't want to lie to her, but—

But I just didn't have the energy.

"Have you talked to Kane at all today?" she asked, gripping the slick bow as the ship pitched over another uneasy wave.

I sighed, a long and thorough noise. Another thing I couldn't bring myself to do. "No."

"What if there's another way? Hadn't he said as much?"

He had, the last time we spoke. After the battle. After my mother's death. After my outburst of power and butchery. Kane had said he was willing to let the entire continent fall to Lazarus to save me from my death sentence. To help me live my life in peace.

But what kind of "peace" could I find knowing how many would suffer at Lazarus's hands because I was holed away in some idyllic city, nameless and hiding from my fate?

"There's nothing he can help me do but run."

Mari pursed her lips. "Perhaps, but . . . He knows more about this prophecy than anyone. Can't you try to have a little hope?"

"I just need off this boat," I said, staring up into the heavy, rumbling storm clouds above.

"I know." She sighed. "This journey has been miserable."

But I wasn't thinking of the rain or the cold or the vomiting. Only getting Leigh and Ryder safely to Citrine, and myself as far from Kane as possible. Somewhere I could be alone until I was needed. A sacrificial lamb, awaiting slaughter.

So I stayed silent as the rain battered my face, searching my heart for an ache, for hope, for even a trill of fear at the thought of my horrific future.

But I found nothing.

I missed my mother.

I wanted to go home.

I wanted to sleep for a long, long time.

"Why won't anyone tell us what awaits us in Citrine?" I hadn't talked to many people the last ten days, but the lieutenants and nobles who were on the ship with us had been very tight-lipped about the secretive kingdom. All we were told was that it was impossible to breach, and therefore about as safe from Lazarus as we could get.

Mari shrugged. "All the texts I've come across just say it's hard to access. On most maps it's either floating in the middle of the Mineral Sea or left off altogether."

I let the ocean's swell rock me while Mari tightened her grip on the wet steel.

"Could it be an island? Like Jade?" The Jade Islands were an equally mysterious kingdom, but at least Mari knew some people who had traveled there and said it was uninhabited.

"Possibly. I guess we'll find out soon enough." Her eyes shone with anticipation. The discovery of something still unknown. "Do you want to go down to the mess? Have some dinner?"

I looked up at the furious sky, purple and blue and gray. Like a bruise, or a mottled pigeon's wing. Heavy, rhythmless droplets landed on my face. "No, I think I'll stay out here for a while." When she frowned, I amended my voice to sound warmer. "But I'll meet you in there." I was doing the best I could, and Mari knew it.

She flitted off with the same spritely energy she always had, rain or shine. The girl was resilient—it seemed nothing, not even the recent battle, pounding storm, or pitching ship could break her spirit.

Heavy footfalls dragged my gaze over to a group crossing the scarred deck.

I knew those boots. That walk.

Kane strode toward the galley alongside Griffin, with Leigh in tow behind them.

The weakest flame of fury, barely a spark, lit in my chest at the sight of him.

His sable hair was wet and plastered against his forehead and the back of his neck. His eyes were ringed in gray from an obvious lack of sleep. A scratchy-looking beard covered his jaw, and he had a swollen face from days and nights of too much drink.

The man was a disheveled mess.

Often I'd hear him, Griffin, and Amelia drinking together into the late hours of the night through the thin walls of my cabin. Laughing, playing cards, singing poorly—any part of me that flared up in vague jealousy at Kane and Amelia's drunken joy I attributed to muscle memory. Sometimes, Mari and Ryder would join them out of boredom. That hurt even more.

I told myself it was a benefit, to feel anything at all.

But Leigh . . . her newly developed bond with Kane had proven to be the most irritating. I would catch them sneaking into restricted sections of the ship, returning with pilfered treats and rusted treasures. I'd hear him tell her of twisted, snarling creatures from lands beyond her wildest imagination. She seemed more than a little enamored of him.

I understood the feeling.

I had been naive and gullible, too, once.

I motioned over to her with a wave. Leigh's curls bobbed against her too-large gray cloak as she said something to the hulking men who walked beside her. They looked like her guard dogs—tall and imposing and powerful. Soaked in rain and scowling. When she strode over to me and they descended down the galley steps, I exhaled.

"What are you doing with those two? They're dangerous Fae, Leigh. Not playmates."

She rolled her eyes.

My skin itched. "What?"

"You're being so hard on him."

She was colder, more serious these days. I understood her pain, and I was trying to be patient, but all her rage seemed directed only at me.

I crouched down to meet her eyeline. "I know you're going through an impossible time. I miss her too."

"This isn't about Mother."

"But your anger . . ." I reached for her, grasping her arm. "I think it may be coming from—"

She shook me off. "Just stop. *You're* upset about Mother. You're upset you couldn't save her." She swallowed, her eyes hard on mine. "You're upset about what you are. And you're taking it out on him."

I bit my tongue against the sting of her words.

"I know you think he's *charming*, Leigh. And you two have this odd little friendship, but he lied to me. He ruined my life." Even as I said the words, they felt hollow. Devoid of emotion. As if I were saying, *He lost my parasol.* This pitch-black emptiness tunneling inside of me was so foreign I barely recognized myself. "You're too young to understand."

The look she gave me could have frozen the sun itself. "He's barely making it through each day."

"We've listened to him sing sea shanties in the captain's quarters every night. Does he sound broken up to you?"

"He's just trying to survive, like we all are."

As if summoned, Kane climbed back out onto the deck, alone

this time, a bottle of whiskey in hand. Our gazes met instantly—I knew he could tell we had been talking about him. I folded my arms and let the ice in my veins reach my face. Kane's brows knit inward slightly before he looked away.

I turned away from him, away from Leigh, and faced out toward the bottomless expanse of uneven, inky waves. There wasn't enough room on this ship to get the hundred miles away from Kane that I needed. Leigh was right. I had been cruel. But he deserved it. Actually, he deserved far worse. He was a liar and a killer, the man who betrayed me, who *used* me. Who took the first shreds of real joy I had ever felt in my life and turned them to ash. Who broke me down until all that was left was a shell. An empty casing where a human person once lived. Barely lived, but still.

This feeling I had for him—this rage—it was easy. The easiest thing in my life, at the moment.

I'd never be able to forgive him.

So instead, I hated him.

# 2

## KANE

I WAS IN LOVE WITH HER. AND IT WAS A FUCKING NIGHTMARE. The way I felt about Arwen—pulse racing every time she spoke, eager to play with her, flirt with her, to make her laugh, make her sigh, frustrate her to the point of seeing that little pinch between her brows, always needing to pick her brain, taste her lips—it was enough to kill a man. I didn't know how anybody survived being in love. It was as crippling as I'd always feared it would be. And . . . terrifying. To never be able to get enough of her. To never be free of these feelings.

Even if somehow we both survived the battle that was brewing—which seemed nothing short of impossible—I would have to walk through the world, for the rest of my life, decade after decade, with this nagging, aching, festering love spooling around my heart and yanking it in her direction.

Worse yet, I had done the one thing I had set out to avoid doing at all costs: once again I had hurt the person who meant the most to me.

It was like a fucking curse.

The ship's pitch over yet another gut-roiling swell shifted me down the rigid wood bench and sent the cabin lantern flickering, casting Amelia and Griffin across from me in ghoulish shadow.

They looked morose.

How had I let this happen? Found the Fae I had been searching years for and fallen stupidly, miserably in love with her? Now I'd have to destroy my father some other way. One that didn't result in Arwen's . . .

I bit down on oily nausea at the thought.

I hadn't discovered an alternative in a century. And it would only be harder now that Lazarus knew who she was. He'd be looking everywhere for her. And he'd find her—inevitably he would. I could only pray to the Gods that by then we would be ready for him.

"Have you finally passed out?" Amelia waved a small, tanned hand in my face. Her voice was getting a little pitchy from all the spirits. The mortal princess rarely drank enough to keep up with Fae like Griffin and me, but tonight she and my commander were both half a bottle in.

And I was on my fourth.

I could only attribute her uncharacteristic thirst to guilt. She had lost everything in the battle of Siren's Bay. Her soldiers, her citizens, her keep—the capital of the Peridot Provinces was utterly destroyed by my father and his men. While she put on a good show, I could see vivid sorrow in her eyes every time she took a sip.

The captain's quarters, paneled in oak and spare besides a few thick flannel blankets and a rusted lantern, had become our crude tavern each night of this abysmal journey. We should have flown to Citrine like we always did—my scales icy against the storm that protected the kingdom, the static scent of lightning funneling through my nostrils—but there were too many aboard the ship to take them with us through the skies, and the few of us who had been to the capital before needed to show them how to enter the city. I slumped deeper into the creaking bench, its wooden slats digging into my shoulders.

"I said," Amelia continued, "before we arrive in Citrine, you need to get word to Dagan. So he can train the girl. Where is he?"

"He stayed in Garnet Kingdom to chase down a lead on the Blade of the Sun," I said. "I'll send a raven."

We had been there to retrieve Arwen's family.

The reminder of her mother's death seized my gut. And the little one—Leigh. The loss had already changed her, something dark and thorny taking hold, finding purchase in her grief.

"Maybe he'll come back with it?" Amelia asked, hope creeping into her voice. "The blade?"

"Doubtful, with our recent luck," mumbled Griffin.

Ah, my ever-positive commander.

Griffin and I had been through more pain, more triumph, and more liquor together than anyone in Evendell. He was more than my commander, more than my ally or my friend. I used to call him my brother. Before Yale's death.

"Come now, Griff. Don't blame our recent luck," I chided, reaching for the next bottle. "We've been terrible at finding the blade for five years now."

I knew every single hiding spot on this continent like the scales on my own wings . . . Where in the damn realm was the thing?

The ship heaved us forward again, and Amelia loosed a nauseated groan. "Hear me out. The prophecy says Arwen will find the blade 'inside her heart,' right? Let's just crack her open and see if it's there. The witch can heal her right after. Frankly, she could even heal herself."

"This joke has gotten very old, Amelia," I snarled at her. "You go near her, and I will kill you. You know that, right?"

"What if it's some kind of full-blooded Fae trick and it's been inside her all along?"

I only scowled.

"I'm serious!"

"As am I."

Amelia hiccupped. *"Infatuated idiot."*

Griffin winced with his last swig. "I'm not saying we should split Arwen open like a log, but it may be time to think outside the proverbial box."

I blamed Griffin's viciously pragmatic general father and a strict, withholding mother for his detachment from people and things. His casual well of endless patience. His lack of any sentiment—any emotion, really. In my more unfortunate moments of temper and impulse I could appreciate those qualities, but right now I wanted to bash in his even-keeled face with my boot.

"Are we running out of time?" Amelia asked.

"In one year we'll be a 'half century past' the day of the rebellion," he said. "That's when 'war is to begin again.'"

"Actually," I cut in, "the prophecy says that's when 'father and child will meet again in war.'"

"But you 'met again' just a few days ago."

True . . . But I didn't want to think about my father. I wanted to be drunker.

"I thought he'd killed you," Griffin confessed. "How did you evade him? Back at Siren's Bay?"

It was a fair question. He'd grown up with my father, too. Had seen him scorch a disobedient guard into white-hot flame or shred a rebellious noble with his own talons without so much as a frown.

Days ago my father and I were a clash of claws and fangs high above the blood-soaked Peridot sands. I knew I couldn't kill him, that nobody could, outside of Arwen with the blade in hand. But it hadn't stopped me from trying. From tearing into his soldiers and mercenaries over and over, relishing each lash and blow, regardless of who they landed on. It was the sound of her cries that had cut through my bloodlust like a hot knife through flesh.

"I heard her. When she . . ." They knew what I meant. When she destroyed everything in sight. The lighte pouring out of her with the force of a split dam, ships, creatures, weapons of her enemies burning in merciless flame across the shallow bay. A breathtaking, violent goddess of fury.

He had let me go to her. He could have annihilated me, but he hadn't. Perhaps he feared her. Or thought she might be able to kill him. But for whatever reason, he let me live. He let us both live.

"She was remarkable." It was the most complimentary thing Amelia had ever said about Arwen.

"Yes." I sipped my whiskey. "She was."

We remained silent for a while, the light from the single lantern overhead beginning to flicker toward extinguishing. I peered through the round windows behind me. Both sky and sea near pitch-black. Thick thunderclouds had blotted out the moon and stars for the third night in a row. The ferocity of the storm meant we were getting closer.

"I'm glad he didn't kill you," Amelia finally offered, sitting back in her chair and pulling her knees up to her chest.

"Bastard fathers. The only thing we've ever had in common." I lifted my bottle to hers in facetious cheers. She clinked mine once and we both drank.

"Eryx seems even more intent than usual on wedding you off to the highest bidder," Griffin said.

"Don't remind me." Amelia wrapped her white fur tighter around herself. The cold weather was especially hard on the Peridot folk. Amelia was well-traveled, as royals often were, but a childhood spent in the most tropical ecosystem on the continent meant she struggled through a slight chill. Tonight she was bundled like a puff pastry, her warm bronze skin a constant contrast to that severe, stark white hair. "Being a chess piece in your father's political game isn't all it's cracked up to be."

"Did you ever discuss your court position with him?" I asked.

Amelia hoped orchestrating the wartime alliance between Peridot and Onyx might prove her use as more than a human bargaining chip.

"He said he'd marry me himself if he thought it would 'benefit the Provinces.'"

Griffin coughed. "That's sick."

"At least our kingdom's pillaging has briefly taken his mind off my vacant ring finger."

"No bidders?" I teased.

"You did, once," she snipped.

Amelia had an arresting sort of beauty, but looking at her now, I couldn't imagine how I had slept with her so many times.

It hadn't been bad. We were friends, so there had been a comfort, a familiarity, when we finally fucked. But now . . . Now I couldn't fathom bedding anyone but Arwen.

Lightning colored the cabin in a flash of pale blue before a smack of forceful thunder rocked the sea.

Just a few hours now, I guessed.

"When we arrive . . ." I trailed off. I wasn't sure what exactly we were walking into with Citrine. My standing with the kingdom was . . . tense. At best.

"I know," Griffin said anyway.

"Oh, no . . . What did you two idiots do?"

"What will you say to them?" Griffin asked, ignoring her.

I scratched at my stubble. "I'll come up with something."

"Hello." Amelia waved at us both. "What happened?" She was beyond drunk now and needed to be put to bed.

"If we have to enter the city," Griffin continued, disregarding her question again, "we should finally pay Crawford a visit."

It wasn't a bad idea. We hadn't ever interrogated the noble regarding the blade, as it went missing from my kingdom's vault about a year after I was banished from Citrine. My spies had kept an eye on him, though, and his renowned stash of unique and rare objects. "If he had acquired the blade for his hoard, we would have known."

"What if he only has information?"

"Citrine won't help facilitate an audience with him."

"Well, they better at least offer refuge to the people on this ship," Amelia said. "They're innocents."

I had no idea if they would. But it would be the least of our asks. "We'll also need their mermagic."

"And their army," added Griffin.

"Right," Amelia slurred. "Because mine was destroyed by demonic Fae soldiers. You know," she said, raising her bottle as she pointed at me, "I actually tried to save her."

My eyes cut to hers as she took a gulp and thumped the glass back down onto the table. "How so?"

Amelia hiccupped. "I told her, back in Siren's Cove, that you were full of it. Using her. I would have wanted someone to tell me."

Something putrid rose in my throat at her words.

*She's right. You're reprehensible.*

It was even worse hearing someone else say it.

"But the girl was over the moon for you. She didn't listen to a word."

Amelia had intended to help Arwen, and now was more than willing to slice her in half to find the blade? "What changed for you?"

Amelia took one final swig and tossed the empty bottle into the depths of the captain's quarters. The sound of shattering glass didn't elicit as much as a blink from any of us. "Now my kingdom is in the hands of scum, my men are dead, and my capital's sacked. So we do what we have to."

The lantern above her pale white head had nearly winked out with the last swell. It sputtered for its life now, casting the cabin in jarring cuts of yellow light.

"We'll have to be careful with Arwen when we arrive," I said. "Now that Lazarus knows her name, what she looks like . . . he'll have everyone in Garnet, Amber, and Peridot looking for her. Soon, the entire continent." I ran a hand down my face. Keeping her safe was going to be an impossible task. "Nobody in Citrine can know who she is."

"We'll say she's our healer," offered Griffin. "It's true."

"For now," Amelia hedged. "But, Kane . . ."

I knew where this was going, and I didn't want to hear it. Not tonight.

Griffin saved me the argument. "Another time."

"Fine," she huffed, standing up with a wobble. "But we do have to talk about it eventually."

"I'm not sure he can."

"Oh, come on." Amelia turned to me, hands splayed on the table to keep her upright. When I didn't argue with Griffin, her eyes widened. "Kane's a little obsessed with the pretty Fae girl, sure. But nothing could stop him from taking down his father. Freeing the people of Lumera. Freeing *our* kingdoms, *our* continent. Right?"

Griffin didn't say anything but glanced in my direction.

*"Right?"* Amelia asked me this time, incensed.

"Right." I gave a bland smile. It didn't matter what she thought. I had made my choice months ago, and would see it through one way or another.

Momentarily appeased, she teetered toward the hallway. "Good. I'm going to bed."

I finished my bottle, as did Griffin, in grateful silence.

The first few lazy, soft rays of sun had begun to glint off the unruly ocean waves and filter into the cabin. My mouth was dry, I was properly drunk, and my stomach was starting to sour. I stood on weightless legs and staggered for the hallway. "I need to piss."

There was no early sunlight in the shadowed hall, but Arwen's cabin door jeered at me from the other end.

I wondered what she was dreaming of. Perhaps lilies. Or that grassy knoll outside her home in Abbington. Even though I reviled Amber, I itched to go there with her. I wanted to touch every single thing she had ever touched. Roll in the grass she had once lain on. I was like a dog with a scent. I wanted to bathe in her.

A petite body slammed into mine in the shadows, and I

steadied my hands on slim shoulders. Arwen, who always smelled like orange blossoms and honeysuckle. I hadn't touched her in days. The contact made my mouth water.

I wrapped my hands tighter around those delicate shoulders for balance. The journey had shrunk her already slender frame. I was practically grasping shoulder blades. Covered in little freckles, like spots on a deer.

"Excuse me," she said.

"You're excused."

"You're wasted." She wrenched free of my grip, and I stumbled a bit with the release and the swell of the ship. She opened her mouth to chastise me, her adorable, pouting mouth and furrowed brow dead giveaways of an incoming reprimand—but the ship rocked and she crashed awkwardly into me once more.

"Easy there." I held her by the middle as the ground danced beneath us, frenetic and jerking, and Arwen gripped my chest as we braced through the tumult. I grazed her hip with my thumb. To stabilize her, I told myself. To keep her from falling.

"Stop that," she snapped, steadying her hand against the wall beside me as another wave teetered us.

*She's right. Inappropriate.*

The ship threw her chin into my sternum. My head was killing me. "I should never have made a move on you in the first place."

A swaying lantern at the end of the hall cast her face in shafts of dim light. Insult bloomed in her olive eyes. Or was that regret? Pain? Whatever it was, I was too inebriated to tell. Clearly I couldn't say the right thing sober, let alone trashed. "I just mean," I tried again, "I knew what was coming. I shouldn't have let us—"

"I know what you mean."

I could feel her little heart racing. She was looking at me like—

That *face*—

Battles had been started over less. Wars.

The ship came to a lurching halt and we untangled from each other, despite all internal alarm bells that blared for me to do otherwise. The exact opposite, in fact. To bind her to me—even if she kicked and screamed—and take off through the sunrise. To leave this war, this prophecy, this revenge to the rest of them, and show Arwen the world. Show her me, for better or worse. Wring her forgiveness from her lips through days and weeks spent alternating between groveling and pleasuring her. I was a simple man—that approach would have worked for me. Perhaps she, too, could be swayed.

I stumbled back toward the captain's quarters instead, nearly losing my balance and introducing my face to the slick, wet floor. Eyes firm on my shoes until a displeased sigh sent them up. Griffin, opening the door at the ship's halting.

He regarded us at opposite ends of the passageway. Surely we both looked guilty, though I couldn't think what of. I bit back a smile at the ridiculousness of it all. How absurdly, vastly out of hand I had let everything get. Arwen must have misunderstood my expression because she huffed like a furious horse.

Griffin shook his head at us both. "We're here."

# 3

⁕

## ARWEN

I TOOK GRIFFIN'S FROWN AS MY CUE TO LEAVE AND scampered up the wooden steps to the deck in record time. My shoulders and waist still blazed with the memory of Kane's large, warm hands. That had been too close—too charged. I inhaled to relax the tightness in my body. Thank the Stones he was so drunk. It was easy to ignore his sensual charm, his roguish charisma, when he couldn't even speak without slurring.

Well, easier, at least.

I pushed through sturdy oak doors and unexpected sunlight washed over my face. The rays tingled on my skin and brought back memories of Onyx—cut grass, white butterflies, cicadas chirping. I'd almost forgotten in our near ten days straight of torrential downpour that it was still summertime.

Time was still passing, the world still turning, despite my mother's death. Despite all we had lost. All I had done.

That sunlight was like liquid gold dripping down the towering masts as they climbed toward the sky. It should have pulled my lips into a smile. I thought of my mother, and how she would feel seeing me frown up at the sun.

But the bath of light only reminded me of all the lives I had taken in my rage, in my unchecked display of power. Flashes of dripping red and cracks of bone sang in my ears, and I felt more seasick than I had when the ship had been tossed like a piece of driftwood among the waves.

Eventually, more passengers made their way on deck, too. Some offered me a wide berth, scattering toward the ship's railings or crowding beneath the billowing sails. Those who had witnessed my power weren't eager to be near me, and I didn't blame them.

But others were just thrilled to witness the storm's clearing, and their chatter pulled my mind free from its tangled, gory web. Even Amelia, who looked pretty sloshed herself, was sporting a rare grin and turning her tanned face to the skies above.

I swore Griffin had said we'd arrived, but there was no land in any direction. I crossed to the other side of the ship to double-check, but we were anchored in the middle of a vast blue ocean—nothing but rippling waves and the occasional seagull high in the air above.

"Holy Stones, it's over!" Mari cheered as she approached.

Ryder followed close behind, as he had the entire journey. He was a terrible flirt, and Ryder's latest infatuation seemed to be my only friend. After a lifetime of sharing everyone with my more charismatic brother, I expected it to bother me, but instead I found a vacant well where my jealousy used to grow. There was, however, someone else on board who bristled against Ryder's interest in Mari.

"Witch," Griffin said to her by way of greeting as he buckled his black leather armor across his chest. "The king requires your assistance." His expression was serious—nothing new there—but he was fidgeting. Fixing his chest plate, tugging at his collar.

I'd never seen him do that before.

"Come on, man," Ryder chided. "You know her name."

"It's better than calling her *red*," Griffin said, gaze so murderous *I* nearly cowered.

But Ryder only grinned and glanced sidelong at Mari. "That's just a term of endearment," he said, twisting one lock of her bright, bouncy hair around his finger and giving it a playful tug. "She knows I respect her enough to call her Mari. Don't you, Red?"

I couldn't help but peer over at Griffin. His glare said he was weighing the ramifications of ripping Ryder's finger clean off and chucking it into the ocean behind us.

I tried to offer him a warm expression. I wasn't sure if he liked me more now that boundless grief had made me sullen or if I liked him more because he never required a phony smile or false cheer. Either way, the new dynamic suited us just fine.

Mari, meanwhile, gave Ryder an easy smile but didn't blush. She was a bit aloof in that way—one of her more unexpected qualities. Men were always interested in her, and she was rarely interested in them unless they had an academic text to offer. While I knew it stemmed less from lack of interest and more from self-preservation—a childhood at the mercy of bullies had taught her to steer clear of men altogether—to outsiders like Ryder, it made her appear confident. Unattainable. The only time I had seen her falter was that bizarre dinner with Griffin outside Serpent Spring, which, try as I might, she was never interested in speaking of again.

"All right," I cut in, sparing all of us more of the strange pissing contest. "Griffin, we'll follow you."

Griffin exhaled in a short burst and we trailed him over to a crowd that had gathered beneath King Eryx. The now-ousted king of the Peridot Provinces stood below the rigging, backed by a crisp blue horizon we could finally see, now that the storm had abated. He rubbed his potbelly absently, looking out over his new, nautical dominion with pride. His waxy, thinning white hair, the same hue as his daughter's, rustled in the sea breeze.

We pushed through the crowd, stopping alongside Barney, who stood beside . . . Kane and Leigh. *Of course.* My stomach soured.

He was showing her his sword's pommel, the sun glinting off the shiny metal and across Leigh's wide eyes. I wanted to cut in, quip something about weapons and their place around children, but it had been days since I had seen Leigh look so interested in anything. Despite his horrible judgment when it came to me, he was . . . good with her.

"Finally, a beautiful day," Barney said beside me, eyes trained on the taut white canvas above our heads, bald head glinting. "This is what sailing should always feel like."

Barney was a delight, and he and Mari alone had accounted for any joy *anyone* on this voyage had experienced. I tried to smile at him. "Have you been to Citrine before?"

"Never. I've only heard great things, though. Some of the kingsguard went with his majesty once and said it changed their lives."

Thank the Stones. I was ready for exactly such an experience. Maybe I'd be like Mari and dedicate my life to seeing and learning new things. Well, what was left of it.

*Ugh.*

My own self-pity was making me nauseous.

*Sunny day, sunny Arwen. Pull it together.*

"It has been a dreary journey." King Eryx's booming voice silenced the tittering crowd. "But the misery has finally come to an end. I have led us to the safest kingdom in all of Evendell." The passengers, still finding their spots before him, murmured their relief at Eryx's words. One overzealous man clapped, and Eryx's grin radiated faux humility.

I fought the urge to roll my eyes.

Eryx continued to address the rain-battered passengers, but Kane's snicker pulled my attention to where Leigh was peering up at him, a mischievous grin across her face. I couldn't help turning to Barney to say, "Don't you think drunk older men shouldn't gossip with ten-year-old girls?"

Barney blanched, looking from me to his king and back. I must've been louder than I intended, as Leigh turned about thirty shades of red before slipping away from us all and deeper into the crowd. I moved after her, but Kane's warm hand encircled my arm and I felt my skin heat with the contact. I ripped free from his grasp.

"Look what you've done," he tutted at me under his breath. "You've embarrassed the little one."

I peered up at him, my glare venomous, only to see the fresh air blowing his hair around his face and sunlight glinting off his silver rings. He looked calm, actually. He released me and tucked the hand into his pocket. "And I'm not drunk . . . anymore."

"That's not possible."

"Shh!" A stone-faced woman whirled around and scolded us before turning her attention back to Eryx.

Shame warmed my cheeks and cooled my rage. I tried to focus on Eryx, who was gesticulating wildly as he spoke about his long and storied allyship with Citrine.

"Your witchy friend brewed me a sobering potion yesterday." Kane interrupted my focus, voice low and velvety. "Will you thank her for me?"

If I had been in a storybook, steam might have billowed out of my ears. He knew how much their camaraderie bothered me, and I could see the pleasure he took in my frustration written plainly across his face. Smug, irritating, lying, piece of—

"And for what it's worth—" His voice was close to my ear now as he bent toward me to whisper, his cedar and whiskey scent like a rush to my senses. "I spend time with Leigh because she's lonely. She needs someone to take care of her."

I didn't bother to fix my livid expression. "I am taking care of her *just fine*."

Our tense silence allowed Eryx's words to drag my focus back. "After many years apart, my dear friend King Broderick will welcome us warmly, I'm sure of it. We need only take a few precautions beforehand to enter the capital city of Azurine."

Ryder spoke up, gesturing to the whipping, open water surrounding the ship. "Enter? I'm sorry, Your Majesty, but there's nothing for miles."

I, too, scanned the sea around us. He was right, but there was no terror, no unease settling in my belly. The other passengers, however, erupted in murmurs of concern. Eryx's beefy kingsguard stiffened slightly at the unrest breaking out across the deck, and the reddening king raised a single hand to quiet them. I couldn't help looking to Kane, who only smirked, one dimple indenting his scruffy cheek.

"The Kingdom of Citrine is not visible to the naked eye," Eryx said, louder now and less composed. "Because it is *below us*. Along the ocean floor."

# 4

## ARWEN

A SUNKEN CITY? WE HAD BEEN PROMISED *SAFETY*.

I gaped at Kane, but he just radiated his usual relaxed indifference, as if Eryx had simply said, *The kingdom is down the street and to the left.*

"Do not fear," Eryx advised. "Have I ever led us into danger before? These precautions I spoke of will help us cross an ocean trench road to the capital's secure beach. Luckily, I have procured for us a talented witch." My eyes fell to Mari, who smiled primly and clutched her amulet. "She need only spell each passenger to ensure they can breathe in the sea. The funnel will do the rest."

Mari, to her credit, maintained a confident grin and dipped her head in acknowledgment of the king. But I knew her well enough to clock the anxiety filling her eyes. She did not want to try and fail in front of all these people.

"Don't worry," Kane purred. "This charm is the least unpleasant. And if it fails, I've heard drowning is only a marginally agonizing way to go."

Finally, after days that felt like years of my heart being nothing but a stone in my chest, a small ripple of fear sent my blood thrumming. It was both awful and all too welcome. I didn't want to speak to Kane a moment longer, but I had to know—

"Unpleasant how?"

Something akin to sympathy flickered across his face, and this time when he answered me, his tone was a touch softer. "It's a surreal sensation, breathing water. But the funnel is quick. It's over before you realize what's happening."

"And once we get to Azurine? Does the whole kingdom breathe water?"

"No, Citrine has its own atmosphere. It's ancient magic, different from witch or Fae. Mermagic that has kept Citrine safe for thousands of years. The kingdom has never been breached."

I nodded despite the shiver that skittered down my spine. I didn't like the idea of being unable to breathe air. My palms were starting to sweat. When I felt Kane's large hand on the small of my back, stroking in little, soothing circles, I went rigid.

"What are you doing?"

For the first time I could recall, Kane appeared at a loss for words. He dropped his hand and swallowed hard. "I thought—you seemed—"

"Don't touch me."

When Kane didn't respond, I looked past Barney to Mari. "How hard will this one be?"

"Not hard at all," she said, still rubbing her amulet. She might've said more, but her eyes widened and she swiftly tucked the necklace into her buttoned linen collar. Ryder raised a brow, no longer listening to Eryx, and instead eyeing our exchange. I followed Mari's eyeline and found Kane staring at all three of us.

"Mari," I admitted. "He knows."

Mari's cheeks flushed pink. "I'm so sorry, King Ravenwood. It—"

"The amulet suits you far better than it ever did me." Mari's answering laugh was more of a sigh of relief. "I will tell you, though," he began, leaning closer to us both. My heart sank. He couldn't tell her now, not before—

"Briar will be very jealous if she ever learns I gave her prized amulet to another woman. And another beautiful witch at that. Let's keep it our little secret, yes?"

Mari nodded her understanding and I breathed out, slow and even.

"Please align yourselves in front of the young witch," Eryx instructed the passengers.

I plastered a smile on and faced Mari. "Good luck."

WITH MARI'S HAND ON MY CHEST, THE MAGIC SWIRLED around us, kicking up my hair and my skirts, kissing my skin, earth and moss scenting the air, until it was over, as quickly as it began.

I didn't feel any different. I scanned my body and was fairly certain I looked the same, too. The rest of the passengers Mari had spelled were guided by Eryx's guards into the ocean, but I stepped aside to wait for Leigh.

Griffin was next. Mari stood at least a foot shorter than him, but still held a confident palm against his chest. She chanted low, eyes closed, wild flamelike hair breezing around her face, while Griffin's jaw held firm, his hands tucked tightly behind his back. He looked anywhere but at Mari, though his cheeks had gone a little pink.

When she was done, Griffin stepped to the side, rubbing distractedly at his chest where her hand had been.

Leigh went next, and after, we stepped onto the plank.

"Dive for the funnel," a guard instructed us. "It's three feet down. Once in, swim hard and try to run when you see land."

"Run?" asked Leigh. "Run how?"

But he was already giving the same brusque directives to the passengers behind us.

Cold, salty air stung my face as we walked across the plank they had affixed to the stern, and I stared down at the churning waves below, freezing and deep, with foamy little caps sloshing against one another.

Fear was beginning to distort my vision. Maybe Leigh and I could just keep sailing. Take this ship and sail and sail and never return.

"Ready?" Leigh's voice punched through my dread.

We gulped in twin gasps of air before jumping from the platform.

Before I hit the water, one singular image flashed in my mind—

My mother's face, devoid of life.

My brain felt the cold before my body. So much colder—I knew it was *so* much colder than I had been expecting. Only moments later did my limbs feel the stabbing sharpness of being enveloped by a biting, bitter sea. I tried to calm my panicky heart—to shake the strange, intrusive memory of my mother. We had to swim. Despite the sting of salt in my eyes and the chattering of my teeth, I pushed Leigh forward.

The ocean was blurry and endlessly deep, but I could see the open mouth of the funnel below us, like a blown-glass vase, opening wide and growing slimmer. We swam toward it without looking back.

The first twinge of the need to breathe rapped at my lungs. To suck in a mouthful of air—not water—but I ignored it. Maybe I could swim the whole length of the funnel in one breath. I had been able to stay under the longest of my siblings when we were younger and played in chilly, rocky ponds.

Leigh and I swam deeper, and once we were through the mouth, the funnel carried us more forcefully down into the depths of the sea. Past schools of silver fish weaving in and out of pocked reefs of coral and porous sponge. Flatter, skinnier fish laced through emerald seaweed that swayed with the current, dusted in sparkling flecks of sand. The lower the funnel shot us, the clearer and colder the water became.

But now my lungs were on fire. I had to suck in a breath, to ease the burning, the pressure building in my chest. Leigh was the epitome of calm, watching two sea turtles pass us by, reaching to touch their marbled backs. She had to be breathing just fine. And I trusted Mari, didn't I? Still, I was terrified that gulp of air on the ship had been my last.

It didn't matter. I couldn't hold out another minute, not another second—

My lungs—

My chest *ached*.

Slowly—ever so slowly—I inhaled through my nose. The water dissolved as I breathed in pure oxygen. I tried again. A tentative mouthful of briny ocean water this time. But I was met with the same result. No matter how much water I took in, by the time it reached my lungs it had evaporated into air. I breathed deeply and swam with more confidence through the sheer tunnel of glasslike water, my limbs loosening with each inhalation.

The sea around us grew dark as ink as we dove toward the ocean floor. Pearly shells had lost the glint of the sun above, and I couldn't tell the color of the starfish or anemones that lay still in the sandy depths. We swam faster—I wasn't sure if the tunnel was only made of water, or some more protective magic, but I wasn't going to wait around and find out between the jaws of a shark.

The funnel fed us through a rocky, pitch-black cave. Finally, Leigh's fingers squeezed mine with unmistakable fear, the crescents of her nails digging into the back of my hand. I tried to squeeze back in reassurance, but we could no longer see the ship's other passengers ahead of us, and the water had grown so cold my teeth were chattering.

I wanted out now, too.

I wanted clean, real air in my lungs. My chest was trembling, from cold or alarm I couldn't tell.

We rushed through the water at a breakneck pace, so fast I realized it wasn't our swimming. It was the funnel . . . purging us. Drowning in pitch-black darkness, I could feel the pressure of it in my eardrums, pushing into my eye sockets and popping in my jaw. Leigh's hand was slipping from mine, the suction of the water tearing us from each other. I strained for her, clawed at her, sucking in strange salty air, eyes sealed shut by sheer force, choking on—

We tumbled onto a hot bed of sand with a *splat*. The grains ripped at my knees and cheeks, my dress whipped up in a frenzy, my hair a web I could barely see through.

But I sucked in a lungful of warm air.

Fresh air. *Real* air.

And the heat was dry and gentle, different from the oppressive humidity and floral breeze of Peridot—different from anything I had ever felt. Leigh had landed on top of me, her elbow implanted in my windpipe. Any fear that spiked inside me was washed away by her childlike giggle.

Knowing she was unscathed, I scooped her off me and righted myself, depositing her onto warm sand, before I spat the grains back onto the beach from where they had come. Unsatisfied, I wiped my tongue on the rough wool of my sleeve.

"Woah," Leigh breathed.

I took in the long, sandy stretch of land before me, bordered by a bustling harbor of vivid blue. Ships of every shape and size—sailboats and tugboats and dinghies—adorned the crush of turquoise waves, milling about and narrowly passing by one another. The harbor was bustling. Men and women shouted from boat to boat, lazing their feet in the water, playing instruments, dropping anchors. It was overwhelming, the sounds, the textures, the brightness, after almost two weeks on a silent, bleak ship. There were more people in this harbor alone than had been in all of Abbington.

I could scarcely wrap my mind around the fact that despite the sun shining overhead, the mountains in the distance, and the ocean that stretched beyond, we were thousands of feet below the sea. Mermagic, indeed.

When I stood, my knees were still wobbly from inertia, but Leigh had already taken off toward the shoreline to feel the crystalline water.

I didn't know why it bothered me.

Taking care of Leigh was my privilege. She was my sister, and I would take a thousand lashes for her.

And yet, I was on edge. I didn't want to have eyes on her at all times. To have to tug her back from the sandy shores, lest another unprecedented tragedy befall her. I didn't have the energy to tether her to my side, and make sure she was safe, and fed, and looked after.

*Kane was right. You're pathetic. And selfish. A pitiful excuse for a sister—*

A stinging on my leg pulled my attention downward and I lifted my skirts to see droplets of red dripping down onto the sand. I had skinned my knee in the tumble in from the funnel. I ran my fingers across the abrasion and tried once again to draw from the air and sun around me.

A glimmer—just a tingle—fizzed at my fingertips.

Thank the *Stones.*

Blessedly, my skin weaved back together, forcing out little pebbles and grains of sand that had been embedded in the flesh.

On our journey to Citrine, I had tried to do that countless times. Late at night in my cramped bunk, I had prayed to feel the light and wind and air pour through my fingertips. To harness whatever unchecked power had poured out of me after my mother's death. Just a little—to light a single candle or blow a door shut with a strong gust. But nothing had happened. Not even a spark.

Well, valuable lesson learned: *use your lighte to obliterate a Fae army, expect to wait weeks for it to regenerate.*

Turning back to the flat, tan beach, I witnessed the rest of the ship's passengers sprawl along the sand, slowly dust debris off their clothes, and pull themselves to stand. We looked like a parade of dreary mourners in our dark heavy skirts and furs, compared to all the light, flimsy dresses—cream and blush and tangerine—in the distance. Down the textured bank stood Kane, Griffin, and

Amelia, not a grain of sand out of place. I walked over to them, my boots trudging across the uneven ground.

"Is there some secret to the funnel that none of us were told?" I gestured to all the coughing passengers, sand woven through their hair and clothes, women wringing their skirts out, before I found more sand in my own braid.

As I dusted it from my hair, Kane's gaze dragged over me with amusement. "Just practice. We've learned to land on our feet. You all right, bird?"

My hands froze on my braid and we both turned pale at his use of the pet name. He hadn't said it since . . .

"Sorry," he mumbled before stalking off.

I drew in a breath that tasted of salt water and pine trees.

"You really did a number on him." Amelia's eyes fell to me. "It's almost impressive."

Then she was walking, too.

I shook the tension from my shoulders and I called to Leigh, still at the water's edge. When she ignored me, I called again, more insistent this time, until she darted over, kicking sand in her wake.

There were about forty of us who had escaped from Siren's Bay—mostly Peridot nobles and their families, as well as a few soldiers. I could only hope more had survived by fleeing to other cities through the rain forest. Though, now that the kingdom was in Amber's control under Lazarus, no city would be safe for those who were still loyal to Eryx and his daughter.

I couldn't see any of Azurine past the large expanse of cypress trees we walked toward, but from what I could tell, the Kingdom of Citrine was nautical and bright, lusciously serene, and brimming with the intoxicating scent of citrus and olive and fig. Warm turquoise water ringed a radiant coastline of pines and limestone cliffs, with whitewashed villas built into them and gulls flapping overhead in a cloudless sky.

Along with the rest of the passengers, I followed closely behind Griffin's towering form, Leigh's hand in mine, as we came to a driftwood-and-rope bridge built over a rock-strewn portion of beach that cut through the aromatic trees and I assumed into the city's center. We crossed it, single file, passing through the needled trees until we were deposited into a bright, sunny sandstone plaza.

A scream sounded in my ears, and I didn't have time to wonder if it had been my own as someone leveled a gleaming scimitar at my throat.

# 5

## ARWEN

A SWARM OF CITRINE SOLDIERS IN SHINING INDIGO armor hauled us from one another, and when the soldier behind me tightened his steel against my neck, my stomach threatened to empty its meager contents all over his hand.

The contingent was large enough to have two if not three men on each of us. It was a sea of cobalt metal and white accents, helmets and spears and shining iron swords. I couldn't see Leigh or Mari or Kane, or—

I fished for that freshly reborn lighte, straining for the power to free myself, but nothing sputtered at my fingertips. The simple act of stitching up my knee had used all of the nearly dried-up well.

"Could this be who I think it is?" boomed an arrogant male voice.

The soldiers parted slightly, and my breath nearly fled my lungs at the sight before me.

The honey-stone courtyard we were being held in led to an expanse of glittering white steps, smooth like abalone and almost blinding in the sunlight. Standing atop them was a lavish palace, different from the intimate, bohemian ranch of Siren's Cove or the gothic, gloomy beauty of Shadowhold. No, this white-peaked spectacle built into the rocky cliffside was adorned with pearls and gold and rubies, each window and spire and turret glistening in the midday sun with clusters of jewels. The lively city of Azurine spread out around the palace before us, but I couldn't appreciate its beauty. Not as I fought to keep my throat from splitting open against a blade.

Standing atop the white stone steps was a regal man with a square jaw and curled hair. Beside him stood a pinched woman with a permanent sneer, earlobes sagging under weighty rubies that hung past her shoulders. The royals were flanked by at least a dozen more of the sapphire-blue-clothed guards.

"King Broderick, what is the meaning of this?" Eryx sounded almost as insulted as he did afraid.

"Your Majesties." Kane's voice was calm somewhere in the crowd. "I think there's been a simple misunderstanding."

Despite my fury with the man, relief washed over me in hearing his cool, deep voice. Even at his most polite, that deadly power—that commanding, predatory intensity—carried out into the court-yard. I couldn't see over the swath of soldiers, but I was sure no Citrine guard had laid a hand on him.

"No misunderstanding," the king on the steps replied. "We recognize your crest, King Ravenwood. And the Provinces'."

"Siren's Cove has been sacked," Kane said. "Burned to the ground by King Gareth of Amber and King Thales of Garnet."

The shifting of the royals before us told me they either hadn't known or didn't much care.

"Please, let us discuss this in a more civilized manner," Eryx called out. "This is wholly unnecessary. Our people here are refugees from battle. We mean your city no harm."

"Not yet, at least," Kane purred, and a chill broke out across my arms. I knew now what he could do. How easily he could massacre this entire group with his barbed, shadowed power.

The regal couple at the top of the marble stairs conferred silently. Agonizing moments passed in which I saw violence, bloodshed, guttural sobs . . . I strained to lay eyes on Leigh or Ryder, and felt the arms around my middle tighten. At best I was looking at another dungeon, more rope around my wrists, more suffering for those I loved, more—

In an instant the guards released all of us, and the blade at my throat was sheathed. I loosed a breath and rubbed at my neck before spotting the royals striding down those sprawling white steps toward us. They must have given their guards the all clear. I scanned through the crowd for my siblings until finally my eyes found a little disheveled blonde head of hair. I pushed through a sea of blue-clad men and reached for her.

"Are you all right?"

"Fine," Leigh said, wrenching from my grip.

I glowered at the soldier beside her and only released his eyes when Leigh forcibly yanked me away. We shuffled through the throng until a warm, calloused hand encircled my arm and pulled me back.

"You'll need to stay with us," Kane said. "Ryder, can you take the little one?"

I looked up to see Ryder shove through blue armor and wet gray clothes. "Yeah, I got her. Go charm some royals."

Since when were they so friendly? Kane hated Ryder.

I peeked down to Leigh. "I'll be right behind you."

My siblings, along with the rest of the ship's passengers, were ushered around the wide bright steps and through a set of great stone doors wreathed in vines and peach wildflowers. Once they were safely inside, and my heart rate had slowed to a more manageable pace, Kane and I climbed the endless stairs behind Griffin, Amelia, and Eryx toward the royal family. I found a few grains of sand still lodged between my teeth, and spat discreetly onto the opalescent stone.

"Not very ladylike," Kane murmured.

"Why don't you find one of those guards with the pointy blades to bother?"

"So violent," he hummed.

"What can I say? I learned from the best."

"I think you're plenty violent on your own," Kane mused as we came to a halt. But something like irritation flicked across his eyes. "The numbskull with the sword at your neck did come close to losing his hand, though."

Eryx bowed when he reached the royals, his pear-shaped body nearly toppling with the performative gesture. They only glared at us.

"King Broderick, Queen Isolde. You remember my daughter, Amelia; King Ravenwood's commander, Griffin Bolt; and this is his healer, Lady Arwen."

"Greetings," the queen said to us all, lips pursed.

I curtsied, and upon rising, my eyes slipped past the Citrine royals and caught sight of a shockingly handsome man leaning against a pillar behind them.

He was lean and tall, with glowing bronze skin, and despite his casual stance, held his arms behind him in a show of respect. The position only highlighted his cut biceps and broad, strong chest.

Even at a distance I found my gaze glued to his confident, resting smile and clear blue eyes, which mirrored the shining, endless ocean behind me. Next to him stood a petite woman, maybe a few years younger than me. She was also attractive, but less magnificently so. That same flaxen hair, heart-shaped face, and stunning sealike eyes.

Although hers looked rather sad, and couldn't seem to pull away from . . . I followed her eyeline, landing on Kane.

*Bleeding Stones.* He wasn't *that* gorgeous, was he?

His strong jaw ticked as he caught me looking at him, inky tousled hair and sleek clothes a powerful contrast to the sunny palace and blue skies around us. He turned a black signet ring around on his pinky and pocketed the hand in one smooth motion, drawing my eyes down to his long, muscular legs.

I swallowed hard and decided I'd better not answer my own question.

King Broderick motioned to the pair behind him, "Eryx, you remember our son, Prince Fedrik, and daughter, Princess Sera."

"Yes!" Eryx exclaimed, overly familiar. "How they've grown! I remember when—"

"No, no need," Isolde snipped, looking down at a single chipped nail.

Fedrik, the handsome man—not even handsome, but artfully, classically beautiful—sauntered over to greet us before giving me a warm, genuine smile and taking my hand in his. "Lady Arwen." Fedrik bowed. "It's a pleasure."

He exuded cheer and ease, as if it were a mere everyday occurrence to find forty wet, windswept refugees in your courtyard, and after this little discussion he'd be off to play some kind of masculine, midafternoon sport and take a dip in the shimmering sea.

A smile itched to spread across my face—he was like sunshine.

Princess Sera offered a fluid curtsy and pinned her eyes even more intently on Kane beside me. I whipped my gaze to him to catch his reaction, but he was expressionless, staring at the castle turrets, silver eyes bored and cold.

This was the version of Kane I had first met. None of his vulnerability showing, no weakness, no warmth. Only cool and casual disinterest, with a well of deadly venom simmering just below the surface.

Eryx marched forward and motioned for Kane to do the same. Amelia moved to join at her father's side, but he placed a single elbow out as he adjusted his belt, very subtly reprimanding her and sending her back to where Griffin and I stood. Shame painted her cheeks with a pink glow.

Unexpected ire burned in my blood. From what I had seen, Amelia was a far fiercer protector of Peridot than her father. She had been the only one concerned about the people of Siren's Cove when the city was attacked.

"We seek asylum," Eryx began. "King Ravenwood's words are true. Peridot fell in the battle of Siren's Bay, and King Gareth of Amber has assumed my throne. Onyx will be next. Citrine is a mighty and powerful force. We will need your vast army if we are to stand any chance in restoring peace to Evendell."

King Broderick didn't even blink. "We cannot help you."

Kane leaned forward. "Broderick, come now—"

But the queen stepped in front of her husband, her pointed chin held high. "If I recall, King Ravenwood, you are not permitted on Citrine sands after what you did. I could have your head on a stake for breathing our air."

Of course.

Of course Kane had done something—surely something unethical, double-crossing, and self-serving—that would land us all without safe haven.

Eryx's boastful face had finally fallen. He actually looked a little bewildered.

"Queen Isolde," Kane tried, as if mustering patience. "She was too young to marry. She's just a child."

Princess Sera went pale, her eyes suddenly fixated on her pink-hued sandals.

"That was not your decision to make." The queen's voice was shrill.

"She was to be *my* wife."

*Oh, Bleeding Stones.*

"Well, I was pleased," Prince Fedrik cut in. "I didn't particularly like the idea of my baby sister marrying a raging Fae asshole anyway. Someone come find me when he's left the city, will you?" He gave Kane a bright smile and a hard pat on the shoulder before walking past him and descending the sprawling, milky white stairs.

*Fae?* Shock coursed through me like a crack of lightning.

But Kane merely scowled.

"Why did you agree to marry our daughter if you only planned to humiliate her?" Queen Isolde pressed.

I was still reeling from the prince's comment. Maybe the entire Kingdom of Citrine knew of the Fae Realm? But how could that knowledge never have spread to the rest of the continent?

"You can do with me whatever you wish," Kane said, ignoring her question. "But do not punish these people for my mistakes. The kind of evil we are up against threatens to destroy every mortal soul. What Eryx has yet to inform you is that King Gareth and King

Thales are allied with my father. Surely, you won't let your pride stand in the way of all the lives in Evendell?"

Queen Isolde's face gave nothing away. Nothing but that splintering rage in her stark eyes. But King Broderick—all I could hope was that he might save this rapidly deteriorating situation. He took his wife's hand in his, though she wriggled against the gesture.

"Personal feelings aside, we cannot risk our kingdom's safety. You may stay here for the night, but we insist that you all leave tomorrow."

No, no no—

What now? I couldn't bring Leigh and Ryder back to Onyx, knowing Lazarus might be waiting for us. And I knew too little about the rest of the continent to even fathom which other kingdoms might offer safety.

Kane persevered. "I may have wronged your family, but—"

The queen's voice was piercing. "*Humiliated.* Devastated our daughter—"

"I know." Kane's eyes were severe. He was done begging. I swallowed hard. "Give me a private audience to convince you both. What I have to say will be worth your time."

Before his wife could sink her claws into Kane once more, King Broderick said, "Fine."

# 6

## KANE

It had been six years since I was last in Azurine, yet the throne room was just as manicured and glitzy as I remembered. Not really my style—I preferred my décor to have a bit more depth to it—but if opal and gold accents on every single door handle and candlestick worked for them, who was I to judge?

What *had* changed was the way both Broderick and Isolde regarded me. As if I were an asp in their garden. The last time I was in their throne room was the night before I planned to wed their daughter, and the royal couple were drunk with bubbled wine, cheering to the union of our kingdoms, dining on giant crab and the roasted tentacles of purple squids.

Their energy today was slightly different.

"All right, Kane. Spit it out."

Broderick looked supremely bored sitting on his gilded throne. And I didn't blame him. He had a kingdom that couldn't be breached. He didn't need to aid our suffering or put any of his people in danger. If I were in his shoes, I likely wouldn't, either. Which meant I'd need to convince him and Isolde the way I would need to be convinced.

"Firstly," I started, looking around at the throne room, empty save for the three of us and their single, exquisitely armored guard. "Among friends—" I winced at the queen's expression. Fine, perhaps not *friends*. "What do you already know?"

"We know about the girl," Isolde said. "The *healer*. That she is the last true Fae from the prophecy."

Arwen was in enough danger as things stood. The thought of anyone knowing who she really was made my hackles rise, familiar along my spine as if I were in my dragon form.

I reminded myself that Citrine royalty had always known of the Fae Realm. Many of the people of Citrine were Mer, a race bred in the depths of the ocean itself. The royals were mortal, but their people—those who could live and breathe underwater with no spells at all—were the lifeblood of their kingdom and had ancient knowledge of Lumera.

Citrine wasn't the only kingdom that knew about my homeland. I had my suspicions about the Pearl Mountains knowing of the Fae, too. It didn't seem possible that the floating city—so focused on the pursuit of knowledge and the worship of the sacred Stones—was entirely unaware of Lumera, but I had never been able to get a straight answer from their ruler, Yervan. And I had no interest in spilling my secrets if he was unwilling to share his.

Aside from Pearl, and my father bringing Garnet and Amber into the fold, for many, many years it was just Citrine, Onyx, and Peridot who knew of the Fae Realm, and thus, the prophecy.

When I arrived in Onyx fifty years ago, I had narrowly escaped a rebellion gone catastrophically wrong and had promised safety to hundreds of Fae. At the time, King Oberon held the Onyx throne, but the wily, liver-spotted man was in his nineties and near death. He was childless, and rumors of civil war were brewing. He had hoped it would be one of his brothers who succeeded him, but he had outlived them all, the old rascal.

I told him of my realm and convinced him of its legitimacy with my lighte. Shared with him the lengths to which I was willing to go to dethrone and kill my father once and for all. And while all I asked for was safe refuge for my people, he had offered me his kingdom instead. He said I was a prince in my own right, and it was time I became a king. Three months later he passed away, and we told the land I was his bastard son.

One of the few lessons of any value my father taught me was to only make one or two allies you can truly count on. Too many, and someone was bound to betray you; too few, and you'd have no support. To the credit of Eryx's far more brilliant heir, Amelia, Peridot and Onyx formed exactly such an alliance.

About eight years ago, when Amelia was only nineteen, she invited the young king of Onyx to Siren's Cove without even asking her father's permission. Amelia had laid out very clearly why our kingdoms were valuable to each other, from our proximity to our crop disparity. Both a partnership and genuine friendship were born from there, and revealing my Fae heritage came only a few years later.

Citrine was my next—and last—attempt at an alliance. Once I met Broderick and Isolde and realized they had secrets of their own, I shared with them my hope of freeing the Fae Realm. They didn't balk—it was a realm they had been aware of for decades. Longer than I had even known of them.

It had only made sense then to promise myself to Sera when she came of age and ensure a sacred and fruitful partnership between kingdoms over the many years to come. Isolde was a wise queen. She knew if I succeeded in destroying my father, her daughter would one day rule the Fae Realm as well. And if I failed . . . well, I'd be dead and she could marry whomever she pleased. A decent deal.

Or it would have been, had I gone through with it—but I had taken one look at young Sera, only thirteen at the time, and realized Isolde and I had vastly different ideas of what coming "of age" entailed. Call it revulsion, ethics, or impulsivity, but I reneged on the marriage and fled the city before the ceremony could take place.

Looking at Isolde now, all I could see was her tear-streaked face that windy winter evening by the sea as she held her inconsolable daughter and roared that I was never to step foot in their kingdom again.

And now, six years later, I had done exactly that.

"You're right," I managed. "Arwen is the promised Fae. And that information needs never to leave this room. Who else knows what she is?"

"Just the people in this room and our highest advisor, Master Aled," Broderick said. "He heard of the healer that had taken up residence in Shadowhold months ago. Some spies informed us of her similarities to the woman who showed an impressive display of power in Siren's Bay. We put the pieces together."

I rubbed at my temples.

"Citrine is safe for her," Broderick reassured me. "We are not fools, Kane. We understand what is at stake here. But outside of harboring the girl, we cannot help you. We have fought hard to keep this kingdom safe. To avoid the pointless wars of mortal men."

"You know this isn't just mortal men." I stepped forward with intent, and the guard behind Isolde lifted his blade, a shimmer of bright blue light dancing across the room.

*Mermagic.*

Stronger than steel, that cerulean glow could lop my head clean off.

I unclenched my fists.

"Even still, we cannot help you," Broderick said, his guard stepping back like a dog called off a scent.

Despite his baritone voice, Broderick's words barely resonated in the glossy, empty room. Such a calm man. I wondered if he ever raged.

I turned to Isolde. I'd have to get through to her somehow.

"I couldn't do it to Sera," I admitted. And then, before she cut me off, "I know, I know. You're her mother, you know what's right for her, but the thought of wedding her. Putting an heir into her . . . She was just a *child*."

"This is your way of convincing us to help you? Insulting how we raised our daughter? How we chose to wed her?"

All right. New approach.

I had not even shared this half-assed, last-ditch plan with Griffin. His sigh of frustration would have knocked me over. "Isolde, if we defeat my father and win the war, someone will need to sit on the throne of Lumera. I am the rightful king, but will abdicate to stay in Onyx. It is my home now."

Isolde said nothing, but folded her hands primly in her lap. I wasn't sure if the gesture was a good sign or a bad one.

"Lumerians will only recognize a Fae monarch, but a mortal spouse would greatly help to promote unity between the species. Especially after my father's quest for a solely full-blooded Fae race. Help us, and I swear to you, I will crown a Fae worthy of Sera."

After a long moment, in which all I could hear was my pulse slamming in my own ears, she angled her head toward her husband and spoke, more to him than to me.

"We do not want to see Lazarus take Evendell, to ruin it as he has Lumera."

My heart flew up against my ribs—

"But—"

And fell like a dove shot out of the sky.

"We cannot lend you our mermagic nor our armies. I will not let my people go like willing sacrifices against Fae soldiers. In exchange for your promise to wed Sera to the next Fae king, we can offer you refuge for the men and women who arrived today. However, you must swear not to spill *one ounce* of blood on Citrine sand. Do not forget how well we know you, King Ravenwood. No lighte, no shifting, no endangering our people."

"Understood."

"One step out of line," Isolde hissed, "and you and every single passenger from that ship will be thrown into our sea."

⚓︎

THOUGH I FOUND THE PALACE AT AZURINE TO BE OVERDONE and bejeweled into frivolity, the castle did have one thing I was exceedingly fond of, and that was their large marble showers.

The room Isolde's guards showed me to was the one I always stayed in when I used to visit the capital. A sunlit suite filled with fluffed sheets and a spectacular view of the whitewashed streets of the city and the sparkling Mineral Sea beyond.

In the washroom, past the soaking tub, was the bathing column. Like a closet of piping-hot, steaming rain paned with glassy emerald tiles.

I peeled off my dirty pants and tunic from our interminable journey on the ship and threw them in the wastebasket with more force than necessary. The mirror before me reflected a pitiful sight. Too thin, sallow, and rough. Patchy beard. Sunken eyes. I needed to stop hunting for peace in mugs of whiskey.

I turned on the water and let it spill out from the ceiling until the whole washroom was damp and sticky before stepping inside and scrubbing every inch of my body until I was raw.

When I was finished, I stood under the hot spray of water and braced my hands on the tiles before me. Little beads of heat dripped between my outspread fingers. A steady stream pounded the crown of my head and back of my neck. I tried not to let my thoughts wander.

Hotter.

That would help.

I twisted the knob until the water was scalding.

And then hotter still, until my skin was as red as a newborn's.

It was no use. I couldn't help but think of Arwen.

I had been putting it off for days. It just felt too dirty, too despicable to make myself come to her image knowing how she felt about me now—what I had done to her.

But I needed a single moment of release. Especially after the empty promises I had made to Isolde. Now, even if I won this fucking war, I'd have another one on my hands unless I married Sera off to some Fae noble. I couldn't even fathom who might rule Lumera if we succeeded. I never let myself think that far ahead. To have defeated Lazarus would mean Arwen had . . .

My fist slammed into the slippery shower wall, cracking the tile and sending debris to my feet.

I couldn't take to the skies, as I so often did when I was this restless.

Gods knew I wasn't going to bed someone else.

And . . . I dreamt of her. Every fucking night. Arwen had invaded not only my waking thoughts but my sleeping ones as well. It was hopeless. Humiliating, to be so wound up, like a coiled wire after months and months of wanting and not having her.

One time, I'd allow myself to think of her. Just this once.

I circled my hand around my shaft and began to stroke in a steady rhythm. The swell of her breasts, bigger than my palm, and her hard, pink-tipped nipples swirled in my mind. The curve of her slender hips, of her wet lips and tongue. What they might feel like wrapped around me. I tried to imagine her still wanting me, riding me, writhing on top of me, begging me to thrust harder, to bring her to the edge. Her core slick and swollen, drawing me in. Her hands, greedy, pawing at me, begging me for more, more, *more*—I pumped faster into my hand, holding the other against the wet tiles to keep myself standing. I came hard and rough with her name on my lips.

The instantaneous shame that followed was even more potent than the desire that had fueled me. I was repulsed by myself.

I rinsed off and threw a towel around my hips. That would be the last time. It was a climax for old times' sake.

Yeah, that made sense.

The knock on my door was a welcome distraction. *Please, let it be someone who wants to punch me in the face.*

I opened the door to Griffin's stoic expression.

"Close enough," I mumbled to myself.

He shot me a curious expression and sat down in the beige lambskin chair next to the fireplace, picking up a decorative opalescent seashell from the table beside him. "I just met with Master Aled." He turned to me, a gleam in his eye. "We may have a way in with Crawford."

My brows perked up. Finally, some good fucking news. "Really?"

"Here, in Azurine. Tonight."

"Great," I said, sinking into the chair opposite him.

Griffin examined me before he let out a brusque laugh. "You look wrecked."

"I'm fine."

"I don't envy you. That"—he gestured at my face—"looks worse than an axe wound."

"Thanks." He'd likely never suffer my miserable fate. I wasn't sure Griffin was capable of romantic love. It wasn't as if he'd ever had an example to learn from. He grew up in a colder home than my own.

"She was too good for you anyway," he offered earnestly.

"I know that."

"I'm not going to talk feelings with you."

"I know that, too," I mumbled, letting my head fall back behind me. The ceiling had a swirled, wavelike design chiseled into it.

"Good," he said.

"They're going to let us stay."

"Also good."

"I had to promise Sera to whoever takes the throne in Lumera, if we win."

"Less good."

I smirked.

"Who will it be?" he asked. "You?"

I lifted my head and found humor in his eyes. "Of course not. How about you?"

That humor died instantly in exchange for crackling contempt.

"We'll keep thinking, then," I said. "What's our route to the collector?"

"A private event he hosts. We can attend with the prince." Griffin dipped his head, studying the shell still in his hands.

I furrowed a brow. "What aren't you telling me?"

"No obliterating Crawford. Not until we get the blade."

"Fine," I agreed.

"Aled said Crawford has been collecting Mer girls. The royals didn't know until he had sold almost thirty of them. *Young* girls."

Bitterness churned in my stomach. Crawford already deserved a long and thorough beating for all the people he had scammed and stolen from. Now he deserved death. "Why didn't they arrest him? Try him for his crimes?"

Griffin looked almost as murderous as I felt. "They don't have enough evidence. Didn't want to risk it given his status in the city. He had one of his longtime cronies to take the fall. Isolde and Broderick hanged the lackey in the city center. Not much of a punishment if you ask me."

Griffin's father was the head of my father's army, and the most brutal man I had ever met. His mother was even icier. In his opinion, hanging was a swift and honorable death. A courtesy almost.

I stood, sprinkling the chair in water droplets. "We'll get any information on the blade that we can while we're in town, then we'll do Isolde and Broderick a favor by exterminating one of their pests."

Griffin stood, too. "Kane—"

"Where do we meet him tonight?"

He loosed a long-suffering sigh. "Now *that's* the fun part."

# 7

## ARWEN

THE BEACH WAS IMPOSSIBLE TO FIND MY FOOTING AGAINST. Each step landed awkwardly, my boots too heavy in the wet mixture of sand and sea. My braid had come undone, resulting in sweaty, crunchy strands of hair plastering themselves against my neck and forehead; my lungs were surely bleeding from the exertion; and my legs were throbbing—a steady, pulsing burn in my quads and arches and ankles.

And yet, the quiet oblivion inside my heart had not yielded.

It scared me more than I could admit—that the salty air in my lungs, the rhythmic pump of my arms, for the first time in my life, hadn't helped.

And my feet—these shoes against the sand—

I came to an awkward, stunted halt and yanked my boots off one after another as if all the suffering in my life were their fault. The patchy, poorly cobbled offenders mocked me from the sun-drenched gold of the Azurine beach.

My face was too hot as I appraised them. My breathing ragged.

Those boots had carried me through the Shadow Woods. Parried in the fields of Shadowhold with Dagan a hundred times. Had trudged up and down the stairs to visit Mari in the library.

They had pressed up against a cold dungeon wall for hours, waiting for merciful sleep to come. Had been kicked into a corner so I could crawl into bed beside a warm and waiting Kane. Those boots had sat folded under me as I held my dying mother in my arms.

My heart raged against my chest as I grabbed the leather shoes and threw them into the ocean with as much force as I could muster.

They sailed through the air on a slight, white arc of energy, landing in the depths of the ocean miles away with a subtle splash.

My eyes found my hands.

They looked the same. Red and blotchy from running under a bright sun.

But—

I had felt something.

And . . . it scared me. My own power. What was thrumming under the surface of my own skin—

"Whatever those shoes did to you, I have no doubt such an execution was warranted."

I whirled at that new, sunshine voice and found Fedrik standing up the beach, backed by a little pastel village. Beyond it, patches of trees were specked with splotches of orange. I wasn't sure how far I had run, but we were clearly no longer near the harbor.

I curtsied, but he tossed his hand in the air dismissively as he strolled closer.

"I must know." He jerked his chin toward the glassy bay behind me, quiet save for the rocking of seafoam against wet sand. "Why?"

"It was a sacrifice," I admitted.

"Then a necessary one," he assured me. "And their honor to serve." Fedrik flashed a grin that outshone the sun above us.

"Are you . . . hiding?" A few hours ago he had abandoned our terse convening on his palace steps to avoid Kane. And now he was here, miles from the city center, alone on this beach with me.

"And what would I be hiding from?"

"King Ravenwood. I just thought . . ."

Fedrik grinned again, handing those genuine smiles out like free sweets. So unlike Kane in that way. In all the ways. "I only needed an excuse to rid myself from the politics. Life's far too short to concern ourselves with brutes like him, right?"

I said nothing, feet growing cold and itchy where the wet sand was drying around my bare ankles.

"Lady Arwen, might I interest you in—"

"I'd better get back. My sister is probably looking for me."

"Sure," the prince said, faintly amused. "Enjoy the city."

~❦~

DROPLETS OF SWEAT HAD GATHERED AT MY TEMPLES AND slid down the sides of my face by the time I slunk back into the palace room Ryder, Leigh, and I had been given for the night. I wiped a hand across my mouth, cool air replacing the moisture above my lip.

Inside I was greeted by the briny scent of the ocean wafting in through our open windows, the sheer drapes flitting in the breeze. The rounded, lavish suite was affixed with two beds, one for Ryder and one for Leigh and me to share, with a marbled balcony that looked down onto painterly manor houses and the cypress-dotted mountains beyond.

A collection of pale blue and ivory hues with a large driftwood table in the center, the room was decorated with solid silver sand dollars and intricate sea glass. Little trinkets of wealth and beauty peppered throughout.

But all I noticed was a new embellishment on the table that hadn't been there before my run.

A small bouquet of flowers, tied with a twine bow.

I picked up the delicate bunch and smelled them. Rosemary, ambrosia, and orange poppies. After reading *Evendell Flora* over and over, I knew ambrosia meant gift of the Stones, while poppies meant consolation, or remorse.

My mother would have loved them. Their colors. Their springy scent. She would have put them in a thick glass vase on our table and told me each day how well they were blooming.

The thought made me want to toss them out our grand bay windows and onto somebody's tiled roof.

Underneath the flowers was a note written in black ink on parchment. Strong masculine lettering read:

*My dearest bird. I am so sorry. For everything.*

Bastard.

Another deceit from a lying manipulator.

"Leigh!" I called into the washroom. The sound of sloshing water told me she was soaking in the tub. "I know you helped him with this."

"I can't hear you," she called back. "And no, I didn't!"

I crushed the flowers in my hand and left their fragmented remains on the pale wooden table. Leigh could report that back to her new ally.

Minutes later, Mari waltzed into our suite dressed in an

embroidered teal blouse and one of the loose cotton skirts I assumed was customary in the seaside kingdom.

"Shall we?"

I raised a brow in silent question.

"Go explore! We've never been anywhere fun together. No way you've seen a city such as this."

"It's been a long day. A long couple of weeks, actually. I was looking forward to resting." I gazed longingly at the puffed sheets on the bed, the squishy pillows. Tempting me to drown everything out with the swift and steady drug of slumber. Even Leigh kicking beside me couldn't make that sound less appealing. "Don't we have to leave first thing in the morning anyway?"

"Word is Kane convinced them to let us stay."

A small mercy. Leigh and Ryder would be safe here. They could stay. Avoid the coming war.

Maybe Kane had agreed to marry Sera. She was older now, and very beautiful. I'm sure they'd be perfectly happy together.

A liar and a princess.

"Come on, Arwen! How about dinner? Then you can come back and sleep for days."

I did want to see the city, but it all felt sort of useless. To see and fall in love with all that I wouldn't get to enjoy again.

"I'm not sure." I twined my fingers in the tail of my braid.

"It's not enough to just survive, Arwen. You have to actually *live*. I don't want to be harsh but . . . I feel strongly about this."

"She's right. Go with her!" came Leigh's muffled shout through the washroom door.

After my run-in with the prince, I had debated going to the castle's infirmary to get a whiff of the ethanol and sanitizing solutions—a smell that used to brighten my spirits and clear my mind.

But I couldn't bring my weary limbs to trek through the expansive palace. I just felt so . . . tired.

Maybe they were right. Maybe this could help.

"Fine. Just dinner?"

Mari's answering smile was almost enough to make my compliance worth it.

# 8

## ARWEN

I BATHED AND DRESSED, TRYING HARD TO IGNORE THE WAY my reflection in the brightly lit, pretty pearl-crusted mirror made me feel. The contrast was stark. My eyes had such deep, sorrowful bags that I looked like I had been pummeled. Many, many times. And my cheeks—washed-out, pallid, gaunt. By the time I found it within me to meet Mari on the palace steps, late afternoon had slipped into early evening.

The sailors in the harbor were anchoring their vessels and ambling into the city center for dinner alongside women dressed in dainty, festive finery. The people here were more beautiful than anyone I had seen in Amber or Onyx. Even Peridot. Unbothered. Relaxed, as if the sunshine and briny waves were enough to make each day worth living, and everything else that happened, good or bad, was simply garnish.

Mari and I strolled through the city at a leisurely pace. I hadn't realized what a luxury it was to not be fighting for my life. Each vined corner we rounded led to a little plaza or a square doused in sunset shades of blush and gold. Ceramic pottery, aromatic lemon-grass and mint leaves, ruby-red grapefruit.

Each café and restaurant—most pressed up against walls of vivid, near-luminous bougainvillea—was accompanied by soft lute music and wafts of garlic, parsley, and thyme. Some narrow passages opened up on one end, giving a peek at the easy waves of the marina, like a slipped-off sleeve of a dress, offering a seductive glimpse to a wanting eye.

The carriages that passed us as we meandered through the streets were impossible to wrap my mind around. Not only because of their elaborate gold filigree and glittery detailing—each hinge and spoke adorned with more opalescent shine than most noblewomen's necks—but because they weren't drawn by any horses. Rather, they moved on their own, powered by the mermagic Kane had spoken of. A blue light—an energy of some kind—spinning the wheels like a witch's spell.

There were more hints of those shimmering, blue rays throughout the town. Subtle, but now I was looking for them—streetlights that glimmered with that single blue flame, an aquamarine glow coming from a cart that seemed to push itself. For a city more vast, more advanced than any I'd seen before, there were no horses, no wells, no aqueducts. Clearly, the energy provided by the sea that insulated Citrine did more than just secure the kingdom.

Eventually, Mari liked the look of one little bustling seafood restaurant and pulled me inside, away from a stuffed, musty bookstore overflowing with pages begging to be read.

She must have been starving.

The owner, a frazzled gentleman with too many customers and not enough help, seated us at a table on a vine-covered patio facing the water with a picturesque view of the golden sun setting over the now-still harbor. Our table was small with a single melting white candle in the center, and we quickly ordered enough food to nearly topple the thing. Squid-ink pasta, chargrilled oysters, roasted heirloom tomatoes—in colors I had never seen, like gold and lime green and rose—and an extraordinary whole grilled fish with the eyeballs still intact served on a plate crafted from a giant clamshell.

Then, emboldened by wine, we ordered more. Milky white cheeses and ruby-red beets, and bread that left my fingers oily and salty each time I ripped a piece off to soak up the watercolor of sauces on my plate.

I had never felt so full in my life.

"If only my papa could see me now," Mari said, stuffing one last piece of sourdough into her mouth.

I raised a brow. "Eating your weight in fish and bread?"

Mari smiled and pawed at her amulet. "No, with this. He always said I'd be as good a witch as my mother. Since she never got to teach me, and he knew so little about her lineage, I didn't have the chance to prove him right. But Briar's the greatest witch to ever live, so maybe her amulet is even better than using my own ancestry. It still makes me feel close to my mother, and I know how strange that sounds."

"No, not strange at all," I said, sipping my orange wine. It was fizzy on my tongue, and the soft focus of my mind from a handful of drinks made the conversation I had been avoiding slightly less daunting. I knew how it felt to have the truth withheld by those you thought closest to you. Especially when they had every opportunity to be honest.

I should have told her. Now would have been as good a time as any. But she was so . . . *happy*. And things were finally, *finally* not completely awful. At least, not for her. Why strip her of her confidence? She'd likely figure it out herself soon enough. She was so bright . . .

I stored away the new guilt deep in the recesses of my heart, and said only, "Just be careful."

Mari shook her head and stuffed her mouth with a forkful of flaky white fish. "Careful of what? It's a blessing, not a curse. I was never able to access a coven growing up. Now I can."

"How is that possible?"

"Lighte draws from the elements, right? From the very earth and atmosphere and forces it out of your fingers. But magic isn't like that. It's not a resource or a tangible plasma or an elixir that can be drained and stolen. Magic is a talent, influenced by a witch's genetics. The more powerful the witches in your lineage, the more magic you can do. That's why covens are so strong: they are constantly drawing from one another."

I tried to soak in what she was saying, but the wine was clouding my mind a bit. As if she could read my puzzled expression, she sighed and leaned closer.

"Think of it like this: Your lighte is like a bowl collecting rain. There can be too much during a heavy storm, or barely a drop in a dry climate. That difference depends on your energy, emotions, and state of mind. The rain can be taken from the bowl and bottled or stored, traded or drunk, and on and on. It's a resource, a reserve, and it lives within you. And after you've used the rain you've collected, you have to wait for more rain to replenish that bowl. My magic is like playing the lute. It's a skill. I can get tired, sure, but it never depletes. I'm likely to be a strong lute player if my mother, and her mother, and her mother before her was, too. And when I pull from other witches and their lineage, I'm not just one lute player, I'm an orchestra."

I shook my head. "How do you know all this?"

Mari only scoffed. "You really are drunk."

Right. Surely she had spent every free moment since I told her of the Fae three weeks ago studying and discussing with anyone who would give her the time of day.

Maybe she was right, and the amulet was real. What did Kane know anyway? I had no energy to argue. "Can you still take the time to research your own line of power? Harness your skill without it? Maybe you can learn the craft bit by bit instead of relying so heavily on—"

"Arwen, why would I do things the harder, slower way when I have a direct line to Briar Creighton? Any other witch who had this opportunity would do the same."

Anxiety bubbled up beneath my skin. The oils and vinegars of our dinner rumbled in my stomach and I shifted against the chair beneath me. "Witchcraft isn't meant to be simple. You're supposed to learn, and make mistakes. It's necessary. It's natural. It's . . ."

"I think that's what people who make a lot of mistakes tell themselves," Mari said distractedly, sponging up some seafood remnants on her plate with the last few bites of oily bread. "Now, why haven't you told me about this prince yet?" She lowered one brow at me with impish delight.

"How do you know about that?"

"I just heard some palace gossip that you two had a *moment*."

Leave it to Mari to be in Azurine for less than a day and already have more inside information than the city's actual residents.

The wine was zingy and sharp on my tongue as I downed my glass and tried to remember what Mari had asked me. "There's nothing to tell. I ran into him on my run. He's very pretty."

"Are you blushing?!"

"I don't think so." It was the wine that was coursing in my veins and reddening my cheeks. "What even counts as a *moment*?"

"A charged tension between you. A zap of energy when you touch."

It only made me think of Kane, and I raised my wineglass before realizing it was empty and setting it back down. "What about you?" I asked. "You know Griffin stares at you every time you're within ten feet of him?"

"Yeah." She snorted, tossing her hair behind her shoulder. "He's so sensitive and romantic, that one."

"Fair enough," I said, harsher than I intended. "They're all bastards, aren't they?"

Mari noticed my change in mood and took a big gulp of her wine before trying and failing to flag down the harried restaurant owner for more. "Don't let one liar stop you from trusting men altogether."

Watching the man dash back into the restaurant's kitchen, Mari huffed and uttered a low hum. She focused her gaze on the cup until it filled nearly to the brim with orange wine.

"Mari," I whispered, leaning closer. "Isn't that stealing?" I looked around. The pilfered spirit had to have come from somewhere. Sure enough, the glasses of one glitzy, distracted table to our left drained as ours refilled while they sat, engrossed in their friends' storytelling.

"It's fine," she assured me, taking a deep swallow. "They didn't even notice."

The spirit swishing on my tongue was enough to replace my ethical concerns with gratitude.

"So you say Kane's a liar, but you make sobering potions for him and drink until the wee hours with him and his friends?"

Mari cringed. "We all grew closer on the journey. But I will gladly never talk to him again if you'd prefer."

"I'd never ask that of you. I want you to have other friends when I'm . . ." I had to stop doing that. I could hear how depressing I was to be around.

"Hey," Mari said, stern. "Whatever happens. Nobody could replace you."

I blinked against the burning behind my eyes.

"And you can't think that way." She tutted.

"Why not? It's the truth, isn't it?"

"It's not over until it's over. Aren't you supposed to be the positive one?"

I laughed—a bitter, tipsy snort. "I can't fight it, so why try? That isn't positive enough for you?"

Mari shook her head, not quite as amused. It almost seemed as if my words had offended her. "How can you say that? You don't have to be so compliant. It's a really awful thing that you've learned."

I sighed. "It is what it is."

"Have you given any more thought to my offer?"

On the ship, Mari had offered to research my true parentage. She figured now that my Fae history was no longer a secret, Dagan might help her hunt down some Fae texts.

If we ever made it back to Shadowhold to see him again.

"I don't really know what the point would be," I said, not sullenly.

I had made peace with never knowing my father years ago. I hoped I could do the same with my mother. Whoever they had been, clearly they hadn't wanted me in the first place. Or, worse, had enough reason to give me up against their will. And now—

Well, it didn't really matter now, did it?

"Speaking of Fae," I remembered, "the prince knows about the Fae Realm. He knew what Kane was."

"Interesting . . ." Mari's eyes widened. "I wonder if the whole royal family does. They did agree to wed their daughter to Kane. Maybe it was a political move. Not just for power over Evendell but the Fae Realm as well."

Given Queen Isolde's ferocity, I didn't put it past her. She likely valued her political dominance as much as her daughter's pride.

"Maybe I'll ask the prince myself," I said, raising my chin.

"I think you should." She grinned back at me.

For a moment we sipped our pilfered wine contentedly as we listened to the ambient sounds of the restaurant. The mild notes of a flute, the clinking of glasses, and the chatter of merry patrons. Just beyond the patio, Azurine citizens laughed and chatted as they strolled with no haste along the still-warm cobblestones, taking in the dappled cerulean light. And in the distance, those constant waves lapped softly against a restful shore.

"So, what now?" I asked, rubbing at my sated stomach. Thank the Stones for the light cotton dress that hung off me like a luxurious sheet. I would have burst through a corset.

"I suppose we have to go back and sleep. We did say only dinner . . ." Mari's grin held only mischief.

I pressed my mouth to my glass to suppress my laugh. The wine was buzzing in my mind and legs, the city alive all around me. I wanted to drown in it. To be someone else, just for an evening. Mari had been right: getting out had helped, if only slightly. Like cheesecloth over a stab wound. "No, no. You've sold me. I'm in for the ride. Where to now?"

"Dancing! Dessert? Both!" She stood up and grabbed my hand,

leaving a handful of coin on the table and pulling us out down a narrow street lined with potted lemon trees.

~❦~

THE AFTER-DINNER CROWD WAS EVEN MORE LIVELY. THEY popped in and dipped out of stores, cafés, and taverns, carrying small baskets stuffed with wine and candles and fruit.

We strolled alongside them into parlors flooded with sweets—I was too full to even look at the sugary morsels—and shops replete with leather goods that smelled like pine and citrus. Azurine was filled with more life, more sound, more *energy* than anywhere else I had ever been.

Turning down a white cobblestone road lit in watery shafts of mermagic streetlight, we heard the rhythmic beat of gentle drums and string instruments.

"This way." Mari drew me through a tavern door, into heat and noise and joy—a jostling throng of revelers dancing and singing, as if they were one sweaty, euphoric mass—and plunged us into the depths before I could object.

Wafts of vanilla and lemon fought for dominance against a heavy fog of sweat and spilled liquor. But the beat took control of my hips and feet, swaying my body and clearing my mind. It was like running—the more I danced, the less I could think or worry. Only this time, the harmonious, rising music succeeded in drowning everything out.

The vibrations of the strings silenced my mind, the lyrics of the bard filled the chasm in my soul. Handsome men with glistening chests and hair glued to their foreheads with sweat twirled and dipped me, cheering and chanting for me to move more sensually, display my body, spin for them—and I did. I allowed myself to be swallowed up by their revelry for hours, until it was well past midnight. Until time slowed to a rolling yawn. Until my hair was a damp mess around my face, my dress had torn, and my feet screamed at me in agony—blisters already blossomed, popped, and peeled.

Still, I danced.

The pleasurable swell in my feet and legs welcome, I writhed and shined and shimmered under the torches that filled the room, singing to the folk songs I knew and the ballads I didn't until my lungs burned. Roared at me. Begged for reprieve.

But I couldn't stop. I moved to the pulsing sounds of the band, the rhythmic beat, the ocean I swore I could still feel lapping in the harbor outside, glittering and kissed by the moonlight. I wanted to be gobbled up by it all. I'd simply never leave.

"I can't dance a minute longer!" Mari shouted over the drumbeat.

"No, let's stay!"

"What?" she screamed, her face pink and shining with sweat.

"I don't want to go back!" I yelled again.

"A snack?"

*Bleeding Stones.*

"Come on," Mari shouted, dragging me toward the exit and squeezing past men and women clambering to push in farther toward the center of it all, deeper, louder—to be fused together with all the others. Made whole.

We stumbled out of the tavern door onto the now mostly empty street. My dress was sodden with sweat and clinging to me, and I lifted my hair off my neck to cool down.

"That was spectacular," I confessed. "My ears feel like I'm underwater."

"Same here," slurred Mari. The river of ale she drank while we danced glazed her words, while my Fae nature had sobered me up all too quickly.

"Come on, let's get you home." I tucked my arm around her waist and walked her back down toward the palace.

"What about the snack?"

"Really? It's likely one in the morning. Will anything even be open?"

"Of course, Arwen. It's Azurine!"

"You say that like you didn't just arrive here today."

"Let's go find a lemon custard!" And with that, she gave me the slip, teetering down the street, and swinging open the nearest café door.

"Oh, Stones," I said to nobody in particular, sliding my sandals off with a wince. The cool street felt divine on my swollen, bare feet. Unsanitary and *divine*.

This quiet café was nothing like the lively spot we had just abandoned. There were only two other patrons, a couple in the corner lit by the flickering candle dripping onto their table, whispering and eliciting soft murmurs from one another. One lone barkeep stood behind the counter, and Mari was already perched on a stool before him, digging into a creamy lemon dessert.

I sat down beside her. "Happy?"

"Thrilled," she said, mouth full.

"Anything for you, beautiful?" The barkeep's eyelids seemed propped open with effort, as he clearly struggled to stay awake through the late hour.

"I'll take one, too." I pointed to Mari's decadent treat, which she was currently struggling to lick off her arm as it slid toward her elbow. "Let me help you, come here."

*"Don't you dare!"*

A male voice, ragged with distress, rang out into the café. The barkeep kept his head down. That thunderous voice had come from somewhere in the back, behind him. I did a quick scan of the room, but there was nobody else in the place besides the amorous couple, who were now looking up, spooked.

The voice called out again. *"I'm begging you, please—don't do this!"*

Mari's eyes met mine, filled with concern.

"It's fine. Stay here."

"I'm not staying anywhere," she said, face paling. "We should go." Mari scrambled off her stool, taking the half-eaten custard with her. "Hurry."

*"Please! I'll do anything!"*

I whirled again, my heart finally starting to patter lightly.

*"Please!"*

The outline of a door stood out to me, concealed with the same sage paint as the back wall. I didn't think before hopping over the counter in one swift motion, barely grazing glass bottles and sliced lemons.

"I can't let you go back there, miss—" The barkeep tried to cut me off, but I dodged him, pushing my way toward that voice raw with fear.

"Arwen!" Mari screamed.

*"No!"* The voice was frantic, pleading.

*"You must know these are the rules."*

Did I recognize that velvety answering tone? I threw the door open with a thud, bracing myself for the very worst.

# 9

## ARWEN

O F ALL THE THINGS I EXPECTED TO FIND IN THE DIMLY
lit back room of this café in the middle of the night, Kane,
Griffin, Ryder, and Prince Fedrik gambling amid a haze of smoke
and liquor was not one of them.

It took my eyes a beat to adjust to the low-burning oil lamps.
The oval table they sat around—built of rich mahogany with a
raised lip to keep the coin and cards from slipping off and carpeted
in a pine-green fabric of some kind—took up most of the room. It
was crowded with mismatched glassware, some with an amber
spirit, some empty save for a ring of burgundy. No windows, no
clocks. No way to see how many hours had been lost, or how much
coin. Aside from a shadowed back door, the walls held nothing but
those soft lights and rich, polished walnut paneling.

And smoke—a din of hazy smoke filling the room from the
men's cigars, puffing out in soft clouds, casting a wraithlike fog over
the lamps and burning my nostrils with its spiced, leathery scent.

"Arwen?" Ryder looked even more shocked than I felt.

The exhausted barkeep saved me a flustered, unintelligible response by barreling into my side. "My deepest apologies, Lord Switch," he blubbered to the muscular man seated at the far end of the oval table. "I tried to stop her, I swear it. She hopped over the bar!"

Kane chuckled, but his eyes stayed on his cards. Had he even looked at me since I came in?

"It's fine. Beautiful women are welcome at my game anytime." Lord Switch, who must have been the game leader or owner of the café, gave me a sinister smile that had the opposite effect of what I thought was intended. He was thick and strong and heavy, with a coarse sable beard, his teeth a brilliant white, and his clothes fine and detailed. His small, bright eyes were like coins and topped by thick, masculine brows, and he dragged them over my entire body with unabashed interest.

I swallowed a ragged breath, still trying to slow my shuddering heart. Kane finally looked up from his playing cards with bored curiosity and followed the man's gaze over to me. Only then did my cheeks go hot. Misted in sweat, feet blistered and dirty, hair frizzy from the heat and hours spent dancing . . . I must have looked horrendous. My fingers itched to tuck unruly hairs behind my ears.

"What are you doing here?" Ryder asked. I turned to my brother as he puffed out a thick cloud of smoke.

"I should ask you the same question. You're supposed to be watching Leigh."

Why was I always the one who had to make sure she was taken care of? Anger simmered inside me. Why was Ryder able to gamble and play and *live* while I had to—

"Calm down. She's with Barney. They're probably rescuing puppies or something."

Before the irritation could combust into rage, Fedrik leaned forward. "Good evening, Lady Arwen."

I curtsied belatedly. "Your Highness."

"No need for such formalities. Not after this morning."

"Fedrik, then," I conceded.

"What happened this morning?" Kane's voice was casual, but something else sparked in those silver eyes.

"I caught your healer sacrificing her boots to the sea."

"It was a mercy killing," I joked.

Kane didn't smile.

But Fedrik ignored him. "You look lovely. How did you hear of our card game?"

A blush crawled up my cheeks. "We were just having dessert after dancing and I . . . I thought I heard someone crying out for help."

Griffin looked up from his cards. "We?"

"That was this oaf." Kane jerked his chin toward a skinny man, so thin I almost missed him behind the other players. "He doesn't like losing his coin, do you, Trevyn?"

Trevyn shook his head ruefully. "I'll get you on the next one, though, pretty boy."

Kane raised an eyebrow. "Will you, though?"

Griffin leaned forward with intent. "Arwen, who's *we*?"

I opened my mouth to respond, but the man beside Trevyn released a hearty chuckle. "If Trevyn doesn't take half your stacks next hand, I will." He had a nose that protruded from his face like a doorknob and smiled wide as he smacked Kane on the back with a grin.

Kane's answering laugh sounded suspiciously like a grunt of pain. "And this is Rhett." He turned to the game leader at the head of the table. "And, Crawford, this is my healer, Lady Arwen. Ryder here is her brother."

My smile was wary as I greeted him.

Crawford only turned to Ryder with a menacing grin. "Unfortunate to have a sister that looks such as this one, no?"

Ryder and I made twin faces of disgust. "Well." I turned to leave. "Have a good night."

"Lady Arwen," Prince Fedrik called. "Don't let Crawford's poor manners end your evening. It's just that our finery suits you so well, he's blinded by it."

I felt heat rise along my neck, and while I didn't want to stay, I still smoothed down the layers of thin white cotton on my dress and muttered my thanks.

Fedrik's golden cheekbones lifted at my words. "I think it's all of us who should be thanking you."

Kane slammed his cards down on the table. "I fold." He stood, his chair scraping across the wood floor forcefully. "Lady Arwen, a word?"

"What's happening in there?" Mari's singsong voice echoed through the café on the other side of the doorway.

Griffin's eyes cut to mine and narrowed dangerously. "Get her out of here."

I felt my brows pull together in confusion. The rest of the table, which had continued playing their game despite my interruption, stalled to peer at him as well.

"Relax, Commander. The ladies are leaving," Kane said before crossing the room to me and wrapping a gentle yet firm hand around my waist. "After you."

But Mari bounced through the door, plopping down next to Ryder in one of the two remaining open seats at the table. She still had a dollop of lemon custard on her elbow, but it seemed that eating had sobered her up a bit.

"What are we playing? I love cards."

Kane and Griffin released simultaneous groans. Crawford feasted his eyes on Mari's every movement as if she were a present wrapped in a bow just for him. Even sweaty and covered in lemony sugar, Mari was a vision.

Griffin ground his jaw shut. I could almost hear his teeth fusing together. "*We* aren't playing anything, witch." He turned his concrete glare to me. "You both need to scram. Now."

"Or you can stay, Red," Ryder said to Mari, his expression eager. "I can teach you how to play."

Mari's eyes shone at his offer, and my stomach fell. The alcohol had all but fully left my system and a numb fog was beginning to cloud my mind once more. That frivolously stuffed bed was calling to me.

"Why such a killjoy, Commander?" Trevyn asked, sipping his overflowing mug of ale and spilling a bit on the fabric of the table. "The more the merrier!"

"Indeed," Crawford drawled. "And this one seems less shy."

Despite the urge to sneer, I couldn't help but look at Mari with envy. She was having the night of her life. Laughing, drinking, about to play cards with handsome, affluent men without a care in the world. I already missed who I had been when I was filled with drink and dancing until my feet were raw.

And I could feel Kane's hand on my ribs like pure heat.

"No, Griffin's right, it's past this one's bedtime." Kane gestured at me, shrugging in faux disappointment, and sending humiliation twisting in my chest. He wasn't my keeper.

"Actually, I think we'll stay."

Kane's eyes were spears as I slipped from his grasp. The single look alone was enough to light my blood on fire. I nearly hummed.

*"Arwen—"*

"King Ravenwood," Prince Fedrik interjected. "Isn't Lady Arwen just about old enough to decree her own bedtime?" I bit back a smile. My savior—the prince who despised Kane. "Surely you can't be so afraid of gambling with a woman? I promise not to heckle when she takes you for all you're worth."

Trevyn and Rhett chuckled, Ryder already teaching Mari the rules of the game. He halted only to wipe lemon cream off her bare arm with a single outstretched finger, and Griffin held his cards so tightly I could have sworn they ripped at his thumbs.

"Fine. But I'll need that word with you first." Kane's eyes held such lethal command I didn't dare argue.

"Fine," I mimicked, following his towering form through the door and out into the café.

# 10

ARWEN

THE CAFÉ HAD CLOSED FOR THE NIGHT. CANDLES HAD ALL been snuffed out, the front door locked, even the intertwined couple had left, likely off to knot themselves into one in the privacy of their own bedroom. My gaze lifted to Kane, my breath hitching in my lungs. As usual, it was an effort to tear my eyes away. His unruly dark hair was hardly tamed by the hand he so often ran through it, that broad hand always adorned in sleek, masculine silver rings that matched his piercing eyes.

But he only cut me a cursory glance with that same bored, if not slightly annoyed expression I had come to hate all those months ago in Shadowhold. "Dessert and dancing, huh? Where was my invitation?"

"I had others to keep me company. The men here are impressive dancers. Very *sensual*."

Kane's eyes were hard and bright, but his expression stayed the same. "How titillating."

His dismissal caught me off guard, and silence bloomed as I couldn't think of a witty retort.

"Nice catching up. Time to go."

"What is your issue?" I hissed at him. "Mari and I can't join your little boys-only card game? I didn't realize Amelia was the only woman you deemed acceptable to socialize with."

I could tell by his rigid jaw that Kane had been about to lay into me, until amusement seized his eyes. He ran a hand down his face—a habit of his that still had a shameful effect on me—and took a deep, soothing inhale. "Let's come back to your jealously over the time I spend with Amelia later. I'd like to dig into that. Maybe over dinner tomorrow night?"

I scoffed, rolled my eyes, and might have even snorted as well—just to make sure he really understood my lack of interest in such a proposal—but he continued as if I hadn't done anything at all.

"Those men are dangerous. Crawford Switch isn't just a Citrine noble; he's a crime lord. And Rhett and Trevyn are his thugs." His expression softened only slightly. "I'd rather you and the witch were nowhere near them."

"Why are you here, then? Playing cards with crooks?"

His smile was cruel. "Is that not behavior fitting of a monster like me?"

I wouldn't dignify that with a response. It was too easy.

His jaw tightened. "We think Crawford might know where the Blade of the Sun is. He's a . . . collector, of sorts. Procurer of fine and rare objects. His card game was the only way to get near him without risking Broderick and Isolde's fury. The three of them are close."

"Why is Fedrik here?"

"Your lapdog plays in the monthly games." Kane made a tutting noise as he straightened a ring on his thumb. "Horrible habit, really."

I couldn't roll my eyes at Kane anymore; I'd go cross-eyed soon. "And Ryder?"

"I invited him. The kid seemed like he could use a break."

"You brought him just to torture Griffin?"

"I can't help it—their feud over the witch tickles me."

"You really are a monster."

"So I've been told." His smirk was wicked as he leaned closer. "Now go grab your inebriated little friend and get back to the palace."

But I didn't want to go back there. I didn't want to sleep for days anymore. Or lie awake in bed, beside a sleeping Leigh, and think of nothing. To toss and turn as if I could roll away from all the emptiness.

No, I wanted the delicious, exhilarating spike in my bloodstream every time Kane was angry with me. Every time his eyes bored into mine in reprimand or thinly veiled ire. The light and airy warmth I felt around Fedrik was a summer sprinkle compared to the heart-rattling monsoon of chemistry that doused Kane and me. We had been speaking again for less than two days and already it was wreaking havoc on my psyche.

"Now, Arwen," he said, taking my wrist in his hand gently, but firmly enough to convey his severity.

The touch sent stars through my veins. Humming. Combusting. He could probably feel my pulse as it raced.

"I told you not to touch me."

I yanked free and slipped back into the game room, even smokier now than it had been before.

"You finally joining us? I have a great hand." Trevyn lifted his brows at me.

"Yes," I chirped, before sitting down. "Deal me in."

"Woo!" cheered Mari.

After a beat standing behind me like a headstone, Kane sat back down next to his commander.

"Coin on the table, ladies," Rhett drawled. "Ten thousand to play."

My mouth hung open. *Ten thousand?* I should have known. An elite private game for nobles and royalty—*shit, shit, shit.* I searched through my satchel and found a handful left over from dinner. Maybe seventeen or so. "Will this do?" I tried to bat my eyelashes.

Rhett and Trevyn laughed like rabid animals at my insufficient coin, nearly to tears, but Crawford's icy expression was what made my stomach turn.

Kane chuckled. "Well, it was fun while it lasted."

Griffin sighed in relief.

"I'm happy to loan you both some. Kane fronted your brother his dues," Fedrik proposed.

It was a kind offer, but I didn't want Fedrik's coin. Especially not after Kane referred to him as my *lapdog.* I didn't want any of their help. "There has to be something else I can use?"

Crawford looked at Rhett before turning to Mari and me. "The only other currency is surely too lewd for women such as your-selves."

I swallowed hard. "Try me."

"Your clothes." His broad, sharklike smile gleamed and a chill clawed through me at both the sight and the suggestion.

"Nobody wants to see that," Ryder groaned.

"Enough, now." Kane's voice was lethal as he stood, shaking the table beneath us and sending towers of chips cascading over the floor.

"Watch it, man!" barked Rhett.

I couldn't stop my gaze from flicking to him. Sheer, punishing rage simmered in his eyes. I couldn't tell if it was from the way Crawford was toying with me or the thought of me stripping for all these men. Or if it was how impotent he was in this moment—unable to control me or anyone else. Whatever it was, I *loved* it.

"Fine." I surprised myself with the assuredness in my voice.

"Me too! Stripping and cards—how fun." Mari hiccupped.

"Why don't you sit this one out?" I said to her, low enough for only her ears. She was too drunk to agree to something so stupid.

"Oh, come on, Arwen," she whispered back. "You take everything so seriously! Wasn't it you at dinner who said we should try making some mistakes?"

"I meant— Never mind."

Rhett dealt us in, and I couldn't help but glance at Griffin, whose pale green eyes were boring deeply into mine. He was less upset when we were under siege.

I shrugged at him. It wasn't my fault Mari was a spitfire. Most likely she'd be incredible anyway and take all our coin without losing so much as the shoe on her foot.

~✦~

I HAD DISCOVERED THE ONE THING ON THE CONTINENT THAT Mari was atrocious at. Maybe it was the orange wine and ale and sugar flowing through her system, but Mari couldn't bluff for the life of her. When she had anything halfway decent, a rosy pink glow would spread across her cheeks. A lousy hand and she'd frown at her cards, as if they had gone out of their way to disappoint her.

I wasn't quite as inept as Mari was, but hadn't been doing much better, either. I had lost the meager coin in my satchel, both shoes, an earring, and the white silk ribbon from my hair.

Kane—who was an excellent gambler, and was leading with more than half the coin at the table, and most of Mari's and my accessories—hadn't given me more than one single glare etched in steel since we began playing, but I didn't care. I liked the gameplay, the rush of betting, and the anticipation of the win. I liked the dangerous men's eyes on me. The illicit thrill. Kane's anger and possessiveness over each slice of my body that I offered to these gluttonous men was an added bonus.

Rhett brought us each another round of drinks, and I drank my bitter, pungent spirit down in a single long swallow before asking for two more. The current hand at play was down to Mari and Griffin. He had significantly more coin than there were items of clothing left on Mari, and had chosen to raise.

"Just fold," he said to her, on edge.

"But I have great cards." She smiled coyly.

"I can tell from your face that you don't."

"Don't listen to him, doll," Rhett jumped in. Then, not as quietly as he intended, he muttered to Trevyn, "I want to see that blouse come off."

Ryder shot Rhett a foul glare and leaned forward to shield Mari from their eyes. But Mari hadn't even noticed their exchange as she cross-referenced her cards with the five laid out on the table.

Griffin leaned closer to her. "Will you please fold?"

"You'll just have to wait and see," Mari retorted, still trying to add her cards up in her head. As if realizing she *did* indeed know what she was doing, Mari beamed. "Oh! I call."

Griffin's face became stone.

"How about with that stunning necklace of yours?" Crawford mused. I wondered if he knew something about the piece, being the collector that he was.

For the first time all evening, Mari's smile slipped. *"No,"* she said too quickly. The table shifted in uncomfortable silence. "No," she tried again, more pleasant this time. "I call with my blouse."

Griffin's eyes went as wide as the coins on the table.

"Woah there, Red, you sure?" Ryder asked.

"I'm sure," Mari said, laying down her cards with pride. "Not too bad, huh?"

They were actually decent. A pair of sevens. With the other seven on the board she had three of a kind.

She looked up at Griffin, her eyes lit with the challenge. "And what do you have, Commander?"

The entire room had narrowed in on them. Even Crawford was absorbed in their standoff. Griffin's jaw was rigid, his green eyes like frosted glass as he didn't even look down to his cards once before saying, "You've got me beat." He pushed his stack of coin toward her gently, and buried his cards back in the deck.

I raised a brow at him as Rhett groaned.

Mari whooped and hollered. "I did not expect that!"

"Nice one, Red," Ryder said with a half laugh.

Kane caught my gaze, looked to Griffin, and then gave me the tiniest shake of his head, confirming what I already assumed to be true. Griffin had not really had the lesser hand.

"Where's Princess Amelia tonight?" Fedrik asked Kane, before sipping his mug of ale.

Ugh. Not him, too.

"How should I know?"

"I assumed you two were . . . ?"

I attempted a semi-interested smile as Rhett dealt the next hand, though my brain was screaming.

Kane said only, "You assumed incorrectly."

"Ah, my mistake, then." Prince Fedrik took a peek at his cards before throwing them in the center of the table to fold.

"Are you interested?" Kane asked. "I assumed King Eryx would have had the agreement drawn up for your nuptials the minute he entered the city."

"Eh." Fedrik leaned back in his chair with ease, exposing a thin band of tanned abdomen. "My parents have given up on arranged marriages. Didn't go so well the last time, if I recall." He shot a half smile at Kane. "And," he added, "she seems a bit . . . intense."

"She is intense," I said. "But she protects her kingdom and her people with that intensity. She's twice the ruler her father is."

Kane raised his brows at me, and I offered him a small shrug. It was true.

"More importantly, she's a famous beauty," Crawford said to Fedrik. "You'd be lucky to own such a woman. I'd bed her every morning and night."

"He wouldn't own her," Mari said, and I remembered that she didn't know how dangerous Crawford was. "They'd be wed to each other, as equals."

Crawford regarded Mari with curiosity, as if just seeing her for the first time. "Did the commander call you *witch* earlier because of your grating voice or can you truly do magic?"

"She's an exceptional witch," Ryder chimed in. "More power in this one than I've ever seen."

Mari's eyes filled with warmth before she caught herself and looked down at her cards.

"What would you know of it, thief?" Griffin leveled his gaze at my brother. I couldn't tell if he had bristled against their flirting or wished to hide Mari's abilities from Crawford or both. The bizarre dynamics of this game were starting to hurt my head. I had another sip of my foul drink.

"When will you let that go?" Ryder huffed. "It was one time."

"He stole from you?" Crawford asked Griffin, interest piqued.

"He stole from *me*," Kane amended, before giving Ryder a bland smile. Ryder fidgeted in his chair.

Crawford glowered, unamused. "I've stripped men of their skin for less."

Tension dripped off the walls of the game room like the condensation on Crawford's mug. Only the sounds of coins being stacked and cards being dealt echoed in my ears.

"You're getting pretty decent at this, Arwen." I appreciated Fedrik deftly changing the subject, and with that same relaxed ease. "Do you gamble often?"

"No." Kane drained his drink. "She's not a degenerate like you, Prince."

Fedrik ignored him. "What do you think of Azurine?"

I took in a breath to answer but Kane cut me off again. "Not much."

"Does he always speak for you?" Fedrik asked lightly.

"No," Kane and I said in unison. I glared at him, trying to slice his tongue off with my mind.

"Your city is breathtaking," I managed. "I've never been anywhere like this."

"Well, I'll have to show you around sometime—"

"We leave tomorrow," Kane interrupted.

I spun to him. "We do?"

"Yes." His mouth cut a tight grin. "Bit too hot for my liking."

"Well, I'm staying."

"You are my *healer*. You will do as I say."

My blood boiled.

"Raise." Crawford threw fifty more coin onto the table.

I looked down at my cards. Two hearts. And two already on the table. All I needed was one more to make a flush. "Re-raise." I pushed in all the rest of the coin I had won.

"I'll raise both of you," said Rhett, adding at least a hundred more.

"I call." It fell out of my mouth.

"With what?" Crawford's eyes gleamed at the neckline of my eyelet lace dress.

I could renege. Claim I had miscalculated and see if they would let me off the hook. But seeing the looks on their faces, knowing how desperately the crooks wanted to see me cower, it only made me more determined. Bolder. Braver.

I looked down at myself, appraising. I couldn't give up my dress and risk nudity. I wasn't even wearing a chemise or corset, which weren't customary in this kingdom. That only left . . .

"My undergarments."

"Absolutely not," Kane bit out.

The last time I had felt this heated and restless and electrified . . . was in his arms. I chased after the feeling. "You don't own me. Or my undergarments."

Crawford's eyes gleamed with vicious pleasure. "I hope you know what you're doing. I have a full house already."

I needed that heart now. Any heart would do. Rhett dealt out the final card.

*Bleeding Stones.*

It was a four of clubs.

# 11

## KANE

ARWEN STOOD UP, DELICATELY TUCKED HER HANDS under her dress, and pulled down the lace garments. Then she threw them onto the table.

"There," she said. The chair beneath her scraped along the floor when she sat back down.

I bit down on my cheek until I tasted copper. A wisp of fabric shouldn't have this kind of effect on a man. And yet a spike of lust so powerful it made me dizzy rushed through my blood. I couldn't look at the others. I wouldn't be able to control my rage.

"Arwen! You minx," the witch lilted.

"I didn't think the dainty thing had it in her," Crawford muttered around his cigar.

But his eyes were so pleased. I wanted to carve them from his head.

Not being able to shift at all in Azurine was making it that much harder to control such urges. It was a release, it was exercise, and it staved off loneliness, bad impulses, and all my other brutish behavior. Though shifting used a lot of lighte, I wagered it was worth it, as I got myself into fewer scenarios that required I use my power in the first place.

*Deep breaths.*

Rhett's coins clinked, the sweet, rich rum of Griffin's drink filled my nostrils, and beside me smoke puffed from Trevyn's fat cigar, making the lamplight hazy.

I studied Arwen. The petal-pink blush that had bloomed on her cheeks and across her nose, her barely parted bee-stung lips, the surprising look of success, of pride—despite losing the hand—that danced in her eyes.

She felt . . . good. Perhaps a little frightened. But bold. Attractive. *Alive.*

Two weeks of watching Arwen move through the world like a ghost, and tonight she had returned to the land of the living. I wasn't naive to the siren call of sex and drink and danger. It had been my own lifeblood for many years.

"I'll never be able to scrub that image from my mind." Her brother groaned in disgust.

She laughed. Actually *laughed*. It had been weeks since I'd heard the sound. Like the ringing of temple bells, I felt that harmony in my entire body.

Nothing was safe. Not her bewitching smile when she laughed, nor her death glares when they were turned on me—on a daily basis, it was taking every inch of power in me, both lighte and sheer will, not to drop to the floor and beg her to put me out of my misery.

"You could have a promising career as a very specific type of entertainer, bird." Finally she looked in my direction, only to shoot me a withering glare. I clenched my jaw to suppress a smirk.

I narrowed all my dwindling focus down to the cards in my hands instead.

A pair of aces. Excellent.

I appraised Crawford. He had been drinking all night, slowly bleeding coin to the rest of us, and had just crossed his thick arms in thought—a sign I had discovered hours ago reflected a mediocre hand. This was the moment I had been waiting for all night.

"I'm all in," I crooned, shoving heavy stacks of coin and women's accessories into the center of the table.

"I'll call." Crawford's eyes were cool, even as anxious anticipation flashed in them. He turned his attention to Arwen, the only other player in the hand. "And what about the lady?"

Arwen considered her cards, then looked up at us. "All I have left to wager is my dress."

"You had a good run." I couldn't help myself. Flirting with her was the most pleasurable thing I had ever done. "I'll win your lacy underthings back for you."

A challenge flickered in her eyes. "I'm in."

"Arwen, you'll be naked," I nearly sputtered.

"Bleeding Stones," Ryder spat out, before tossing his cards into the center to fold.

"But I want something more than your coin for my final piece of clothing," Arwen said to Crawford, ignoring us both.

He lifted a menacing brow. "Anything for the daring maiden."

"What can you offer me?" Seduction crept into her voice.

"Rubies? Diamonds? Name your price." Crawford ran an eye along Arwen's neck. A game now to him.

"Hmm." She tapped her finger to her lips in thought. "I travel with a king, so have no need for more jewels. Maybe I underestimated your reach? I was hoping for something a bit more . . . special." She frowned down at her cards and waited.

A huntress setting a trap.

"My reach is unlimited. What would excite you? Texts? Weapons? Something less . . . refined?"

Arwen's mouth soured at Crawford's implication.

I was tempted to shear the skin off the man right then. To inflict as much agony on him as he had on others. On the Mer girls. It was beyond an injustice that he would never pay for his crimes in full.

But Arwen covered her revulsion with a weighing frown. "What kind of weapons? Anything impressive? Please don't bore me with a shiny sword."

Crawford leaned in from his side of the table. "I have just the highly sought-after prize you seek. But it's worth a lot more than one naked woman."

Griffin stiffened in his seat beside me.

"Careful, Crawford," I murmured. I didn't care if he had the blade in his breast pocket—the pig didn't deserve to look at Arwen, let alone insult her.

But she just sat back, the picture of calm. "No, King Ravenwood. He's right. Maybe I could just . . . see such an item?"

Crawford grinned. "That can be arranged. If you win."

"Let's play, then."

Rhett dealt the cards out to Crawford, Arwen, and me.

A spread ideal for a flush—four of the five were spades.

My aces of diamonds and clubs rendered worthless.

Crawford's eyes had gone viciously black. "Flush," he said, laying out his king and ace of spades. "Sorry, pretty." Venom crept into his grin. "Now *strip* for me."

If Arwen so much as stood to undress, I'd reduce this room to kindling before she got a single cotton layer above her knee.

But she only smiled. Not a phony, performative grin. But that genuine, brilliant, dazzling Arwen smile that made it hard for me to walk straight.

"No, *I'm* sorry. I believe I have a full house." Arwen splayed the cards out in front of her. She did indeed have a full house—the only hand that beat Crawford's.

Victory rang in my ears. My gorgeous, sneaky bird.

Crawford said nothing, but Rhett let out a slow whistle.

"Well done, Arwen," Fedrik murmured.

Arwen pulled the mass of coin and clothing into her, handing back Mari's shoes and belt. Crawford didn't move a single muscle as she slid her undergarments on beneath the table.

"Now, about that prize," she purred.

A dark cloud had settled over the collector's competitive mood. "Come by my villa tomorrow night, and I'll show it you."

"We leave Azurine tomorrow, as my king said."

*My king.*

"I'm afraid I don't have the weapon on me at the moment." He jerked his chin down to his oxblood tunic, with its fine gold threads and his heaps of thick jewelry.

"I'll come to your villa tonight, then," she pushed.

The table shifted in discomfort, Ryder picking at his nails, Fedrik looking out the window at the moon's pale glow—but I only relaxed into my chair.

"Come on, Crawford, don't disappoint the lady." I grinned. "A deal's a deal."

"I don't keep it at my villa," Crawford said, his knees bumping against the table as he stood.

Arwen stood, too, face still a bit pink and flushed. "Then where?"

Griffin straightened in his seat. Crawford's cursory gaze cut from me to him to Arwen. Then to Mari, and I wanted to kick Ryder for outing her as a powerful witch. I could see Crawford sizing up his odds against this room. My fists twitched with the thrill of the looming fight.

Lurching forward, Crawford grabbed his coin and barreled toward the back of the room, Rhett and Trevyn close behind him.

Now that, I actually hadn't expected.

Crawford was fast for such a hefty piglet, but I was on him in seconds, my shoulder just narrowly edging open the distressed door at the back of the room they had slipped inside of, its wood marred by nicks and stains.

"Fuck off, Ravenwood," Crawford spat through the crevice.

I would have laughed, had Arwen not raced toward the back room as well.

"Stay out there."

"No chance in the Stones," she huffed as she slipped with immeasurable grace through the narrow gap Crawford and I had inadvertently held open for her.

I had forgotten how damn lithe she was.

Promise to Isolde forgotten, I slammed the door open with shards of pure black mist, nearly sending the rickety thing off its hinges and knocking Crawford and the two men to the ground in a heap.

Crawford practically mangled Trevyn trying to lunge for me, swinging and missing by a mile. One swift kick to the gut sent him back down to the threadbare rug of his clandestine office.

The walls of the dimly lit room were plastered in antique oil paintings and framed clippings from local Citrine papers. But other than a shelf of tattered books, it held nothing but a soiled green love seat, a dented metallic barrel—filled with some kind of thieved spirit, I was sure—and a leather chair behind a single desk that at one time might have been richly carved but was now tired and worn.

I heard Mari squeak from the poker table as Griffin strode in beside me. "Should I knock the two goons out?"

"You can't be serious," Fedrik said, a lilt to his voice that petered out as he, too, stepped inside and met my eyes. "My parents and Crawford can come to some kind of agreement to suit you and your healer. All this over a mere gambling debt?"

Spineless twat was not only unobservant, he was a puppet for his parents. Always had been.

"Listen to the prince," Crawford groaned from the dark carpet. "We can work this out easily."

"No, I don't believe we can." I rolled my shirtsleeves up and stepped closer to Crawford. Rhett flinched and Trevyn scampered into the corner on all fours. "Fedrik, if you would so kindly take my healer, her brother, and the witch back to the palace, Griffin and I will be right behind you."

When Crawford tried to crawl for his desk, I dug my boot into his outstretched fingers until I produced a satisfying *crunch*.

His pained moan curved my lips upward.

"I'm not going anywhere," Arwen said, arms folded. "I'm owed a blade."

"Arwen," her brother chided. I cut a glance back at him, still out in the game room, one arm wrapped around Mari's shoulders. "Come on."

"Go back to the palace, Ryder," Arwen said. "And take Mari with you."

He didn't need to be asked again.

Ryder and Mari filed out with haste and Fedrik only looked back at us once before following after them.

I faced Griffin. "Make sure he doesn't go straight to the queen."

"Yep." Griffin jerked his chin back toward Arwen, as if to say, *And what about her?*

"She'll be fine."

I wasn't sure, but for an instant it seemed like that was pride gleaming in Arwen's eyes.

# 12

## ARWEN

KANE HAULED CRAWFORD UP BY HIS TUNIC AND THREW him deeper into the room with a grunt. Then he turned to Rhett and Trevyn, the latter's collar trembling at his bobbing throat. "Do not call for help. Do not alert anyone that we are here or neither of you, nor your employer, will live to see daybreak."

"Now, wait one moment," Rhett began, voice weak—

Kane slammed the door shut with only that vicious split of shadowed mist, shaking the thin walls around us and producing a yelp from Trevyn. He crawled on all fours to the door, wrenched it open with quivering hands, and dashed out the other side.

"And you?"

Rhett wasted no time abandoning Crawford as well, even going so far as to close the door politely behind him. Kane smirked.

"You're demented." Crawford's eyes shimmered with the first hint of fear as Kane stalked toward him, small tendrils of wicked power unfurling around his feet as he moved.

The burly noble didn't waste a second to see what Kane had

planned. He threw himself against the wall at the back of the room, sending two paintings in antique frames clattering down to the floor. Bathed in the dim candlelight, he tried to climb toward the window above like a scurrying rodent. But it was too tall, just barely out of reach even for a man of his stature, and his feet couldn't find purchase against the wood.

Kane closed in on him with ease and turned Crawford to face us, wrapping a large hand around his throat and holding him high against the wall he had tried to scamper up, his feet jolting uselessly in the air.

"You'll regret this," Crawford swore. "I'll keep your eyes in a jar in my villa." He scraped and clawed, trying to grasp at Kane's face, but Kane had the more significant arm span. Even Crawford's kicks barely connected.

"The Blade of the Sun," Kane said. "Immediately. Before this café becomes a pitiful pile of stone and playing cards."

"I've never heard of such a weapon."

"Bullshit," Kane thundered, bashing Crawford's head into the wall.

I couldn't help my flinch.

But the rest of his words were lost on me. Kane's violence had dislodged a few paintings and debris from the walls, and something was poking through shattered glass on the floor. It looked—

No, that couldn't be possible.

It looked like a drawing.

A drawing of *me*.

The sound of wet pummeling echoed through the room as I knelt to examine the paper clipping. Sure enough, the parchment in my hands read *Have You Seen This Woman?* and below that, *Wanted for Treason* alongside a near-identical drawing of my face.

*No, no, no—*

A chill pumped into my veins.

"Fine, fine—" Crawford spit, heaving after another round of Kane's blows. "I may know of the thing, but I don't have it. I never did."

"Who does?"

"If I knew, why would I tell you?"

Kane reared his fist back, thorns and shadow twining along his palm and up his forearm, before crashing it into Crawford's jaw with force. Enough to break the bones, but not enough to knock him out. Or kill him.

Crawford bit back a groan. Coughing, he spit blood onto Kane's other hand, still clenched around his neck.

Under my breath, and turning my face from Crawford's bloodied, pulpy one, I whispered to Kane, "He has a wanted poster of me. It was framed on his wall."

When Kane's quicksilver eyes met mine, it wasn't anger that simmered in them. It was fear. And that fear laced into his voice like poison as he turned back to Crawford and said, "Unfortunately, you've just become worth more to me dead than alive."

Undiluted terror pooled in the man's beady eyes. The realization that he would die this evening. That there would be no narrowly escaping with his life, no respite from the pain, the dread.

That it was over.

Crawford thrashed against Kane's hold and his grim eyes cut to mine, pleading. I winced as Kane let his fist loose again, slamming into Crawford's gut and then his kidney. He sputtered, unable to breathe, until he sucked in a lungful to moan in agony.

"Why?" he asked between breaths, bright red coating his teeth and lips. "Because of *her*?"

He spat again, but Kane's choke hold only tightened. Gasping, he tore at the hand around his throat.

Kane was going to kill him before we learned anything.

And all because he knew that I was—

Maybe . . . maybe that was it.

I moved toward them, skin tingling with fear and . . . anticipation. Some kind of grisly exhilaration. "You know who I am?"

*"Arwen—"*

I shot Kane a look in an effort to convey the new ruse we were playing. No longer subservient healer and dark king, but instead, powerful Fae outlaw and human brute.

Though he remained silent, there was an uncanny interest in Crawford's beady eyes I had missed before. How could I have been so oblivious? He had looked at me just as Lieutenant Bert had. He had known I was Fae all along.

Kane tightened his grip.

"You knew all night."

"Yes," Crawford spat. "I have a dignitary friend in Garnet. He told me that you're . . . *different.*"

"My king wasn't lying. He'll strangle you to death."

"It'll be easy," Kane swore, "like juicing a lemon—"

*"But* what I'll do to you will be far, far worse. Give us the location of the Blade of the Sun, and leave with your life."

Crawford studied me, and despite my racing heart, I suppressed the urge to fidget. Then his eyes landed on Kane. "Tell your animal to release me."

I motioned for him to do so, and Kane only hesitated a moment before dropping the criminal without pretense. Crawford fell to the floor like a deflated ball, face slamming into the moth-ravaged rug, sputtering and puckering for air.

Kane wiped his bloodied hands on his pants.

"A year ago I heard it was in Reaper's Cavern," Crawford said when he had caught his breath. "Nobody was ever going to retrieve the thing without dying. So I said it was in my possession. People believed me. It was good for my image. That's it." He spat blood onto the floor and rubbed his jaw and throat.

Kane paced across the room to lean against the carved desk, and it creaked under his weight. "I thought Reaper's Cavern was a myth."

I prowled closer to Crawford's hunched form. "If you're trying to trick us—"

"No!" He cowered. "I'm not! It's not."

Playing with Kane had been one thing. The thrill, the hunger in it—but this was something I had never felt before. Crawford's wide-eyed expression sent a wave of pleasurable sickness through my system.

He *feared* me.

*Me.*

He feared what I could do to him. I had never felt less like a victim in twenty years of being alive. No, I felt like a nightmare. A dangerous, tantalizing *nightmare.*

"The cave sits outside the town of Frog Eye, in the Peridot Provinces. I watched thirty of my men walk in there to recover the treasure. Not one made it back to Azurine."

"I'm getting very bored, Crawford." The raw dominance in Kane's voice nearly bowed *me* into submission. "How do we get there?"

"How should I know? My men had the only map, and like I said, they all died."

Kane pushed himself off the scarred desk, stalking over to us as he rolled his sleeves, and drove his foot into Crawford's gut with enough force to send the man back into the wall. "Where do we find a *fucking* map?"

Crawford doubled over, retching onto the ground below us,

putrid ale and stomach acid seeping into dark threads. Kane seethed at him, disgusted.

"You'll never know," he croaked. "The Garnet dignitary I spoke of, the one who told me what you are . . . They're onto you. Unnatural abomination . . . Even when I'm gone, they promised me a piece of the Fae girl would live on in my collection." Crawford's eyes pinned mine. Fury, fear, and . . . acceptance.

No, no, no—

"They promised me her *heart*." His grin, pinned on Kane, split his face in dripping red and pearly white.

I wasn't breathing. My eyes shot to Kane. "Wait, don't—"

But Kane snarled as he unleashed the power that had been so fiercely fighting to escape all evening, a thin rope of smoke ripping from his wrist and looping around Crawford's neck. He fought— limbs spasming in every direction, reaching for Kane, for me, gripping at the rug. But it was useless. Kane bared his teeth in feral pleasure as the wisp of pure, black night tightened and tightened and *tightened*—

Until Crawford slumped over, gray and cold, his coin leaking out of his pockets like a greedy pool of golden blood.

Palpable silence rippled through the room.

I wanted to look elsewhere.

Anywhere but those vulgar, blood-filled, vacant eyes.

But Kane's expression was even worse. Crawford was vile, and surely deserved death. But it was Kane who looked . . . *alive*. More *invigorated* than he had in weeks. All because he had snuffed the life out of someone. Exiled them into nothingness.

Something that had destroyed me, shredded and shattered my soul so intensely that I was now a walking shell, Kane did effortlessly and without remorse.

And then, he grinned.

A wild, heartless smile that crept into his jaw and lips as his lighte receded up his forearms and back into his body.

I had run in here after a man like this? After all he had done to me? Out of some revolting need to make sure *he* wouldn't be in danger?

"How . . . how could you have done that?" I wasn't sure which of us I was talking to.

Kane sucked in a steady lungful of air. "Save your lecture. The map's in here. He kept looking around the room."

In a daze I swept the space. "Maybe the walls . . . they're covered in—"

But Kane prowled over to that ornate, creaking desk. I watched, waiting for him to scavenge through the drawers, the papers crowding its face, the inkwell in its corner. Instead, he nudged it a few times. Tentative, studying—looking for something. He prodded it again and I realized he was hunting for the source of the wobble. The weak leg that couldn't sustain the weight of the hefty wood. When he found it, he knelt and yanked the thing clean off, toppling the desk altogether with a loud *crunch*.

I jumped at the sound—the papers floating across the floor, the ink that soaked into the carpet below.

Kane returned to me with the desk leg—an intricately engraved wooden stake—and held it out for me like a dog with a bone. His hand was shaking.

Before I could breathe a word, the door behind us flung open.

Trevyn rushed in, raising a silver machete that glinted in the candlelight. "Leave him alone!" he sputtered, red in the face and sweating furiously.

"Fuck," Kane swore, unsheathing his own sword.

But Trevyn froze, eyes not on Kane, but rather on Crawford's slumped body. He gasped, the machete now pointed out as if to keep us at bay rather than to attack, panic worming its way through his slender face and quaking limbs.

"Trevyn," I cautioned. "You tell everyone Crawford choked to death on his dinner. All right? You found him like this. Live the rest of your life with that secret, and we'll spare you."

"We won't be doing that," Kane said, more tired than anything.

Guilt slid through my chest. Even a seedily employed man like Trevyn had a life he cared to live. Hopes and dreams and possibly those whom he loved. Those who loved him. And I didn't want to see Kane murder another man. Especially not one who had only tried to protect his patron.

"If Trevyn swears to never tell a soul what he saw," I said to Kane with as much severity as I could muster, "then we can."

"Why should we?" Kane's eyes were predatory on the crook.

"Because I *said so.*"

I was placing a lot of faith in Crawford's big mouth. In the hope that he had told his underling what I was. What I was capable of.

"I swear it," Trevyn stammered. "Whatever you say." The machete clanged to the tattered rug.

I stalked even closer to him, my hair beginning to feel a bit like static. "I will know if you're lying. I know *everything.*"

"I believe you," he whispered.

"If we find out you betrayed us, I will come to your home and drench all whom you love in blood. You'll be cleaning them out from under your fingernails for weeks."

"I think you proved your point, *oh powerful one,*" Kane said with irritation. "It's time to leave."

## 13

### ARWEN

Y OU DIDN'T HAVE TO WAIT FOR US," I SAID TO FEDRIK.
     The streets were empty at the strange hour—too late for the now-weary revelers, too early for the morning risers. We were alone save for a sleeping beggar and a stray tabby cat. I could smell the freshly caught fish and garden-grown kumquats from the nearby taverns, and I sucked in a lungful.

"I was too worried to go back with your brother and friend," Fedrik said, placing a hand on the small of my back. Griffin pushed off a stone column he had been leaning against to walk beside us. His expression was tight, being stuck outside with Fedrik clearly not how he wished to spend his night.

Fedrik guided me down a narrow alley on the way back to the palace. I had hoped his palm against my back might soothe me, or elicit something pleasant, but it didn't. Only that same suffocating hollowness settled back into my bones.

"What happened in there?" he asked.

"We got a map to the blade," Kane said to him, stepping into pace beside us.

Kane wiped his brow against the temperate night air. His shirt was coming unbuttoned and revealed a glistening, broad chest, and his sleeves had been rolled up to allow for seamless violence. His raven hair, so befitting of his namesake, curled at his neck from the humidity. A petrifying nightmare and bewitching dream all at once.

"And," he continued, with that tilted, murderous curve of his lips, "I killed Crawford."

Words lodged in my throat. Was he gloating?

Fedrik looked bewildered.

"Told you," Griffin huffed to Fedrik.

We weaved through a couple of disheveled fishermen making their way home from a tavern after what—given the rich odor of rum that permeated the air as we neared them—must have been a raucous night of heavy drinking.

Jealousy swamped me. I wouldn't have minded another glass of that orange wine myself.

"For men who could be tried for murder, you both seem quite glib." Prince Fedrik's words were coy but his tone was cutting. I stepped closer to him, and Kane studied the movement as if it were a personal insult.

"For someone who just lost a gambling buddy," Kane said, "you don't seem all that bereft."

"He wasn't my *buddy*. He was my parents' friend."

"I didn't know there was a difference," Kane hissed, and then, before Fedrik could defend himself, "You weren't aware he traded stolen goods?"

"You think petty thieves deserve to be murdered? You really are as ruthless as they say."

"The trafficking of young Mer girls isn't *petty thievery*."

I shut out the unfathomable images that flooded my mind. Fedrik, too, said nothing, rendered silent by disgust.

Kane only nodded, his eyes cold on the prince. "Some ruler of the kingdom you are. Commander Griffin can escort you back to the castle. I require my healer's assistance." Kane lifted his hand to us, knuckles bloody.

Fedrik turned in my direction. "Do you need me to stay?"

"She's *fine*," Kane thundered.

But Fedrik's eyes stayed on mine, and an incomprehensible giggle nearly burst from me. Maybe at the raw fury Kane would unleash if I said yes. Or maybe at the naive idea that if Kane wanted to hurt me, there was anything at all Fedrik could do to stop him.

"He's right," I finally said. "I'm fine, thank you."

Fedrik lifted my hand to his mouth, pressed a single kiss there, and retreated to the palace without so much as a look to Kane. Griffin watched him go but made no move to follow.

"Pathetic," Kane spat.

Under flaming turquoise streetlamps, the city was bathed in uneven tones of blue and black and gold that painted him like angry brushstrokes.

I folded my arms against the wind as it sailed through the city streets. "What is? Leaving when I asked? Respecting someone's wishes? Can you even fathom such a thing?"

"No," he snarled. "Not when it comes to your safety."

"Clearly the only thing I need to be kept safe from is you." I gestured to the café and the dead body that was still cooling within its walls.

Kane sighed, drawing a hand over his forehead. "He had to die."

"Funny, I've heard you say that before."

"Probably because it was true."

"Or because you get off on it. Because you're sick."

He prowled toward me, eyes black. Pure poison black. When he was so close I could smell his leather and sweat, he murmured, "I'll show you what I fucking get off on."

"All right," Griffin cut in, jolting me and slicing the tension between us. I had forgotten he was standing there. "I think that's enough for tonight."

"Go home, Griffin," Kane snarled, eyes never leaving my pursed lips. "We're fine."

"You could have turned Crawford in to the king and queen. Why did you murder him?" I pressed. "Do you like it?"

"He knew who you were. He also traded little Mer girls like candies to his friends. You don't think a man like that deserves death?"

I spun on my heel with his words and walked away from the narrow courtyard, out into the wider street where I could breathe. "That's not the point. You will always find the worst men and kill them. Not because they deserve it, but because you *want* to hurt."

Kane stepped into pace beside me, Griffin already strides ahead, sick of our bickering.

I was, too.

"And what?" Kane pressed. "You'll save every trembling asshole who says *please* until one of them turns around and slices you clean through?"

"There is *nothing* wrong with showing people *mercy*. I shouldn't have expected a savage like you to understand."

"You know what? That's good. *Be* angry with me. *I'm* angry with me. About Siren's Bay. The prophecy. Your mother—"

I stopped cold. "Don't you *speak* of her—"

"I welcome your anger. Relish it, in fact. Much better than watching you walk through life like a corpse. So give me the worst of it. I'll take anything you've got. Just stop putting yourself in situations like that to *feel* something."

Shame coated my throat. "Situations like what?"

"Drinking recklessly, taunting Crawford, taking your damned *clothes off*—you're going to get yourself killed trying to feel alive."

"You think I *want* something to happen to me?"

"I'm starting to think that's exactly what you want."

"That's not— I'm not— You know nothing about me." I tried to cut around him and nearly toppled into his chest. Looking past him, I realized we were alone. Our only company the distant sound of waves crashing against the shore and crickets chirping in the lush cypress trees.

"Don't I? I know what you fear. I know what you pray for. I know how you like to be touched, how you *taste* . . ."

When his eyes lit with something raw, something primal, I raised my hand to hit him. To channel my fury into something palpable and tangible like his smug, male face. But my fist collided with his palm instead of his jaw. He held my hand in midair as he stepped closer, invading my senses.

"I let you do that once, bird," he murmured. "It won't happen again."

We were pressed together now, and I could feel his body against mine, warm from wanting and hard like stone. His thumb stroked softly along my still-wound fist, and I hummed involuntarily at the sensation.

His eyes emptied of all silver. Pure predatory pupil.

And I could admit it to myself.

How badly I had missed his body. His smell. His muscled chest—both comforting and deadly powerful.

But now there was something else, too. The need to follow that surge of pure heat. The rush expanding my lungs, the fire funneling through my blood when he looked at me with that excruciating, near-predatory lust—I was spellbound by it. And a bit insatiable.

I reached higher on my toes, needing to feel that heavy, thick weight that was pressing against my stomach a little lower. Just a little—the friction at my core as I pressed myself against him brought another hum from my lips.

He grunted. "What happened to *don't touch me*?"

"Who said anything about *you* touching *me*?"

"Such a cruel, wicked little bird."

"Maybe so." I wasn't sure what I was asking for, but still I said, "Please, Kane."

"Fuck," he groaned, finally, *blessedly*, releasing my fist to run his hands up my sides—those *hands*, like they were made for my body—and scoop me into a bruising kiss.

All I could make sense of were our tongues, and our mingled, hissing breath, and my hair, twisted in those massive hands of his, and him, as he cradled my head, coaxing rushed breaths and whimpers from me—

I knew I had missed the curve of his lips against my own, knew I had been craving him like a habit I couldn't kick, but had never expected—never *known*—it would be like this. Like breathing again after weeks and weeks and *weeks* without air.

Kane backed me against the sandstone wall beneath a covered balcony—long dress tangling underfoot as he maneuvered me by the rib cage to exactly where he pleased—and palmed my ass and hips hungrily, lifting me against him. Kissing roughly as if at any moment, I was going to change my mind. The shameful truth was that I could do nothing of the sort—I was already damp for him between my legs, and each soft groan that rumbled from his broad chest made me wetter, that pulse in my core more demanding.

He deepened our kiss—a raw, searching, messy thing—taking his time, slowing to be more thorough, and when his thumb lazily circled my pointed nipple through the sheer fabric, I groaned into his mouth.

He hissed in pleasure, aligning our bodies so his cock pushed harder against me.

I writhed along him, clawed at him, nails scratching at his neck so hard I thought I might draw blood. The image only ignited me further. Under the vines above us, cloaked in night, I swirled my tongue along his, swallowing his grunts and sighs, feeling his hands work their way lower, lower, *lower*—

"Can I?" he ground out against my lips, when his thumb grazed between my thighs.

*Yes, yes, yes.*

Sparks and flames were rushing through me, lighting me from the inside out.

Wild, reckless, stupid, but *alive*—

I nodded my head vehemently, my lips wet against his. He was breathless as he groaned my name. Like he was suffering interminable torture.

I fished for his leather laces. I felt no shame—he wanted me. And that single truth thrummed through my entire body like liquid lightning.

His lips found the base of my throat—licking, lapping, teeth and breath—as he rubbed me, making me mewl. I whimpered again as he sucked my collarbone, palmed my breast, holding my body like it was precious—

*Delicate*—

Something worth worshipping.

The kiss was turning. Becoming emotional. Intimate. He was cradling my face with such reverence, fusing his body into mine with care and effort. Giving me such space, such freedom with his body . . . Poignant, personal, so much so that I could almost hear his heart—

"Stop," I rasped. "Let me go."

He shuddered, but lowered me to the ground instantly, pants still half-unlaced. His breathing was as heavy as my own.

I stared at him, unable to form words around the piercing ache in my chest.

"Don't look at me like that," he managed. "I can't *breathe* when you look at me like that."

All the boldness in those eyes—all that lust—gone. The moon was a bath of light across his charcoal hair, his knotted brow, his heaving chest.

"What do you want from me?" he asked, voice too low.

Angry tears burned behind my eyes. I swallowed against them. My lips stung.

I felt like screaming.

He shook his head, gazing toward the harbor, where the moonlight was fading, making way for a prying sun.

"I don't know . . ." I shuddered in a ragged inhale. "You broke—you broke my heart."

He flinched at my words. The look of shock on his face would have been priceless an hour ago. I would have reveled in the triumph of surprising him, of eliciting such a reaction from him.

But not now.

"You asked me once if I thought love was a weakness," he said, too low. "You, Arwen. *You* are my weakness."

"Then I'm doing you a favor." My voice sounded cold even to my own ears.

My whole life I had been all too weepy. An easy crier in both joy and despair.

Now, I couldn't produce one single tear.

I sucked in a steady inhale, the confusing emotions already retreating. Spinelessly slinking under that foundation of numbness.

Kane's eyes were as hard as granite and just as sharp. "You're scared. To be with me, to feel something, now that you have to face all that I tried to protect you from." He inhaled, too, running a shaking hand through his hair in exasperation. "I understand, I do. Just don't say you're doing this to save *me* the pain. It's too late for me."

I wanted to say it was too late for me, too. That I was doomed. That I wouldn't have enough time left in this world to heal from his lies, his betrayal, from the trauma of the last few weeks, and then, after I had repaired all the parts of me that had shattered, to see if there was anything left inside that was capable of giving him another chance.

Giving *us* another chance.

Under the last dregs of pure moonlight all I found to say was "I'm sorry."

# 14

## ARWEN

THE KNOCK AT THE DOOR OF OUR SUITE THE NEXT DAY WAS inexplicably familiar. Solid and controlled, nothing musical to it—not Mari, then. Kane's was more demanding. Leigh's little fists didn't make as much noise. Ryder's were more impatient. I finished rinsing my hands in the washroom and swung the suite door open, only to find the wrinkled, kind eyes I had missed so terribly the past few weeks.

I threw myself into Dagan with open arms, enveloping him in a hug I don't think either of us expected.

"What are you doing here?" I asked, my face pressed into his layered tunics. He smelled like black pepper and seawater. He must have just arrived in Azurine this morning.

"Hello to you, too, Arwen," he said, patting me squarely on the back as if I were his associate.

That was all right, I'd take what I could get.

When I could feel Dagan growing uncomfortable with the length of our hug, I released him and peered up. He appeared happy to see me, but there was a deep sorrow behind his eyes. "I was very sorry to hear of your mother's passing."

"Thank you," I said. "Do you want to come inside?"

"It's been quite some time since you've last trained. I'd imagine you're out of practice. Shall we fit a lesson in before you leave for the Peridot Provinces?" He turned to show me two glinting silver swords strapped to his back.

"What do you mean?"

I had run back to the castle last night and crawled into bed, eager to drown everything out. When I awoke to the breeze sending the white linen curtains into my room like sunshine specters, Leigh and Ryder were gone. The note on the table said they had tried to wake me but I couldn't be roused, and they were spending the day at the shore.

"The king is leaving this evening to pursue the Blade of the Sun in Reaper's Cavern. I take it you know the importance of the blade in the prophecy?"

I gave him a slight nod.

"Arwen," he said, gentle but stern. "Shall we train?"

I drifted into the washroom to change before following him out into the open-air hallway. Servants and handmaidens milled through a hall marked with potted lemon trees and pearlescent fountains overflowing with fresh, clear water. Between the pillars I could just make out the pine-fringed coves and vine-covered villages in the distance. The morning breeze swept that scent of ever-present salty ocean—tinged with the roasting of pork and chickpeas—through the palace, but even the vibrant day and savory scents couldn't salvage my mood.

Last night had been a catastrophe.

Kane and I—

I shuddered at the memories. "Only Kane and Griffin are going to Peridot? No soldiers?"

"The commander will remain here in the capital. But King Ravenwood is bringing Mari. Her powers may be needed to access the cavern that holds the blade. They hope to keep a low profile now that the kingdom is ruled by Amber. No battalion."

Griffin wasn't going with Kane? "And what about you? You just got here."

"I am going to stay in Citrine with Eryx and Amelia for the time being and strategize on the battle that lies ahead. Back in the Fae Realm of Lumera, wartime strategy was part of my job as the head of Kane's guard."

"And you and Kane were always close?"

Dagan smiled mildly as we took a few shallow steps down to a courtyard of shocking green. It wasn't as private as our glade back in Shadowhold, but the grassy annex was still slightly off the palace's beaten path. "He is my king first, and my friend second."

"So your king asked you to convince me to join them in Peridot because he was too cowardly to ask me himself?"

I knew I sounded sour. The sun was bright and hurt my eyes. I wanted to go back to bed.

"I requested to discuss the matter with you."

I squinted up at him. "Why?"

"If you stay, it will give us plenty of time to work on your skills, both sword and lighte." He gave me the closest thing he could to a comforting look. "But I fear training isn't the reason you would avoid the voyage."

"I don't want to talk about him—it. I don't want to talk about *it*."

"You know I am glad to avoid that specific subject matter." His face contorted with a grimace. "That relationship isn't my utmost concern."

"I really don't need to go with them, though," I argued, clinging to something, though I wasn't sure what. "I'll just wait out the rest of my days here, in the sun and the sand, and Kane can call for me when they've found the blade, the battle plans are ready, and it's time for me to do the honors." I mimed a stabbing motion, and then a suffering-a-terrible-fate-and-dying motion. Neither provoked even a smirk in Dagan.

*Stones*, I had missed him.

"The blade will beckon you to find it. Like a pig searching for truffles."

"Gee, thanks."

"They need you."

"And I need to stay with Leigh and Ryder. We've only just found each other again."

A palace maid walked through the grassy corridor with a high stack of linens, passing under the pearl arch behind us. Dagan examined my face, waiting for me to continue, somehow knowing there was more.

"And they've lost so much."

I refused to conjure her face. Her auburn hair. Her dresses that smelled of sage and ginger—

"Let's harness your lighte. We can discuss Peridot after, if you want." Dagan unstrapped the swords from his leather holsters and leaned them up against a tan stone pillar. Then he sat on the grass beneath us and folded his legs.

I shifted on my feet. "Don't you think that's a little pointless?"

"Pointless?" He craned his neck to look up at me, squinting one eye against the sun. "The more you use your lighte, the stronger you will be, and the faster it will regenerate."

"Even still, all I really need to do is to drive one blade through Lazarus's heart. I'm not sure healing or . . . whatever it was I did that day on the ship . . . is going to help me."

"You think harnessing the essence of the air and sun and wielding them in your favor will be useless in your effort to slay the mightiest Fae in existence?"

Well, when he put it that way.

"Point taken." I sat down gingerly in front of him, blades of soft grass cushioning my ankles. "Where should we start?"

Dagan considered me, curiosity and maybe . . . sympathy in his eyes. Then, as if a light had gone on inside his mind, he drew in a breath that lifted his brows.

"What?" I asked, more edge creeping into my voice than I intended.

"You've given up."

And with that, he stood, returned his swords to his back, and began to walk away.

"Hey!" I scrambled from the grass beneath me. "Where are you going? What do you mean?"

He didn't turn as he headed across the courtyard, bougainvillea and full, plump peonies cascading around him. "I can't teach you anything if you haven't the spirit to fight. And I've heard Azurine has a delicacy made with giant clams that I've been hankering to try."

"Dagan." I tugged on his sleeve. "Stop."

He whirled around with more speed than I anticipated, and I had to remind myself that he was the fittest elderly man I'd ever met. Maybe who had ever lived. He stared into my eyes for so long I became self-conscious and tried not to fidget.

"For someone so concerned about staying with her kin, have you thought of what your resignation might do to them?"

A wave of guilt slammed into me even as I said, "No. I mean, Ryder, Leigh, even Mari . . . They're fine."

The brief disappointment that flitted across Dagan's hazel eyes cut deeper than a dagger. "Is it not cruel to make them suffer because they care for you?"

I fought the way my face wanted to crumple, how my limbs wanted to give out and reunite me with the ground at my feet. "I'm not making anyone suffer."

"Aren't you?"

"Stop answering me with questions. What if I don't want to take care of everyone else anymore? I just want to be alone. To be free for a little while before it's all over. Is that so wrong?"

"So staying behind while Kane and Mari travel without you is freedom now? Lonely, isolated, simply waiting for death? Wishing for it?"

"Dagan, will you drop it? I just don't want to go. I—"

But he stepped closer. "Forcing everyone to abandon you because you are too cowardly to do it for them? Pushing and prodding, until they choose to—"

"Stop it," I bit out, louder than I intended. Two birds flew from the cypress tree that bathed us in shade. For a moment all I could hear were my rushed breaths and water gurgling from distant fountains.

Dagan regarded me with curiosity. "When you first arrived at Shadowhold, Griffin, Kane, and I each tried our best to keep you at arm's length. Do you know why?"

"Because you're a curmudgeon, Kane was trying not to get in my pants—unsuccessfully, might I add—and Griffin doesn't like people?"

Dagan stared at me in utter silence. He was making it impossible to keep the conversation away from pesky, painful emotions.

"No," I conceded. "I don't."

"Only the three of us knew what you were destined for. We knew how painful it would be to one day tell you of your fate. How both realms were counting on you: a twenty-year-old girl from a small Amber town, with the weight of the world on her scrawny shoulders."

I swallowed the lump that had lodged in my throat.

"We did not want to be vulnerable."

My heart twisted for him—for the man who had lost his wife and daughter and didn't want to let anyone else in. Kane and Griffin had also lost their families at Lazarus's hand. Suddenly, Griffin's difficulties around Mari, and people in general, seemed cloaked in tragedy.

"Just as *you* are avoiding leaving Citrine for fear of what the voyage may make you want. I told you once there is power in harnessing your fear. There is also power in vulnerability. It is what makes us human, and gives us something worth fighting for. Sometimes, that is also something worth dying for."

I rubbed at my neck. "I can't let myself want to live, Dagan. I can't turn my back on the prophecy. As you said, look at all the people that are counting on me."

"I know how frightening it is to allow yourself to want something you know you can never have. Sometimes, we tell ourselves that it's easier not to care at all."

I folded my arms and looked out toward the sea in the far

distance. I tried to be there in my mind. All alone. An island. Where I wouldn't have to face any of this.

"But there is power in hope too. You have no real knowledge of what is in store for you. It's a long and winding road for all of us, prophecy or not. Do not spend what little time you may have left in this world shutting yourself out of it."

"I can't—" I heaved in a shuddering sigh. I hadn't realized I was out of air. "I can't be weak anymore. I was weak and afraid my whole life. It feels better to accept my destiny, to be strong."

"Admitting you do not want this fate doesn't make you the same timid girl you were when you arrived in Shadowhold."

"Well, that's not how I feel," I said, my eyes finding the blades of verdant grass beneath my shoes. "I'd rather just keep my head down and move through each day until it's time to do what I need to."

"*Move through* the last year of your life?"

I bit my tongue against the nagging hurt in my heart. It wasn't too different from what Kane had accused me of, and Mari, too.

"*Much better than watching you walk through life like a corpse.*"

"*It's not enough to just survive, Arwen. You have to actually live.*"

"Fine," I said, my eyes landing back on Dagan. "I'll go."

But his expression wasn't one of satisfaction. "And what about Kane?"

I sighed. "What about him?"

"Do the same rules apply?"

Ire simmered in my veins. "Aren't we done here? I agreed to go."

But Dagan persisted. "You wish to deny what you feel for each other, lest you open up your heart only to be wounded again?"

"Are you taking his side? After all he kept from me?"

"I didn't tell you of your fate or your lineage, either, Arwen."

"Yeah, well, I didn't fall in love with you."

Dagan stood there quietly, letting my words sink in.

A mild breeze carrying the freshness of the pines tossed my hair around my face. A single seagull, stark against the clear blue sky, pulled my gaze overhead. It rose over the shining castle spires and toward the sea.

I had never spoken the words out loud.

Not even to Mari.

But those feelings hadn't died with Kane's betrayal. With all of Lazarus's men that I butchered. With my mother. The scars of what I had felt for Kane were as pronounced as the ones Powell left across my back.

"You did that on purpose," I finally said, bitter.

"If you really are *doomed* as you keep saying"—Dagan's lips curved with the faintest hint of a smile—"I have very little time to teach you quite a lot about life. I'm simply trying to speed up the process."

"Now who's making the dark jokes?"

Dagan loosed a sly laugh and sat back down on the grass. After a beat, I joined him.

# 15

## KANE

Everything was killing me. My head, my heart, my eye sockets.

It was worse than those excruciating days on the ship sailing for Citrine when Arwen could barely look at me, and I had wanted to throw myself overboard for lying to her. I had known I was bad for her then.

Now I knew I was terrible.

*"You broke my heart."*

Each time I pictured her saying the words, I drowned in a fresh onslaught of misery. And I had almost *fucked her*—her first time, too—in some nondescript Azurine alleyway. Fucking deplorable.

I hated myself for all of it. I'd never stop.

And somehow, reliving last night's misery wasn't even the worst part of my day.

"What are we waiting for?" Mari whined as she trudged past me through the uneven sand.

I couldn't seem to place another foot forward, my eyes glued to the capital city as the sunset painted the sandstone and pearl.

Arwen was staying in Citrine.

I had hoped Dagan might convince her otherwise, but I hadn't heard from either of them all day. And after what I'd done to Crawford . . . I couldn't afford to stay in the city a minute longer. The royals would put the pieces together soon enough.

"Nothing," I mumbled, though Mari was out of earshot.

I couldn't blame Arwen. It was probably safer here. Though, I might argue she was always safer by my side than anywhere else on the continent. But her family was here, and I understood why she didn't want to be anywhere near me. Let alone traverse enemy territory together hunting for a blade that was most likely already in Garnet hands.

I had asked Griffin to stay here and keep an eye on her. I trusted Dagan with my life, but he wasn't Fae. With Lazarus after Arwen, I needed Griffin or myself with her at all times. Knowing that he would watch over her while I searched Reaper's Cavern was a small mercy. One I probably didn't deserve.

Griffin, though, was miserable about it, which was yet another reason for my splitting, acute headache. He claimed he didn't want me to find the sword alone, to risk death and dismemberment—but I knew the truth. I had to take the witch with me, and it was ripping him apart to be away from her. Clearly, I knew the feeling.

But he'd never admit such things to me, so he just grumbled through the day in a foul mood that matched my own. The two of us sniping at each other like a crotchety old couple until Mari and I headed off.

Calm waves rocked slowly against the wooden dock behind me and the many ships it held, the sun setting but still high enough in the sky to cast a warm glow against the back of my neck. Mari looked positively morose as she read over King Eryx's parchment one more time before casting the breathing incantation on the both of us. She said the spell with so little energy, the magic barely kicked up the sand around her feet.

"Perhaps you need some hair of the dog?" I offered.

Her blistering eyes were like coal on mine. Not even a hint of a smile.

"Come now, witch." I tried to salvage the mood for both of us. "We'll be there and back in no time."

"Will we pop out of the funnel back into the middle of the ocean?"

"Pretty much."

"What if our ship is gone? Lost to pirates or battered by a storm?"

"It likely is," I said as we walked toward the cavern. "But we won't need a ship." I leaned toward her conspiratorially. "Dragons can fly."

Nothing. She just pursed her lips and stalked forward, mind elsewhere.

Arwen would have liked that. At one time, back in Shadow-hold, had I been truthful with her, we might've laughed together over my beastly, winged side. I could have shown her the Shadow Woods from the clouds. My favorite view—

"Wait!"

Hope clouded my vision at that familiar voice, ringing through the quiet sunset-draped harbor. I twisted to see Arwen running down the dock onto the beach below, long chestnut hair swaying around her, dressed in her leathers and with a small pack at her side.

"Wait," she repeated, sand kicking up at her heels, only a little out of breath as she caught up to us.

"Hello, bird."

She regarded me thoughtfully, her gaze searing along my jaw, my lips. If she noticed I had shaved, she didn't say so. "I'm coming with you."

Mari's entire mood shifted, as if the rain cloud above her head had transformed into sunshine with Arwen's declaration. "Oh, thank *the Stones*!" she said, throwing her arms around her friend. I wished I could do the same.

"And that means . . ." I didn't even have to finish the sentence.

Griffin tramped onto the beach, deliberate as always, though his eyes held a subtle brightness. He had gone from a glorified babysitter stuck in a foreign city without his friend or his woman, to a man on an adventure with the only people in this world he even remotely liked. I would call this version of Griffin almost gleeful.

He gave me a single nod and I swiped a hand down my face to hide my grin. "And then there were four." I glanced sidelong at Arwen. The setting sun was radiating off her rosy cheeks. "What changed your mind?"

"Dagan did. Ryder and Leigh will be safe here with him and Barney. I think Ryder wants to learn more about our war strategy, so I told him to stick close to Amelia and Eryx. It's what's best for them. And this is what's best for me."

Pride swelled in my chest. Brave as ever, and thoughtful, and determined—

"Good," I said.

We resumed the walk toward the darkened cavern, Griffin at the front, Mari slightly behind him, and Arwen in step beside me, a few paces back.

"So, who will watch over Shadowhold?" she asked. "With Dagan here?"

A half smile curved at my lips. Perhaps she still cared for the keep. For my home.

"We sent word to Lieutenant Eardley after the battle of Siren's Bay. He has the Onyx army divided among my largest cities, the palace in Willowridge, and Shadowhold."

Arwen stayed silent, mental wheels clearly turning.

"By now my father must know we made it to Citrine. I'm less concerned about Onyx falling than I was that day in the Shadowhold gardens." I swallowed against the memory. I'd stared at her face then like a lovesick teenager and battled every instinct, every bone and fiber in my body, not to touch her. Not to kiss her. I had gone and done it anyway, of course, like the selfish bastard I was. *You are bad for her*, my mind chanted on repeat.

"How come?" she asked.

"Our army is the fiercest on the continent. Beating them would cost Lazarus many of his men. He lost at least a hundred due to a certain powerful Fae outburst. And he knows Onyx would never bow to him the way Peridot has. He only wanted to take Shadowhold to get to me . . . and you. But now we're here."

"Except we're going to be in Peridot."

"Right. But he won't know that. Not if we keep a low profile."

"Right," she said, eyes on the grains of sand moving under her feet. "Good."

The ocean lapped pleasantly against the sandy shore. I wouldn't have too many more opportunities to say this in the coming days in such close proximity to Griffin and Mari. I braced myself and stepped in front of Arwen, cutting us both off.

"Arwen—"

"Don't."

I swallowed thickly. "I just want to say one thing."

"What part of *don't* is confusing to you?"

That smart mouth. I tried not to think of our kiss last night. Of her hurried lips on mine. Her hot hands in my hair. My fingers itched to reach for her, so I clenched them into taut fists at my sides.

"You were right," I said, trying to keep my voice even.

She pursed her lips, waiting for me to continue.

"We shouldn't be together. It was wrong for me try, after . . . Just know I will never lie to you again. I care for you and . . ." I shook my head. "The point is, I'm sorry for yesterday. For everything. I'm not going to harass you anymore. Or kiss you anymore."

It was all true. Every inelegant word of it. I wouldn't hurt her again, and I'd change my behavior to ensure it. No more depression beard. Or depression drinking. No more flirting. Fighting. Impromptu kissing . . .

"Kane—" she began.

"Wait up!"

We both whirled around at the eager voice, only to see Prince Fedrik bounding toward us.

Dear Gods, he was carrying a pack.

"Wow, Arwen," he said once he reached us. "You look beautiful."

"Fedrik, we're right in the middle of something." *Leave. Now.*

"The king and queen have requested I join you on the expedition for the Blade of the Sun."

"Sorry. Team's all full. Better luck next time." There was no world, no reality, where I brought this imbecile along with us so he could insult me and ogle Arwen for the next few days.

"You'd be wise not to fight me on this one, King. Even your advisor Sir Dagan agreed to my joining the expedition. Despite your clear lack of morals and piss-poor personality, you and I actually want the same thing."

I would have some very choice words for the old swordsman when I returned. "And what might that be?"

"Without our army you have no shot against Lazarus, and if you lose, we all do."

"Your parents will not risk their people, nor their resources."

"If I deliver the blade to my parents, it'll be hard for them to argue against the odds. They only want to know our win is assured."

"Broderick and Isolde don't think I'm capable of retrieving the sword myself?"

"Their words were more along the lines of, 'We don't trust him for shit.'"

Arwen's melodic, playful laugh and the bright smile he shot her in return made me feel insane. But he could have told his parents what I'd done last night. And he hadn't. If he thought there was a chance they could be convinced to utilize their armies on our behalf, I couldn't refuse him. "Fine. It's going to be a miserable journey. I hope you like to get your hands dirty."

Fedrik grinned. "I'll fare all right, though I'm touched by your concern, King Ravenwood."

"Kane's fine."

"I reserve that kind of familiarity for people I actually like."

And with that he strode forward, sidling up next to Mari and Griffin, leaving Arwen and me alone in the sand.

A mischievous glint sparkled in her eyes as she said, "This is going to be great fun."

❦

WE FLEW THROUGH THE NIGHT UNTIL WE REACHED PERIDOT. What had taken eleven days by tumultuous sea took Griffin and me only one evening in the silent skies.

The trip gave me a chance to clear my head—as flying often did. This . . . jealousy . . . was new to me. When Arwen once harbored feelings for Halden, it had been rage bellowing through my bones. I knew he was a murderer, a liar, a manipulator. I would have rather had anyone else be the object of her affections. I would have rather had it be fucking Barney.

But this wasn't that same icy, slithering thing that bit through me then. Familiar, from when my father abused his own people. Or when I had been betrayed by those closest to me, or defeated by them. Not that same temper that was always right there under the surface of my skin, snarling and begging to be set free so I could demolish and destroy.

No, though I had imagined crippling Fedrik a thousand different ways, each more creative than the last, none felt remotely satisfying. And not because I didn't truly wish to injure the prince—I really, *really* did. But because this wasn't rage at all—it was *grief.*

I would not be able to endure her with someone else. I wasn't strong enough. I had never been strong enough to lose her.

And even if it wasn't him pursuing Arwen, that's exactly what would happen. She was beautiful beyond comprehension, fiercely loyal and compassionate, and had the biggest heart of anyone I had ever met. As long as she lived, there would be no shortage of men who wished to be with her, and eventually she would reciprocate those wishes.

What mattered now was not what those thoughts did to me, but finding a way to give her a chance at actually making such a life with someone.

To take my mind off the mountain of odds stacked against my success, and the pain I'd feel regardless of whether I succeeded, I thought of Shadowhold, and how pleasant it would be to return one day. I had been away too long already, and missed the keep terribly.

Not just Acorn or my dusty library or my quiet study with my childhood chess set.

Not just the ample silence, the way nobody spoke to me unless I wished them to, or the peculiar majesty of the Shadow Woods.

I missed the feeling of being *home*.

Once we were soaring over enemy territory, we swooped low, flitting through the humid tree cover to avoid any prying eyes or watchtowers. The blanket of night helped, too, but day was breaking, and now that Peridot was overrun by Gareth's men, we couldn't risk the Amber soldiers seeing us. It was time to shed our creature-forms.

I swung my tail toward Griffin to signal our descent.

We landed amid a deep, shadow-shrouded jungle. Even though the sun was rising, the trees above were so dense they swallowed up nearly all the dawn light. The air was wet, and each breath felt like steam in my lungs. If it was this humid in the early morning, I shuddered to imagine what the unfiltered afternoon sun would bring. My claws squelched against an equally damp forest floor covered in tangled vines and emerald moss.

Arwen and Mari had been sleeping, but landing shook them awake and they dismounted still cloaked in a thick layer of slumber. Fedrik tramped onto the muddy ground as well before Griffin and I shifted back, grateful for the spells from childhood that kept our clothing intact.

"Where are we?" Mari asked.

The palm and nut trees around us had trunks the circumference of small homes and waxy, bright green leaves that dripped dew and moisture like rain. Amid the varied palette of greens were splashes of vibrant color—oblong pale blue fruit, spiked pink flowers, yellow moths with wings larger than my outstretched palm.

"We're a few miles outside the town of Frog Eye."

"Are we near Siren's Cove?" Arwen asked, and I suppressed a frown at the expression bare on her face. The regret in her eyes over the capital's siege.

"No, we're on the other side of the kingdom. Not nearly as affluent over here, and mostly populated by pirates, sailors, and smugglers who roam the Ocean of Ore a few miles west." I tramped past two monarchs, tangled in flight. "So be careful, and no stupid plans."

"Stupid plans? You can't be talking about us." Arwen gestured to herself and Mari.

"Amulet heist, Shadow Woods wolfbeast disaster, Halden escape scheme . . ." I counted on my outstretched fingers as I recalled each harebrained plot. "Need I go on?"

"The Shadow Woods wolfbeast disaster was all her." Mari pointed to Arwen.

"Traitor," Arwen muttered, though her lips twitched.

"Dare I ask what a Shadow Woods wolfbeast disaster entails?" Fedrik asked Arwen, nudging her playfully.

"No," I snapped before walking away from them and deeper into the jungle, cautious not to trip on any roots or vines, which covered the forest floor like snakes.

I heard Arwen gently assuage the prince and I marched farther through the symphony of chattering monkeys and exotic birds.

"More or less than three days before I decapitate him?" I asked Griffin as I slapped at a greedy mosquito getting plastered on my forearm.

"That's a wager I'd prefer not to win."

He was right. If Fedrik had any chance of convincing his parents to fight alongside us, he was worth something to me alive.

Behind us Arwen's laugh rang out alongside the resonant hoot of a toucan. I squinted into the tangle of trees above us for the creature—anything to avoid watching Fedrik make her smile—but only made out a kaleidoscope of leaves, like stained emerald glass. The morning sun was already beginning to filter through, and the heat brought moisture to my back and neck. We couldn't hike now and risk heatstroke. "Shall we go find a lagoon while we wait for nightfall? I'm already sweating like a pig."

Griffin sighed, looking back at the rest of our party. "Do we trust Fedrik to protect them?"

My eyes landed on our group, setting up camp. Mari ordered Arwen and Fedrik to hold a canvas tarp higher, and then even higher still, and then more to the left, and then even *more* to the left. I cut a glance to my friend—his eyes on the witch were almost pained.

I wondered how long Griffin would let his aversion to intimacy stop him from pursuing her. The fact that he'd not had a single romantic relationship since I'd known him told me not to hold my breath. Still, witnessing him struggle with his duty to protect his king and his urge to never leave Mari's side was wretched even as a bystander. "Fine. Stay with them."

"No way." Griffin's brows pulled in with distaste. "I'm coming with you. Someone has to have your back. You're the king of Onyx—I think you forget it sometimes."

The whirl of earthy wind pulled our attention back to the campsite, and we watched as all three tents built themselves with ease. The canvas grew taut, bags and packs emptied themselves, and pallets unfurled next to a laundry line, which strung itself between tree trunks. A thin chalk outline drew itself around our tents and campfire. Mari murmured her spell, copper hair flying about her face, until the dirt and leaves settled and we beheld a well-furnished campsite.

Mari appraised her handiwork, lovingly grazing Briar's jewel around her neck.

"You think there's any chance that amulet has the kind of magic she thinks it does?" Griffin asked under his breath.

"No," I said. "Not that I know of."

"It's messing with her head," he muttered. "She's too attached to the thing."

"Nice work," Fedrik said to the witch.

"Oh, it's nothing. You two needed the help."

"What's the white circle?" Arwen asked, looking at the boundary Mari drew.

"A cloaking ward. Our camp won't be visible to anyone outside the chalk. Like Amber soldiers, bounty hunters, bandits, pirates, wild jungle cats, Lazarus—"

"That's enough, thanks." Arwen swallowed hard. "I see the value."

Mari smiled sheepishly.

"Don't worry," said Fedrik. "I can protect you from at least three of those."

"My hero," Arwen replied with a sweet smile.

My gut twisted, and I moved for the tree line. I needed a cold body of water.

Or a stiff drink.

# 16

---

## ARWEN

**H**OW CAN I BE OF SERVICE?" I ASKED MARI AS SHE PUT THE rest of the site together piece by piece with her magic. We needed to camp out in the jungle to avoid the cities filled with Amber soldiers who wanted our heads. I didn't mind much, but Mari wasn't thrilled about it.

"Nothing. Just make yourself comfortable. I've got it," Mari said, folding each tent's furs and hanging each lantern from the comfort of the tree she leaned against. Two iron pots unpacked themselves and a cluster of metal mugs stacked in midair.

My feet shifted beneath me, and I folded my hands into my blouse. "Are you sure?"

I hadn't seen Kane in the last few hours. I wasn't worried about him in war-torn Peridot by himself. I was just antsy. And hot. When would he be back? How long until we hiked for the cavern? How would this blade call to me? We had not even been here a day and already I was sick of my own anxious thoughts.

"What's Griffin doing?" I motioned to his massive back, hunched over something by the fire.

"He's actually quite the fisherman." A slight color had risen to Mari's cheeks. "He caught some fish wherever he and Kane went. He's gutting them now. But no cod, of course."

I tried not to smirk. "Of course. Because you hate cod."

"Everyone hates cod. It's bland," she said, brow furrowed. "Obviously."

I looked back at Griffin, slowly and methodically slicing the fish into filets. Fish he had caught at Mari's instruction. I imagined him throwing every cod back in order to please her, and my heart tugged a bit. But he looked as pleasant as he ever did. The meticulous, solitary hobby suited him.

"If you're looking for a job around camp," Prince Fedrik said, slipping out from his slightly larger, more stylish tent, his blond hair fluttering in the dappled sunlight, "I was about to gather some firewood. Care to join?"

Mari gave me such a forcefully encouraging expression she might as well have waved a flag overhead that read, *Go, you idiot!*

"Sure." I grabbed the axe and followed him into the depths of the rain forest.

After flying past miles and miles of night-drenched, unspoiled, fertile farmland and lush green hills on the back of Kane's dragon form, I had expected serenity and peace, but this side of Peridot was not nearly as pleasant as Siren's Cove. It was wild and tangled and verdant. A little overwhelming. I missed that clear blue bay and sparkling pink sand. I wondered if anyone had cleaned up the wreckage that now adorned it. If you could even clean blood from sand. Or if the peaceful waves of Siren's Bay had taken on the gruesome task, washing away each body, each stain with the restless tide.

"Nervous for tonight?" Fedrik's words jarred me from the bleak image.

"No," I admitted, traipsing through roots and vines and little critters that scuttled at our feet. I chose to leave out the truth: that I hadn't felt much of anything in weeks until my poor choices the other night.

As if reading my thoughts, Fedrik said, "With Crawford . . . That was . . ." He scratched at his bicep. "How often do you end up in situations such as those with your king?"

"Never," I lied. Fedrik cut a look my way and I cringed before amending, "Occasionally."

"How did a lovely woman such as yourself end up as the personal healer to a king like that?"

"Dreadful luck?"

When he grinned in response, all his glittering white teeth sparkled in the sunlight. "Your bad luck is my good fortune."

A smile pricked at my face. It was so easy, talking to the prince. So easy to pretend I really was just a castle healer, my biggest problem the moods of the royalty I served.

"Why not retire from your post? I have some sports injuries; I'll employ you as my own healer."

Briefly disarmed, I faltered for a sufficient response. "I wouldn't do that. Wouldn't abandon him. Personal frustrations or otherwise."

"Well," he said after a pause, "it's brave of you to stand by King Ravenwood. To travel alongside him," Fedrik continued, stopping at a fallen tree and smoothly taking the axe from my hand. "Especially on a risky journey such as this one."

How funny. I hadn't been brave a moment in my life for twenty years—crippled by anxiety and worry—and in the span of just a few months I was facing fears left, right, and sideways without as much as a hair raised on my neck.

Fedrik reared back and swung the axe into the supple, mossy wood, splitting the log with one clean stroke. The muscles of his back rippled through his damp white shirt as he struck once more with a grunt and knelt to hand me the split pieces.

"I'm not usually like that," I said, clearing my throat. "My brother and sister are the brave ones."

"Really? And you're the . . ."

I chewed my cheek in thought. "Responsible one?"

Understanding glinted in his eyes. "You and I play similar roles, then. So your siblings, are they actually brave or just reckless?"

"Most of the time Ryder doesn't understand enough about a situation to realize he *should* be afraid. And Leigh is too young to know how much there is to fear." I regretted the words as soon as I spoke them. She had seen now how vicious the world could be.

Sensing the bleak direction my thoughts had taken, Fedrik took my shoulder in his broad hand. His grasp was warm and supportive. Strong and sturdy like the wood cradled in my arms.

"At the risk of sounding rude . . . when I first met you, you seemed, well—you seemed a little sad. I'm sorry. For all you and your family have had to endure. If you ever need to talk, I'm around. Healers are too often forced to witness the carnage of battle."

I wanted to laugh. I *was* the carnage of battle.

"Thank you," I said instead.

"I have a younger sister, too. I think you met her briefly in Azurine. Sera?"

"Yes, are you two close?"

"Very," he said as we sloshed through a patch of mud. "We fight like cats and dogs . . . or maybe wolves and kittens. But at the end of the day, she's the most important person in the world to me."

I offered him a small smile that I hoped conveyed how much I related to his sentiments. "So, who's the wolf and who's the kitten?"

"Oh, I'm the kitten without a doubt. She decimates me."

A rare laugh bubbled out of me, and we both smiled at the sound. Something new was blossoming inside me. More than just appreciation for his chiseled jaw and bright blue eyes or the way his kindness toward me irritated Kane. Fondness, like a warm, brewed cup of tea, seeped into my heart. I liked this sunshine prince. Quite a bit, actually.

"I'm sorry about her betrothal to Kane. I know it ended poorly."

Fedrik shrugged. "It was a blessing. They wouldn't have made each other happy."

I rolled my next words around on my tongue, debating whether I really wanted to know the answer. Curiosity won out. "Was part of your objection to the marriage the fact that Kane is . . ."

"An asshole? Or Fae?"

I gave a shallow nod indicating the latter.

"I'd be lying if I said I didn't think it was strange. I mean, he isn't human, is he? He would've outlived her, outlived their children . . ."

I pursed my lips, nodding again.

"But," he said evenly, "I'm no bigot. I probably wouldn't have cared if he had been a decent man." Fedrik half smiled, though his eyes were forlorn. "But, of course, he wasn't."

"Was that why you joined us? To judge him for yourself?"

Fedrik set down the logs in his hands to hack into another fallen trunk. His muscles tensed with each blow and I tried not to ogle the bronze skin of his forearms sparkling with sweat.

"Here," he huffed, handing me more fresh firewood, and carrying the rest himself. "I wasn't lying on the beach yesterday. I want Citrine to fight for the side of good, and my parents are more likely to be convinced if we have the blade."

"You just also don't know if Kane *is* good."

"*Good* is a general term. Do I think King Ravenwood is a good man? No, not particularly. Do I think his desire to end his father's reign and halt his conquest of Evendell is honest? Yes. And he'll need our army to do that."

I fought the anxiety stirring in my stomach. "But your parents, they refused him."

"They're very set in their ways."

"And that bothers you?"

"I'm not afraid of change, like they are. But I am afraid of them."

"So what can be done?"

"If we have the blade, it'll be hard for them to ignore the fact that King Ravenwood and the Fae from the prophecy stand a real chance. And if we can't get it, I hope to convince them to change their minds about him as a person."

A slow breath sailed out from my lips. "I don't feel Kane has showed you his best side quite yet."

Fedrik's lips curled up. "Does he have a good side?"

I tried to answer honestly. "He has a better one, but I don't expect you'll see it on this trip."

"King Ravenwood doesn't frighten me."

I almost said *he should*, but chose only to nod. Better for Fedrik not to know what being Fae truly meant. Not to know exactly what Kane could do to him if he felt so inclined.

"If I may be so bold," Fedrik said, as if he were mustering some kind of courage, "what is the nature of your relationship with him? I know you are his healer, but . . . he seems a bit possessive of you."

Oh, *Stones*.

"He and I . . ." A searing image of Kane's hand around my waist, pressing me against him in a moonlit alley, jumped into my mind. Maybe partial honesty was the path of least resistance here. "We kissed."

Fedrik raised his brows. "And now?"

I wanted to tell him I had been asking myself the same question. Partial honesty won out again. "We are working through some of the discomfort. We probably shouldn't have acted on our mutual attraction."

"I can't say I blame him," Fedrik said, though he kept his eyes on the glossy leaves around us. I still felt heat rise in my cheeks. "And Griffin and Mari?"

"That's an even more fraught entanglement," I said, relieved to move on from Kane and me. "Feelings seem to be blossoming right under Mari's own nose, but I don't know if she can see them for what they are quite yet."

"You should tell her as much."

"I've tried. I'm not exactly the pinnacle of romantic success these days. I probably wouldn't take advice from me, either."

"And for Griffin?"

"Oh, he's completely gone for her. Every time she's nearby he rubs at his chest with a baffled expression. Like, *What is this feeling I only get when the witch is around?*"

Fedrik laughed like I was an absolute delight, and I beamed at him. "He won't even refer to her by her name."

Still smiling, we rounded a tree and stumbled right into Griffin with his fishing gear and a shirtless, sweat-slicked Kane. Griffin's face was steel. He had clearly heard every word. Kane chuckled low and soft as he leaned over to remove his boots, a small yet shimmering lagoon rippling behind them.

I tried to think of anything but Kane's body, sweaty, glistening, and soon to be submerged in cool water.

"Oh—Griffin." I blanched, guilty. "We were only teasing."

"It's fine." But he stalked off like it was very much *not* fine.

Kane tutted at me. "Bird, you have such talons today."

I rolled my eyes. "Me? You torment him more than anyone."

"I *challenge* him. You're no better than a bully."

But I was only half listening. I couldn't take my eyes off his flexed, shiny, defined abdomen. The deep rumble of his voice . . .

When I finally looked up, Kane was grinning like a wolf.

I wanted to say something rude, but my traitorous mind was still trying to pull its jaw off the floor.

Fedrik responded instead. "Where's your shirt?"

Kane gestured to the green pond behind him and began to unlace his leathers. "Care to stay for the show?"

"We'll pass." Finally, speech had returned to me. "The reviews were terrible."

"Witty and beautiful." Fedrik regarded me with a lifted brow. "You might be dangerous."

"Don't worry," I teased. "I'll spare you."

"And merciful? We're all doomed."

"No." Kane's eyes narrowed at Fedrik, all humor gone. "Only you."

That voice carried such lethal promise it sucked all the floral Peridot air out of the jungle and left the lot of us silent.

Fedrik only frowned. "Here, Wen, let me take those logs back to camp."

I smiled primly to hide my grimace as I handed the logs to Fedrik.

"*Wen?*" Kane asked, voice dripping with distaste once Fedrik was out of earshot.

I bristled. "So?"

"So it sounds like a name for a horse."

I stared at him dryly. "*Bird* is a literal animal."

"Fair point." A grin curled his lips.

"He's nice," I admitted. "He doesn't look at me with pity."

Kane's face fell as he brushed one hand absently across his chest. He needed to put his shirt back on immediately. I turned from his broad shoulders—that muscled, tanned chest *gleaming*—and walked stiffly until I sat myself beside the crackling hearth.

I could have used a cold plunge myself.

---

WE HADN'T NEEDED THE FIRE FOR WARMTH GIVEN THE balmy heat of the jungle even once the sun had set, but Griffin roasted his fish over the open flame, and after, we washed supper down with tea and ale. Mari made sure the protective ward was twice as strong before we let the fire build. Its brightness within the dark jungle would have been a dead giveaway to unwanted guests.

"When we arrive at Reaper's Cavern," Kane continued as we ate, "I think Arwen should stand guard outside."

The fish soured on my tongue. "What? Why?"

Kane didn't look at me as he addressed the others. "Just while we ensure some precautionary measures are in place."

"Why?" I asked again pointedly.

"The cave is said to be inescapable." His voice was cool, but his eyes gave away the gravity of his words.

"Lore says you'll go mad before you find your way out," Mari added.

A cold sweat broke out across my neck. When Kane snarled softly at her, she shot me an apologetic look.

"I intend to mark our trail as we go, as to never lose our way," he continued. "I'd just like to make sure the cave will let me do so."

*"Let you?"*

"It's said to . . . have a mind of its own."

Fantastic. Fantastic news. "What about everyone else?"

"I'm not too worried about a mortal legend affecting two Fae and a witch. And what happens to Fedrik is unimportant."

Fedrik almost laughed at that one. I might have, too, if my heart wasn't in my throat.

"But I am worried about you," Kane continued. "And your aversion to enclosed spaces." He wasn't mocking. The warmth in his tone told me as much.

I knew he meant it. That he was worried about me, but—

It wasn't just my fear. It was what he couldn't say in front of Fedrik.

It was my *value*.

He couldn't risk losing the prophesied full-blooded Fae before she could enact her destiny. Before she could die.

"No."

"Arwen, it's not—"

"No. I came with you to help."

"Arwen," Mari tried. "Even I don't like the sound of a cave that traps all who enter. Let us just get inside and make sure we can get back out."

"Does she have to go in at all? Could she stay at camp?" Fedrik asked.

"No, we're just bringing her along with us for our own amusement," Kane said. "Good one, right?"

Fedrik's expression was humorless. Kane looked as though he felt similarly.

I pinched the bridge of my nose as I inhaled. "I spent my entire life being afraid. Sitting outside while the rest of you risk your lives . . . I'm not going to do that again."

The loud hoot of an owl echoed through the trees to my right and Kane sipped from his mug. "Fine. Your coffin."

All the air suctioned from my lungs and Mari squeezed my shoulder.

*Prick.*

"What will we use to mark our path?" Griffin asked.

"How about petals?" Fedrik offered, gesturing to a tangle of plumerias behind him.

Kane narrowed his eyes at the prince with such vitriol, it was almost awe.

"My magic," Mari supplied. "I can leave a trail of light to guide us back."

I felt my lungs expand. That was reassuring—a light to lead us out of the darkness. I no longer wished to imagine all the ways tomorrow might result in my demise. I had a perfectly well-cooked fish on my plate and people beside me I enjoyed spending time with. As Dagan instructed, I would try to appreciate it while I had the chance.

I leaned back, rubbing my stomach. "This is surprisingly good."

"I'm touched." Griffin took a final bite before tossing his plate toward our packs. The resonant clang sent a frog hopping into the leaves beyond our camp.

"Was probably the lack of cod," Fedrik added, shooting me a conspiratorial look. Clearly, he had heard my earlier conversation with Mari.

Mari grinned. "Exactly! Who likes cod?"

"Actually, I do," Griffin said.

Mari rolled her eyes. "Of course you do."

The firelight gleamed in Kane's eyes. "Why didn't you catch us any, then, Commander?"

I tried not to smile.

But Mari saved Griffin a response. "Why couldn't we have stayed in Frog Eye?" She tried to nestle into a wide tree's roots, curling her feet up underneath her, but couldn't seem to get comfortable. "At an inn? With a mattress?"

"We're enemies of the kingdom, witch," Griffin said, kicking over an empty linen pack, which Mari slid between her back and the gnarled tree. "We can't risk being seen by Amber soldiers."

*And the entire town, if not the whole kingdom, is likely peppered with sketches of my face that say* Traitor. I focused on Fedrik, examining the condensation on his metal mug. While I relished the fact that he had no idea who I was, he also had no idea how dicey this excursion was. Guilt and envy fought for dominance.

"Arwen could slice them to bits in a heartbeat," Mari huffed to no one in particular.

"You know how to wield a sword?" Fedrik asked, impressed.

I blushed a bit. "Just the basics."

"Don't be modest, Arwen, your skills even impressed Griffin." Mari dipped her head toward the commander in question.

Kane's brows quirked up beside me. "When did you two train?"

"In Serpent Spring," I said. "On the way to Peridot, the first time we came here."

"She was better than I expected," Griffin added, eyes dancing. "But I was faster."

"Griffin said the same thing about the woman he tossed from his bed this morning," Mari quipped.

I spun to face her. No way he had revealed anything so intimate, and to Mari, nonetheless.

"I'm kidding." She smirked. "We all know Griffin's never touched a woman."

Laughs erupted around the campfire. Even a wisp of a smile cracked at the corner of Griffin's mouth.

"The witch is welcome on every one of my doomed adventures," Kane said, wiping a hand down his face to quell his laughter. Mari gave him a look that said, *Lucky me.*

My heart stirred with warmth. Maybe their friendship didn't bother me as much as I had previously thought.

"You know," Kane said to me, under his breath. "If you ever wanted, I could show you how to beat him at his own game."

"Who, Griffin?"

"Or anyone who has a bit of experience on you." His quicksilver eyes gleamed in filtered moonlight, as if it was drawn solely to him, like the rest of us were. "I'm not as good as Dagan, but I'm here, if you'd like the help."

"Thank you." I swallowed, our détente feeling slippery and new. "Maybe another time."

Kane gave me a subtle nod of his head, but his eyes were solemn.

"I never thanked you for letting Trevyn live," I added, the words serving as my own olive branch. "For letting *me* let Trevyn live."

"I didn't do it for you," he admitted, eyes focused on the rim of his tin cup. "He was harmless, we weren't going to be in Citrine long . . . I didn't think I'd stay up nights worrying that Trevyn would be the one to get you."

"Do you do that? Stay up nights worrying about who will get me?"

His silence was like a knife to the heart.

"You brought a lute?" Griffin said to Fedrik. My eyes cut up to see the prince rooting through his pack.

"I thought it might help to pass the time," Fedrik said, pulling the instrument out. "But I'm not very good."

"Kane is," I announced. "He's exceptional." I thought back to the night in his quarters when I was sick with fever and he strummed me a melancholy lullaby.

Mari whirled to face him. "No . . . You? Have a hobby?"

A dark rumble of a laugh spasmed out of Kane. "Yes, but it's been a long time."

"Play a song for us, please," I asked him. I had meant it to be bratty, playful, but it came out so sincere I was almost embarrassed.

Kane's gaze was like liquid heat, and he stood without another word and strolled over to Fedrik.

"May I?"

Fedrik handed him the wooden instrument and Kane sat back down next to me.

He strummed tentatively at first, his large hands still finding purchase on the strings. His rings were near luminous in the firelight, especially the silver and onyx signet that always graced his left pinky. Those hands continued to move and then halt, testing chords and tuning strings, until finally the music took on a rhythmic cadence. A gentle, melodic song weaved through the balmy night, a symphony among the crickets and bats and croaks of frogs. I could feel Kane's notes in my bones, like a story I knew word for word.

I studied Kane's concentrated face, his soft yet focused brow, as his deft fingers played a tune I thought might have been about rolling hills and birdsong the day after a horrible storm. About forgiveness and rebirth.

I had probably just had too much ale.

But nobody spoke while he played. And when the song ended, and none of us uttered a word, he played another. This one more of a bright and joyful jaunt that conjured images of dancing and clinking glasses and spilled liquor. And after that another, and another. I fell asleep to the sound of Kane's lute, my head against the indulgent moss of the forest floor.

# 17

## ARWEN

THE MAP ETCHED INTO THE WOODEN DESK LEG THAT KANE had found was a mystery to me, but took Mari only a few minutes to figure out. She had smothered the peg in mud and turned it out onto parchment like a rolling pin, revealing a fairly basic map to Reaper's Cavern and then how to find the treasure within.

We left an hour before sunrise, when it was cool enough to hike but light enough to see our way. The trek there took us through a near-impenetrable expanse of palm trees and over steep, grassy hills. After wading through a lukewarm river and climbing across fallen, algae-covered trunks, I was dirty, damp, and covered in all manner of bug bites and scratches. I had thistles and twigs lodged in my hair and leathers, and despite leaving with the moon at our backs, the sluggish heat was now back with a vengeance, and I was coated in sweat.

And all the while, my thoughts were elsewhere. I had woken up to a handful of jungle flowers—two pink orchids and a bird-of-paradise—tied to the inside of my tent, despite being sure I had drifted off beside the campfire. I had dropped them in the jungle when we left camp, unable to keep them, nor crush them like I had the others.

"We're here." Kane's voice cut through my wandering thoughts and pulled my eyes to the mouth of the cave in front of us: a wide pitch-black expanse like the open jaws of a primordial beast, wreathed in wilting vines and ancient sage-green moss.

Griffin retrieved three torches from his pack and lit them, two of which he handed to Kane and Fedrik; the last he kept for himself.

"It doesn't even look that ominous," said Mari before stepping into the cave. Griffin didn't hesitate to follow after her, and Fedrik after them.

Kane stepped closer to me, and I was reminded once again of his looming height. "How are you feeling?"

"I'll be fine. Why?" I was anxious enough as it was. "Does something look wrong?"

"Did you get my flowers?"

"Which ones?"

"Either of them."

"No. Now answer me."

He shrugged. "I was just checking. If you faint, I'll be the one who'll have to carry you for miles through the tunnels."

I made a face. "You'd love that, wouldn't you?"

It was only a joke, but Kane cut a harsh line with his lips. "Sometimes your naivete baffles me."

His words stung, as they so often did when they struck a nerve. "I used to prefer things that way," I admitted. "Not knowing the truth."

"I'm sure," he mused, eyes on the jungle behind me. "Much easier to make me the villain in a story missing so many pages."

My blood stilled. It was true. Hadn't it been easier to see him as only my savior or my enemy? Hadn't that made all these wretched feelings that much more bearable?

"You're right," I said on a breath. "Now I barely understand the world, and even less so, my place in it. It's harder to be optimistic having seen how complex and ambiguous things really are." I chewed my cheek. "Even you used to appreciate my blindly positive outlook."

"I did—I still do." Kane ran a hand across his damp brow in frustration. "Don't you know why I call you bird?"

"Because you locked me in a cage?"

His silver gaze simmered like hot smoke. "Because when I met you, for the first time in as long as I could remember, I felt hope. And not just hope that I might beat my father, though of course, I can't deny that."

Acid roiled in my stomach, but those eyes held mine, and I found myself unable to look away.

"That's what birds represent. Stranded sailors look to the sky to be led by them back to dry land. Birds soar through the dawn each morning, as sure as the sun rising in the east—the promise of something new, regardless of what came before." He sighed and ran his hand through his hair. "Hope always has wings."

I searched for a response and failed, but Kane tramped toward the cavern's gaping mouth, soon swallowed whole by desolate darkness. I steeled myself and hurried after him.

The sound of my shoes slapping on the ground below echoed off the stone walls, cracked, jagged, and jutting, as my eyes adjusted to the hollow, dank space. My fingers were already tingling, adrenaline racing through my veins in the confinement of the tunnel.

I moved past Kane, Griffin, and Fedrik to catch up with Mari, still leading the procession, holding the parchment map out in front of her as she walked. Behind her a little bouncing ball of light dawdled along, painting a single glowing line on the dirty cavern floor. It didn't look too dissimilar from my own lighte, though instead of resembling stark, blinding sunbeams, Mari's magic was more like the fuzzy glow of a star.

"That looks promising." I gestured to the iridescent orb dancing between her legs.

"Beautiful, isn't it?" Mari smiled, her freckled nose lit by the quivering torchlight close behind us. "We'll be able to see this from anywhere in the caves."

"What spell is it?"

"It's called luster. It can last for days." She toyed with the shimmering, softened light as it flew up between her fingertips and coated them in a dripping glow before skittering along the ground beneath us. "Much better than breadcrumbs."

"How deep does the map say we have to go?"

Mari's nose scrunched up like it so often did when she was a little stumped but didn't want to admit it. "It's not very clear. The map was more helpful in finding the cave. Inside, there are so many turns, so many dead ends . . ."

I swallowed acid. "So you, the smartest person I know, aren't sure how to get us out of here?"

"That's what the luster is for," she said, waving a glowing hand through the damp air. "Have a little faith."

We forged ahead, heart in my throat, sharp stalactites like an inverted mountainscape hanging from the cave's roof above us. I peered up at them—they were not made of mineral deposits and filament, but rather semiprecious gems like luminous aqua adamite and iridescent moonstone.

A holy, glowing cave.

My childhood teachers back in Amber would have wept at the sight.

We rounded a corner and made a left at a snake-tongued fork. Crystals lodged in the rocks behind us cast the passage in dim, violet shafts of light. We maneuvered around oddly shaped boulders and under dripping water that I didn't wish to know the origin of until we passed a shimmering pool that lit the dark cavern an otherworldly blue. When I looked closer, it was a cluster of slow-moving, shining jellyfish that gave it that vivid glow. If I wasn't so nervous about becoming trapped, or so cold—the temperature had dropped significantly upon trekking deeper into the cave—I might have been able to appreciate its beauty.

But I had sucked in one too many deep, awkward intakes of breath to calm my racing heart, and had made myself dizzy with too much air.

*"Lore says you'll go mad before you find your way out."*

At my sharp inhale, Fedrik appraised me. "Scared of cave monsters?"

"No." *Splendid response, Arwen.*

"I've been to every kingdom in Evendell at least twice, scaled mountainsides and plunged off cliffs and crawled through mud. Trust me, these caves are child's play."

That was actually helpful. I needed the distraction. "Some kind of thrill seeker, are you?" I imagined Fedrik traipsing all over the continent, a beautiful sunbeam prince hunting for adventure.

"Just a bit. Does it interest you at all?"

My eyes spied a phosphorescent insect scuttling into a crooked, skinny crevice. My heart picked up speed. "What? Travel? Sport?"

Fedrik shrugged as if to say, *Does anything?*

"I actually haven't seen too much of the world. I'd love to scale a mountainside. I'd settle for just seeing a mountain range."

"Well, I'll take you sometime, if you find yourself available."

This was the benefit of Fedrik not knowing that I was the Fae from the prophecy. With him, I had ample time to go on mountainous adventures. I grinned at him in the darkness, his blond hair backlit by illuminated crystals. "Where would we go?"

"The Kingdom of Amber has some spectacular mountain ridges. Most around the city of Rookvale."

Rookvale was only three hours north of Abbington by carriage. Right at my doorstep. So much of that insulated life, self-imposed. I shook my head.

"Wait," Mari said, stopping us and her path of luster in our tracks. "I think we have to go back two turns. This is a dead end."

The words sent my stomach into a state that made nausea preferable.

"Lead the way, witch." But Griffin's eyes remained focused on something that had skittered into a crevice in the walls.

I reached for Mari's hand, my chest feeling too tight, until a voice rang through the abyss.

In one graceful stride Griffin stood in front of us, his hulking form shielding both Mari and me from whoever else was down here.

"Could be the Garnet soldiers Crawford spoke of," Kane said, suddenly beside his commander. I hadn't even heard him behind me.

"Or regular folks hunting treasure," Fedrik offered. "Shall we go ask before we rip heads off? Just a thought."

Kane rolled his eyes. "Be my guest."

To my surprise, Fedrik did as Kane said, and sauntered down the tunnel, torch outstretched, until I heard him exchange warm pleasantries with a shadowed form.

We trailed behind. Standing there with Fedrik, hands folded around a map of his own, was a rugged man, likely in his late twenties, skin leathery from some sun-drenched occupation and covered in nautical tattoos.

Fedrik gestured toward us. "This is the rest of my party." Then, to us, "This is Niclas."

"What brings your group to Reaper's Cavern?" Niclas's voice was as rough as his weather-beaten skin.

"Just looking for a little adventure." Kane's casual voice could have fooled even me. "Who were you talking to?"

"The caves," Niclas answered, eyes pinned on Kane as if testing him. Goading him to mock. "Sometimes they talk back."

"You sound in desperate need of traveling companions," Mari said cheerily. "You're welcome to stick with us. However, our map is from a desk leg I had to smother in mud, which we only got from this seedy nobleman who *died*, which is a whole other story, but he traded all these stolen goods in Citrine, which is underwater, so who knows how much access he even *had* to the outside world, meaning I'm not sure if we can really trust this thing," Mari said, wagging the map at Niclas before taking off down the corridor, luster following after her like the dust of a shooting star.

Niclas's eyes flicked to us in confusion and a bit of concern, but Griffin only walked after Mari with a resigned sigh. "She just means our map is a little faulty. Don't . . . don't worry about the rest."

"Where did you say you're all from?" Niclas asked with suspicion. "Some place . . . underwater?"

"I grew up outside of Willowridge, in the Onyx Kingdom," Mari called back to him as we walked. "And you?"

"Pitney."

"That's in the Quartz of Rose, right? In the south?"

It was no surprise that Mari knew where Pitney was, nor that she could make friends with a stranger such as Niclas with ease.

"Yeah. I've never met anyone from Onyx. You're . . . more upbeat than I expected."

"It's not as bad as people think," Mari said, distracted by the map she was turning around and around.

I rubbed at my neck until she settled on an orientation and continued forward.

"Doubt that," Niclas huffed. "Your king is a sadist."

I held a hand across my mouth to hide a snort. My eyes caught sight of Fedrik's shaking shoulders.

"It's horrible, isn't it?" Kane asked, forcing Niclas to turn around and face him. "Someone should remove him from the throne."

"Oh, they will," vowed Niclas.

"Where'd you hear that?" I asked.

"From all over."

So my assessment of a sailor or a smuggler had likely been right. We were lucky that our new companion wasn't from Onyx and couldn't recognize the terrible King Ravenwood on appearance alone.

"What kind of treasure brought you here?" Mari asked.

Niclas loosed a gruff laugh. "You don't want to hear my story."

"Correct," Griffin mumbled.

"Sure we do," Fedrik said at the same time, stepping around a boulder.

"After the south of Rose fell to the north, the Scarlet Queen punished everyone who fought against her. My family still lives in poverty due to her sanctions. But our most famed historians were said to have kept two ledgers, one of which contained the names of those who won the war for the north, and one which identified every southern dissenter by name. As you can imagine, the latter became quite valuable—a physical document of those responsible for the revolt." Niclas's grin was a flash of white in the torchlit darkness. "But my grandfather was a peaceful man. He never took a single northern life. He was a wind chime maker, for Stones' sake. That second ledger will exonerate my family, and it's here, in these caves."

Niclas's plight was more honorable than anything I had been expecting. "Why would the ledger be in here?"

"You know the name Drake Alcott?"

I shook my head.

"He was the most brilliant thief to ever live. And from Pitney, too. More than a burglar, this man was an *artist*. He stole from lord and criminal alike and evaded capture for over forty years. He's one of the only men to make it through Reaper's Cavern, and he told the men of our city that when he saw the Peridot pirate's treasure, it contained the ledger."

"Why didn't he take it?" Fedrik asked.

"He didn't take anything from the cavern. Wasn't in it for the gold. Just the glory."

"What happened to him?"

"He eventually made a misstep. I heard he was sent to Hemlock Isle five years ago, so he's probably long dead. Careful," Niclas cautioned, and I looked down just in time to see my foot nearly crush a human rib cage.

*"Bleeding Stones."* I walked around the fragile skeleton and picked up the pace, adrenaline making my palms itch each time I remembered how deep underground we were.

"At least we've made it farther than that sorry—"

A guttural rumble erupted below our feet, shocking the breath from my lungs.

Kane was beside me in a heartbeat, and I gripped his arm without thinking as the walls shook and roared, my heart spasming in my chest.

"What's going on?" Mari shrieked.

Small rocks unearthed from the larger stones around us and fell to the cave floor like hail.

"The cavern is moving," Niclas said, unnervingly calm.

The roaring grew louder behind us.

I spun just in time to hear the groaning of shifting stones and watch with stunned dread as a slab of pure gray crashed down on the tunnel behind us, slicing off Mari's luster path—and our only way out—like a knife through marbled meat.

# 18

ARWEN

No!" THE WORD PUNCHED OUT OF ME, AND I LURCHED FOR the closing exit.

I knew it was Kane who yanked me back by the middle before I could get myself squished trying to escape.

"It's going to be all right," he whispered against my hair.

No, no, no, it was too late. We were sealed in.

The path Mari had left—

My light in the darkness—

We'd never find a way out now.

My heart pounded violently in my chest, like the wings of a hummingbird. *Out.* It was all I could think. I needed out *right now.*

Out, out, *out*—

I backed up into stone and slid down, cool rock jagged against my loose blouse. Sucking in air by the gallon, I heaved—

Tears.

There were tears slipping down my face.

Pungent salt on my lips when I sucked in one huge breath after another.

I screwed my palms against my eyes, and when that offered little relief, held them to my stomach as if I could still the nausea or make myself *breathe* or even calm the trembling of my palms, but nothing was working, nothing was *helping*—

Some part of my hysterical, frenzied mind could hear Griffin and Mari attempting to move the slab of stone. Their bickering and frustrated grunts only intensified my fear.

We were trapped. Preserved in here. Like insects in resin.

No, no, no—

Kane crouched down in front of me and pried my hand from my chest, where I was attempting to physically press my heart into slowing.

He held my palm in his, rubbing it soothingly. "Don't breathe too deeply. Sip the air, Arwen. Like water."

Adrenaline as shocking as lightning shot down my legs. I was having a heart attack. I couldn't sit still, shifting and shuddering and shaking. My throat was constricting—so tight I couldn't talk.

"What's wrong with her?" Fedrik asked, hovering over me.

"Nothing's *wrong* with her. She's panicking. She doesn't like to be confined."

"You're fine, Wen," Fedrik said warmly. "I doubt we'll be down here for long, and we have plenty of food and water if we are stuck."

*Oh, Stones.*

*Please, please, please,* I begged to no one and nothing. *I need to be free, please.*

"That's not helping," Kane hissed at him. "Leave us before you make it worse."

Fedrik hesitated, looking down at me. "I'm sorry, Arwen. I—"

"*Now*, you dolt. Tell the rest of them to keep walking. We'll catch up."

Scolded, Fedrik backed off, his eyes swimming with remorse.

I would feel awful about that later. But I couldn't think right now. About anything other than the overwhelming, raging urge to be out of these caves and *breathing* again.

"You're," I said between heaves, "so harsh." Another gasp. "With him."

Kane chuckled roughly. "He deserves it."

"He's a kind person." I gasped in more air. "Far kinder than you."

"But isn't it such fun to watch him writhe under my thumb?"

"So cruel. I can't believe I ever tolerated you. Let alone kissed you."

"I can't believe it, either," he said, still swirling his unhurried thumb against my palm. Then up and down my wrist. Up. Down. Massaging my fingers until my hand became jelly in his. "What was our worst kiss? Interrupted in Peridot?"

But I couldn't answer. I couldn't breathe. I wanted to be unconscious. Anything but this—

"Alas, now that you've realized what a bad idea we were," he continued, "I'll have to go back to Amelia's bed. I hope she's kept it warm for me."

Rage, bright and hot, swarmed in my vision.

"Good," I spat. "You two fickle demons deserve one another."

"She's quite the demon, indeed. Sometimes I'd leave her bed with bite marks."

"I hope she bites your head off." My anger surprised me. So much so, I could barely think. I breathed in and out evenly to quell my fury. So what if he was revolting? A revolting, nasty prick. He could do whatever he pleased.

Kane assessed me, eyes raking up and down my face, my throat, my chest. He held my wrist in his hand like it was the most fragile flower and pressed his thumb to my pulse.

"Ah," he said. "Much better."

And with that he stood and offered me his hand. "Come on."

I shook my head. Had he— "Was that . . . like that first night in the cells?"

"Anxiety lives only in the mind. If your thoughts are elsewhere, you can't panic. It used to work well for my brother."

As soon as he said it, both our expressions shifted. My heart rate slowed further.

"You have a brother?" I placed my still-shaking hand in his and took another slow inhale.

"Had," he said.

"*I bring pain wherever I go. I hurt people. Often those I care about most.*"

"*They're dead, Arwen. Because of me.*"

My heart ached at the memory of us in my bedroom in Shadow-hold.

"He used to dislike heights about as much as you dislike being confined."

I wanted to know more, but it didn't feel like the right time to probe him about his family. Not when I had just snapped at him over a woman he hadn't slept with in years. And while, once again, he was helping me quell my panic. I didn't know how to explain that my jealousy had more to do with me than with him or Amelia.

Kane spared me the attempt, pulling me from the ground with ease. We walked cautiously down the cool stone tunnel, following after the rest of the group. I inhaled slowly through my nose, even when the rustle of wings somewhere above us spurred my legs faster, and Kane kept pace in silence. I preferred the glowing yellow eyes or the strange carvings of symbols on the walls to any of the eerie sounds. I'd rather see whatever was lurking in the cave with us than be forced to imagine it.

When my breathing had truly calmed enough to speak, I peered up at him. "Thank you."

"Don't worry about it."

He kept his eyes on those paving the way for us, plodding forward as they shared stories and dropping back to peek at the map. More gemstone stalactites overhead. More twiggy, bioluminescent critters scampering at our feet. Antennae and shimmering wings.

His silence was making my chest ache.

"I'm sorry for my behavior back in Citrine," I said. It was a start. "For stripping, and goading Crawford and . . ." *And throwing myself at you.*

"I don't give a damn about any of that. Only your safety. The rest was a sight to behold." Kane gave a tilted smile at the memory. "When you told Trevyn he'd be cleaning his loved ones out from under his fingernails for weeks." He laughed, low and rough. "That one was dark even for me."

I laughed, too, and allowed myself to look up at him. "Maybe we could try something new."

Kane's eyes twinkled in the varied torchlight. "And what might that be?"

"Whoops, wrong way," Mari called from the front before turning on a heel and passing us. We fell to the back again and I tried to remember Kane's instruction to sip the air like water.

I willed my voice to be casual. "Friends?"

Hurt flickered in Kane's eyes, there and gone in an instant. But he jerked his chin in casual agreement. "Whatever the bird desires. I could always use more friends. I'm very lonely, you know."

"Do you mean that?"

Kane breathed out evenly through his nose. "A little."

Always so cryptic. I wanted to open his head with a pickaxe and crawl inside.

"What's that look?"

"I was thinking about taking a pickaxe to your brain." I flushed. It sounded so much more absurd out loud.

"Dear Gods, I've broken her."

I cocked my head. I had heard the phrase before at Shadow-hold, but never growing up in Amber. "Is that what you worship? Gods?"

Kane scratched at his jaw. "It may be more information than you can handle right now, bird."

I sighed. How much more could there possibly be? "Try me."

He scanned the dark expanse around us, contemplative. "In Evendell, legend says nine stones, each one a kingdom's namesake, formed the continent's core. You worship them, the Stones. Have temples built to them, curse them, pray to them, and on and on."

I nodded. Amber was the most devout kingdom, with more temples, priests, and priestesses than any other kingdom, except maybe Pearl. I had grown up studying the Stones in all my classes.

"The Fae, my people—our people—believe in Fae Gods. Immortal beings who created our realm, and all the others, including Evendell."

I wasn't as shocked as Kane expected me to be. Maybe because to him, this was a great truth—the creation of his world. But to me, it was just a story.

"So the Fae don't believe in the Stones at all?"

"No, we do. We believe mortals mistakenly refer to the Fae Gods as the Stones they created. There were nine original Fae Gods as well. The Blade of the Sun was hewn by them, and they are the ones who infused the hilt with their nine stones."

"Original gods? Now there are more?"

"So they say." Kane shrugged. "It's not as if they walk among us in Lumera, and I'm not quite as knowledgeable on deity lore."

The Fae history and folklore—*my* history and folklore—fascinated me. Almost as much as hearing Kane speak of the antiquities he loved so dearly. I wondered how much of this he learned as a boy in his classes, and how much came from his big, dry books.

The unmistakable smell of decaying human flesh hit me like an ocean wave and I dry heaved before clasping a hand over my face. Kane strode faster for the group before us. Everyone had stalled before . . . something. Without a torch of my own I couldn't see what it was in the assaulting darkness.

But I could *hear*.

The slithering of their scaled bodies. The bloodcurdling screech they produced—

And *smell* the putrid remains of whatever they had killed.

"What is that?"

"I have no idea," Mari murmured, which was always disconcerting.

"They're reapers. Hence the name of the cave," Niclas said.

Fedrik grunted. "And what is a reaper, exactly?"

"Why does it matter?" Niclas snipped. "They won't stop us."

He made to push toward the undulating, screeching sounds.

"I wouldn't do that," Kane said. Kane, a man I had never heard caution anyone—except me—against anything dangerous in his life. The least risk-averse person I had ever met.

Niclas scoffed. "We make it this far, and your balls shrink to grapes at the sound of some lizards?"

My eyes widened at his vitriol.

Not one to pick fights with those he deemed beneath him, Kane said nothing. Niclas appraised the rest of us, but no one dared to move.

"Fine. I'll go alone."

He inched forward, and the group parted to accommodate him, granting me a better view of the torchlit scene.

A vast pit extended before us. The expanse was bisected by a single plank of stone, like a thin bridge, that could only fit one foot placed in line after another. A deadly balancing beam to the other side. I couldn't see into the depths, but I could smell the rotting flesh of those who had not succeeded in crossing it. And hear the creatures that had no doubt torn them apart.

But beyond the thrashing, seemingly bottomless pit was the only reason for Niclas's bravery. In the distance, on the other side, was a rocky archway, lit from inside with scintillating, luminous light. Light that clearly reflected off pure gold, diamonds, and jewels. Sparkling, glittering, radiant.

The treasure. Just out of reach.

"You can't," I breathed.

"Watch me."

"Nobody wants what's through that passage more than us," Fedrik said. "But it's not worth your life."

Niclas considered Fedrik's words, eyeing the creatures that slithered through the pit.

Griffin cut a sidelong glance at Kane. "So what now?"

Kane's jaw stiffened. "Take them and find a way out the way we came. I'll go on my own."

"No." My knees buckled beneath me.

Kane gave me a pointed look as he lifted a shoulder, and I remembered that he would not need to cross the narrow bridge on foot.

"No way I'm letting you bunch take what's mine." Niclas shrugged Fedrik's hand away and, despite our shouts urging him to wait—to please listen to reason—stepped onto the narrow bridge. He inched along, one foot after the other. When he teetered, Mari nearly shrieked and twisted Griffin's arm into a vise grip.

"Holy Stones," she whispered. "I'm going to vomit."

Niclas narrowly righted himself and somehow continued walking. All the while, the snaps, slithers, and screeches of the scaled beasts below echoed off the cavern walls.

"Fifty coin says he drops before he makes it halfway." Kane smirked.

"I'll take those odds." Griffin's eyes were glued to the wobbling sailor.

"You're both sick," I hissed.

Niclas was making good progress. He was fast enough not to sway, but slow enough to be deliberate. I wondered if years of balancing on an uneven boat deck had granted him great steadiness. Maybe he would make it to the other side, find his ledger. Maybe even the blade . . .

And then what? Kane would probably pluck it from his hands and toss him to the reapers himself.

"That's fifty coin to me," Griffin muttered. Kane only grunted his response. Niclas had nearly made it to the end. The man was clearly disturbed, but I was rooting for him. I thought we all were, standing there watching him place one careful step after another.

Until his left foot landed wrong.

And that was all it took. He tried to course-correct—hands lunging out for support that wasn't there, flailing through the air like ribbons—before he disappeared into the writhing pit.

I got one look at a reaper in a dim shaft of torchlight as it sailed up to meet him. Sleek, agile body of an enormous snake, flexible and fluid. But that face . . . like a piranha. Ferocious, serrated teeth—layers of them—and rabid, oily red eyes, sunken deep into a face that hadn't seen daylight in likely millennia—

Then, the violent gnashing of teeth ripping Niclas into chunks as ebony reptilian skin mingled seamlessly with the pitch-black shadows of the pit. Mari squeezed her eyes shut and glued her hands to her ears against the gory sounds as Fedrik looked away, wincing. Niclas's death was instant—a savage, instantaneous dismemberment—and I thought it was a mercy that he had felt little pain, but that didn't stop me from retching onto the cavern floor at the sight.

Kane rubbed a comforting hand down my back but said nothing, no witty barb or gallows humor, and I thanked the Stones for that. I wouldn't have been able to stomach it.

Before any of us could comment on the horror we had just witnessed, the ground beneath us rumbled once again. My hand slung out to Kane's and clutched, so tight his fingers would have been pale white had I been able to see them in the darkness.

Would the stalactites above fall like heavy spears?

Would another moving partition crush us into paste?

Two twin slabs of stone jutted out from the walls that bordered each side of the pit and moved inward toward the bridge Niclas had tried to cross. The rocks scraped and groaned, the shuddering reverberating in my teeth and bones until the slabs met each side of the bridge, sealing the pit completely. What had just been a pond-sized expanse was now flat ground. No more pit, no more reapers, no more Niclas.

"How . . . ?" Fedrik tried, but words seemed to fail him.

I could still hear the faint gnashing and shrieking of the reapers underneath the stone floor. Kane pushed past Mari and Griffin gently and placed a tentative foot onto the fresh ground. My breath hitched in my lungs—but when the stone didn't give way under his weight, he strolled elegantly across and turned to face us from the other side.

"Come on in, the water's fine."

I wheezed out a breath and tried not to think that Niclas had somehow offered a sacrifice necessary to cross the reapers' threshold. We followed after Kane, heels echoing on the stretch of fresh, new stone, until all five of us stood on the other side and faced the dazzling, glittering reflection in the corridor entrance.

"Shall we?" Kane offered, before taking a step toward the stone arch.

But a sinister feeling sank through me, and without thinking I flung my hand out in front of his chest to stop him.

"No," I gasped out. "Don't."

"What is it?"

"Something isn't right." My gaze swept the space. "The passage is a fake. A trap."

"It's too obvious," Griffin added.

"A catchall for anyone who makes it through the reapers," Fedrik tutted. "Horrific."

"There!" Mari's voice bounced off the cavern walls as she dropped to her knees beside a hole in the stone to our left, cobwebbed and tucked out of sight behind a jagged rock. Too large to be a creature's den, but too small for a grown man. Some kind of tunnel.

"No, witch—"

But Griffin's warning was too late. Her small frame, illuminated by our now fading torches, disappeared into the tight entrance with ease. My stomach seized at the sight. My worst nightmare come alive.

"Someone needs to go after her," Griffin said, crouching down. His broad shoulders would never make it through.

*"Holy Stones!"* Mari's voice was muffled through the rock.

"What is it?" I called.

Griffin nearly jammed his entire body into the solid stone.

*"The treasure . . . It's . . . it's all here."*

Fedrik dropped to a crouch beside Griffin to inspect the narrow passage.

There was almost nothing across the continent I could want to do less than this, but . . . if the blade was in there, it would call to me.

Kane's eyes fell to mine, my intention clearly plain across my face. "You can't. It's too tight."

"I'm the only one the blade will speak to," I said quietly, Fedrik out of earshot.

"Fine," Kane said, a muscle in his jaw jumping. "I'm right behind you."

But we both knew none of the men could fit.

Only me.

In my own little tomb.

I knelt and squeezed past Fedrik and Griffin, my elbows and

knees scuffing against the dirt and dust. My head swam with the earthy stench: clay and mildew and decay. My heart beat like a drum in my ears, my brow beading with sweat. So tight. So narrow. And all submerged in stark, pitch-blackness. I was shaking now, not from the cold but from the fear. I nearly gagged on it. This would be the single most miserable way to die, trapped in here, left to suffocate.

*No, no, do not think like that.*

I scraped and slinked, but the tunnel was only constricting the deeper I crawled, and we were so far under the ground, and air was escaping me. With each heave, I lodged myself farther, and farther still—until I turned with the angle of the stone and saw where the tunnel would deposit me. Hurrying my elbows against the floor, I clawed and crawled and slid through to the other side, landing in a room where everything was glimmering.

A sparkling room, lit with candles—and laden with gilded treasure.

"Arwen," Mari said, overcome.

My eyes squinted to adjust to the glow. To take it all in.

Stacks and stacks of copper and silver and gold coin. Life-sized marble statues of virile men and women cloaked in gauzy bedsheets. Bejeweled tiaras and serpentine scepters. Jade votives and ages-old scrolls now petal-thin. Fierce, glinting weaponry. Beads and vases and crowns.

So much my eyes could barely devour the small, overflowing room. They swept up to the ancient wrought-iron candelabra implanted in the stone of the ceiling. The light that flickered there— enchanted pillar candles that had probably been lit for centuries.

*"Arwen?"* Kane's voice called through the tunnel.

"Yes," I called. "The treasure—it's here."

*"The blade?"*

I drank in the four walls shrouded and bloated and filled to the very brim with riches, my eyes assaulted by the flickering glow and sparkle. I pored over every inch. None of the longswords, daggers, or scimitars had a hilt with all nine stones. No song that sang only to me. No blade.

"I don't think it's here," I called. I heard Kane curse. "But I'll keep looking."

"There is so much history in here," Mari said, voice soft. Awed. "Stories and scrolls and books from eras and eras ago . . . I could weep. Am I weeping?"

"Just don't touch anything," I murmured, my eyes greedily gobbling up an entire wall of resplendent, glittering bejeweled spears.

Despite Azurine being the most lavish place I'd ever visited, and everything in that palace—even the little golden soap dishes adorned with fine pearl latticework—likely worth more than my whole home back in Abbington, nothing, *nothing* I'd seen there could compare to the wonders that filled this room.

"Oh, my Stones," Mari whispered.

I whirled. "You found it?"

"It's the ledger . . . just like Niclas said. With all the names in it . . ."

Before I could caution her against it, Mari reached her hand out and closed it around the book's dust-flecked leather, and every candle in the room winked out.

# 19

---

## KANE

THE DARKNESS CLOSED IN AROUND ME, SEDIMENT AND dust showering down, the ground rumbling and cresting beneath my feet, the sound of stone on stone blaring in my ears.

Arwen's scream pierced the tumult like a fang through skin.

My hand slammed into the stone that separated us, hard enough to send a crack rippling through the trembling rock. "Arwen!"

They were calling to me, she and Mari both, voices faint through the stone.

Muffled further by the absolute *roaring* of the cave collapsing on itself.

I pressed my ear to the wall, its shaking plane cold against my face, but I couldn't make out words.

The reverberations below my feet had become almost too strong for me to keep myself upright. I locked my knees and steadied my palms against the rock.

Solid, suffocating rock—

Power menaced at my fists as I readied them against the barrier between us.

But I didn't get the chance to strike.

My instincts sent me to the left, barreling into a spiky cluster of fallen crystals just as a boulder the size of a carriage dropped directly where I had been standing.

"Kane!" Griffin's voice.

I whirled. He and Fedrik were trying to make their way to me, dodging falling sheets of rock and crumbling, jagged stalactites.

"You have to go back," I yelled over to them.

Another angry layer of rock broke loose and plummeted from above, right over their heads. I raced for them, but I wouldn't make it—

In the split second before impact, Fedrik shoved Griffin out of the way.

And the sheet landed on the prince with a sickening *crunch*.

My gut clenched at the sight.

Fedrik screamed in agony, his leg pinned underneath the slabs of rock.

"Go!" I roared to Griffin once I had made it to them. "Get Arwen and Mari."

Griffin was way ahead of me, sprinting through the hail of boulders. I couldn't hear the women anymore. Panic thrummed through every inch of me, the lighte under my skin demanding that I crush, break, *tear* everything apart until I reached them. Until I reached *her*. So fierce I nearly had to brace myself against the rocks atop Fedrik.

I assessed the damage: even with my strength, I couldn't lift the heaviest stone clean off him. I'd have to slide the largest one, likely mangling his leg.

The prince seized my shin. "Kane, leave me," he gritted out. "We both know. There's nothing . . ."

"Don't be a martyr. Can you imagine how much your parents would hate me *then*?" I shoved with as much strength as I had, drawing the lighte from the soil deep beneath the cavern floor. Fedrik choked on anguish as the mass slid along his leg, shattering his bones.

Finally, the thing heaved off him. The ground continued to shake.

"Can you move?" I didn't have time for anything else. I needed to get Arwen.

"Yes," he said. "Run."

Fedrik heaved onto his stomach in an attempt to drag himself toward—

Toward what?

There was no safety down here. Not with these rocks falling, the cave collapsing. He'd be squished like a snail underfoot.

He needed to get out. We all did.

"Griffin!" My commander's glossy emerald power had barely made a dent in the enchanted stone that held the treasure room. "Get Fedrik back to camp. I'll find them."

Griffin gave an agonized look toward the wall he had been slicing through—

"Now," I roared.

He hurtled back to us, slinging Fedrik's arm around his neck and taking off without so much as another look in my direction. They barreled across the stone platform above the reapers, following the path Mari's luster had left. They would only make it as far as the cave-in and then . . .

I didn't have time to think about what might happen then.

It was all I could do to dart back for the wall to the treasure room, over crushed stone and dirt and debris. I heaved what rocks Griffin had broken loose away, one by one, sweat rippling on my brow, muscles straining at the effort. My lighte spilled out of me, wisps of barbed smoke and thorn cutting through the stone where Griffin had etched deep grooves with his own power. My arms, now two of eight, the wisps working in tandem like I was a creature of great myths.

"Arwen, can you hear me?"

Nothing.

I wasn't breathing.

"Mari?" I roared. "Arwen?"

*"Kane."*

"Yes, my love." *Sweet relief.*

*"We're trapped!"* Mari screeched, the walls now thin enough to hear through as my lighte broke down and shoved boulders the size of wheelbarrows out of the way.

"Try to stay calm."

Skin was ripping off my hands in coin-sized chunks. There was too much rock, too much stone, even with my shadow arms of smoke and thorn and wings. I pulled and pulled, until there was nearly a path through for me above the tunnel they had crawled through.

But still—more rock. More stone. Each bigger than the last, the more I broke through it . . . Was the wall between us *rebuilding*?

Fuck. I couldn't do it alone.

"You have to use your lighte."

*"It's not working—I'm trying but it's not working!"*

"Breathe. This is nothing for you. You have endless power. Draw it from the air." But I was no Dagan. There was no sun. Not much air left to draw from. I could only hope Arwen hadn't come to the same realization.

*"Kane, get yourself out of here. Get Fedrik and Griffin to safety."*

"I'm not leaving you."

*"You have to. The whole cavern is going to collapse. We'll find another way out."*

"I'm almost through."

But I wasn't. I had just narrowly squeezed into a carved crevice, and it was already sliding back together. I'd have to rebreak through solid, ancient, cursed stone. I slammed all the lighte I had into the wall and tiny fissures spider-webbed along it. I struck again, bones in my hands cracking, muscles in my back aching and screaming in protest.

*"No, you're not. I can see the wall re-forming."*

"Kane!" Griffin's voice. I spun, but it wasn't a call for help.

It was a warning.

The reaper pit was opening, the platforms that had sealed it sliding back into their original slots in the cavern walls. Reptilian screeches joined the earsplitting chorus of thunderous falling rock.

Gods *damn it.* This death trap had been a Gods-forsaken, failed waste of fucking time, and now it would claim all of our lives.

"Kane!" Griffin, again.

"I heard you," I shouted back.

*"Listen to me."* Arwen's calm voice was barely muffled through the stone anymore. I was so close. *"We found another way out. And you can't get through. Not in time. I will never forgive you if you die trying to save me. Do you understand? Never. You get everyone else out. We're going to be fine."*

There was a fail-safe. There had to be. A way out of the treasure room, for the pirates or Gods or sorcerers or whoever had moved the goods in there over the many decades. Warring against every instinct, every cell in my body, I pressed my hand to the fissured stone and yelled back, "Fine. Hurry."

*"You, too"* was all she said, and then I knew she was moving, and I had to do the same.

I dove for the sliding platform, now only a ledge against the cavern wall beside the pit, a hair wider than the beam along the middle. The pungent smell of rotting human flesh stung my eyes and tongue. The stone was growing narrower, and I sprinted past a single bloodstained fang that reached up to scrape my boot.

Tumbling onto the ground on the other side with a mere second to spare, I watched between heaving breaths as the slab sank fully back into the wall from which it came.

My chest constricted as I beheld the writhing pit of screeching reapers that now separated us. I had left Arwen. And I was going to tear this entire world to pieces if she didn't make it out. Starting with myself.

I careened back down the same tunnels we had come through, following Mari's line of painted light, until I reached Griffin and Fedrik at the solid stone wall that had trapped us inside mere hours ago.

Fedrik was on the ground, Griffin slamming arcs of emerald lighte into the wall where Mari's luster ended.

"It rebuilds itself."

"Where are they?" Griffin bit out.

"They'll be fine."

Fedrik's face leeched of all color. "You *left them to die?*" He turned to Griffin. "We have to go back."

"I left them because Arwen begged me to save *your* life." The words were like ash in my mouth. "She said they found another exit."

Fedrik panted. "How could you—"

"Enough," Griffin barked. "Arwen and the witch will survive. They're strong. I need Kane's help so we can do the same."

Drawing every last drop of lighte that I had inside me, pulling from the very marrow of my bones, I drove a wall of black mist like a knife against the stone. Griffin did the same, his translucent, tourmaline lighte funneling out of his palms like blown glass. Layering on mine, filling in gaps where I was ragged, patchy, faltering—

Slowly—*agonizingly* slowly—our powers carved and splintered the sediment until a single crack cleaved the stone in two.

I heaved, bracing my hands on my knees. I heard Griffin spit into the dust beneath us.

And still that merciless, uncompromising, ravaging force shook the ground beneath our feet.

"Quick," I breathed. "Before it reconstructs."

Griffin helped Fedrik up and grunted as his lighte flowed out of him once more in an incandescent aura, pushing one side of the crack we carved with his shoulder and trying to force it open like a jammed door.

I moved next to him and did the same, my boots grinding into the shuddering floor. The cave wall that had come down of its own accord was silent against my pressed ear, and yet awake . . . Listening. Breathing. Restless.

The solid rock held firm, and that peculiar feeling fueled me to push harder, and *harder* still, until at once it rotated open, enough for us to release our hold and gulp in matching breaths of air.

I could smell the twinges of the rain forest, the slight heat that was slipping in through the tunnel we had split open.

Fedrik limped through on his crushed leg with no further urging, Griffin after him. I slipped out last, allowing myself one final look at the crumbling cavern behind us. But I felt no release of the oily dread that coated my throat.

She would make it out.

She had to.

We ran for the mouth of the cave, each step bringing another bird's call, a waft of fresh air, a fragrant damp breeze, until we were spat out where we had entered.

I sucked in steadying gulps of humid, floral air as Griffin lowered Fedrik against the trunk of a palm and knelt to inspect his leg.

Not a minute later—when we had scarcely caught our ragged breaths—a deep, guttural roar erupted from the mouth of the cave. Hideous groaning rang through the trees, sending creatures rustling overhead and at my feet.

The cavern . . . it was closing.

Sealing shut—

I moved without thinking, faster than I'd ever moved in my life—

Thicker than the stone I had used nearly all my power to break through, a slab from the top of the cave's open mouth crashed into the earth long before I could reach it. I slammed my fists against what just mere moments—*seconds*—ago had been the wide-open jaws of Reaper's Cavern.

Against what was now a mountain of solid rock.

# 20

ARWEN

THE NEXT CHUNK OF ROCK THAT CRASHED DOWN SENT MY body sprawling over Mari's. The force knocked my vertebrae against one other as I curved, prone on top of her, shielding her while she screamed, and that roar of shaking, crumbling, violent stone continued everywhere. The fragments, the dust that painted my tongue—it was all the tunnels, undulating and caving in. Burying us.

And the disorienting, insidious, leaden *darkness* that we had been marinating in for minutes, or hours, I wasn't sure.

I couldn't hear myself beg Mari to quiet down. To stop screaming. To please, stop screaming.

"Holy Stones, we're going to die."

"No." I heaved. I still couldn't see. I couldn't *breathe*—

"I don't know any spells for being entombed." She thrashed underneath me, my body still bent over hers. My lighte didn't sense any blood, any snapped bones, any internal bleeding—

I rolled off her and strained to breathe slowly. Like Kane said. To sip the air.

"We're going to suffocate and die. Or be crushed to death. Or both." Mari did not know how to talk to people who were deathly afraid of enclosed spaces. "We're going to decay, and rot in here, and one day someone will find our skeletons along with all this treasure."

"Mari," I snapped at her, breathing slower than felt natural. "That is not going to happen."

"Why did you lie to him? He was almost inside!"

"He wasn't, and he was going to die trying to get to us. You and I just have to focus. There has to be another way out."

"I need my grimoires."

But I didn't. I sucked in the stuffy air around me, pointed my hands where I thought Kane had been cutting through—a mere guess in the stifling blackness—and tried to summon my lighte. A spark, a beam of glittering power, a single ember, anything.

*Come on, come on—*

My hands cramped from flexing and I ignored the tendrils of dread that unfurled inside me. What had Dagan said back in Azurine? I couldn't remember now. My mind had been filled with such silent roaring back then. I hadn't listened. I couldn't *remember—*

Earthly wind rattled thin metal and pages of ancient books around us.

"What spell are you doing?" I called in the darkness. She was on the other side of the room now.

"The luster!"

Good. The room was pitch-black without the candles. We'd need—

My eye caught a sliver of light dancing across the mountains of golden treasure, still shaking with the tremors.

"Stop!" I cried. "There's light, coming from somewhere. Over there . . ." I traced my hand along the engraved walls, feeling around in the darkness. I could hear Mari doing the same. We had a wealth of knowledge and determination between the two of us. We didn't need lighte or magic. We could find our way out the old-fashioned way.

"Wait, come here—" Mari called from the other side of the room.

I pawed my way to her voice, grasping at candlesticks and pointed crowns, banging my hip into a suit of armor and wincing as pain bloomed along my side.

"What is it?" I asked over the earsplitting noise.

"I think I feel . . ."

Knocking into her shoulder with my knee, I squeezed past her frame and reached my hand down over hers where the light was slipping through. My pulse thrummed with hope. "Hinges."

"It's some kind of false wall."

I examined the crevice with my fingers until I felt a spiked knob at the base of the hidden door and rotated it with all my strength. As the rusted stakes slid through the flesh of my hand, the door groaned and shifted.

Despite the shrieking pain in my palm, I turned the knob, and then turned it again.

With a low reverberation, barely audible over the shaking and falling of sediment around us, the door opened enough that Mari and I could crawl through.

The corridor was chilling.

The roaring, silenced.

Preternaturally still, lit with iron candlesticks that glowed with that same abnormal fire, the kind that didn't flicker with the wind. A dim, unwelcoming passage to our left, a slightly lighter passage to our right lit with more of those candles as far as my eye could see, and whittled stone at our feet that became stairs guiding us down, down, *down*—like the cave was inviting us to stay, a volatile and easily offended host.

"Which way?" Mari asked me.

We halted before that darkness, that deathly crypt below us— likely taking us so far beneath the jungle floor the air would become too heavy to breathe. Air that had probably been trapped down there since the Stones birthed the continent.

The thought made me sick. But the other paths again felt too easy. And the cave had the spirit of a trickster. A cheat. A fraud—

But if we descended those fatal, nightmarish stairs, would we spend eternity down here? Had the others—

I couldn't let my mind drift to Kane or Griffin or Fedrik . . . if they, too, had been deceived by Reaper's Cavern. Or simply crushed. If I would never see them again . . .

Mari loosed a sigh.

I tried to do the same. "I think we have to try. You wait here, and I'll call for you if it—"

"Arwen!"

My eyes were still adjusting, but I heard it, too. The clunky, disjointed tremors. The earsplitting reverberation, like the roar before a wave pulls you under the sea. An avalanche of rocks tumbling toward us from the lefthand passage.

*"Bleeding Stones,"* I breathed.

Mari grabbed my hand and hurtled us down the musty, depthless stairs and into an even darker, danker corridor. We ran through the stone, like the old corn mazes of my youth, sliding and skittering against the dirt beneath our feet. Tearing through—left, right,

right again, sharp left, dead end. Doubling back to go right, *not* left, and then left again.

"Why the stairs?" I called, doubting our choice, ice sluicing through my blood with regret.

"It seemed so wrong . . . it had to be right?"

The avalanche grew louder, rumbling and reverberating through my ankles, my shins. I could hear Mari whispering behind me, trying to cast some kind of spell, but nothing materialized. It was slowing us down. We had to keep running, keep moving, despite the never-ending twists and turns the cave presented us with.

I was faster than her and was starting to drag her behind me like a rag doll. But we couldn't stop. Didn't dare to face the crush behind us. The way our bodies would be buried under the earth for centuries.

True fear—genuine and harrowing and poison black—assaulted me. Worse than the panic. Worse than the vacant nothing, the numbness.

I did not want to be entombed in solid rock.

I did not want to die.

We had to get out.

*Out*—

The world, the cave, the avalanche yawned away but for that single word. We just had to get *out*.

Our path stemmed narrower, forcing me to propel Mari forward. My legs were tired. I just needed one break, one spot to breathe, to think, to formulate some kind of—

"Arwen, look out!"

We screeched to a halt, nearly falling on top of each other as the last corner we rounded deposited us in front of another unexpected fork lit by those same ancient candelabras, the ones I knew in my bones had been here long before any of us were even thoughts.

We careened left, Mari's hand clammy and slipping in mine, tears burning at my eyes, blood in my lungs, I was sure of it, and—

There.

Light.

Blessed, beautiful *light*.

Reflecting from an archway on the far left of the passage. Light that could only be from the sun. My knees could have buckled with relief were it not for the propulsion, the raw horror driving us inexorably forward.

We were so close now—

So close to fresh air—*any* air. To being *out* of here—

But the roaring had only intensified. Louder, and more violent. As if the cavern were a living, thinking creature, and saw hope in our eyes.

I made the unforgivable mistake of looking behind Mari's wind-swept curls.

That wave of crumbled rock crushed through the tangled maze behind us, faster now, gaining and gaining speed, like a flood in a storm. A goliath boulder, greater than both our heads, dislodged from the landslide and shot toward us.

*No, no, no—*

The sphere of lighte I had flowered around Leigh and me weeks ago in Siren's Bay blossomed around me and Mari, rippling, shimmering, and protecting us from the projectile. Mari screamed—I couldn't tell if that was from relief or dread—and the shimmering, flexible orb grew thicker, as if bolstered by my need to defend her. More sharp daggers and pellets of stone rained down and bounced right off the domed top of my lighte.

Thank the ever-loving Stones.

We were close enough now.

The light of a lush, green day beckoned to us, the smell of moss and rain . . .

And I knew we'd never slow our inertia in time.

That we would be crushed before I cut a hard enough turn to allow us both into the passageway.

Demolished.

Reduced to limbs and hair among a sea of speeding rock.

There was only one way out of this.

We flew past the open corridor, and for a heartbeat that sunlight spilled through, across my face, the exit summoning me—

And I used every ounce of strength to push Mari inside the narrow passageway with all my strength without breaking my stride.

I could just barely hear her agonized scream of protest, make out her crestfallen face—unruly hair backlit by beams of sun and verdant leaves—as I kept running, deeper into the cavern's suffocating corridor, tailed by that roaring wave of debris.

There were no corners to duck behind, no turns to make. The narrow passage was endless, growing darker and darker, thinner and thinner, and all the while the avalanche behind me echoed.

And my legs were getting heavy. So heavy. If the flickering iridescent bulb around me was any indication, my lighte was already dwindling. I couldn't keep the shield up much longer.

And I was so, so tired.

This was as good a time as any to give up. I had saved Mari. I couldn't outrun the crush forever . . . My feet slackened—

Only to see the slightest sliver of light, like a crescent moon, glowing in the distance.

And maybe it was the pain I feared. The pain of being flattened by a thousand tons of solid rock. Or maybe a slice of hope was all I needed to try—to fight to live. But whatever it was that spurred me, I threw everything I had into my final steps, and prayed the light was indeed an exit.

And then I got closer, and saw what it was.

A cliff.

The tunnel led out to a protruding cliff. A chute for all the stones behind me to flush out any of the cavern's unwanted visitors.

I didn't have time to think. I raced with all my strength, out into the blinding, pure white sunlight. The air was hot and thick and fresh in my lungs, and before I realized I had come to the cliff's edge, I threw myself off, the tumbling rock behind me falling down as well, just barely missing my head.

For a single, unbearable moment—suspended in midair, arms flailing, legs wheeling with inertia—I felt an inexplicable itching at my shoulder blades. Like needles buried under my skin, rising to the surface, impatient to stab through.

But then I fell, down, down, down, past the palms, past a soaring parrot, and into a deep pool of green water, the rockslide splashing into the lagoon behind me. The cold rush of water pulled me under, and consciousness slipped away.

# 21

## ARWEN

THE HAND ON MY CHEST WAS NOT ONE I RECOGNIZED.
Etched in blurred, blue ink that might've once been bold tattoos, tipped by fingernails caked in dirt, and missing half a middle finger, the hand rose into the air and slammed down on my chest again, dislodging more water from my lungs. It was all I could do to roll over, gagging and spitting onto the grass.

"Atta girl."

I hacked again before air flooded my lungs. Humid, and scented with plumeria and algae.

Rubbing my eyes, I pushed to stand from the wet seagrass and nearly tumbled back into the vast expanse of water beside me: a lush, clear emerald lagoon, as deep as it was sprawling, produced by misty streams of water that cascaded down the rocky ravine I had fallen from.

A bird's squawking pulled my eyes up, past the overrun canyon of verdant green and gushing blue and into a sky smudged with a few angry purple clouds. The sun had slipped behind one, making the edges glow. I searched for the ledge I had jumped from, but the limestone amphitheater's cliffs were all the same and I couldn't see where the cavern had expelled me.

I glanced back to the man who had saved my life. Scruffy hair framed a kind face creased from sun and wind and dirt, with brows both overgrown and patchy. Leather draped him, as well as colorful beaded necklaces and jewelry on both ears. His wide grin was populated by few teeth.

A pirate.

I crawled backward like a crab, only to knock my tailbone against someone's boots. I flicked my gaze up.

More men. About seven or eight of them. In tunics and pants that had once been vibrant, with hats to block out the unforgiving sun on an open sea. Some had intricate tattoos so often seen in Peridot, others obscene piercings I hadn't ever seen before through their noses and lips.

Where had Mari ended up? Not in this rocky clearing, evidently. I could only hope she had fared better than me and wasn't lost in the jungle somewhere.

I scrambled to my feet and said, "Don't touch me," with as much strength as I could manage. My head pounded.

"That's one way to thank a fella," the first man replied, standing as well before stalking closer.

"I'm serious, come any closer and I'll kill you."

Half-hearted male laughter echoed against the cliffs.

"Leave her, mate," someone called.

"Don't you think if we wanted to harm you," the man said, inching forward slowly like I was a skittish animal, "we woulda while you was sleeping?"

Realization struck me so fiercely it was like being pulled under the water once more. I grabbed at myself, my soaking pants and shirt, but nothing seemed out of place.

"Oh, Stones, we didn't touch you. Just saved your bloody life."

A twinge of embarrassment tickled my spine. They didn't hurt me. They didn't even leave me to drown. "Thank you."

"Look! You found your manners. I'm Studs."

I wrung my hair out with both hands as I said, "Arwen."

"Pleasure. You really took that leap like you wasn't afraid to die, Arwen." Pride must have colored my expression because he shook his head at me. "Not a flattering thing, stupidity."

A flush worked up my neck. "I didn't have a choice."

Studs didn't seem to care much either way as he walked past me and back to his men.

I swept my attention over the clearing. I had never seen any of this before. The cliffs, the rolling hills, the lagoon. I had no clue where I was, or how I would find everyone else.

"Wait!" I called to Studs and his men, who were already heading off through the jungle. "Where are you all going?"

"Back to Smuggler's Beach," Studs said, halting. "We sail for Rose tomorrow."

"You're fleeing Peridot?"

A man with a face like a bulldog snarled at me. "We ain't *fleeing*."

"The land's gone to shit since Amber stole the throne," another added.

"I know you don't owe me anything," I started. "And you already saved my life. And then I accused you of . . . But might you help me find my camp? On your way, maybe?"

Studs mulled my offer over, stroking his chin and scrunching his nose.

One of the men called, "How much coin do they got on 'em?"

"Because you were dry as bone," another added sheepishly, his too-large hat tipping over his face, which he scrambled to right.

I folded my arms and stared daggers at Studs. "So you *did* touch me."

"Only to search you for coin." He shrugged. "Didn't touch none of your frilly bits."

I should have known riches would be the easiest way to a pirate's heart. "I'm traveling with a wealthy lord. He will reward you handsomely for my safe return." I had become such an excellent liar I was nearly vain about it.

Studs's jaw tightened, but the gleam in his fellow men's eyes was enough to tell me I had struck gold. "Where were they last?"

"In a jungle camp outside of Frog Eye."

Studs chuckled. "We could have you there by sundown."

"I would be so grateful."

He turned to his men. "One last night in Frog Eye before we go?"

⚓

"WHO'S THIS LORD YOU JOURNEY WITH? YOUR HUSBAND?"

Studs tramped through a muddy puddle and I swerved to avoid the backsplash as I considered his question. The journey to Frog Eye would be hours. I didn't want to trap myself in a web of lies, nor be too honest given my fugitive status. Better to keep the focus on them than on me. "Mhm. So what do you export? Jewels?"

Two men laughed like I was *very* naive and I cocked my head to Studs in silent question.

"We seem rich to you?"

I shook my head and hoped that was the least offensive way to answer.

"Mainly spirits. Sometimes furs and pelts to the colder regions."

A man in front of us with a knotted white beard scoffed. "That's why we're still working in our old age."

"Settle down, Gage."

"There are more lucrative endeavors is all I'm saying."

"It's all you're ever saying."

I tilted my head. "Like what?"

"Nothing you should worry your pretty little head over."

Gage barked another laugh at his captain. "You afraid the lass'll faint? Or squeal?"

All eyes fell to me, and a prickly sweat broke out across my back. There were only a few exports I could think of that would produce anything close to a *squeal*. I braced myself, even as I said, "Try me."

Studs leaned in close, his breath hot and stale on the shell of my ear even in the jungle humidity, and said, "You ever heard of Faerie lighte?"

Horror swamped me. "No."

"Course you haven't. It's not your fault. They don't teach it in the fair lady classes I reckon you took."

"What is it?" I asked, finding my voice as we climbed over the wide roots of a kapok tree.

"Type of witch called a Fae. Their power isn't magic, but something they can pour right out like you and I piss. Sells for more coin than you could dream of in Smuggler's Beach. Even more in the black markets of Rose and Garnet."

Hadn't Kane told me about this? The memories were fuzzy and

saturated with spirit, but I remembered him explaining it to me once, in his wine cellar.

*"It could be bottled and sold, used to fuel anything. It could heal, build, destroy."*

"But you don't sell it, even though Gage wants you to?"

"Doesn't seem right. Like selling blood. Men have to live by some kind of code, don't they?"

"How do those that do even get it? From the witches called the Fae?"

"Curious little badger, aren't you?" Studs said, mussing my hair roughly. "There are other men that hunt the Fae down. It's a specific skill, the harvesting. And a perilous one. Those Fae are powerful things."

Whatever harvesting was, it didn't sound pleasant. My veins itched at the mental image of having my lighte drawn out of me against my will.

"So why don't they—the harvesters—just sell the lighte themselves? Keep all the profits?"

Studs made a clucking noise and I noticed a sparkle of silver there, embedded in his tongue. "You have to be *known* here in Smuggler's Beach. Any old harvester can't just walk up and sell their wares. Too many try to sell fake goods. My pop was a runner and seafarer, and his pop before him. I've built a booming business for myself with this crew. We run a tight ship—get it?"

My answering laugh was surprisingly genuine. "Well, then, thank you again, for changing your schedule to accommodate me."

"It's no trouble at all. I like to take the slower route when I can. Spend another day in the jungle, in Frog Eye. Who knows how many days any of us got left? I like to look at the iguanas and things. See the pretty women. Drink the ale."

"Why do you say that? Because Peridot is more dangerous now, you fear for your life?"

Studs's laugh was a hard braying noise. "Stones, no. In our line of work, it's always one wrong step and you're missing an appendage."

"And yet, you could be doing anything else, and you choose to smuggle. Because it was your father's business?"

"If I was a goatherd instead, then I'd be afraid of losing one of my goats. There's always something to fear. That's the price of doing anything worth doing."

"That's . . ." I smiled as I searched for the words. "Pretty poignant, Studs."

Studs turned to face me as we rounded a banana tree. "And here you were thinking we were just a bunch of—"

A silver arrowhead flew through Studs's eye, and warm, red blood splattered my face. Copper landed on my tongue. I spat at the ground over and over in shock—pure, horrifying *shock*—as the kind pirate crumpled to the grass beneath us.

Dead.

Ice cut through my veins at the sight.

The single arrow lodged in his skull. His still, slack mouth, mid-sentence.

Shouts of pain pulled my eyes from Studs—

The rest of the men had scattered, running for the mossy hills, the trees, the limestone cliffs—swords drawn, knives at the ready— but the hail of arrows rained down on most of them, wilting the men like roses in heat.

I could barely hear their screams over the ringing in my ears. I whirled into an armored breastplate, and my mind, my *bones*, shuddered. I knew it like my own leathers. The golden stone detailing, the rust-colored, intricate filigree.

Amber armor.

The soldier grabbed my shoulders and threw me to the ground, mud and pain blurring my vision as my head smacked the grass.

"We have to stop running into each other like this, Arwen."

The voice registered so strangely in my heart. Like a comfort, warped by twisted, recurring nightmares. His boots strolled toward my face, which was held against the ground by another soldier above me. He crouched until I could see that white-blond hair.

*"Halden?"*

# 22

KANE

I HAD BEEN STARING AT THE SEALED ENTRANCE OF REAPER'S Cavern for what felt like hours. Though grief beckoned like a siren, I wouldn't give in quite yet. Instead, I'd focus on bafflement. On how I could have been so supremely stupid. How I could have let Arwen and Mari both slip through my fingers.

Fedrik moaned as Griffin attempted something with his leg behind me. After a few long, tedious inhales and the stomp of boots behind me, Griffin arrived at my side. I was still confounded by my own horrible, inexcusable decision-making, when he appraised the solid rock alongside me. "How's the staring going?"

"How's the prince?"

"He needs help."

"We have to wait for Arwen. We can't risk an infirmary. The towns are swarming with Amber soldiers . . ."

A miserable groan pulled our eyes to the tree that Fedrik leaned against as he tried to adjust his position. Griffin hadn't been wrong:

the prince's face was nearly gray, his leg tied off with a tourniquet below the knee.

"That leg will be septic soon," Griffin said. "We should get him back to camp."

"We can't. Not yet."

"You think I *want* to leave them?"

I knew we had to help Fedrik, but I couldn't move. Couldn't or wouldn't, I wasn't sure. But the solid, cratered stone mass before me was taunting me. And I couldn't leave, wouldn't *fucking* leave without—

Mari's voice cut through my thoughts like an arrowhead. "Holy Stones, there you are!"

*Thank the Gods—*

Griffin moved like a man possessed as he bounded for her. He reached Mari just as she cleared the tree line, only to stall out a foot in front of her. A loaded pause followed as he scratched his arm before saying, in relieved greeting, "Witch."

Mari only huffed and traipsed around him. "Fedrik, are you all right?"

Fedrik only grimaced in response, his eyes elsewhere. He and I were both staring at that same leafy green spot in the jungle Mari had just plowed through.

Waiting.

A beat—

And then another.

Before my eyes stung. Before my hands clenched into fists. Before acid burned my throat.

"Where is Arwen?" Mari asked it first, her voice smaller than I'd ever heard it.

Fedrik looked stricken. "She isn't with you?"

My whole body went still, my pulse halting in my veins. "*You were just with her.*" My sight had gone red, like a fog of blood. "What do you mean, *where is she*?"

Griffin stepped in front of Mari smoothly, his face a mask of calm.

"Fuck, Griff, I'm not going to hurt her," I bit out. "Mari, tell me what happened."

The witch swallowed audibly. "We escaped the treasure room and made it through this terrifying stone maze and then there was an avalanche of rock that was barreling toward us and we were *exhausted*, I've never run that much in my entire life, but even Arwen was tired I could tell—" She paused to swallow again. "It was horrible and so much faster than us and we were just going deeper and deeper into the caves until we saw this corridor that opened up to the jungle, and she . . . she . . ."

*Finish the thought before I rip it from your tongue—*

"She saved me. She used her lighte." Mari said the word quietly. "To protect us both and push me in even though there wasn't enough time for her, too. She would have been squashed, so she just kept running. And I tried to go back, but the tunnel was impenetrable because of the landslide. I tried a disintegration spell, which is most commonly used on wood that's been infested by termites, but it didn't have any effect on the stone, and I don't have my spell books, and—" Another swallow. "All I could do was hope she made it to you first, but now . . . I don't know where she is."

For a moment it was silent. Nothing but the caws of birds and the humid breeze rustling in the waxy leaves around us.

"I have to go back in." I wasn't even sure if I had spoken the words aloud.

"You heard the witch," Griffin said. "There's no way back in."

"Arwen is probably trapped in there. Her *greatest fucking fear.* I have to—" I couldn't think. What could I even do? I whirled to Mari. The look in her eyes said my expression was as horrifying as it felt on my face. I tried to school my features. "Mari, you have to do something."

"Like what?" She clutched at Briar's amulet again.

"A locator spell," Fedrik groaned against the tree, his face very pale.

"I just told you." Her voice was getting frantic. "I don't have my grimoires. I don't know these spells off the top of my head. I'm not an encyclopedia."

This was not the time for Mari to start doubting herself. As if reading my thoughts, Griffin held her gaze and said firmly, "You know enough. What about—"

"Oh yes, you know all the spells! Rattle them off for me, will you?"

I nearly knocked myself unconscious. "Please, Mari. Skewer the commander with your wit *later*. Think *now*."

Griffin, the brave bastard, only stepped closer to her. "Clear your mind and think of your grimoires. You've read them all cover to cover."

Mari chewed her lip. "Maybe a binding spell? To tie one of us to her. It'd be a bit like running around blindfolded, but they'd know if they were getting closer. They'd be able to feel her."

"Me. Send me. Do it *now*."

"I need a memory of you and her. To bind you together."

A dark cloud passed over the shining sun and a chill crawled up my spine. "What kind of memory?"

Mari shut her eyes. "Anything with a strong emotion." She brought her hands up to the sky, fingers taut and spread wide toward the tree cover, and murmured words in a language I didn't recognize.

"There was an evening." I cleared my throat. "A few months ago, when she spoke during a forum I held. She had great insight. I remember feeling unbelievably proud of her . . . the way she had braved the room. I knew my people still scared her, and yet—"

One of Mari's eyes peeked open. "I'm going to need more than that, Kane. You have to actually *feel* something."

Rare heat flamed up my neck—I did not embarrass easily. "Fine," I gritted out. The memory that she needed bobbed to the surface from wherever I had sought to suppress it the past few months.

"The night the wolfbeast attacked Arwen." I prickled against Fedrik's and Griffin's curious eyes. "I had been flying back from Willowridge. The whole way home I was kicking myself for leaving her. I had this . . . feeling. That something would happen to her while I was gone. That I would be punished somehow. Perhaps because we had grown so close the night before. Or, because the people I cared about so often wound up dead.

"When I got back, I raced to her room. I was going to make up some flimsy excuse for visiting her, but she was gone." My knuckles went tight against the memory of her empty bedroom. "It was like finding a limb missing. Running through the woods, I think I made a promise to every single God for her safe return. And when I found her in that clearing . . . saw her *blood* leaking onto the forest floor . . .

"I thought my very heart lived outside my body in that moment, and I was watching it wither and die. I would have given my own life ten times over to save her from that pain. From the fever, the nightmares, the agony. It was the longest night of my life. When she awoke the next morning—healing, laughing—it was like dawn breaking over a thousand years of darkness. She—"

"It's done."

I hadn't even noticed the wind swirling around us—or that I had closed my eyes—but when I opened them, Mari's hair was falling softly around her face and thin, reedy leaves were fluttering back down to the ground.

Like a bath of light and warmth, I felt Arwen's spirit flitting about inside my chest.

*Alive—*

She was alive.

I clutched at my heart. "She's all right."

"Thank the Stones," Mari breathed. "You should be able to sense where she is. The feeling of being tied to her will only intensify as you get closer. Once you touch, the spell will end."

I made sure I still had my sword on me and gathered my pack.

"We'll meet you back at camp," Griffin said. "We won't risk finding a healer in Frog Eye unless we have to."

I nodded and took off toward the layers of greenery ahead of me.

The sensation of my hands being tied stopped me in my tracks. Monkey shouts and bird calls were swallowed by pure silence as I looked down, but my arms were hanging at my sides, despite the feeling telling me otherwise.

"What is it?" Griffin called.

Fear—true and genuine *fear* hammered through my heart.

"I think . . ." I could feel what Arwen felt. Could feel her being tethered to something, my back, mirroring hers, bound to some kind of pole. "I think someone *has her.*" My voice was hoarse.

Horror knotted both Mari's and Fedrik's faces.

I didn't waste another moment before hurtling for the trees.

# 23

## ARWEN

The amber soldiers' encampment made our three tents look like—well, three lone tents.

I tried to hold my chin up as Halden's officer led me past the sentries stationed at the wood-crafted fortress gates, but I knew. I knew this was the end. I was amazed none of them had killed me already. Wasn't I all that stood in the way of their leader's eternal reign?

Halden guided us along a wide dirt path. His hair was shorter now. Cropped and clean-cut, but still that pale, yellow blond. His expression was stern, his armor adorned with more gold, more filigree, but he was the same boy I'd caught toads with in Abbington. The first boy I kissed.

The same one who told his king where Kane and I would be. Who brought the armies and fire-breathing creatures to Siren's Cove. Who ensured the death of men, women, children—

My mother.

Soldiers around us sharpened swords and carried stacks of

shields and helmets, insulated by canvas tents and burning hearths. We passed a crude stable, too large for mere steeds, and the smoke billowing in bursts from the open roof told me it was filled with salamanders. Their ashy scent and guttural snarls sent cold dread swirling in me like a dark tide pool.

I hoped at least my death would be swift. A beheading, maybe. The slashing of my throat. Stabbing was painful, but if deep enough, wouldn't last long. Just not burned alive by salamanders. Or drowned. Or eaten by something rabid and snarling.

*Please*, not that one.

I had hardly gotten a look at the hog roasting over the massive spit or the horses decked in familiar Amber caparisons before Halden ordered me into a khaki tent and observed as his soldier tied me to the pole at its center. I grunted as my arms were angled behind me and twisted around the splintering wood.

"Hold still," Halden said, his expression as hard and cold as steel. "You'll only hurt yourself."

A bitter laugh bent from my lips.

"Leave us," he said to his underling.

Halden's modest tent clearly belonged to some kind of low-ranking general: a stark desk with a map of Evendell and an ornate paperweight, a small hearth emitting a low heat, and a pallet with matted furs and an out-of-shape pillow. Halden sat on the chest at the foot of his makeshift bed and stared at me.

"Someone got a promotion."

He looked tired. "Mhm."

I let my disgust show plainly on my face before the question blurted from me. "When did you realize what I was?"

"After we were conscripted, Ryder and I got blind drunk. He

said you had some magical healing ability. I never thought of it again until Gareth told me what I was to do."

"Murder Fae."

His eyes flicked to mine, and he bit at his nail in thought. "Right."

*Revolting prick.*

"I saw the way Kane protected you," he continued. "And I took a chance. Told Gareth what I knew of your abilities. Of the way the king of Onyx was keeping you in his home like his own little prize. And then we sailed for Peridot."

A long-familiar guilt screwed itself deeper into my heart.

I *had* been the one to doom Siren's Cove. By telling Halden of Peridot and Onyx's alliance.

"You *killed* people. Innocent people, Halden."

"Lazarus is going to take Evendell whether we like it or not. He's more powerful than anyone, even your Fae prince."

"Kane is a *king*."

"He's the son of a king," Halden bit out. "You'll never find the blade, and that's the only way to kill him. There are only two people who can speak truths such as this prophecy: the seer who decreed it, and her daughter. Their words are binding with greater magic than anything you could possibly understand. And even if somehow you do find the blade, you'll never beat Lazarus in battle. Don't forget how well I know you, Arwen. The look on your face tells me you know I'm right."

I strained my face into neutrality. Did he realize what he'd just told me? There was another seer?

"I chose to align with the winning side," he continued. "In the new world, when Lazarus rules both realms and uses all the lighte he's mined to make Evendell worlds beyond what we can even imagine, I'll be spared. So will my family, and anyone else I care about."

"Like Ryder?"

A glint of emotion in his brown eyes. "I hope he'll see reason and join us, yes."

"The Halden I knew never could have stomached any of this. It would have kept him up every night, all night, sick with guilt."

The look that flashed across his face told me I wasn't completely off base.

"If you're going to kill me, just do it already."

"Where's that Arwen optimism? My orders are to bring you back to Lazarus in one piece." I didn't have time to catch a relieved breath as he said, "But first, I need to know if you did indeed find the blade."

"You must know I can't tell you that."

His jaw tightened. "And you must know we have other ways of getting information out of people."

A quiet dread rippled through me. "You wouldn't," I breathed.

"I don't want to, but I'll do what I have to do to heed his orders. Now tell me—where is the blade?"

I couldn't tell him we hadn't found it and give up the only leverage we might have. I couldn't lie and tell him we had it and send his men after all the people I cared about. The reality of what might come next had been soaking in for a minute now, and I steeled myself. "Do what you have to do."

He opened his mouth to speak, then closed it before he tried again. "Arwen . . ."

But I held my tongue.

Halden strode behind me, and I could only feel his fingers

along my spine as he unclasped my bodice and let it fall limply to the floor. Revulsion wasn't all that coursed through me. Shock, too—shock at feeling his strangely familiar hands in such an intimate place.

He came to stand before me and lifted the hem of my blouse. I squirmed away from his touch as he raised the fabric up and tucked it gingerly, chastely, underneath my breasts.

Relief but also *panic* sang in my blood as he moved for the hearth and picked up the metal poker that had been resting beside it, weighing its heft in his hands. I fished for my powers, like tiny little buds not quite ready to bloom. I had used so much lighte to save Mari and myself, I had almost nothing left.

*Come on*, I urged my body. *Fight.*

He let the poker heat in the fire while I struggled, apparently not concerned that I might escape. When the rod was white-hot, he pointed it at me, hovering the metal right in front of my exposed skin.

Angry heat radiated off it in licks.

"Aren't you afraid of me?" It was all that might persuade him now. "Of what I can do to you?"

"Come on, Arwen." He laughed. "Heal me to death?"

I shook my head. "They didn't tell you what I did at Siren's Bay."

"You mean what your Fae prince did? You're trying to take credit for that? To scare me?"

I couldn't tell if it was brilliant or senseless. Lazarus, in all his pride, did not want anyone to know just how much power I held.

"Just tell me," he said. "Where is the blade?"

But I stayed quiet, unable to think of anything to save myself.

"I'm sorry." He winced before pressing the scalding iron against my stomach.

Pain like nothing I had ever felt before splintered through me as the poker shrieked against the skin of my abdomen. I cried out before biting my tongue until blood pooled in my mouth.

The more relentless the pain, the more I reined in my sobs. He would not earn the satisfaction of my screams.

"This hurts me more than it hurts you."

"I hope that's true," I said through my teeth.

"Where is the Stones-damned Blade?"

He removed the brand, taking my melted flesh with it, only to place it back into the crackling flames. The tent smelled like cooked meat, and I gagged and spat blood on the ground. The burning wound blistering above my navel stung worse than any lash Powell had ever landed on me. I could not endure another brand.

"Don't make me do it again," Halden said, as if he had heard my very thoughts. His voice was like sandpaper.

But something was bubbling beneath my heart. In my bones. My lighte was coming back, I could feel it. Maybe it was spurred on by the pain and the urgency of my predicament, as it had been in the tunnels hours before. I just needed a little more time. Mere moments.

Tears burned my eyes as he lifted the hot poker and brought the glowing end closer. But he hesitated. "Please," he begged. "Just tell me where it is. I don't want to hurt you again."

"Do it, you coward."

The agony this time was blinding. I recoiled from the iron but had nowhere to go, and couldn't hold in the scream that erupted from my throat. I thrashed against my bindings, the burning pressure and searing pain ratcheting up my spine, down to the arches of my feet, through my lungs—

*Focus, Arwen. Pull from the atmosphere.*

"Tell me where it is and let this end for both of us!" Halden roared, withdrawing the sizzling brand from my stomach and tearing my shirt up to press it into the top of my breast.

I moaned in agony, the skin too sensitive, too thin. Blinding, endless pain, my toes curling, my head swimming with it, but—

But it was enough.

Enough to resurrect my power, and energy coursed through me, drawn in from the very air in his tent. The lighte sputtered outward from my hands, disintegrating the rope around my wrists into ash.

With free arms, I shoved the poker off my breast and punched Halden as hard as I could in the jaw.

"What the—"

Only momentarily stunned, he lunged for me, but sheer fury coursed through my heart, along my skin, and out of my palms. My lighte, an explosion of bright, white energy, spun out, engulfing Halden and the entire tent in ferocious golden flame.

I could feel my body lifting. The weightlessness, the heat, the wind—

More ropes of white fire sprayed from my fingers as I roared at Halden, who fell to the dirt floor, bellowing in agony. He screamed and screamed, and the scent of his burning flesh seared my nostrils.

*Good,* I thought. *Burn.*

I wasted no time watching him writhe around on the pallet in anguish, as flames licked the bed, the furs, the canvas of the tent. I bolted through the opening as smoke billowed out behind me, and I emerged to a cool jungle dusk and a camp that was, for the moment, unaware of my escape. I ran for the crude wooden barriers.

The makeshift fence was tall, but I could make it. I jumped up and latched on to the beams, just as I heard voices spot the fire and then call for my capture.

My nails dug so deeply into the wood that splinters crammed underneath the nail bed. But the pain in my stomach, my chest, the burns being stretched as I climbed up, up, up—that pain was beyond anything . . .

My lungs were raw from screaming by the time I toppled over and down the other side.

There was no time for triumph—the voices were rising to a pitch and making their way to the fence behind me. They'd never stop coming after me. I'd have to run all night. As if the sky were a mirror to my mood, my fury, my urgency, a clap of thunder snapped through the trees above, bathing the rain forest in its namesake.

I sloshed through mud in the sudden downpour, pressing my palm to the burns under my blouse. The lighte I had left sputtered and fizzled against my skin. Not enough to heal the blistered flesh. I wouldn't have anything left to repair myself for some time.

The thunder was a roar in my ears, rain dripping into my eyes and over my lips. I was so tired, so flooded with aching and exhaustion. The endless downpour trickled through the palm fronds and over my body until I collapsed and coiled in a heap. I couldn't tell the droplets from my own tears, but I knew that I was crying.

And shivering, though it wasn't cold.

The sounds of sloshing footsteps in the mud behind me should have spurred me up, *up* and off the ground. Into another sprint. But I had nothing left. I folded even farther in on myself and braced to be dragged back to the encampment and tortured again.

"Arwen!" Kane's voice cut through my despair like a single ray of resplendent sunlight.

I opened my eyes and took in his soaking form, his raven-dark hair swept back with rain, and his face.

His murderous, livid face. Inconsolable, incomprehensible,

bewildered rage. I had never seen such fury glow in his eyes in all the time I'd known him. It rippled off him in waves.

How could he possibly— Did he know what had been done to me?

He knelt to my tangled form and scooped me up and into his arms.

I winced as my burns folded in on themselves. "How are you here?" My voice sounded like I had come back from the dead. I wasn't even sure what I was asking.

"I never should have left you." He held my head against his own.

"It hurts," I admitted, grasping at my stomach.

"I know," he said, voice like gravel. "But you're safe now."

He stood and carried me all the way back to our camp, the insistent rain an urging at our backs.

# 24

---

## ARWEN

**W**ITH INCREDIBLE CARE, KANE LAID ME ON MY TENT'S pallet, draped in the fox fur cloak he had given me so many nights ago in the Shadowhold dungeon. The single hearth in the small space was barely flickering, casting a steadfast low glow along the gray canvas. The pitter-patter of rain that had drifted in and out as Kane carried me back was now a full-blown storm, angry droplets and a screeching wind assaulting the canvas above. It was the coolest night I'd had in the jungle thus far, and I sat up, wrapping myself more tightly in the fur before I winced.

The pinching, burning pain where Halden had branded me stung, but the shame was almost as potent. Shame that he'd laid a hand on me, and even more so that, after everything, it still felt like a betrayal.

I grazed my own stomach. Barely any lighte bloomed at my fingertips. Maybe I had used too much power escaping Reaper's Cave and blasting whatever that was at Halden. I healed what I could—spare drops of lighte calming blistered skin—and tried to make peace with the discomfort.

A small inkling of pride shone inside me.

I had summoned my lighte, and not just to heal. I had used it to protect myself.

Kane was facing the tent entrance. The rain continued to batter the canvas.

"Did you find Mari? Did everyone make it out?" My voice sounded like an instrument missing strings.

Kane turned to face me, still drenched, still rippling with that unwavering fury that I didn't fully understand. "They're all fine. I told them you needed sleep."

His words soothed me. "Did she take the ledger with her?" I asked through my fingers, massaging my temples and brow. What a Stones-forsaken day it had been. And no blade to show for it.

"I didn't ask," Kane forced out.

"What is wrong with you?" His anger was making *me* angry. I was the one who'd been seared like a cut of meat. I shuddered at the memory, and Kane's eyes grew more lethal.

I couldn't hold that gaze a minute longer. Dirt and splinters had lodged underneath my fingernails, and I began to pry them out one by one.

Kane released a slow breath before sitting on the pallet beside me. His damp shirt brushed my shoulder as he wrapped one large, warm hand around my own and pulled it into his lap. Cautiously, like I was a mouse in a trap, he plucked the hair-thin slivers of wood from my bloodied nails.

My frustration melted like snowflakes on warm skin.

His voice was still low, but softer as he said, "How are you feeling?"

"I've felt better."

"I thought I had lost you. Thinking you had been . . . It was . . . unendurable."

"I'm sorry."

He lifted his eyes from my fingers. "Don't be sorry. Not for anything."

"But you didn't lose me. I'm right here, and still—you're so angry." If he knew somehow who took me . . . Maybe he thought I had admitted that we didn't have the blade.

He drew a hand down his face in frustration, the other still clasped around my own. I tried to shift, to face him better, but the sharp pain in my stomach and chest was like being stabbed, and I grimaced.

"Don't move," he murmured, releasing my hand and helping me sit back. But every time something touched my burns, they stung. I repositioned myself again.

We both looked down at my blouse, soaked in rain and blood. Studs's blood.

"Off. I need it off," I blurted. "It's sticking to the burns."

Slowly Kane slipped his hands under the fabric, his calloused knuckles sliding along my sides and sending a very different kind of shiver up my spine.

"All the way off?" His voice was strained.

I hummed my agreement, and in one swift movement, the blouse flew over my head and landed in the corner of my tent in a heap.

And then I was topless. In front of Kane. In the very small, dimly lit tent, only thin canvas and the backdrop of thundering rain to insulate us. His eyes fixed on my burns. If I had thought he was angry before . . . the look on his face now could have ended worlds.

I crossed my hands over my breasts, avoiding the burn as a flush crawled up my chest and onto my cheeks.

"Someone *branded* you?" The canvas of the tent shook. Birds flew from trees, creatures scampered away in the rain. I wanted to flee, too. He was terrifying. More terrifying than I had ever seen him.

"I thought—" It barely made sense in my own head. "That somehow you already knew? The look on your face when you found me . . ."

"Mari bound me to your spirit. To find you." His jaw clenched. "I felt what you felt."

Oh, Stones.

"Your hands being tied. When someone—" He nearly grunted. "When someone removed your clothes, lifted your blouse. When they *burned* you. I didn't know where you were. Who or what was harming you. The pain—I assumed it had to be magic . . . That you were still in the caves. I didn't realize it was a mortal with . . ." Kane examined the burn above my navel. "A fucking hearth poker?" His eyes were like silver flames of lethal rage. "That and a fucking death wish."

"Kane, I'm all right. You're getting all worked up for nothing."

*"Nothing?"*

"I'm here now. I'm safe. You *saved* me."

"Not soon enough."

I glared at him.

"Sorry," he said, blowing out a long slow exhale. "I'm trying to be less of a vindictive asshole these days."

"You are?" I wished I hadn't sounded so incredulous.

"And I didn't save you," he said, ignoring me. "You got yourself out."

His words buoyed my spirits. It was true: I had escaped Halden on my own.

Kane released an uneven breath. "Who were they?"

"If I tell you, you'll go after them. Word could get back to your father that we're here."

"Do not play with me right now, little bird. I have been watching you flit in and out of a pitiful sleep for hours. I felt you flinch. Listened to you weep. You have no lighte left to heal yourself, which tells me you were forced to put up one damn good fight to escape. Someone needs to be ripped limb from limb for laying their hands on your precious fucking body."

His words stirred something in me. Heat rose up my neck. "Promise me you won't go after them tonight."

"No," he growled.

If he went to the Amber encampment, at best he'd murder numerous men, some of whom might be just like my brother. Conscripted, unsure what or who they were fighting for. At worst he could draw attention to us, or be harmed.

"Please," I tried. "Stay here, with me."

His eyes skipped from shocked to pained. "Tomorrow then," he relented. "At first light."

"Give me your word."

His silver gaze softened on mine as he said, "You have it. I won't go anywhere tonight."

I sighed. "It was Halden."

Blistering silence. And then, "I should have killed him when I had the chance."

"I made it out of the tunnel, and was rescued by pirates—"

Kane rolled his eyes. "I can't lose sight of you for even one moment."

"They were going to set sail a day later than planned to bring me back to you. But then Halden and his men found us and murdered them." I hadn't let that pain soak in yet, and my heart sank. "I begged them to help me, and got them all killed."

"No, Halden and his men did that."

A single tear leaked down my cheek. I tried to wipe it awkwardly with my shoulder, my hands still covering my breasts.

Kane wiped the tear from my cheek with his thumb before tucking a strand of hair behind my ear. "You don't have to hold your hands like that. I wouldn't look. Especially not when you're wounded. I'm not *that* despicable."

"Right." I frowned. "I know that." I didn't know why I was being so modest. I doubted my nakedness in this state did much for him.

"I should check on the others anyway." Kane stood and walked back over to the entrance of the tent.

I uncovered myself and lay back until I was comfortable. I couldn't help the way my lips curved up as relief flooded me. I could have laughed. Kane looked back once more before leaving. "Now, that smile . . . *that's* distracting."

With that I really did laugh. When he came back, I'd—

"Wait!" I called, and he poked his head back in, splattering rain. Kane was not a do-gooder. Not a *check on people* kind of person. "Check on them? Check on them *why*?"

Kane's eyes cooled, and a sliver of fear clanged through my body.

"Who is it?" I breathed, sitting up with a wince.

"The prince had a small accident. Nothing worth concerning yourself over—"

But I was throwing on my blouse, cringing at the pain, before he could finish the sentence.

# 25

## ARWEN

I STUMBLED PAST KANE, OUT INTO THE MERCILESS RAIN. MY burns singed against the wet cotton of my shirt.

*Please be all right, please be all right.*

"Arwen!" Kane called after me, but I could hardly hear him over the sloshing of my shoes.

I flung the canvas of Fedrik's tent open.

Mari and Griffin were sitting on either side of him. I went still.

Fedrik looked like a corpse.

His usual radiance had been replaced with a ghoulish, gray pallor and he was sweating, despite the wind and chill of the tropical storm.

And his leg.

His poor, ruined leg. Someone—my guess was Griffin—had done as much as they could, wrapping the pulverized thing in bandages and a tourniquet, but it was not enough. Based on the blotchy plum and dull blue under his skin, he was bleeding internally, and even if we could get him to an infirmary, he would likely lose the leg below the knee. I needed my lighte to heal him tonight if he had any shot of keeping the limb.

"It's fine," Fedrik croaked before I could speak. "Not as bad as it looks."

"No, it is," I cautioned. "It's actually far worse than it looks. You're just very handsome."

A tiny bit of that exceptional Fedrik glow inched its way back into his eyes. But not enough. Not nearly enough.

"You're here," he said. "That's what's important."

My stomach sank. "No, no, *no*," I muttered. My lighte was coming back too slowly. "I can't—" How could I explain? "I can't heal very well right now."

"No." Fedrik laughed—a dry, rattling sound. "I meant only . . . you're alive."

Kane slipped into the now very crowded tent behind me. His woodsy scent was amplified by the rain, and it assaulted my nostrils. I whirled on him, wincing at the pinching from my burns, and slammed a fist into his chest.

"How could you not have told me when I first woke?" I seethed. "And after all that you said about being less—"

Fedrik interrupted my tirade. "I asked him not to."

"Begged, actually," Kane amended.

I spun to Fedrik. "Why?"

"Kane said when he found you, you were in rough shape and needed to rest." Fedrik's eyes met mine, pain sweeping across his face. But not for himself . . . for me. "It's just a leg," he said, more buoyantly. "I do have two, you know."

"Oh, stop." It almost came out like a sob. "You have made a life of exploring. Climbing, hiking—" I shook my head. "Of course, you can do all that with one leg, but . . ."

"He can't do it at all if he's dead," Mari muttered.

"Mari!" I snipped at her.

Fedrik stiffened a little.

"She's just being theatrical," Griffin reassured Fedrik. "I've seen worse on the battlefield."

Griffin was lying, and if I could tell, Fedrik could, too.

They hadn't taken him into town. I had to believe that wasn't just to avoid the prying eyes of enemy soldiers. They had been waiting for me. To fix him. And I had returned without my lighte. I was sure it was the only reason Kane had kept me in the dark—he knew there was nothing I could do.

Well, even if I had no lighte to use, I was still a healer. I could still help.

I crouched to sit beside Fedrik. "I'm going to try to set your leg. I need two long, sturdy branches, and as many bandages as we have," I said to Mari. "And if you can conjure ice, that would help as well."

"I'm on it." She stood and maneuvered past us.

"This won't be pleasant," I warned him, wincing as I shifted around. I could actually have used some ice as well.

"Distract me," he said, holding my eyes with his. "Start by telling me that isn't *your* blood on your shirt."

"Not all of it," I said drily as I began to clear space to work.

"Wen," Fedrik soothed. "What happened to you after we escaped the cavern?"

"Some pirates offered to help me return to Frog Eye. But they were ambushed and killed in front of me by Amber soldiers. They took me . . ." I swallowed. "And hurt me. An old friend did, actually."

"Halden?" Griffin's low growl rattled the tent around us.

I couldn't look at him. I didn't want to see the rage on my behalf.

"Yes." I felt Fedrik's shin, assessing the damage.

"How did you get away?" Fedrik asked through gritted teeth.

"I got very lucky. Kane found me outside the Amber encampment."

"Right." Fedrik fidgeted. "Watching Mari cast that spell was . . . illuminating."

I was aware of both Griffin and Kane shifting around me. What was I missing? Griffin's words cut through my confusion. "Why'd the Amber boy hurt you?"

"What, and not just kill her?" Mari asked, returning with my supplies. "Holy Stones, Commander, have you no tact?"

"That's not what I meant," Griffin grumbled, but his downcast eyes told me otherwise. Maybe Griffin was an even worse liar than I was.

The tent had grown too crowded for its size. Mari knelt in the corner beside me as I leaned over Fedrik, whose pallet bisected the floor. Griffin sat on the other side of him, his considerable frame cramped alongside Fedrik's many packs. Kane stood at the entrance, hunched to accommodate the sloped canvas. I wasn't sure if he preferred to stand or if there was just nowhere left to sit. The hearth in the corner fought to stay alive.

"He wanted to know where the blade was. If we had it." But I had thought it was strange, too. If I was dead, per the prophecy, there would be no one left who could kill Lazarus. Why didn't Halden take me out when he had the chance? "If I said we had it, they would have come after you all. But I couldn't tell them we didn't and lose any leverage we might need." I swallowed bile at the memory. "So I just . . . let him."

The sound of screeching, twisting metal shook me from my work.

I whirled to see Kane's hand around a mangled mug.

Fedrik's eyes widened. "Quite the grip you have there, King."

"Why don't you go get some *air*," I said to Kane pointedly.

His response punched through clenched teeth. "Plenty of air right where I am, thanks."

I huffed at him and turned to place the long branches Mari had found along Fedrik's leg, aligning the bones as close as I could to where they should have been. From what I could feel, his shinbone was cracked down the center and needed to be worked back in line with his knee and ankle. The swelling was tough to feel around, but at least that was a clean—or *cleaner*—break. The smaller one, his fibula, was practically shattered. Not much to do there but wrap it tightly with bindings around the branch and support the jutting bits back in the right direction.

Though Fedrik had to be in great pain, he hardly showed it, aside from the beads of sweat he couldn't help but loose onto his tunic, and the occasional slow inhale or grunt.

The more I elevated the limb, and the tighter I bandaged it, the more the swelling went down.

My heart rate had lowered, my thoughts flowing in a slower, more even pace. I had missed healing. Had missed helping people, with or without my lighte. When Fedrik grimaced at a tight yank of the dressing, I recalled how I was supposed to be distracting him.

"Halden did say one thing that stuck with me. That the seer had a daughter. He said they're the only two Fae to ever have visions such as these. I know the seer died decades ago, but could her daughter still be alive?"

Silence enveloped the tent.

"What is it?" I asked.

"I can't believe they tracked her down," Griffin murmured.

"And for nothing," Kane mused. "Esme never inherited her mother's gift."

*Esme?*

"Why would Gareth's army think that she did?" Griffin asked.

"I'm not sure," Kane said. "We'll have to pay her a visit, won't we?"

"Yes. The blade isn't here and I've never sweat so much in my life," Griffin said, wringing out his shirt and exposing a sliver of cut abdomen.

"Go where?" Mari asked, though she sounded distracted.

My lighte tingled at my fingertips once more, regenerating faster the more I used it, as Dagan had once told me it would. With Fedrik's leg reset, I snuck my hand under his bandages and fused his bones back together with careful precision. His leg would be able to bear weight by morning, and might even function fully by the next day. It would look like a miracle.

"To Crag's Hollow," Kane said.

Finished with Fedrik's leg, I climbed over Mari to sit in the corner, wiping dampness from my brow that had gathered while I worked. "Back to the Onyx Kingdom?" I remembered Crag's Hollow from a map in the Shadowhold apothecary. It was a coastal town outside of Willowridge.

Kane ran a hand through his damp hair. "It's worth a shot."

"How do you know the seer's daughter?" I asked.

"I doubt she remembers either of us. Griffin and I helped her escape Lumera when she was young. After her mother was killed during the rebellion, we brought her here to Evendell and helped her set up a new life."

"Unguarded?"

"I never thought they'd come for her, all these years later. There was no reason to."

"We'll find out why they think she has her mother's visions," Griffin said. "It's the only thread we have to follow." My heart chilled with the unspoken words: *Since the blade wasn't in Reaper's Cavern, and we have no other leads.*

"Maybe the seer had another daughter? Or a son?" Mari suggested. "And Halden was mistaken?"

"Only women Fae are born with the ability," Kane said. "And the seer only had one daughter. If Halden knows about Esme, there must be a reason she's valuable to them."

"If she's still alive," Griffin added.

Silence swallowed us whole once more.

"I hate to burst everyone's bubble, but I don't know if Arwen or I will be in any shape to travel tomorrow."

I bit my lip and cut a sidelong glance at Fedrik. "I just need to brew some potions overnight. I have a feeling we'll both be healthier come morning." I had already slipped my hand underneath my own shirt, wincing at the burns as my palm pressed against them, cupping my breast to heal the blisters there and lacing together the skin of my palm, still shredded from the treasure room door.

"You're the healer, but I don't think this"—he grimaced, gesturing to his leg—"can be fixed with a potion of any kind."

I wanted to tell him the truth. It was the right thing to do. But when Fedrik looked at me, he didn't see the weak, naive girl from Abbington or the full-blooded Fae fated to save the continent. He didn't see a child who had been beaten or a fearful, anxiety-riddled coward or a woman with a year—if that—left to live.

He only saw me.

"Trust me," I said.

His eyes held mine with nothing but avid affection as he took my hand. "I do."

His skin was smooth and soft, so different from Kane's calloused fingers. I looked down to see his tan hand dwarf mine. He smelled warm and soothing, like figs and bergamot.

"I've got to piss," Kane huffed.

My face and neck burned, and I pulled my hand from Fedrik's.

Griffin shifted awkwardly in his corner before standing. "And I've got to gather the . . ." He scratched his jaw. "Leaves. Got to gather the leaves." Griffin left almost as fast as Kane had.

I cut a glance at Mari, and tried to say *don't you dare* with my eyes.

"And I'm going to leave." Mari stood. "Because this is awkward."

She slipped out of the tent, leaving just Fedrik and me.

An involuntary laugh slipped out of me, but my pulse was racing. The sensation felt more like anxiety than lust, but didn't it make sense to be jittery? After all the adrenaline, and fear, and—

"Hey," Fedrik said, taking my hand in his once more. "I'm sorry. About what you went through today."

"It's not that bad."

"May I?" he asked, gesturing toward my stomach.

I nodded stiffly and he let go of my hand to lift my shirt, ever so slightly.

*"Bastards,"* he hissed when he saw my healing burns. Fedrik looked back up at me, his eyes simmering.

"I'm all right," I said, and meant it.

"I'm not," he retorted, his breathing uneven. His blue eyes had regained some of their vivid color, and it was as if two boundless oceans were staring back at me. When I remained silent, he lowered my shirt.

"I'm glad he was there. To help you."

"Me, too," I confessed.

"I know it was more than just a kiss . . . with him."

I knew this would come out eventually. I sighed up at the apex of the tent. The rain had softened now, and was barely pattering above us.

"It was extremely complicated," I said, thinking of my conversation with Kane before we entered the caves this morning. How sometimes I had a tendency to see things in black-and-white.

Fedrik's brows knitted inward. "You must know . . ." He pressed his lips into a line as if debating his next words. "You must know he's madly in love with you, right?"

I felt my eyes go wide. It wasn't that I hadn't had the thought. I just hadn't expected Fedrik to be the one to say it.

I had hoped as much, once. Wanted it to be true more than I wanted my heart to beat. But the energy between us, the jealousy and possessiveness, the constant poking, taunting, the push and pull—it wasn't what I imagined love to look like. And truthfully, he had needed me to serve a purpose. That was what drew him to me. My life—my *death*, rather—was what he had always been after. Somewhere along the way he had become attracted to me, and then—

"No." I shook my head. "He's not."

"Wen—"

"I'm like a plaything to him. A game. And he doesn't like to lose." I bit my lip. "Or have other people play with his toys."

Fedrik's eyes glowed with heat. "Are you implying I want to play with you?"

Had I not seen the clear desire written across his face I would have flushed with embarrassment. But lately the only tonic to my misery was being bold. "Don't you?"

Fedrik laughed, a little guilty. "I don't wish to interfere somewhere I am not wanted."

Did I?

Want him?

Not really.

I liked Fedrik immensely. He was sophisticated and kind, worldly and easygoing. And he offered me something nobody else in my life could: the ability to see myself through the eyes of someone who didn't know my fate. I had grown so much in the past few months I felt like stretched-out skin—so worn from the changes I'd been through that I wore them across me in long pale streaks.

Fedrik made me feel supple and new.

But still . . . No. Try as I might, I didn't *want* him. Not wholly and thoroughly the way I always wanted Kane. Not even in the childlike way I had wanted Halden—longing for what he could be one day rather than what he was.

But before I found the right way to say all of that—if there *was* a right way to say any of it—he gave me the slightest catlike twitch of a smile, mistaking my silence for affirmation, and leaned in to brush his mouth against mine.

# 26

KANE

Rain pelted my face as I finished pissing and pulled myself back into my pants.

The bottle of bourbon still dangling from my hand was mocking me. I had been determined to drink less, but today happened to be one of the more unpleasant of my life, and I needed something to take the edge off. Or several somethings, to take off several edges.

Grief was a curious thing. After so many tenuous years of it, I'd come to recognize what might induce greater pain than usual. I didn't avoid those prompts—the mention of my mother's or brother's names, playing the lute. I had built up enough scar tissue that such heartache now only felt like a twinge. The dull scraping of a butter knife.

The true threat, I'd realized, was when I *wasn't* prepared: when something wholly unexpected conjured them to the forefront of my mind. Then that butter knife became a battle axe.

Trying—and failing—to drink less produced one such unforeseen, agonizing ache.

My mother never drank. Not in celebration, not in misery. Not even for show. I didn't know if she enjoyed spirit but abstained for some surely admirable reason, or if she loathed the stuff entirely. If I could have told her I was trying to kick the habit, and for a woman, no less, she might've doubled over in fits of laughter. Yale would've without a doubt.

Or she might've been hideously proud. Pulled me into a hug I knew I was too old for, but would have accepted nonetheless, and assured me I was capable of anything I set my mind to. I'd try to change the subject—move away from praise I didn't deserve—but she'd proceed as if I hadn't said a word. She'd ask me when I knew I was in love. When I'd introduce her.

But my mother would never get to see how being in love changed me, for better or worse.

She'd never get to meet Arwen.

And it was those thoughts that ripped at the wound in my heart, cleaving it open anew.

A sudden chill swept through the wide, flat leaves surrounding our camp and splattered me in sideways rain. I took another pull from the bottle.

My mother definitely would have encouraged me to lay off Citrine's prince. Truth was, Fedrik was kind of a decent kid. He had tried to give his life for Griffin in Reaper's Cavern. So what if he was a bonehead, completely unaware of how quickly a Fae like Griffin would have healed from his same wound? He was a *decent* bonehead.

He had pleaded with me to let Arwen rest after her ordeal, despite his shattered leg. Had been fairly tough through one of the more grisly injuries I'd seen.

By the time I found myself back at camp, the storm had

thoroughly ousted our campfire and faint light only emanated from two of the three tents. Mari and Arwen were probably sleeping by now, Griffin likely sharpening his blades.

Time to be less of an asshole.

"Fed," I said, ambling toward his tent, "I've got this bourbon—it might help with the pain, and I'm actually trying to cut back—"

Under the lifted flap of the tent's entrance was Arwen, laced in the arms of the prince, lips glued to his.

I nearly retched all the liquor in my stomach onto their crackling hearth.

Arwen pulled away from Fedrik faster than he could realize what was happening, and his dopey, lust-addled gaze took a minute to meet mine.

He had kissed her.

He had been *kissing* her—

I was going to skewer his innards and feed them to him—

"Kane," Arwen shouted after me, but I was already stalking from the tent.

It wasn't even that he had kissed her.

*She* had kissed *him*.

I wouldn't listen to her fuck him in the tent beside me. That would—I would . . . There would be nothing left of me then.

*Don't be a possessive, territorial brute. She isn't yours.*

And hadn't I known this was coming? Plagued myself with the possibility of it like a self-inflicted wound? And my conclusion was always the same: She deserved some joy. Some pleasure.

My legs carried me deeper into the jungle, past Mari's chalk boundary, past limp leaves that slumped into my path, past drooping moths soaked in rain, fluttering out of the way with a swat of my outstretched hand. I took another swig until the liquor burned my throat and stomach. Then another.

I whirled at the sound of soft footsteps behind me.

Arwen was misted in rain that forced her blouse to cling to her body. "I'm sorry that you—" She swallowed hard against the storm. "That you saw that. But I didn't expect him to— I don't even like—"

"It's fine," I said softly, the words blades across my tongue. I turned from her and kept walking, scarcely able to suck in enough muggy air to slow my breathing.

"Really?" she called after me, her feet trampling through wet leaves and mud.

Couldn't she leave me alone?

I spun to find her olive eyes bright and wide, like the stars the jungle hid from us.

"Yes, *really.* Cocky might be the only thing that doesn't look good on you, bird."

Her face hardened and her nose pinched, making my heart twist in my chest.

I loved that look. I loved that nose.

"I just thought that you—that we—"

"I don't care what you do, Arwen, as long as it makes you happy."

She shifted, her flimsy shoes squelching in the mud beneath her feet. She really needed some new boots. "So you're . . . fine?"

Every single nerve in my body battled the urge to grab her by the shoulders and roar. *Fine? Fine with this? I would be more* fine *with a javelin through the gut. I would barely feel it compared to this. You're mine. You will always be mine. Nobody else should be allowed to touch you. To look at you. To make you laugh. I want to take you from this jungle tonight—continent, blade, prophecy be damned—and go somewhere nobody can find us. Somewhere I can keep you like buried treasure. Where I can feed you cloverbread, and read to you, and fuck you when I please, and worship you every day and every night for the rest of our lives.*

"Sure," I said, nearly grinding my teeth to dust. Fierce rain pounded at my skull, on my shoulders, along my neck. Palms and nut trees shook with the force of it, clawing up toward the night sky. "Sometimes you make a poor choice because it feels good. I get that better than anyone."

I hadn't meant it like an insult. I'd done the same a thousand times.

But Arwen folded her arms and bared her lovely teeth at me. "Every 'poor choice' I've made has been in an effort to *heal* from you. You lied to me, Kane. Worse, you made me think you had feelings that you didn't so you could *sacrifice me.*"

"That is *not—*"

"Oh, right." Arwen didn't cower. In fact, she stepped forward, forcing me to crane my neck down to maintain eye contact. "You changed your mind when you decided you wanted to sleep with me. *How noble.*"

I opened my mouth but she cut me off. "What did you want me to say? That day on the ship, when I learned everything . . . What did you expect me to do?"

A hideous clap of thunder, like the roaring inside my head, shook the forest. Neither of us even blinked.

"I don't know, forgive me? Use some of that token positivity of yours to see the horrific position I was in and how hard I had tried to save you? Choose to be with me despite the mistakes I'd made?"

She pursed her lips, as if forgiveness, or perhaps just being with me, was the most repulsive thing she could imagine.

"It's true," I conceded. "I made egregious faults in judgment. I'll never deserve you. I never could have. But don't kid yourself, Arwen. You're not running from this because I lied. Or because you don't care anymore. Or because of some prince. You think I treat emotion as a weakness? You're *terrified* of letting yourself feel anything real. You've let the prophecy become a shield you can hide behind. Nothing matters if you're going to die, right?"

"Fuck you," she spat.

I nearly flinched. I had never heard the curse from her lips before. Her anger was coal tossed on the fire simmering in my veins. I pressed closer until her breath hitched. I felt the little noise in the base of my spine. "Right here?" I snarled. "Little needy bird. It's a bit damp for my taste, but you must know I'd fuck you anywhere you asked."

"You would, wouldn't you? Rut like animals on the forest floor."

I smirked. "Look, she listens for once."

"I don't think about you that way, Kane. Not anymore."

"I don't believe you."

"Then you're a fool." Her voice was nearly breathless.

"No, you think about me constantly. As I do you. Every day, every night. Every single waking hour until it's so all-consuming, I can hardly hear myself when I speak."

Arwen shook her head. "You said you were going to leave me alone. Back on the beach in Azurine."

"I guess we're both liars, then."

Movement rustled the trees behind us and we both spun, breathing hard.

Eight masked men emerged from the tree line. Wielding swords and bludgeons, trays and bark as shields—bandits.

My eyes fell to the forest floor. We were past Mari's fucking boundary.

Arwen inhaled sharply.

There was no need to risk my lighte with Amber soldiers looking for us. Not with mortals such as these. I unsheathed a dagger from my boot, rotating my wrist and shaking out my shoulders, adrenaline pouring through me—molten hot and in search of blood.

Just the release I needed.

"Get back to camp. Get Griffin."

Arwen did no such thing. "This man here," she said, jerking her chin toward me, "is deadly. You will not survive him. Leave us now and save yourselves."

The heftiest bandit, his face obscured by a leather mask, stepped forward, feet sloshing in wet sludge. "I'm no scholar, but I can count. You're two and we're at least triple that. Our band is even larger. Forty men strong and right behind us." He stepped forward another inch and I placed myself in front of Arwen. "Not sure if you've seen, but things aren't too pretty around here since Amber laid their claim. We need food. We need coin. You'll just have to do. But I swear not to use your lady. We ain't that way."

My low growl shook rain from nearby leaves.

I thought I heard Arwen say my name once in warning, but it was too late. My steel dagger clashed with the bandit's sword in a violent clamor, and then they were on us like a swarm of bees.

Another masked man charged me, and I drove my knife through his improvised pot-lid shield with ease. He'd been running toward me fast enough that the blow sent him careening toward Arwen's feet, where she kicked him square in the temple.

"Arwen," I grunted, shoving back a kid with a block-shaped head into a wide, wet tree. "Back to camp. Now."

But she slid up against me, her chest pressed to mine, and my heart attacked my rib cage like a cornered animal. Before I could articulate my confusion, she pulled my longsword from its sheath and plunged it into something—or someone—behind me.

"Watch out," she breathed.

I pivoted from a thug swiping at us with a crude butcher's knife and ducked his next blow, though I felt the stinging scrape of the blade against my forearm. I reared back and drove my dagger into his gut until the hilt met skin and a gruesome groan gurgled from him.

Two more men hurtled toward me. Unable to swiftly dislodge my dagger, I knocked them to the ground with the man still impaled on my knife like a human wrecking ball.

The whisper of a single arrow soaring through the air pulled my attention behind me. It was headed toward—

No, no, *no*—black wisps of my lighte reached from my hand and just narrowly slipped around the bolt, inches from Arwen's back.

The wood splintered into sheer mist, and my stomach fell to my boots.

Far, *far* too close.

But she was none the wiser, driving my sword into non-vital organs. Thighs and arms and shins. Her blade singing through the night as she feinted to the right and used her pommel to smack an assailant hard in the temple, knocking him to the ground.

That move actually looked familiar.

"Where'd you learn that?" I called, as my knife landed on another bandit's club, mere inches from my kneecap.

"Griffin taught me," she gritted out, heaving an eager assailant off her with a grunt.

I had to admit, the thought of fighting alongside Arwen had terrified me. But she was . . . astounding. So strong, so poised. Strangely merciful, which made no sense to me, but was so innately Arwen. Each of her movements executed in striking harmony like a ballerina. A graceful goddess of force and precision.

"Kane!"

Her voice cut through my affectionate thoughts just in time for me to rear my arm back and deck a lanky kid sprinting toward me square in the face. He clattered to the ground with a wheeze, another already charging. I absorbed the bandit's impact and we both went down. Driving my knee into his groin, I pushed myself up and planted my knife in his windpipe.

And then there were more—so, so many more.

"Ah, fuck."

As promised, dozens of bandits crawled from the tree line, drawn to the sound of the brawl. Surrounding us on every side.

I cut a glance at Arwen, her sword now soaked in blood and her brow gleaming with sweat.

We couldn't take them all. Not without help.

I rolled my shoulders back and undid the top few buttons of my soaked shirt. The power I fought to keep at bay inside me—fighting and squirming for release—galloped out with the speed of a prized stallion. It spun and curved around the glade, a single obsidian rope from my palm, sprouting spikes like razors and slicing cleanly through six men.

At the sound of Arwen's grunts and metal against blunt wood, I sent the next wave of twisted power in her direction. The shimmering smoke spun around her ankles, almost tenderly protective, before spinning outward and suffocating the three men that surrounded her. She shot me an appreciative nod.

I opened my mouth to tell her once again to *go find fucking Griffin*, before pain bloomed in my shoulder blade.

Real, bruising pain.

I whirled on two bandits wielding bats. Poison-black vines wrapped around their necks, constricting like snakes until both men were mere pale, gray husks on the ground.

*Fuck*. I rubbed my shoulder.

More power, more lighte, billowed from my palms, my forearms, and filtered out into the clearing.

Rain slammed against my face—

My power slashing, cutting, suffocating.

My dagger sliding into man after man, artery after artery, limb after limb—

Arwen, heaving with the force of her sword, backing up behind me for protection.

More lighte.

More blood—

Until—

At least three dozen men, two groaning in agony, lay at my feet on the wet forest floor. It was still drizzling through the trees above, and I wiped my brow of both rain and sweat. One last bandit circled Arwen, his bow outstretched toward her.

I prowled forward, ready to end this foul night.

"I can handle him myself," she bit out, eyes still on the bandit.

"Clearly," I said, gesturing to the men that littered the ground. "But I'd be honored to take care of it for you." I shot a feral glare at the bandit, who backed up a single step.

Arwen raised her sword, and I sighed.

The rustle in the bushes sent all three of us whirling.

Relief sang in my veins. Mari, in her nightgown, dusted with the light rain, and Griffin close behind her, still rubbing sleep from his eyes.

Arwen sighed. "Thank the Stones—"

The whistle of an arrow flashed through the clearing—

And struck Mari in the chest.

*No*—

My heart seized as she fell to the ground like a stone through water.

## 27

## ARWEN

I DIDN'T RECOGNIZE THE NOISE THAT BLEATED FROM ME.

A howl? A sob?

Panic had turned my voice to acrid ash.

*Not Mari, please, no—*

*Not after Mother.*

I tore for her, slumped and inert in the mud and leaves—

Feathers unfurled above me, and a lionlike snarl told me Griffin was shifting overhead, his limbs snapping and stretching, legs becoming the great, muscled hinds of a lion and ending in gnarled talons. The mighty beating of a plumed wingspan that nearly touched the trees on either side of the glade was only silenced by that *roar*—

The roar of a punishing predator.

Then, a single jaw-splitting scream.

The last of the bandit's life. I cringed away from the squelching sounds of razor-sharp teeth digging into human flesh and sank to my knees by Mari's side.

Kane was already there.

"Is she breathing?"

"I'm fine," Mari croaked before he could respond. Her hands clutched at her chest. Nails caked with dirt.

Shock. She was in *shock*.

I moved her hands aside and searched her for the entry wound, the blood—but there was none. Just a dusting of ash above her heart, as if Mari had been struck by lightning.

She coughed violently, the wind knocked from her, before pressing her hand to mine atop her chest. "The amulet. It protected me." She reached for the necklace at the base of her throat.

And then her light eyes widened as she felt her vacant neck.

"Mari," I cautioned, releasing my hand from her heart. "You're all right." I wasn't sure if I was comforting her or myself.

But she only searched frantically through the muck and leaves, her hands moving over the arrow that had been cleaved in two by the force of her power. "Where is it, where is it . . ."

"Mari . . ." But I couldn't think of anything to say as she salvaged the shattered necklace from the ground and let out a sorrowful, horrified sob.

"It's all right. You're fine—"

"*Fine?*"

"Mari, can you look at me?"

But she only scrambled up, wobbling on her feet. "All of it, gone—"

Griffin, back in his human form, jogged past Kane and straight for us. "What's wrong? Is she in pain?" I didn't glance back at where he had massacred the bandit. The slain man's blood clinging to the commander's arms and chest told me enough.

Griffin reached one rust-colored hand toward Mari, but she swayed from his touch.

"I just need—" She fished for words. "There has to be a way to fix it."

I swallowed against my lungs, nearly erupting from my throat. "You don't . . . There was no power in the amulet."

"What?" Mari's voice was softer than I'd ever heard it.

"I should have told you. It was so wrong of me to keep the truth from you—"

"Should have told me what?"

I looked to Griffin and Kane for help. Nothing but pity welled in their eyes.

*Pity* for strong, independent Mari. Reduced to tears over a necklace.

I steeled myself. "There isn't any magic in the amulet. I've known for some time, and thought you would be better off unaware. It was wrong, and I'm genuinely, awfully sorry."

She stared at me, her expression unreadable.

"Briar gave it to me years ago," Kane added. "An exquisite gift. Very generous . . . but that's all it was. A gift. Just . . . jewelry."

"But you've seen the magic. The things I've done. It just *saved* me."

"No," I said, my voice breaking on the word. "*You* saved you. You don't need it, Mari."

Kane's voice was low. "We should leave before any of those Amber men come looking for the source of the commotion."

"We should fly for Crag's Hollow," Griffin said softly. "There's nothing left for us here."

But Mari held her ground. Nightdress soaked in rain. Bare toes in cold mud.

Kane and Griffin exchanged one more look before stalking ahead of us toward our makeshift camp.

"You all kept that from me? For weeks? I've looked like such a fool."

"No, you haven't. Not at all—"

"It's . . . it's . . . humiliating."

"Nobody thought that—"

"Finally, I think I've made one real friend—"

"Of course I'm your friend. So believe me when I promise you, you *will* do magic without the amulet. You already have. And you'll be better for it now because you'll finally face your fear of . . . failing." My words trailed off, but it was too late. I had already said them.

Mari winced before pushing past me and making her way into our camp.

*Bleeding Stones.* Not phrased right. Not at all.

I had seen her angry before, many times. But never hurt. Hurt was so, so much worse.

Kane and Griffin were already packing up our bags when I followed her back to our camp, incessant rain still pelting my face.

"I heard shouting," Fedrik said, limping from his tent.

"Your leg—you're putting weight on it." One small mercy in a catastrophically dreadful night.

"I know. I didn't think I'd be able to walk again. You are some healer, Wen." Fedrik shot me a warm look.

Our chaste, heatless kiss flashed in my mind, and I said nothing.

Fedrik swallowed. "What's going on?"

My head swam. I didn't know how to begin to explain all of it to him. My vicious fight with Kane. The bandits . . . That I had been lying to Mari.

That I had hurt her.

I went with, "Everything's fine." And when he frowned, I

added, "Are you able to pack up? We intend to leave for Crag's Hollow." Mari milled past us before he could respond, stuffing wet, rain-covered mugs and tins into a large canvas sack. "I can help you in a moment, I just need to talk to Mari."

"Please don't," she said, grabbing her dress and blouse from the clothesline we had rigged between two palms.

"Mari, come on—"

She scoffed, turning to face me, the barest hint of hesitation twinkling in her eyes. "I have wanted to be a witch my entire life. I finally find a way to do so—to feel that glory, that success, to feel close to my *mother*—and it's all a fraud? That's painful. But what's worse is my closest friend, who I have stood beside through countless tragedies, lying about it to me for weeks and then saying I'll be *better for it*." She shook her head. "I know you don't care about yourself anymore, but I thought you'd at least give a shit about me."

I felt the words across my cheek like a slap. "What?"

"Damn it," Griffin huffed, discarding his half-filled pack and sitting down on a tree stump as if to say, *All right you two, get on with it.*

"Oh, come on. You don't care about anything these days, least of all the people around you. Watching you toy with Fedrik and Kane? Who *does* that?"

Something stickier than shame ran through my veins. "*You* were the one that encouraged me to pursue something with Fedrik."

One of the men swallowed a noise of surprise but I couldn't tell who. I didn't want to.

"I thought it would make you happier!" Mari's voice had risen too many octaves. "But I get it now. You don't truly want human connection with anyone. That's probably why you haven't told Fedrik yet."

"Mari," I warned.

"Told me what?" I cut my gaze from her to Fedrik, but only confusion rippled in his eyes.

Griffin saved me an unintelligible answer. "Come, now, witch. That's not—"

"And you." Mari whirled on him. "Talk about emotionally stunted. Holy Stones."

Before she could further tear into the man who had just killed for her, I cut in. "Give the commander a break. You're one to talk about leading people on."

Griffin stood, his fisted hands nearly shooting clean through his pockets. "While you two fight like whining alley cats, I'm going to go find some . . ." He took a ragged inhale. "I don't know. Some peace and quiet."

"Nobody was talking to you anyway," Mari huffed. Griffin just pinched his brow in a practice of patience and made for the wet palm fronds. "We are *friends*," Mari spit at me. "A word I am beginning to think you never understood the meaning of."

"And what about Ryder?"

"What about him?" She was nearly shrieking.

"You, like everyone else in the world, are totally enamored of him." The words stung me, too, as I said them. Another person who preferred my shiny, charming brother. The sibling that wasn't scarred and bruised and broken. "Did you forget how he left me to risk my life when my family fled Abbington?".

I was surprised by the venom in my words. I had never realized how much that hurt. That he had allowed me to practically walk to my death.

Mari straightened, as if preparing to say something she had

been debating for a while. "No, I never did. And you should tell him that you haven't, either. But it's easier not to, right? To hold everyone at arm's length so it won't all hurt so much? I mean, Arwen, you barely even mourned the loss of your own mother."

"She wasn't my mother." The words slipped from me before I could process them.

Mari flinched as if hit.

"She wasn't . . . Not really."

"This is exactly what I'm talking about. *Of course* she was your mother, Arwen. Whether or not she gave birth to you is beside the point. I never knew my mother, but if I had, I sure wouldn't come up with a reason to say her death didn't matter."

"I *never* said that."

"No, but you act like it. And worse, like yours won't matter, either." She shook her head and patted down the fabric still bunched in her arms as if our argument had wrinkled the fabric. "I'm going to go find Griffin. He can't see well in the dark."

And with that she stalked off into the forest.

Somewhere in between a senseless squabble about boys and Mari's analysis that I didn't so much as mind my mother's brutal murder, the rain had ceased. The smell of soaked leaves stung my nose, and the rustles and chirps of forest creatures no longer seeking dry shelter filled the silence between the remaining three of us.

Kane stood from the tree he had been leaning against and quirked a brow at me. "Nobody knows that about Griffin."

"Yeah, well." I sighed, rubbing my face in frustration. "She's very observant."

I could feel both Kane and Fedrik's eyes on each of my movements.

"She's just taking her anger about the Stones-damned amulet out on me," I said. "It's fine. It'll be fine."

Kane's jaw feathered in thought. "Actually, I don't think that's what she's upset about."

The softness in his voice made me want to wring his neck. I crossed the campsite to him and drove a pointed finger into his chest. "Don't even start. I wouldn't be dealing with any of this if it wasn't for you."

Only a warning danced in his eyes. "Are you finding that denial to be working very well for you, bird?"

"Hey, don't talk to her like that."

Kane turned to Fedrik, his voice terribly calm. "I will end you."

But Fedrik only chuckled, almost brazen. "You have nobody to blame but yourself for ruining things with her."

"Why don't you ask Arwen exactly how that happened? It's a funny story, actually."

"Let me guess, you mistook murder for courtship?"

I couldn't take this a minute more. Fedrik's protection that I didn't deserve. Kane's jealousy, Mari's searing truths—I seized a shuddering inhale. "He's right," I blurted. "They all are. I've been keeping something from you."

Fedrik studied my face, allowing me to continue.

But I needed to get out of this damp, sticky, Stones-forsaken forest. I didn't want to spend another minute here in Peridot.

I didn't really want to spend another minute anywhere with myself.

"Can we talk? In private?"

Fedrik jerked his chin toward his tent.

The heat from the small hearth inside was stifling. The canvas glowed a rich, burnt orange from the flames, its low, slanted ceiling closer to the crown of my head than it had felt hours ago. I swallowed nothing, crossing my arms once before unfolding them again. Fedrik watched me warily.

"Kane and I stopped seeing each other because he never told me that I was the Fae. From the prophecy. The last—"

"Full-blooded Fae," Fedrik supplied, his expression more cold understanding than wide-eyed shock.

I faltered. "I—"

"Lied," he supplied again.

"No. I mean, yes. I did. Mari was right. I didn't want to tell you because with you, I could ignore it. But that was selfish and . . . and I'm sorry."

For a moment, no one said anything. The tent suffocated our breaths. Fedrik shifted on his feet.

"It felt good to be a version of myself that still had a future."

"Sure. But . . . you didn't even give me a chance to take on that suffering with you."

"Nobody else needed to suffer."

A few spare shafts of light fluttered around the tent from the deteriorating hearth. I grabbed one of Fedrik's tunics to begin packing for him, only to see my palms streaked in splotches of red. Bandit blood.

Fedrik limped across the tent in one long stride until he was beside me and took the tunic from my hands, placing it back on the pallet beneath us. I cast my eyes to the floor, fixated on the dirt under my shoe, but he lifted my chin gently with his finger. "It's a strange time to begin a relationship with anyone. There's a lot we don't yet know about each other. The very fabric of our world is in turmoil, grave danger awaits us all, et cetera. But . . . I enjoy spending time with you. And I'd like to give this a real chance, if you would. Prophecy and all."

I wanted my heart to soar—

But it was still Kane's face that rippled in my mind before any thought of being with Fedrik could crystalize.

"I can't, Fedrik. I shouldn't have kissed you."

"Well, actually, I kissed you—"

"I still feel something for him."

Fedrik brushed a thumb across my jaw, his devastating blue eyes more solemn than I'd ever seen them. "I know you do."

"That doesn't bother you?"

"You're human. Broken hearts don't heal overnight."

I cringed, slipping from his grasp. "Well . . . I'm not really. Human, that is. That doesn't bother you, either?"

A half laugh. "No."

"Even still. I don't . . . see you in that way. I hoped I would, really, I did. But I fear we might just be good friends." I couldn't help the relief that swept through my limbs. It was a truth that needed to be said. No matter what happened next.

"He'll never be what you deserve."

"I don't know if I deserve too much right now."

"Well," he said, considering. "You could start by apologizing to Mari. I think she's more betrayed that you accepted your fate so . . . flippantly . . . than she is about the amulet. It's as if in doing so, you've abandoned her."

"A lot of people have," I murmured. "Abandoned her, I think."

He tilted his head at a contemplative angle.

"That's pretty good advice, Fedrik."

"You're lucky to have a friend like me."

I smiled a bit. I was, actually. "She wasn't wrong, though. I'm different now. Maybe I can't be what she needs."

"Why don't you let her make that decision?"

I moved to walk around him and out of the tent to do just that, but Fedrik pulled my hand into his. "Kane will never stop looking for that blade. And while he drags you across Evendell to hunt for it, you'll keep getting burned and beaten. And not just by your enemies. He's *bad* for you, Arwen." Fedrik drew in a breath. "Let me take you back to Azurine. No expectations. Nothing implied. I just want you to have a life outside of all this madness. Outside of Kane. Let me offer you a different way to live."

I stiffened at his words. "But the prophecy—"

"You can enjoy whatever time you have left. And I'll be by your side until the very end. As a friend. Or as anything you want me to be."

"The blade is supposed to call to me."

"He's hunted for it without you for years. It was out of his own selfish need that he brought you along in the first place."

"I chose to come."

"And I'm saying maybe you shouldn't have."

The hearth crackled softly as we stood there, wet clothes still clinging to our bodies, my bloodied hand still wrapped in his.

"Thank you," I croaked. "For the offer."

"Will you think on it?"

"Arwen? Fedrik?" Griffin's voice drifted in from the campsite.

Fedrik cleared his throat. "We're in here."

I slipped past him to where Kane and Griffin were surrounded by our canvas packs, their tents broken down and bundled up. I couldn't meet Kane's eyes. I didn't want to know what he was thinking. What he might or might not have heard.

Griffin cocked his head toward us. "Where's the witch?"

My breathing was still uneven, but I managed to say, "She went looking for you."

The commander's eyes widened a bit at my words, and he looked from us back to Kane, whose eyes narrowed in concern. "So, no one knows where she is?"

A furious shiver ran up my spine, but I steadied it with a slow inhale. "I'm sure she's fine." I moved for the knot of darkness and leaves surrounding us. "Mari?" I called out. "Mari!"

I didn't care if there were more bandits, more soldiers—

"Mari!"

"I'm right here, Holy Stones," she mumbled, stepping out of the trees.

A breath whooshed from me.

Griffin nearly sagged with a sigh of his own. "Hurry up," he murmured. "We're leaving."

"I was looking for *you* in the first place! Let me just pack up." Mari lifted her hands to conjure the spell.

But I couldn't wait. I had to fix this. "Mari, I'm so—" I started, the exact moment her body crumpled to the ground.

"Mari!" I yelled, rushing to her.

Lifting her face from the ground, I wiped the mud from her cheeks. But the sight—

Her eyes.

Her huge golden-brown eyes were stark. Clear. Wide open.

No, no no—

I pressed my head into her chest and exhaled every ounce of air that had been growing stale inside me when I heard a solid, rhythmic heartbeat. And air, flowing in and out of her lungs.

Despite the pale, sickly pallor of her face, those unmoving eyes, the cool blue veins along her arms and jawline, as if she were a corpse—she was breathing. It didn't make any sense.

Griffin was already next to me, cradling her head in his hands as it lolled to the side, painstakingly brushing twigs and leaves from her full red curls.

"What's wrong with her?" he asked, voice more frantic than I'd ever heard it.

"I don't know." My shaking hands summoned lighte and I urged it toward her, but there was nothing to heal. Not a stroke, not a seizure . . . Again, I felt for the steady pulse in her veins. "She's . . . healthy. Medically speaking, nothing is wrong."

"Something is wrong, Arwen. She's fucking unconscious!"

I pricked the cool pad of her finger with the jagged edge of my nail.

A reflex.

Griffin sucked in a breath. "Is that good?"

"She's not paralyzed."

"That's good," Fedrik said from behind us.

But it didn't explain—

"It makes no sense," I said again. "My lighte . . . I would— I don't understand . . ."

Griffin's voice was far too low as he leaned close to her. "Mari?"

Her eyes didn't so much as flutter.

I spun back to Kane, still holding Mari's hand in both of mine. "I can't heal her like this. I need—"

"We'll find an infirmary in Frog Eye—"

"She'll need blood tests, ointments, potions . . . Will they have that?"

Kane shook his head, eyes still fixed on Mari's head supported by Griffin's hands. "We need a bigger city. Frog Eye is a small smuggling town . . ."

Griffin shook his head. "Siren's Cove is sacked. It's too dangerous. We have to fly for—"

"Willowridge." Kane crossed his arms.

Onyx. Back to Onyx. "Your palace?"

Kane shook his head. "We can't risk it. It's not as insulated as Shadowhold. Lazarus could be waiting for us."

"*Where, then?*" I asked, rage coating my voice. Mari's hand felt too small wrapped in my own.

"Briar's." Griffin's voice was barely a whisper.

"We haven't seen her in fifteen years," Kane warned. "I don't—"

Griffin said in a voice so raw it sent my stomach guttering with dread, "Now, Kane."

## 28

### ARWEN

I T WAS STILL THE DEAD OF NIGHT WHEN WE ARRIVED IN the Onyx capital of Willowridge.

Mari never so much as stirred the entire ride. Griffin and I had watched her without a single blink between the two of us. Fedrik sat beside me all the while, patiently and wordlessly. If she hadn't been breathing, I would have thought—

But she *was* breathing. She *wasn't* dead. She was going to be fine. Briar would know what to do.

She had to.

Otherwise I'd never forgive myself.

We landed on a roof of tiled terra-cotta, and in the dark I could just barely make out a hilled city beneath us, streetlamps illuminating the clean, cobbled roads in buttery light. I could have licked the air itself in gratitude—it was finally, mercifully *chilly*.

I had missed Onyx air more than I knew how to articulate. The familiar smell of lilac and gardenia hung in the dry breeze that kissed my face. Now we were only two hours by carriage from home, and no longer in a kingdom where I was wanted for treason.

I fished out my fur cloak from one of our hastily thrown-together sacks and dismounted. Kane's significant wingspan retracted, those sleek, smooth, snakeskin-like wings tucking into his spine before polished obsidian claws and horns became neat fingernails and stacked silver rings. He led us down a steep set of stairs, Griffin carrying Mari behind me. The wood creaked under our feet.

I surveyed the city, the fears I used to harbor of Willowridge feeling more and more like someone else's memories. From what I could see, which wasn't much due to the hour and the mist, Willowridge was filled with elongated homes topped by terra-cotta or slate roofs and solid unused chimneys. I could only imagine what the city was like in the wintertime, though, when wispy smoke must have drifted from each one against the faint evening snow, dancing along to the sound of bundled carolers.

These homes were different from the whitewashed villas of Azurine or the farmhouses and cottages of Abbington. Sturdier, with their rich brick or limestone, and more gothic as all things in Onyx seemed to be—tinged with something dark and haunting and a little sorrowful. Like the romantic wrought-iron gates or the lanterns on each home that gilded front steps and doorknobs or the hand-painted signs in that bold, swooping print that marked the street corners.

Kane walked through the night, leading us down a narrow, elm-lined street. At its end, a wide, expansive iron gate stood, bathed in a pool of gentle light from a streetlamp. Through the twisted metal I could see a vast and sprawling manor, grander than the townhomes two streets over, with delicate roof tiles and great windowpanes just outlined by moonlight. Griffin held Mari beside me, squinting into the dark stretch of land before us, as Kane approached the gates.

"Briar!" he called into the night, his voice accompanied only by the music of a lone busker and his accordion and the percussive clack of horses' hooves on cobblestone somewhere deeper in the city center, away from the homes.

I waited, trying not to fidget, until the chill had seeped through my fur and into my bones.

Finally, the gates rattled open on their own—no guards or soldiers to pull them apart—and Kane gave us a shallow nod.

"A good sign?" I asked Griffin.

"We'll find out."

We marched onto a rolling lawn. The moon was high in the sky, and rows and rows of lavender filled either side of the brick path beneath us, which led to the stately manor's porch, lit by more lanterns beckoning us inside. A single white-painted bench hung from dark wooden beams above.

Kane grasped the weighty door knocker and its clang rang out too loudly into the night. When Briar opened the front door, her beauty nearly stole the wind from my lungs.

Almost as tall as Kane, and just as arresting, her long, dark hair was piled into a crown of braids atop her head. Her skin was white as snow and clear as the sky after a good rain, so smooth it was like porcelain, and carved with as much care. Strong jutting cheekbones, full lips like rose petals, and a slight, pert nose. Her eyes weren't severe like Amelia's—who knew why that comparison was on the tip of my tongue—but rather warm and open. Bright violet eyes like I had never seen, as if she was actually a mythical creature disguising herself as a young woman.

I wasn't so far off—she didn't look a day over thirty-five, but of course, she was.

She looked from me to Kane—both of us still unkempt and wet from rain and soaked in blood and dirt—to Griffin, holding an unconscious girl, to Fedrik, leaning on the column of her porch to support his weak leg, and bared her flawless teeth at us. "Kane, you shouldn't have. All this fun, for me?"

"My witch is hurt. Possibly spelled or struck with a curse of some kind. She's unconscious but my healer says completely healthy. She needs you."

Briar stared at Mari's face.

Inspecting. Studying.

My stomach roiled on itself.

"Bring her inside," Briar finally said, wrapping her dark robe tightly against the night's chill. "There's a spare bedroom on the second floor that Cori can help you to."

"Thank you," Kane said, gesturing for Griffin to bring Mari inside. The commander exchanged a nod of familiarity with Briar as he crossed her threshold.

Through the bleary light of what had to be two or three in the morning, an ornate yet cozy foyer gleamed under a crystal chandelier overhead. Sophisticated artwork peppered the walls of the wide maple-wood staircase Griffin carried Mari up, trailing behind a woman in a clean, white uniform whose face resembled the moon, both in serenity and shape.

I could just make out a long hallway farther down, which must have led into Briar's elaborate home, but she guided us immediately to the left and into a dark sitting room furnished with a rich violet carpet that matched the sorceress's haunting eyes.

Briar stepped one slipper-clad foot inside and the whole room lit up with warmth—white pillar candles ignited, a stone fireplace roared to life, and soft string music emanated from a harp in the corner with no player that I could see.

"Sit, sit," she told us, folding her slender limbs into a plush chair. "Cori will make up the bedrooms. I have three spares and a small library with an extra bed on the second floor."

I did as I was told and gathered my tired body into a ball in the corner of the leather settee. Fedrik sat next to me and Kane across from us.

Where had Cori taken Griffin and Mari? I arched to see where the staircase led.

"Cori will get her settled," Briar said to me. "I need information from you before I see what I can do."

"Anything," I said.

"And who are you?"

"This is Lady Arwen, my healer, and Prince Fedrik of Citrine. Broderick and Isolde's son."

Briar greeted us both before turning back to Kane. "Tell me what happened."

Kane leaned forward, bracing his elbows on his knees. "She was—"

"We were attacked by bandits," I blurted. "Mari—the witch—came to help, but Kane and I had already disarmed most of them. One bandit was left, though. He shot an arrow at her before we could get to him. I couldn't see really, but I think it hit a necklace she was wearing." I cringed. "It was yours, actually. She thought it made her stronger. She was doing magic far beyond her reach as a young, new witch. Her mother died in childbirth, so she never got to learn from anyone properly.

"Anyway, she was fine. I mean, completely fine. She fell back with the force, but got right up moments later. No head injury. No chest wound. Then she collapsed about an hour later. Completely unresponsive, but her breathing and heart rate are normal." I sucked in some air, and Fedrik placed a warm hand on my shoulder and gave a squeeze. "I'm a healer, as Kane said. I can tell you with certainty, she isn't ill."

Briar had listened intently before she spoke. When she did, she turned to face Kane. "Why did she have my amulet?"

"I gifted it to her," he lied seamlessly.

"Are you sleeping with her?"

I nearly choked on sheer air.

"No." He furrowed a brow, but didn't look in my direction. And why would he? The question had nothing to do with me.

Briar stood, smoothing her robe down her lean legs. "Very well," she said. "What am I if not a walking favor for Kane Raven-wood?"

She breezed past us and up the stairs, leaving Kane, Fedrik, and me in the harp-twinged silence.

"What did she mean?" I asked Kane. "About being a favor to you?"

He grimaced. "She's done a lot for me over the years. I'm very grateful to her."

Bleeding *Stones*. The thought of her pleasing him, doing him *favors*, made me want to pitch myself into the sizable fireplace in front of us.

"You don't know?" Fedrik asked me, confusion dotting his crystal eyes.

"No, Prince, she doesn't. And I don't think now is the time, do you?"

"Know what?" I asked. I had developed a very unpleasant

response to the thought of Kane hiding anything from me. My palms had already begun to itch and I folded them into my skirt to halt the fidgeting.

"My grim history," Kane snarled at Fedrik.

My stomach tightened at the words. I knew very little about Kane's failed attempt to take his father's crown—only that it resulted in many deaths and forced him and others to flee to Onyx. I didn't blame him for not feeling as if he could open up to me now. Not after all our progress had just been washed down a bloody, rain-drenched drain.

Especially not when another man was seated beside me, a supportive hand moving up and down my back. Kane's eyes were glued to the motion. A beast with its prey.

I hadn't told him yet about Fedrik and me—that I wasn't pursuing something with the prince.

But I couldn't think of that right now. I couldn't think of anything but Mari.

Kane stood abruptly. "I'm going to make some coffee."

"I'll take one, too," Fedrik said.

Kane regarded him with such distaste I nearly laughed. But I didn't, and Kane walked out of the sitting room in silence, his heavy footfalls echoing as he trudged down the long hallway behind us.

"My mother told me about the Fae when I was eleven," Fedrik said, eyes on the flames before us as they waved and jumped. "She said there was another realm, beyond Evendell, and it wasn't on any map, or taught in any classes. A secret place, where very magical creatures called Faeries lived.

"It wasn't so foreign to me—Citrine is a peculiar kingdom, as I'm sure you've gathered. The magic that keeps our kingdom safe is ageless, elemental, born from the seas themselves . . . But unlike Citrine, my mother had said, the Fae were kept in their realm against their will. Then she told me of the rebellion.

"Briar was one of Kane's followers. That's what she means by doing him favors. The last one she did for him lost Briar her husband, her home . . ."

I pursed my lips, my mind already moving back to Mari. Whether Briar would help her if she blamed Kane for the loss of her life back in Lumera.

"Briar is going to know what's causing Mari's illness, Wen. I'm sure of it. She's said to be the most powerful witch of all time because she has the longest lineage. Her ancestors were the first-ever witches to exist, back when there were no mortals, only Fae Gods."

"You know of the Gods?" I asked. His answering smile turned me sheepish. Of course he did. He was so worldly and educated. He had seen so much, been so many places. Explored, adventured, learned.

"I'm not sure what I believe. If you go to the Jade Islands, they worship something entirely different. It's all relative, isn't it?"

I nodded, though I knew nothing of the Jade Islands, or what they believed in. Where was Mari when you needed her? My heart protested as if I were pressing on a fresh bruise. I shot my eyes back to the top of the staircase.

"Shall we take our minds off it for the time being? Favorite place you've ever traveled?"

*Siren's Cove, with Kane.*

Fedrik was trying so hard to be helpful. He actually was a good friend. Maybe my second or third ever. But thinking of Siren's

Cove made me think of Kane, which made me think of our stupid, violent argument earlier. And what might have unfolded between us had we not been interrupted.

"I'm going to head upstairs," I said, standing abruptly.

Fedrik stood as well. "Of course. I can come with you?"

My eyes widened.

"That's obviously not what I—" Fedrik shook his head. "I'm exhausted as well. I just meant, if you don't want to be alone—"

"Thanks, but I just need some sleep." In the last twenty-four hours, I had been trapped in a cavern, tortured by a boy who used to kiss me, attacked by bandits, and I might have lost my closest friend in the world. I didn't think I could take another moment of being awake.

I slipped from the bewitched living room, through the foyer, and up the maple staircase. Dark specters of night cloaked the hallway, but I could still make out elegant tapestries on the walls and vases of Onyx's lush lavender and lilac tucked into shelves and placed atop ottomans. I walked until I reached one of the rooms Cori had made up for us.

Inside it was like a little forgotten dresser drawer. Cramped, dusty, and overflowing. A long-abandoned hearth at the foot of the patchwork bed still held coals. The room wasn't small, but it seemed as much due to the sheer number of books that had been stacked, piled, and lodged inside its four walls. Rows and rows along the floor, on every shelf, filling a hand-painted ladder and open chest, piled in the corners, stacked in columns on a vanity— this must have been Briar's makeshift library, though I doubted she could find anything in this maze of parchment and leather. Mari would have blown a gasket.

The one saving grace was the room's balcony, where a propped-open door allowed for a cool breeze and the mild rhythm of cicadas to waft inside.

I bypassed the bed to peer outside and down at the swing on Briar's porch below. The wooden beam creaked under my hands as I leaned over, and I watched as two fireflies flitted through the lawn that sprawled beneath me. I closed my eyes and leaned my head back, letting the moonlight brush over my face and clear my mind.

How nice it must be for Briar—to wake up in the mornings and walk out to her quiet porch, survey her bountiful lavender, and read a book on the softly rocking bench.

Lonely, sure.

But peaceful. Untouched. Unthreatened.

Nobody to worry over. To grovel and beg and pray for their safety.

Nobody to hurt.

No ticking clock. Just a long, endless life, all alone.

A pang of envy clamored through me.

I wanted her solitude, her serenity. She had built this life for herself that would ebb and flow for the next century.

My life would end within the year, and what had I built before it was ripped from me?

Turrets and spires and ramparts of sheer cowardice to protect me from my own pain and suffering. Now I might never be able to tell my closest friend how profoundly sorry I was. I'd let my grief over my mother's death carve a chasm between my siblings and me. I'd broken my own heart and had no idea how to untangle the knotted mess between Kane and me. I had definitely led Fedrik on in my pursuit of normalcy. And all the while, the walls I'd built did nothing to protect me from a fate I had no control over.

For so long, my sorrow had felt like an untouchable foundation under the structure of my life. A base I had to build atop—any joy, any progress erected over that same buried, stagnant, inaccessible grief.

And now, I realized all I had built was an abundance of pain.

My heart seized with the intensity of how much I missed my mother. She would have had thoughtful, soothing words to remind me why things could always get better.

But she wasn't here.

And even if there was a chance of my survival—even if I could let myself believe in such a thing—I didn't particularly *want* the life that would stretch before me.

I lay in bed for hours as that thought gutted me over and over and over.

I finally fell asleep, my legs twined in lilac-scented cotton, alongside the rising sun.

# 29

## ARWEN

"Arwen, wake up." Kane's voice was a caress. "Briar has news about Mari."

My eyes flew open and peered past Kane to find Briar, face solemn, standing in the cherrywood doorway, her near-translucent skin shadowed by pale, evening light.

I shot up, nearly colliding with Kane's head. "What is it? Is she—"

"She's going to be all right."

Solace and concern warred in my heart. If Mari was going to be fine, why did Briar look so worried?

I launched myself out of bed and scrambled for the silk robe that Cori had hung beside a birdcage stuffed with more of those wrinkled, flaking books. Kane and Briar strolled down the dark, carpeted hallway and I rushed after them.

Had I slept until evening?

In the last bedroom, Mari lay, still unconscious under white quilted bedding. An impressive sunset flirted through the window that looked out across Willowridge's cityscape. Cori laid a damp cloth on Mari's forehead, then took her pulse, writing something down in a worn journal on the bedside table.

I crossed the room to Mari, taking her cool palm into my hand. The lack of warmth sent my power rippling at my fingertips, but there was still nothing to heal—a deeply unsettling sensation, like trying to see out of a blinded eye.

I almost missed Griffin, leaning forward in a leather chair in the corner of the room, elbows pressed to his knees, palms tightly clasped, eyes ringed with lack of sleep.

"Has she woken at all?" I asked.

"No." His voice was hoarse.

"She will, she just needs rest," Briar said behind me.

I turned. "What happened to her?"

"She's been poisoned," Briar said, folding her arms elegantly and leaning back against the windowsill. Purple shafts of sunset highlighted little floating specks of dust hovering in the room's still atmosphere and painted Briar's angular face in warm contour.

"Cori and I checked for injuries, ailments, curses, hexes, charms . . ." She furrowed a brow at the memory. "The amulet she wore . . . I fashioned that amulet many, many years ago, for my closest friend, Queen Valeria Ravenwood."

I had never heard Kane's mother's name before, but I swore I could feel the air in the room deplete as Kane sucked in a sharp breath.

"It held a simple spell. To protect her from death at the hands of the Fae king in the months leading up to our plot against him." Briar cut a sidelong glance at Kane. "He wasn't such a doting husband even before then, if you recall."

"How come my mother never suffered the same fate as the witch?"

"Valeria was not of my coven. She could never have pulled from my lineage when she wore it. The amulet only served its intended purpose around her neck. However, Mari here seems to have found a way to use the power I forged the amulet with to bolster her own."

Mari had been right. The amulet *had* been boosting her power. All this time . . .

"You say she was doing magic far beyond her skill level?"

Kane nodded at Briar, his mind turning alongside my own.

"And she wore it day and night?"

"She never parted with it," Griffin said from his corner.

"Once the amulet came off, the debt demanded to be paid. Months and months of bolstered magic . . . The overindulgence led to withdrawal. Her body is making up for lost time."

"So, if she rests, she'll wake up eventually? Fully recovered?"

"We hope."

"And Mari's mother . . . she must have been part of your coven, right? Mari knew the amulet was helping her reach her ancestors."

Briar's mouth twisted as she glared at me. "No. As I told you, your friend must have found a way to steal my magic against the wishes of nature. My coven has been extinct for centuries."

"She would have told me if that were the case." Mari would have been thrilled if she had discovered such a loophole. She would have shouted it from the Shadowhold rooftops.

"Perhaps she was delusional," Briar said, eyes chilling. "Believed her own lies."

Something about Briar's callousness felt false. Like she was the one putting her faith in made-up stories. "If that's really what you think," I pressed, "why do you look so afraid?"

I only registered Cori's sharp intake of breath as Briar stepped forward, and despite my better judgment, I flinched. But she only walked past me and toward Kane.

"Your castle healer is too bold," she said, lips lifting upward. "I'm tired of her voice. If anyone is keeping secrets, it's *you*, Prince Ravenwood."

There was something so sinister about referring to Kane as a prince rather than the rightful king of Onyx. Reminding him, and everyone else in the room, who he used to be—who he came from. My mouth turned with distaste.

Kane's face hardened. "None that I can recall."

"You've spent the past fifty years looking for the last full-blooded Fae. Now you've been traveling with a witch pilfering my magic, the prince of a kingdom that despises you, and a healer who has been rumored to have obliterated an army just a month ago in a combustion of light and flame . . ."

Kane's crushing silver eyes only flickered. But his lack of response was enough to stoke the tempest within Briar.

"How could you not have told me? I sacrificed everything for you. My life back in Lumera, my power, *Perry*. And still, I welcomed you into my home, healed your ailing witch, and you planned to leave and never tell me that you *found her*? After all this time? After all we lost? How *dare* you?" The glass window behind Briar shattered with her rage and sent a gust of cold air through the room. I jumped at the sound and Cori shuffled out through the door like a well-trained dog.

"Briar, darling," Kane's words were coy, but his eyes flashed. "Control yourself."

"I will do what I *please*," she said, with deadlier calm than I had ever heard someone speak around Kane. "I have half a mind to show you exactly why you were wise to stay away all those years—"

"You're right," I said, the words spilling from my lips before I could catch them. "I'm the full-blooded Fae. He didn't tell you because I begged him not to. Too many people are after me . . . Kane told me how much he trusted you. I was foolish not to listen."

I could hear Kane's frustrated sigh, but I kept my eyes on Briar. I expected wrath, or violence, but when she turned back to face me, it was satisfaction that pursed her lips. Some kind of . . . acceptance.

"Right," she said evenly. "I figured as much." And with that she drifted out of the room as if on a wisp of smoke, and left the rest of us in silence.

❧

KNOWING MARI WOULD WAKE SOON, AND THAT, AT LEAST for the time being, Briar would not kick her out of her home, we had decided to leave for Crag's Hollow in the morning. Griffin, still glued to Mari's bedside like a barnacle on the bottom of a sunken ship, had brushed off the call to supper, choosing to eat in his leather chair that surely held the distinct imprint of his backside by now.

But I was starving.

Now that I didn't fear Mari's impending death, air flowed through my lungs more easily, my tight limbs had loosened, my appetite had returned . . .

Along with a flood of emotions that must have been kept at bay by all my worry.

Memories of Kane and me, shouting at each other in the wet, muggy jungle. Accusing and admitting in equal measure things I was sure we both wished we hadn't said.

And Fedrik, urging me to abandon Kane for my own safety.

And Kane, still believing Fedrik had kissed me. Which he had, but—

Believing it had meant something entirely different than it had.

After bathing and dressing, I descended the stairs to find Kane and Fedrik in the dining room, and Briar, dressed in a fine navy gown and decadent fur shawl. "I have a dinner engagement of my own tonight, but Cori's roast is scrumptious," she said to Kane, as if she hadn't just threatened his life mere hours ago. Then she closed the front door primly, leaving me with two beleaguered men and one glistening, savory roast.

The three of us sat down in silence and began to eat, the sound of metal on porcelain a conflicting accompaniment to the harp that played itself in the next room. I brought my fork to my mouth and tried to appreciate the rich flavors, but each bite curdled on my tongue as I thought of all the pain I had brought the three of us.

I tried to cram those thoughts into some cluttered corner in my mind, but the recesses of my psyche were becoming too crowded—each painful thought I shoved in forced an even less pleasant one out.

More cutlery grated on porcelain. More haunting harp music, the strings in the next room plucking themselves. More insufferable silence.

I could think of nothing at all to say to Kane, so I turned to Fedrik. "Have you been to Willowridge before?"

"Yes, a few times, actually." He finished his bite and looked from Kane to me before continuing, if not a little awkwardly. "The city is quite special. You would love it, Wen. The art here—the galleries. The sculptures alone are some of the best crafted marble I've had the pleasure of viewing. And the food. I once had this entire rack of lamb, served out of a—"

"Yes, it's my favorite of my cities," Kane said, as he sipped his wine. "I quite like that herb-crusted lamb myself."

Fedrik frowned, clearly not having intended to directly

compliment Kane's capital. "Where else do you and Briar like to go when you're here visiting her?"

I lifted a brow, to which Fedrik only shrugged. But he knew what his question implied. That Kane was a cad, a dog—that he wined and dined beautiful witches and took them to bed after visiting galleries and eating racks of herb-crusted lamb.

Kane's expression was one of unflinching calm as he put down his fork and said, "There's a charming bacchanal off Till Street where they fuck sheep and drink the blood of virgins. Shall we stroll by after dinner?"

Fedrik smiled stiffly, but I could tell he wasn't sure if Kane was joking. I was about to relieve him of his concern, when the mention of Briar brought a strange thought to the surface of my mind.

Kane had slept with his dead mother's closest friend.

Briar had slept with her friend's son after she died. A boy she had likely watched grow up.

Suddenly the relationship that had felt so sensual and threatening to me was imbued with sorrow, remorse, and shared grief. It gave me a dull, cloying stomachache, like a too-hot, winding carriage ride.

"I'm full," I said as I pushed my chair from the table without poise. Fedrik stood, too, polite as ever, while Kane's silver gaze from his seat stripped me bare. I let my feet carry me down the candle-lit hall and up the stairs. Closing the door to my room with such force the books quivered, I dumped myself onto the bed like a rag doll.

But the silence was too loud up here, too. Too oppressive.

I appraised the walls and walls of books, leaning closer to read their weathered spines. A pink-hued leather tome that had clearly once been cherry red reminded me of Niclas and his family's story. *A History of War in Rose.*

I pulled it from the shelf and walked down the hall to Mari's room. I didn't know if she'd be able to hear me, as I didn't fully understand the comalike state that she was in, but Cori had encouraged us to talk to her, and Griffin had to be going mad with boredom in his corner. The book was as much for him as it was for Mari.

He appeared to be sleeping when I sat down—those huge hands motionless against the arms of a chair that, in comparison to his large body, appeared comically small. I read aloud quietly so as not to wake him, the troubled history of Rose a welcome reprieve from my own mind.

The kingdom was like a continent of its own, with such a large population spread out among so many varied landscapes that its people had developed two different ways of living. In the south lived a simple, peaceful people. They weren't too different from the men and women I grew up with in Amber. Which made sense, as we were practically neighbors. The lower hemisphere brought warm weather and bright, consistent sunshine. Amber would have enjoyed the same sun and temperate heat had it not been tucked into the insulated valley that kept us in a permanent state of autumn. The southern people of Rose relished their bountiful crops, which they sold in vibrant outdoor markets. Their year-long produce was so robust, the entire region abstained from animal meat altogether.

Conversely, in the north of Rose lived a people of industry and hedonism. Influenced by the nearby unruly Opal Territories and culture-driven Onyx, this region of Rose was focused on commerce, finery, and decadence. Though I liked reading about the sultry melodies that came out of unfamiliar metal instruments, and the short sparkly dresses the women wore, I skimmed over the section about the sensual dancing in hidden, smoke-filled rooms, as I worried Griffin was only pretending to be asleep.

Eventually, these two sides found themselves imbued in an endless war until the north triumphed via . . . I flipped through the pages twice to see what I had missed. Serrated scraps dotting the book's spine told me a handful of pages had been ripped out.

"Sorry, Mari," I said to her motionless face. "I know you don't like cliff-hangers. Maybe Briar has another book on the subject."

"The Scarlet Queen had a secret weapon."

I turned to Griffin in his worn leather chair, but his eyes were still closed.

"I knew you liked story time," I said, unable to hide my smile as I put the book on the table beside Mari's bed. "Why do they call her that? Queen Ethera?"

Griffin sat up slowly, blinking his eyes open and scratching his jaw in thought. "Because the streets of the south ran scarlet with blood after she won the war for the north. The southerners say it like an insult, the north like a badge of honor."

"Do you love these dry history books as much as Kane?"

"I'm not much of a reader," he said mildly. "It hurts my eyes."

It was by far the most personal thing Griffin had ever told me about himself.

"So how do you know about the queen's secret weapon?"

"He was a friend of ours."

"Was?"

"He pledged to fight beside us in the rebellion. But he turned us in to Lazarus days before, in return for his freedom. And his army's." Griffin scowled at the memory. "For some reason, once he made it to Evendell, he and his people fought for Ethera. He's been in hiding from Kane ever since."

"A Fae?"

Griffin nodded, rubbing his neck.

"Griffin," I said as gently as I could. "That chair looks uncomfortable. Go sleep in one of the guest rooms. I'll stay here with her."

"I'm all right."

*"You think about me constantly. As I do you."*

Kane's words rang though my mind like a church bell. All the time we could have saved, the pain spared, the suffering. Griffin was no better.

"Why do you fight it so hard?"

Griffin furrowed his light brows. "Fight what?"

"Your feelings for her."

I had expected him to balk, to argue, to ignore me completely. But he cleared his throat and said, "If I never try to have her, I never have to lose her."

He angled his head toward the window that Briar had shattered with her magic only hours earlier—Cori had cleaned up the shards of glass, but the cool night wind still funneled into the room, blowing wisps of hair around my face.

I wasn't sure I agreed with the commander. We had all almost lost her. And had the unthinkable happened, Griffin never would have had the chance to tell her how he felt. He would have had to live with that his entire, near-unending Fae existence.

When I realized he wasn't going to say any more, I reached for the book, but my eyes had grown weary and I couldn't see the fine text.

"I think I'm going to bed," I said.

But Griffin had finally dozed off. His golden hair fluttered across his forehead with every unhurried exhale, his face melting into his hand, which sat propped on the chair's stiff, cracked arm.

When I stood, I noticed a spine-creased book next to the chair that had become his home, tucked beneath one of its clawed feet.

I smiled. Griffin must have been the most fiercely loyal person I had ever met. He was honest beyond belief, probably to a fault, but still. He didn't suffer from pride or ego. I was lucky to call him my friend. So was Mari.

I stood and kissed her forehead before walking back to my small, book-filled alcove.

The bed depressed under my weight and my eyes fell to the glass doors of the balcony before me—the soft blue curtains that hung imperfectly around them allowing a single sliver of the world outside to slip through.

I rolled to my side, cool sheets on my face like a kiss.

But sleep never came.

*"You're terrified of letting yourself feel anything real."*

*"Nothing matters if you're going to die."*

I turned to my back and let my eyes focus on the dainty cobwebs and cracks on the ceiling above me. I had loved Kane, once. And he had broken that. Broken *me*. Lied to me, used me, tricked me, stolen me away—

But even as I rattled off his offenses in my mind as I so often did, they carried little weight. Maybe I had spent too long blaming Kane for every profoundly awful thing that had ever happened to me.

And worse than blaming him for my misfortune, maybe I had been using *him*.

Using him as a catchall for my pain, my suffering. As a punching bag when I needed to feel fury. As an answer when I wondered, *Why me? Why did I have to die?*

And buried deepest of all, bared wide open in the silent, dark room that smelled of bound leather—maybe I had been saddling Kane with all my pain, using him to diffuse it, long before the battle of Siren's Bay.

At Shadowhold, when so little made sense to me. When the world as I knew it was being dismantled minute by minute, piece by piece. When all Kane wanted was to show me the rest of the blossom while I was fixated on the stem. And I had fought him tooth and nail.

Maybe now that he had done the one thing he always swore he wouldn't—try to let me in, allow for the vulnerability he always saw as weakness—I owed him some vulnerability of my own.

Or at least an apology.

I couldn't watch him fight for me, protect me, desire me from afar—all while I hid my feelings for him. That was true cowardice.

What those feelings were, I didn't fully know. Attraction, chemistry, friendship . . . I wasn't sure I could feel anything the same way I once had. Not when this numbness, this darkness, this bleak, revolting dread slithered through my veins.

But maybe I'd say exactly that.

That I hadn't figured out what I wanted or how I felt—but that I missed him. In the depths of my soul, in my hands when they twitched to touch him, in my ears when they searched for his voice in every room. *I missed him.* If it wouldn't be too wrong to ask him to be patient with the selfish, fragmented parts of me. To give me a chance to discover what I wanted, even if we both knew I didn't have much time left to do so.

Maybe I'd just ask him to try.

It was all he'd ever asked of me.

# 30

❧

## KANE

I̸T HAD BEEN HOURS SINCE DINNER, AND THE MANOR WAS cloaked in sleep. The very bricks of the walls might've been sighing in peaceful slumber. I, on the other hand, hadn't slept since the night before Reaper's Cavern, and feared I wasn't likely to ever again.

My next swig of bitter lavender spirit burned considerably less than the first. I sank deeper into the couch, watching the low, crackling fire. It flickered and twirled like a beleaguered dancer, once passionate but now half-hearted and lazy—tired of its own routine.

I was tired, too.

How could I have raged at Arwen like that back in Peridot?

I had been nasty, crude, entirely immature—

I had promised to keep my distance, and now that she was finally finding happiness— I ran a hand down my face in aggravation and groaned into my palm.

"Would you like a small violin to play alongside your brooding?"

Turning, I spied Briar, unclasping her fur and hanging it up in the foyer. I shut my eyes and leaned into the leather, hearing only the tinkling of ice against crystal and the patter of shoes being kicked off. A brightness behind my eyelids pried them open, and I beheld the previously guttering fireplace now fierce and roaring as Briar slunk into the chair across from me.

"I preferred the dark."

"Of course you did." Briar smirked. "King of Darkness, Prince of Shadow . . . Don't you tire of your own misery?"

"Yes," I said honestly. "Who was your mysterious dinner with?"

"Another witch. One of the Antler coven back in Lumera."

"Did they have any news?"

"Broderick and Isolde are concerned. Word is spreading that they have aligned with Onyx."

"But they haven't." Nobody but myself and the royals knew of our plans to wed Princess Sera to my successor. "They offered hardly forty people asylum."

"I relayed as much, but my companion said they fear Lazarus will get wind of such notions."

"Wonderful," I growled. More complications. "I'll send the prince to Shadowhold to meet with Lieutenant Eardley. They can find a way to contact his parents."

"Plotting to have the Fae girl all to yourself?"

The fire snapped at us and I felt the licks of heat across my face. "I'm in no mood tonight, Briar."

Her voice was softer when she spoke again. "What is it you hope to do in Crag's Hollow?"

I had wanted to ask her this since we arrived. "Did you keep in touch with Esme over the years?"

"No," Briar said, swirling her drink and staring down at the little caramel whirlpool she had created. "I haven't spoken to her since we left Lumera."

"She was like a daughter to you."

"And she still feels betrayed like one. Her mother died fighting alongside us."

"Think she feels betrayed enough to work with Amber?"

Briar pursed her lips. "Why do you ask?"

"Amber knows of her, somehow. I'm not sure how they found Esme, or what she's offering them, but it's worth finding out. We have no other leads on the blade. I'm fishing for a miracle."

Briar clucked her tongue. "I doubt she can do much to aid your search. She inherited very little lighte from her mother, and none of her seeing abilities."

"I know." I shook my head. It didn't make any sense.

Briar leaned in closer. "You shouldn't have kept her from me."

I had been waiting for this. "I know that."

Briar's mouth twisted. "And even if Esme somehow helps you find the blade . . . what then? You cannot save the girl, Kane."

I held my face neutral. "Then I'll go to the Pearl Mountains."

The last and only trick I had up my sleeve. A theory from decades ago, that because the prophecy spoke of my father's death at the hands of the second-born son, I might be able to carry out the deed in her stead. After my father, and Arwen, I was the closest to full-blooded that existed.

"Ah." Briar clucked her tongue at me. "To take her place."

"I've read everything that exists about Pearl's libraries, their scholars, their priests. I've studied every interpretation of the seer's words. And all of her sister's prophecies and her mother's for good measure. It might be possible."

It was a relief of sorts, to speak the words out loud. The plan had been stored in the recesses of my mind for years. A plan I never thought I'd have to attempt once I found the final full-blooded Fae.

"The prophecy says final Fae of full blood *born* at last. You are not full-blooded. You cannot be reborn."

"It also says a king doomed to fall at the hands of *his second son*. That's me." I gave a sardonic grin.

"What about a king that can only meet his end *at her hands*?" When surprise lit my face, she smiled. "You thought you were the only one who had read the seer's words a few hundred times?"

"It's vague, as all prophecies are. Perhaps he takes his dying breath in her arms after I've killed him. Or, maybe by meeting her, it led to his end. Look, Briar, either way, I have to try. I love her."

Briar appraised the crackling flames before us. "Would you still go if she felt the same for you as you did for her? You'll lose what little time you might have left together."

"I'd still go," I answered truthfully. "But it helps that she doesn't."

There was no possible outcome in which I allowed Arwen to pay the ultimate price for the safety of the realms. The only way to save her from such a fate was to find a way to take her place. If anything, it was a mercy I'd be long gone before I had to watch her grow old with someone else, Fedrik or otherwise. I could almost ignore the jealousy that infested my mind, crawling across every jagged cleft of my brain until I grimaced.

"I don't know much about Pearl's priests or scholars," Briar continued. "But there's only one man who can help you: the White Crow."

I raised a single brow at her.

"He resides on a remote peak in Pearl's Vorst region. I don't know if he still practices magic, but if anyone can turn you from nearly full-blooded to true Fae, it's him. The White Crow is chief among the most gifted sorcerers to ever grace Evendell. Be warned, though," she said, her lilac eyes dimming. "He's never been right-minded. Be wary of what you let him do to you."

For a while we sat in silence, listening to the cracks and whistles of the enchanted fireplace. I sipped my whiskey and thought of Mari upstairs. Her resilient spirit so like the flame that flickered before us. Her hair, too.

"You were a Foxfire, right? Before you married Perry and became a Creighton?"

Briar dipped her head slowly, eyes now down on her own drink.

"Why do you fear Mari is part of the coven, if they have been extinct for so long?"

"She used my amulet to bolster her magic. She is channeling our lineage. It wouldn't have done anything for a witch from another coven."

"What is there to fear? Your last one still living."

Briar's eyes fell to mine, fraught and unreadable. "Perhaps you're right."

Briar, too, was from a family whose . . . beliefs she didn't share. Perhaps that was why she was so quick to join my cause all those years ago. My plight against my father was one she knew well.

As usual, the thought of him turned my stomach rancid. The heat from the flames was beginning to radiate into my wool shirt and make my skin crawl. I stood and stretched my legs. "Thank you. For everything."

"Good luck, Kane."

I wasn't sure what she was referring to, but I needed luck in so many different ways I didn't bother to ask.

With effort, I dragged my tired limbs up the creaking maple stairs into the dark hallway. I wouldn't be able to sleep, but perhaps lying in silence could bring some peace to my mind. I'd try not to think of wartime deals or sadistic covens or mad sorcerers.

I'd try not to think of Arwen.

My hand was wrapped around the doorknob of my guest room when light footsteps pattered into the hall behind me. My heart shuddered.

"Why are you awake?" I said into the door. I almost couldn't bear to look at her. I knew what the sight of Arwen, barefoot, hair mussed, and wrapped in that silky robe from this morning would do to me.

"How did you know it was me?"

Such a silly question. As if I couldn't sense her the moment she stepped into a room, smell her orange blossom skin, hear the musical tone of her sighs and hums.

"Lucky guess," I said, finally turning to face her.

Gods, I had been right—she looked like a night-blooming vision, born out of starlight itself. Her long dark hair pulled into a low ribbon but still messy from tossing and turning, unable to sleep. The silken white robe veiling her like a divine spirit. I wanted to worship at her feet. I would, if she'd let me.

"I was going to make some tea," she said. "Do you want some?"

*Yes. Anything you are willing to offer me. I will drink it from your very lips.*

"No."

Her face fell slightly, but she made no move to walk past me.

"Good night," I said, my voice sounding more like a growl than I intended. I cleared my throat. "Sleep well."

I should have apologized for my outburst after seeing her with

Fedrik. But I compelled myself to enter the guest room and close the door before I did something idiotic instead like kiss her. Or ask her to marry me.

I needed my head looked at.

Kicking off my shoes and clothes, I crawled into the stiff bed. My skin was hot, my heart restless in my chest. Being stalled in this manor together was the problem. We needed to get back on the road. Perhaps I'd—

When my door squeaked open, it was honeysuckle and orange blossom that drifted through the room.

# 31

## KANE

ARWEN WALKED OVER TO THE BED, SHOCKING ME—A MAN rarely surprised, if ever—by climbing onto the mattress and folding her legs underneath her. "Can I stay with you for a while?"

I squinted at her in the darkness. "Are you feeling well?"

A small laugh. "I just can't sleep."

"If this is about . . . I'm sorry. For lashing out at you after—"

"Don't be." She wrapped the robe tighter around herself. "I shouldn't have let him kiss me in the first place. Fedrik and I are just friends."

"I meant what I said before, though. If it makes you happy, then that's what I want for you." A depressing thought blared through my mind, and I added, "But if this is . . . I'm afraid I can't help you self-sabotage. Can't give you another reason to hate me."

"I don't hate you." She sighed through her nose. "And there's nothing with Fedrik to sabotage. You're so fixated on him."

Then why . . .

Oh.

*Oh.*

I was an idiot. I had done this my entire life, and yet somehow didn't recognize Arwen's need for release. A distraction from the horrors of her own mind. A quieting of the constant roar.

Cautiously, I lifted the cotton sheets up for her, like offering a sugar to a wild horse. More of an invitation than a challenge, but she still took in the open sliver of bed for an extended beat.

In the end, she crawled forward and slipped underneath with a shaky exhale.

And then Arwen was lying in my bed.

Next to me.

Her body heat and honeysuckle hair overwhelming all my senses.

And in this moment—these peculiar, private witching hours, when Arwen was serene and soft, and starlit, her placid eyes appraising mine—her beauty was *merciless*. It was . . . beyond anything I could comprehend. After all these months and months of wanting her, the tether tied around my resolve had frayed to dust.

*Relax*, I told myself.

Still, my heart hammered, a near-fearsome pace against my ribs.

*Perhaps she wants to flirt. To cuddle. To feel something, but she isn't even sure what yet. Do not think about her body directly beside you. Barely covered by such thin silk. Her hair still a little damp from bathing—Gods, do not think about her bathing. About licking her sudsy wet breasts, sucking at the gentle skin of her neck, her smooth inner thighs . . .*

My breathing had become rushed and shallow. I'd just test her out. Give her morsels and see what she did with them. Let her set the pace.

"Actually, bird," I said, my voice now something lower, rougher, "it's you I've been fixated on. Specifically, what's beneath that little silk dress of yours."

I braced for that fierce, scrunched nose. That preloaded insult—

But Arwen didn't so much as scoff, and the silence warped into something charged and hungry around us. The room, bare of candlelight, was illuminated only by the nearly full moon beyond the lone windowsill. Arwen's chest was rising and falling almost as fast as my own in a pool of watery moonlight.

The muscles in my lower stomach clenched. "Arwen, what did you come in here for?"

Her hesitant gaze, now fixed on the beams of the ceiling, was almost enough to stop me right there.

*See, you've already gone too far. Pushed her too much. You're deplorable. Out of control.*

Arwen shifted, staying silent, biting that full, plump lip—

"Ask me for it," I nearly ground out.

*Tell me to stop, or I won't be able to. They'll have to pry me from you.*

Arwen's breath hitched. Finally, she said, "What are you offering?"

"To have you moaning for me like a woman possessed."

Her legs pinched together at my words. "And how might you do that?"

"Let me taste you, and you'll find out."

"Fine," she breathed, restless eyes finally landing on my own. "Kiss me, then."

My fingers nearly ripped through the thin sheets surrounding us. "That's not what I mean."

Her brows pinched inward before rising in realization.

This was a mistake. I knew it was. Even though she was asking me to take her, she was vulnerable and acting out. If I was stronger—not so fucking useless around this woman—I would stand up and leave the room. Perhaps this manor entirely. The city. I'd need to put thousands of miles between us to keep myself from her. I'd walk and walk and never look back.

But I wasn't stronger. I was weak.

"Do you trust me?"

After everything, all I had done to her, it was the only question that mattered.

"Yes," she breathed. "Always."

I could have devoured her.

Instead, I inched closer, slower than I thought my muscles could allow, hearing her breath suck in, brushing one stray hair from the spot where her slender neck met her shoulder and palming her hip through that slight, near-liquid silk. Like paper. I could have sheared it. Could already be feeling the white-hot heat of her body against my palm. But I didn't want to scare her. And if she knew the things I wanted from her. The things I wanted to *give* . . . She would be scared.

*I* was scared.

Grunting quietly without meaning to, I brought my lips down to her breasts, her stomach, mouthing her through the thin material.

And I was hard.

Already unbearably hard, just being this close. The tie at her slender waist fell away with my hand, and I spread the robe open, exposing the short nightdress underneath.

"These little dresses of yours drive me fucking crazy," I groaned, my mouth against her stomach, careful to avoid her healing injuries. Lifting up the satin, like unwrapping a gift, exposed her smooth thighs and . . . and the dainty white lace between them.

*"Fuck."*

Arwen laughed breathlessly, her delicate fingers now in my hair, at my brow. "And you say I have a mouth like a sailor."

I licked the skin of her thighs. Cream and honey. Like dessert.

I wasn't going to make it through this—every *inch* of her was dizzying. Her hands gentle in my hair, scraping lightly along my scalp. Her breath hitching when I cupped her round ass in my hands to drag her closer. The memories that swamped me as I sucked indulgently, indolently, on her hip bone: Her too-loud laugh when she was genuinely, truly amused. How her yawns rewarded me with that dopey, satiated expression I sometimes dreamt of. The way her eyes grew dark and determined when she ran—fast and precise and graceful.

Arwen's thighs fell open and a sigh slipped from her lips. She *wanted* this.

I licked across her smooth lower stomach, just above that slip of fabric still covering her. Accepting her invitation, that silent ask for *more*. She twitched as my tongue skated over her skin.

Wrapping my hands around her hips, I pulled the undergarment down to her ankles and off, hearing the fine lace tear from the force of my grasp.

Arwen's long hair was loose against the pillows, her white ribbon having come undone, her cheeks flushed, her wet lips parted . . . And those green eyes, as she held my gaze without a blink . . . such *trust*—

That look. I knew it was that look alone that had ruined me.

But then my eyes fell to her legs—casually, comfortably open. Relaxed. Wanting. And between them—wet and slick, pink and glistening and perfect.

My cock pulsed painfully. Near unbearable.

Gods have mercy.

I tossed the lace to the floor and wrapped my hands back around her ass, bringing my mouth down to the inside of her thigh, right beside her warm center. Arwen squirmed and clawed at me, making my cock twitch again.

She was going to have to hold still. I splayed a hand across her stomach and pinned her down to drag my tongue across her without interruption. Arwen bucked, moaning, and I nearly came apart myself.

"You taste like my dreams."

She mumbled something incoherent, and I laughed into her, making her writhe again.

I kissed against slick, sensitive skin, exploring every inch of her, drinking in her heat and honeyed scent. Every sigh, every arch of her hips, every time her fingers reached feverishly—I would taste her like this for hours. Days. Weeks. I would never feel full of her. I would always, *always* need more.

I ran a single finger through her soft, wet center and groaned in satisfaction. She was drenched. Pooling at her entrance, dripping down the inside of her own thighs. So wet that I knew she was aching. That she couldn't bear much more.

It was enough to pull all the air from my lungs as I stroked my finger back and forth in her wetness, my tongue dragging over her but never that bud, that sensitive peak—teasing, taunting her, losing myself until she was practically panting.

She mewled plaintively.

The sound turned my limbs boneless. "Is there something you want?"

"Please," she begged as I dipped my tongue inside of her this time. "Kane," she said in a choked whisper.

When I finally pressed my tongue to the spot she'd been pleading for, she breathed out in a rush and dug her nails into my shoulders.

She tasted so sweet, her little noises so desperate, that as I slipped my finger inside her and felt her walls clench around me, I had to shift to relieve pressure from my cock against the bed. But she was wanton and breathless and gripping me wildly, squirming as I thrust my finger in time with my tongue, flicking back and forth across that spot at the apex of her thighs.

She began to tense and stiffen, at the precipice of her release, so I withdrew to kiss along her swollen lips lightly, running my fingers up her sides to graze the swell of her breasts.

Perfect. All of her. Too perfect to be real.

Arwen arched and let out a frustrated little whimper. "Kane." Like she couldn't bear another moment. Like this was agony.

I understood. I wanted her release almost as badly as she did. Had wanted to feel her come apart on my tongue and fingers since nearly the moment I met her.

I traced my tongue across her once more, lingering on that spot at the apex, but never staying for long. I could barely think past this very, present moment—what she was allowing me to do to her. What she wanted from me. The only other thought, like some far-off call in the distance, was the knowledge that soon I would stroke myself only to this single memory. The memory of tasting her soft skin, hearing her little hums of pleasure. The knowledge that nothing would ever feel as good as being trusted by her, and indulging in her like this.

When I peered up, Arwen's eyes were screwed shut, her chest heaving with uneven breaths, her hands fisted, one in the sheets and one in my hair. When I swirled my tongue against her, she let out a low hiss.

"Open your eyes," I murmured to her.

She sat up on her elbows, pupils huge and dark, breath panting out of her.

"Look what you're doing to me." I reached into my breaches to grip my cock, swollen and heavy, before licking long and slow up her center.

"Oh, Stones," she hummed, throwing her head back, and I grasped myself harder at the sound of her voice.

When I sucked on the little bud, she cried out and squirmed almost violently. Letting go of my shaft, I ran my finger once more through her wetness before pushing inside. Pumping until my hand was drenched.

"More?" The grit in my voice made me sound like I had been choked.

"Kane, please."

I drove another digit inside, giving her time to stretch and pitch around the intrusion, stroking my fingers in and out, cupping them up toward her innermost wall. She writhed and keened against my mouth and fingers until I was forced to hold her down against the bed.

More suction, more pressure until—

Tensing, she cried out as she reached her peak. I thrust into her over and over and over, holding her open and sucking and licking through each pulse and contraction.

Once she was shivering with aftershocks, I stood from the bed to find the lace undergarment I had tossed away in my lust-addled fervor. "Here," I said, voice gravelly even to my own ears. "Sorry I ripped them. I'll buy you a hundred more."

She assessed me, limp and dazed. "What are you doing?"

"What do you mean?" I could barely think past the pulsing, thrumming, liquid-hot need in my groin. It was impressive, frankly, that I was still standing upright.

She sat up, hair tangled like I had never seen it, before her bright, playful eyes fell to my tented breeches. "I think it's your turn."

My cock was harder than it had been in nearly two hundred years of living. My balls aching and heavy, and the woman I would kill for, would die for, was offering to make me come.

And I was the half-wit who said, "Don't worry about me."

I really did need my head looked at.

"Why not?"

"Let's call it an abundance of caution. Otherwise, trust me, I'd beg you for it."

She frowned, sleepy and satiated, and my heart cracked open. "King Kane Ravenwood, begging me to touch him. That's a sight I'd love to see."

She really didn't get it. I was moments away from getting to my knees and begging her to touch me every minute of every hour of every damn day.

She might have said more, but a yawn overtook her.

And I—I was learning a new, painful lesson. Not too old, then, I guessed, for that.

I wasn't as strong as I had once thought. Or, I just wasn't strong enough. To have her, but not *have* her. Not wholly. Or perhaps I was just too selfish. I wanted her too much.

Still, that knowledge didn't stop me from climbing into the bed and smelling her sweet, honeysuckle hair as she tangled into me. Listening to her breathing become relaxed and steady, her head tucked underneath my chin, her heart beating in time on top of mine.

I had been right—I wouldn't sleep tonight.

I wasn't going to miss a single second of what it felt like to hold Arwen in my arms.

# 32

## ARWEN

I HAD BEEN AWAKE FOR AT LEAST TEN MINUTES, KEEPING my eyes closed against Kane's glorious, chiseled chest, not moving a single muscle—not my arms wrapped around him, nor my legs twined in his. If I stayed still enough, maybe I could pretend to sleep forever. And never have to face the reality that I wanted to be with Kane again, desperately, desperately, *desperately*.

I'd crawl over crushed glass to feel what I did last night. Not the pleasure—though that, too, was . . . world-shattering—but the moment I slipped into his bed and saw the look on his face. Surprise and lust and sheer *relief*—that was what had permanently altered my mind. I'd never recover.

The problem was what happened now, in the harsh light of morning. The thought turned my stomach into twisted, angry knots. I reminded myself that all we had to do today was go to Crag's Hollow and speak to Esme. I could tackle the war in my mind and heart once Mari was awake and able to tell me what to do.

"How much longer are you going to pretend to be asleep?"

I buried my face into his neck shamefully.

"I don't mind, except that I'm starting to think you're avoiding me." He said it with a playful lilt, but an edge of desperation had crept in.

"How long have you been up?" I asked into his warm skin.

"Awhile."

I angled my head up to meet his sparkling silver eyes and noticed the puffy bags underneath them. "Did you not sleep at all?"

"I had business to do early this morning. And last night I was a bit distracted," he said, brushing my hair from my face. I pressed my cheek into his hand like a needy kitten. I wanted to lick his whole body. To take a bite out of him. He was like a feast and I was starving. I wondered if he'd let me suck on his fingers—

"What are you thinking?" he asked, arching a brow and running a hand through his tousled morning hair. *Oh, Stones.* Not morning hair. I was already contending with a tan bare chest, jaw like granite, and large masculine hands. I could not handle morning hair, too.

I clenched my legs together. "I'm thinking about breakfast," I lied.

"Perhaps if you want to fuck breakfast, but I know your lusty eyes when I see them."

I felt my cheeks heat from shame. Not for wanting him—*needing* him—but rather that I had let him bring me to the brink of human pleasure and back last night, and hadn't done anything for him in return.

"Fine." I had come too far now to back down. "I was thinking of your wicked tongue."

That earned me a slight grin, but his eyes were lacking their usual intensity.

My heart fell. "Not the answer you wanted?"

"That's as good an answer as any man can hope for," he deflected. "But we should get going." He untangled me from his arms and stood from the bed, still in his breeches. He swept the room for his clothes. "I'm going to ask Griffin to stay here. It's where he'd rather be, I think."

I sat up and pulled the covers to my chest. Something was wrong. "You're a good friend," I said absently. My mind was racing. "He'll appreciate that."

Kane nodded. "Last night Briar told me Citrine is worried about Lazarus. Fedrik left for Shadowhold to meet with Lieutenant Eardley and get word to his parents. We'll be back by evening, and can meet him there, if you want."

"Fedrik left?"

Kane seemed to misunderstand whatever expression painted my face, and he cast his eyes down to thread the leather of his pant laces. "I'm sorry you missed him."

"Is that what this is about? I told you I'm not with him, Kane. We barely kissed one time."

Kane grimaced. "Gods, even still. I don't particularly want to hear about it."

"I don't feel that way about him. I never did, and I told him as much. He's just a friend."

"All right."

"So why are you not in this bed with me?" An attempt at sultry, but my voice came out petulant. I cringed.

When his eyes finally met mine, they crackled with intensity. "We have a lot to do today, and time is of the essence."

I should have just gotten up. What kind of sex-addled lunatic begs somebody to be with them? *Twice* if I were to count the way I threw myself at him last night. But the idea of Kane not wanting me at all anymore, after last night, was gut-wrenching.

Emboldened by the memories of Kane's hands wrapped around my thighs, I sat up on my knees and slipped the straps of my nightdress off my shoulders.

"Arwen," Kane warned, voice like ice but eyes as hot and rich as firelight.

"Kane," I challenged, pulling the silken fabric down until I was kneeling before him, bare save for my ripped undergarments.

He groaned softly at the sight of my naked breasts, gripping the boot in his hand so hard I heard the leather crack. Still, though, he said nothing. Did nothing.

*Fine, then.*

I hooked my fingers along the sides of the remaining fabric at my hips.

"Please don't do that," he gritted out.

But I had come too far now to back down. I wanted him to claim me. I slipped the undergarment off easily, ignoring the heat in my cheeks that mirrored his.

When he still said nothing, I flushed deeper. "You're really going to make me beg?"

"You know what seeing you like that does to me."

"What does it do?"

"Your body makes me see stars." He released a slow, tight breath. "When you're on display for me like that . . . The things I want to do to you. Unspeakable, Arwen. They're *unspeakable.*"

Heat gathered between my legs and I pinched them together. His eyes followed the movement and I whimpered. "Then do them."

But he only crossed the room to my discarded nightdress and

handed it to me. My cheeks went hot, and I pulled the dress over my head like I had been scolded.

"You needed comfort last night." He ran a hand through his waved hair. "I don't blame you for seeking release like that. I've done the same. Far too many times."

"That's not what—"

"But I made a mistake."

"A mistake?" My blood boiled with shame and hurt. "So you finally got between my legs and now you're bored?"

"No—what? Arwen—"

"What, then? Is this revenge? For everything after Siren's Bay? Kane." I took a breath to calm myself. I didn't want to fight with him anymore. "I never should have—"

"Arwen—"

"I know, I know. We have to leave. Maybe to you nothing matters more than getting this blade, beating your father, but to me—"

"You do," Kane interrupted, still holding his boot.

"I do what?"

"You matter more to me. More than revenge, redemption—anything. Don't you know I love you, Arwen?"

His words slipped out like an admission of guilt. All the emotion that had been welling inside me, creeping up my throat, ready to lash out at him, vanished like steam from a boiling pot.

"I'm in love with you." His laugh was rough and tired. "Desperately so. The way those sailors lost at sea love the bird that guides them home."

He pulled his shirt on, still unbuttoned, before sitting on the desk across from the bed. "I know your feelings for me aren't the same as they used to be, but it doesn't change anything for me. Nothing could."

On the verge of crying or laughing or pressing my lips to his, I sucked in a lungful of air.

"It was never my intention to burden you with this, but . . ." His voice was too quiet. "I just can't be that release for you. I hoped I could, but I think . . . I think it might actually kill me."

I merely nodded, all of a sudden feeling very fragile and confused.

So many nights back in the servants' quarters in Shadowhold, I had fallen asleep to imagined moments just like this one—Kane's declaration of love, riding off to that abstract cottage together . . .

But it had never been so raw, so painful.

I ached for both of us. For what we had put each other through.

I had tried to *use* Kane. I had—

I moved off the bed, searching the room for my silk robe, wishing I could disappear entirely. "I'm sorry," I muttered.

"Don't be, please," he said, standing. "Hey, that's the last thing I want. Last night was fun, right?"

I tried to grin, but nothing had ever felt so false. I wrapped the robe around my middle. "Of course, yeah."

"Good, then my work here is done." He gave me that knee-weakening half grin. "I'll meet you downstairs."

# 33

## ARWEN

K ANE AND I FLEW UNTIL WE REACHED THE WOODS surrounding Crag's Hollow and then made our way on foot into the gloomy coastal town. We walked down a cobblestone road that wove between rickety, lopsided buildings shrouded in mist until we passed an off-kilter lighthouse. I smelled the brine and salt before we rounded its faded bricks and caught a glimpse of the dock at the heart of the small fishing village.

Beyond the faded signs for boat rentals and tethered canoes and anchors stretched a washed-out platform that hung over a collapsed ancient, glacial lake. The dark water of Lake Stygian spread like an ink stain against the foggy sky above, and I could barely make out a humped landmass in the far distance, like a huge, slumped figure had fallen asleep in the water.

"What is that?"

"Hemlock Isle," Kane said.

"That's Hemlock Isle?"

Kane cocked his head. "Where did you think it was?"

"I don't know, actually." Niclas's mention of it was the first I'd heard of the place.

"The entire island serves as the largest and most treacherous prison in all of Evendell." Kane's voice was kind enough, but his eyes stayed trained on the milling sailors in the town ahead.

It had been slightly tense between us all day, but I was determined to alleviate the discomfort. "Is it unsafe to live here? Do escaped criminals make it to the dock by cover of night?"

"No, bird. Nobody escapes Hemlock Isle." He didn't smile, but the use of the familiar pet name was a good start. "The island is essentially a deep crater. It's impossible to climb in or out unless you can fly."

I surveyed the wet, windswept little town around us. Rocks and bluffs jutted out on either side of the street, most of the homes built into the dark stone cliffs or suspended high on stilts above the rough waters below. "So how do we find Esme?"

The houses and shops were weathered, splintered, and peeling paint—some even boarded up altogether. But the town wasn't impoverished or dirty, just a bit worn in. I didn't mind. The saline air was refreshing, and I sucked in a lungful, wrapping my fox fur around me tightly.

"We'll start at her shop, the Painted Lady. Are you cold?" Kane began to pull off his gloves.

"I'm fine. I like it."

We stepped to the side in unison as a spectacled man with a fish cart passed by us, a gaggle of children hot on his tail singing a nautical tune about seals that tired sailors mistook for mermaids.

"It's strange," I mused, "but I think I'm actually a little bit in love with this place."

Kane grinned slightly and his gaze fixed on a steep cliff to our right. The rugged stone hung over a small blue café with pale white shutters and a sign that read "Mariner's Pub." "I feel the same. I own that cottage up there."

I had missed a small, crooked house on top of the cliff. With a textured stone chimney, faded gray paint, and two lanterns hanging out front, it sat all alone beside a single plum tree.

"It's beautiful."

Kane chuckled and I looked over to him, catching the sparkle in his silver eyes despite the cloud cover. "I don't know about that, but it's got a pretty breathtaking view of the lake. On the rare cloud-free evening, it's the best sunset in all of Onyx. And right below, Mariner's Pub serves a mean fish and crisps. Quentin brews this cider in the winter with his daughters . . . Greta goes a little over-board with the rum, though." Kane's expression had turned grave. "I worry about her drinking, but she's just at that age."

I stilled. "How old?"

He shook his head. "Four."

A laugh slipped out of me as we continued up the street, brisk air at our faces, watching the lake as it swirled and churned in the distance.

"Esme's is right up this hill."

The road wound like a gray stone snake, dotted with swaying weeds and pussy willows, until it led to a tilted storefront. The shop's thatched roof was sloped downward on one side from years of sea-side wind, and the pin-striped canvas awning out front was so faded I couldn't tell what color it had once been.

We stomped up creaking steps and pushed inside, a copper chime ringing out our entry. The Painted Lady's name conjured images of a bright and colorful store laden with powdered rouge and fatty lipsticks, or fine oil paints and bristled brushes. But

Esme's store was dim and cold, with shelves and aisles barely lit by too few hanging lamps. Each cramped row was stuffed with dusty oddities like glass blown into obscure shapes I couldn't fathom a use for and tiny matchboxes with hand-drawn sketches of babies and dogs.

The store was empty save for a mousy little girl with shaggy hair, who, as soon as her eyes met mine, slipped behind the counter and down what must have been a hidden flight of stairs.

"Did you see that?" I asked Kane.

"See what?" He wiped at his face and coughed. "The cobweb I just swallowed? Clearly not."

I grinned up at him. We were handling the discomfort of the morning rather well. I was actually a bit proud of us.

*"I'm in love with you. Desperately so."*

I gulped at the intrusive memory of his words, feeling my face turn hot, and spun to inspect a miniature pewter toad.

"Esme?" Kane called out into the store. "Hello?"

The countertop and the cupboards behind it were as cluttered as the rest of the store, with rusty jewelry boxes spilling ribbons and tarot cards. Three hooks hung by the slatted, swinging doors, each with a different-sized, well-worn raincoat: one blue, one maroon, and one yellow. Below, three pairs of scuffed, matching boots.

A woman emerged from the hinged doors and greeted us with a bright smile as she tucked her hair back into a nautical scarf.

"Greetings, and welcome to the Painted Lady. May I offer you a tea leaf reading or a commune with the dead?"

"We're actually here on other business." I coughed on dust and swatted at the air. "Are you . . . ?" But the woman had spun her back to us, looking for something. With a nod, she adjusted a rusted tin pail on the floor with her shoe. It sloshed, and I peered upward until I spied a poorly patched hole in the ceiling. "Rain's coming tonight, I think," she said to us, like it was our little secret.

"Esme, I used to be a dear friend of your mother's. My name is Kane. Do you remember me?"

The smile that had been plastered across Esme's face faltered slightly, and she clasped her hands rigidly on the countertop. "Can't say that I do, sorry."

"I'd like to ask you something, if you have a moment."

Esme wrinkled her nose, waiting.

"Is it possible that you inherited some of your mother's abilities?"

The false smile only grew. "Unfortunately not. Anything else I can help with?"

"We have a high-ranking Amber official who tells us otherwise." Kane took a step toward the counter, leaning on it and sliding a casual hand into his pocket. "Now, why would that be?"

Esme's wide smile vanished, replaced by a curt, thin line. "He is mistaken."

"Esme," I tried. "We do not mean you any harm. We aren't with the Amber or Garnet armies." I glanced sidelong at Kane. "Kane is leading the only battle against them. Against Lazarus." I said his name so low it barely slid past my lips. "If you can help us find something from your mother's prophecy, it could give us a fighting chance."

"You're . . . King Ravenwood? Son of Lazarus?"

"The one and only."

"Please," I begged her, pressing myself against the countertop. "Any visions you may have had could help us."

Esme looked like she might cry. She bit her lip and leaned closer, until the three of us were nearly huddled.

"I wish I could help you both. Truly, I do." She turned to Kane. "If you are his son then you already know what Lazarus did to my mother, and that I was lucky to make it out of Lumera alive. But my father was fully mortal. I inherited some lighte, but not the ability to discern the will of the Gods."

"Why does Amber think otherwise?"

"They came here, months ago. Interrogated me, threatened my husband and our son. They didn't believe us when we told them I didn't have the skill. When I realized they wouldn't leave without *something*, I . . . I lied."

"You told them false prophecies?" I asked.

She dipped her chin, and her eyes spied the stairs behind the counter. "I didn't know what else to do. They took my husband. Told me never to share my visions with anyone else if I wanted to see him again." Her face hardened as she came to some conclusion. "I appreciate what you are trying to do, but I need you to leave now."

"What did you tell them?" I pressed.

Esme squirmed, eyes again darting toward the stairs behind her. "I can't risk sharing any more, I'm sorry. Please, just go."

"Of course," I said loudly. Kane's eyes shot to mine, but I ignored him. "We'll leave, then. If you change your mind, we'll be at Mariner's Pub until dark. I promise you, Esme, if you help us find what we need, we will free your husband and return him to you."

"I already told you," she said, brows knitting together. "I don't have the ability you seek."

"I know." I pushed from the counter, tugging Kane with me by the sleeve.

Once we were a good bit down the road, he whirled on me. "Mind clueing me in?"

"I think Esme has a daughter. I saw her right as we walked in."

"So?"

"*So* maybe her daughter is the one with the ability. She only has one kid. The raincoats, the boots . . . only three. For her, her husband, and their child. But she said she had a son, and the child I saw was a little girl."

Kane's brows furrowed, his eyes considering.

"Can't seers only be women?" I pushed. "Why else would she lie unless she didn't want anyone to know what her daughter could do?"

"Even if she had a daughter, and she lied to us about it . . . that girl would practically be a halfling. The likelihood that such a great deal of lighte skipped a generation . . ."

"Esme was definitely hiding something. She kept looking toward the basement, where I *saw* the girl run off. And no chance she's getting away with lying to Halden and his men. She'd get a 'vision' wrong eventually unless she had someone that was feeding them to her. That bit with the rain pail was a classic charlatan trick. They used to come to Abbington all the time and try to swindle our coin by predicting the leaves would fall."

Kane ran a hand across his mouth in thought. "So she creates the ruse to protect her child from Lazarus."

"Right. She saw what happened to her own mother, her husband . . . I don't blame her."

"What makes you so sure the little girl will come find us? It would be an awfully risky thing to do."

I looked back down at the town below us and the dark, inky water beyond the docks. Fish and salt and pine heavy in the afternoon air. "I'm not sure. But I have hope. It's what I'd like to think I would do. To get my family back, if they had been taken. And maybe to help the good side win. We'll have to see."

Kane chuckled beside me, our feet falling on the stone in seamless rhythm. "Bright-side bird. Should I call you that?"

"Too wordy. I like my nickname as it is."

"You do? Well, that's no fun, now, is it? Shall I call you something else? 'Mongoose' doesn't quite have the same ring to it . . ."

I laughed despite myself. "You're ridiculous."

"Only for you."

When I peered up at him, he was fighting off a grin of his own. My eyes widened, shocked that the very earth below us hadn't crumbled and broken apart or the sea hadn't swallowed us whole. Kane and I were getting along. And not fighting. And not sleeping together.

I sighed, deep and even, and faced back toward the town.

Kane's voice was a little like velvet as he said, "Are you ready to drink until dark?"

I rolled my eyes. "Is that all there is to do to pass the time here?"

He lifted a single brow.

I felt a shiver kiss up my spine. "Yes, let's drink."

# 34

~~~

## KANE

ARWEN HAD A SULTRY, CURVED LOCK OF HAIR HANGING in front of her face as she sipped her ale. It was silky smooth and shiny in the flickering lanterns of the tavern. I wanted very badly to tuck the chocolate strand behind her ear. So badly, it was making my palms sweat.

What kind of masochist tells the woman he loves that he's in love with her, knowing full well she doesn't feel the same? Perhaps the same idiot masochist who makes her come with his tongue and then swears never to do it again. Both reckless choices had turned merely being around Arwen into torture.

And now I was sweating over a lock of hair.

Arwen raised a brow at me. "Are you all right?"

"Just fine." I downed the rest of my drink. "Can we get another round?"

The barmaid was a slim woman with a chest too large for her frame. She replaced our empty mugs with fresh, overflowing ones and flashed us a bright smile. I took in the tavern around us, growing busier as the light bled from the sky.

"Are you even thirsty, or do you just like when the pretty server fawns over you?"

"Careful, bird, your talons are showing."

"Am I wrong?"

I put down my ale and appraised her. "You're a very jealous woman, do you know that?"

"That's rude."

"Am I wrong?" I mimicked.

Arwen blew out a breath. "No, I guess not. It's kind of horrible, isn't it?"

"For you, perhaps. Envy is the poison we feed ourselves."

She took a sip of her ale and wiped her mouth with the back of her hand. "I spent a long time feeling less than. And lonely . . . It's my default now, to assume nobody will pick me first. That you'll find other women prettier, that—"

"Mari would rather befriend Ryder?"

"I'm going to work on it." She grimaced. "I think I actually might owe Amelia an apology."

"If it helps, I have eyes for none but you."

It was true, and despite the pain, there was potent relief in being honest with her. I took another swallow of the frothy spirit. When Arwen said nothing, I couldn't help but add, "You, on the other hand, seem to have eyes for many royal men. Is that a power thing?"

Her pinched little nose was going to be the death of me. Why did I love to torment her so?

"You are truly insufferable," she snipped, amusement in her eyes. "It's a wonder anyone puts up with you at all."

"I'm not sure anyone does."

We had been seated at a sticky table with one short leg that made for an irritating wobble, and when I placed my forearm against its surface, I accidentally sent our full mugs of ale sloshing.

"You and I especially," she said, stabilizing the table with both hands while I wiped up the spilled ale, "seem to fight like school-children."

"Do you remember Lady Kleio and Sir Phylip?" I asked, throwing the ale-covered napkins into the barrel behind her as she ducked.

"Yes, they're two of your nobles. They hate each other."

"They're married."

Arwen's eyes lit. "You're kidding me."

"Will be twenty years this winter."

"They can't be happy, though. They tore each other to bits in that forum."

"They challenge each other. They're rather sweet together, actually."

Arwen glanced out the foggy window behind her. The cloud cover was so thick outside it was hard to tell what time it was, but I knew we had been here at least four hours.

"Arwen—"

"I'm not giving up on her."

I swallowed a sigh, her determination as impressive as it was frustrating. "Bird, you don't even know the girl."

Arwen maneuvered to peer out a different window, the one to my right. "You can fly back to Shadowhold. I'll find my own way there later tonight. Maybe I'll hitchhike."

"You're hilarious," I said dryly.

"Let's get one last round from your cute friend and give Esme's daughter another hour. Then we'll go." She trained her eyes on mine with sincerity. "Please? I have a feeling about this."

"Sure." I wasn't in a rush to leave, really. I had everything that mattered to me right here in this tavern.

"Want to play roses and thorns?"

I nearly spat my drink out. "Isn't that a sex game?"

The look of horror on Arwen's face was worth all the coin in my kingdom. "No! What is wrong with you? It's a children's game." She shook her head. "Bleeding Stones, Kane."

I laughed hard into my mug. "All right, teach me this children's game."

She tucked her hair behind her ears, finally moving the rebellious strand from its spot against her cheek. "Your rose is the best part of your day, and your thorn is the worst. My mother used to do this with us each night at dinner when I was growing up." A flicker of sorrow danced across her face, there and gone in an instant. "I'll go first so you can see how it's done. My rose was coming here, to Crag's Hollow. I love the sea air, the gloomy sky, the bustling town. I'm grateful I got to see it."

Her love for my favorite town in Evendell made something soft and gentle swirl in my heart.

"And my thorn—" Arwen sighed. "Almost everything else in my life, if I'm being honest."

I narrowed my eyes at her. "Fun game."

"It's not usually this depressing." She looked to both windows once more. Still no sign of the little seer.

"My turn?"

Arwen nodded.

"My rose is getting to spend an entire afternoon in here with you."

Arwen's eyes grew brighter, and it was enough to make my honesty well worth it.

"And my thorn," I said with a wicked smile, "is that I didn't—"

But her expression lit with surprise at something behind me, and I turned in the direction of her eyeline. There, a tiny brunette girl, nearly skin and bones, was pushing her way through the boisterous crowd. She was the spitting image of her mother, that same warm, brown hair—hers shorn to look more boyish—huge dark eyes, and pointed, dainty chin. She couldn't have been more than seven.

Arwen leapt from our table, sending it wobbling once more and nearly knocking our empty mugs to the floor. I narrowly righted the table in time before strolling after her.

"Hello," Arwen said to the girl brightly. "You must be Esme's daughter. I'm Arwen, and this is Kane."

"You're just as you look in my visions," the girl said.

A chill broke out along my spine. Arwen faltered for words but the girl only stood there, jostled by patrons, eyes full and solid and unwavering. The pub was growing livelier as the evening settled in, and I could barely hear my own thoughts. "Here, follow me."

Arwen offered a hand, but the girl didn't take it, choosing instead to trail us out of the tavern and onto the cobblestone streets. I led them around the corner into a narrow alleyway wedged between a fish market laden with tentacles and scales in crates of crushed ice, and a candy shop with rows of bright green apples dipped in butterscotch.

Arwen leaned down to meet the girl's eyeline. "What's your name?"

"Beth."

"How did you know to come find us, Beth?"

"I overheard you. In my mother's shop."

"You're very bright," Arwen said with a wry smile.

"You were loud." Her voice was ice-cold. Devoid of any emotion. Likely thanks to years of seeing things far beyond what she should—moments she had never and would never live—love and death and loss.

"I know what you seek," Beth continued. "But I don't know where the blade is. My visions of it are too fleeting."

I had lost faith in vague leads such as these a long while ago, but Arwen straightened beside me and grasped my wrist tightly. "We'll take anything you can give us."

Beth, showing her age for the first time, fisted her hands in her trousers and cast her eyes down to the gray stone beneath us. A briny wind carried over the scent of fish from the shop next door. "The blade has been in Onyx all along. It never left."

"That's not possible," I said, not unkindly. "It was stolen from my vault five years ago. The entire keep—the entire kingdom was searched."

Beth shook her head with vehemence, those dark, haunting eyes still downcast. "I'm never wrong. Even when I want to be."

Arwen swallowed hard and straightened to stand beside me. It seemed at once we both suffered the realization that the seer's gift had been more of a curse on the young girl.

"The Blade of the Sun is in Onyx. I have visions of it, thrown beneath heaps of other weapons. Tied to another master, but yearning to be paired with its mate." She turned to face Arwen. "You."

The color had seeped from Arwen's face, leaving her even paler than usual. "What do you know of me?"

"You are the final Fae of full blood born at last. As my nana said you would be. Daughter of the Gods."

Daughter of the *what*?

"What does that mean?" Arwen pleaded, crouching down to the young girl's eyeline once more.

"You don't know?" Beth's depthless eyes met mine.

"Neither of us do. Can you share?"

She opened her mouth, but must've thought better of it and instead took a step back. "What about my father?"

"We'll find him for you, I promise," Arwen swore to her. I fought against my tensing muscles. The man was likely dead. It was a daring oath to make.

"The king beside you thinks he is dead."

I bit my tongue. "A seer and a mind reader. Quite a lot of lighte you've got there, Beth."

"It's why my mom keeps me hidden. The world is not safe for Fae like me."

She was right. Not as long as Lazarus harvested lighte like wheat in a field. "Then why trust us?"

Arwen shot me a devastating glare, and I shrugged at her.

"I know what you fight for."

"We will do our best to find your father, and if he is alive, we will return him to you and your mother," Arwen said. "If I can find the blade, I will kill Lazarus. I will fight to give you a world in which you do not have to hide."

"You will die," Beth said, devoid of emotion, and I tried to ignore the way three words from the mouth of a seven-year-old nearly brought me to my knees.

Arwen, to her credit, kept her voice even. "I know."

Beth turned to face Lake Stygian. The sun had disappeared behind Hemlock Isle in the distance, and the night had become chilling and forlorn.

"The story your mother told you was true. She met your father in a tavern, and they spent the night together. He left the next morning and she never saw him again."

"So she *was* my mother? How is that possible? Was she a full-blooded Fae, too?"

"No. She was mortal. Carrying a full-blooded Fae to term in her womb made her ill. She should have died, from the lighte that poisoned her. But your abilities healed her over and over again. Eventually, she grew immune, and the months of holding a powerful being inside her took their toll."

"You're saying I—killed my own mother?"

Beth, not one for sympathy, only nodded. "But she knew what you were. Your father told her the truth."

Arwen stalled, unable to find words to respond.

"And what was that?" I asked, words forming around my own shock. We needed to wrap this up before Arwen's shattered heart took some final blow it couldn't withstand.

Beth brought her chin up to face me. "That he was a Fae God. And he would father the final full-blooded Fae. A chosen one, a prophesied savior of Fae and mortal alike. And that it was unlikely she would survive the pregnancy."

"But she did," Arwen said. Not a question. "She survived."

"You healed her."

Arwen shook her head. "And then she *lived*. Even after I couldn't heal her anymore."

"Yes," Beth said, face almost careless.

Arwen's brows pinched together, and her voice broke as she asked, *"Why?"*

It could have killed me, to hear so much pain in her voice. I reached for her, but she was fragile, her emotions too precarious—later. I'd try somehow to soothe her later. I flexed my fingers and folded them into my pocket.

"I can only tell you what happened, or what will happen. Not why."

"Perhaps it was her love for her children," I supplied.

"That was what her stepfather thought, too."

Arwen's eyes shot from the ground up to Beth. "Powell knew? He knew what I was?"

"Your mother told him everything."

The beatings. Arwen had wondered why he hated her. Now we both knew. He thought she was killing the woman he loved. It was awful. It was *unfathomable*. It was—

"Thank you, Beth," I said, breathing evenly. "Can you tell us one last thing?"

Beth looked back up to the winding road that led up to her mother's shop. "I don't want my mother to come looking for me."

"Quickly, then. Is there any other way to kill Lazarus? Is Arwen truly the only one who can defeat him?"

"I don't know all that is to come. I only see bits and pieces. I have seen the way of the Crow, if that's what you're asking. It's possible, but the cost will be greater to her than her own life."

The pit in my stomach expanded with the weight of the girl's words. What could cost Arwen more than her very life? The thought terrified me.

"Is there anything else you can tell us about the blade? About where it is in Onyx? About our battle with Lazarus?"

"You must defeat him. You are the only hope either realm has."

"Yes." I gritted my teeth. "That I know."

I waited for Arwen's reprimand of my tone, but it never came. She was looking off toward the lake, and I knew then.

I knew that I had lost her.

It might've been the clamor of my chest caving in on itself that rang in my ears. "Beth, what is your father's name? What does he look like? We'll do our best to bring him back to you."

For the first time the girl's eyes lit up as she said, "Vaughn. He has dark brown hair that reaches his shoulders, and a beard. I haven't had a vision of him since they took him weeks ago. If I do, should I write a letter to you?"

"Yes, address it to Lieutenant Eardley at Shadowhold. Thank you for all your help."

She turned to leave and made it halfway up the slick road before spinning back to us, horror clouding her youthful eyes.

A chill rippled through me.

"What is it?" Arwen managed to say.

"You'll . . . you'll have to make the deal. When the time comes, you'll have to."

"What deal?" I asked.

Beth stiffened. "I don't know. I only get pieces . . ."

All I could think to say was "Please."

"Her face will be wet with tears," Beth said, motioning to Arwen. "And your hands . . . they will be coated in blood."

The storm had moved in, and though the buildings beside us offered some cover, rain had begun to drench us both. Before I could say more, Beth ran back up the hill to her mother's store, and we watched until her silhouette disappeared into the mist.

# 35

## ARWEN

RAIN HAD STARTED AT SOME POINT I COULDN'T RECALL, and my nose and eyelashes were now misted with cool, wet drops. I fell to my knees against uneven cobblestone.

"Arwen." Kane's voice was rough.

The deluge blurred my vision.

That and the guilt. More guilt than I knew what to do with. And shock at Beth's words.

Pure shock.

My hands gripped the cool rock beneath me to steady myself, and my nails scraped against wet, unmoving stone. I wasn't sure what I was clawing at.

"Arwen," Kane said again, crouching down on one knee, the puddled rainwater leeching into his nice pants. I could feel him beside me. His warmth radiating toward my body. Could see the white of his shirt billowing in the static wind.

But he wasn't touching me.

I had murdered—*murdered*—hundreds of Fae soldiers, Mari

was in some kind of magic-induced coma because I hadn't listened to her, Fedrik had nearly lost his leg trying to save me, and now—

I had poisoned my own *mother*. For twenty years, I had made her sick. Brought her to the brink of death. I had practically killed her—

Or, had I caused that, too? She never would have been in Peridot in the first place had I not asked Kane to bring her to me.

I was a healer, and all I had done was harm people.

And my . . . father. A god. A Fae god.

A gruesome laugh slipped from my lips.

"Can you stand, bird?"

I sucked in a lungful of air until my chest grew cold, and it did nothing at all to steady me. My power, my lighte itched and twisted at my fingertips—fueled by guilt and grief, building inside me, ratcheting up my neck and down the backs of my legs and into my ankles and toes.

I tried to stand, and made it halfway up before a dizzy rush forced my arm against the wet exterior of the sweetshop to hold me upright.

"Arwen."

I whirled my eyes to Kane and could only make out the thin trail of a raindrop dripping down his nose. My vision was tunneling.

"Take a deep breath for me?"

The wind was shallow in my lungs. I shut my eyes against the storm and Beth's words and all the pain and all the agonizing power, and willed the cool droplets to soothe the burning in my heart.

"Let's get you home," Kane said.

"I don't have a home."

"Don't get self-pitying on me now, bird. Shadowhold will always be your home."

"It's everyone else I pity. Everyone who's unfortunate enough to grow close to me."

His broad hands grasped my shoulders—so gentle, and yet with enough firmness to drag my eyes upward. "You were a *fetus*. You didn't sicken her on purpose. Your mother loved you, Arwen. She knew what you were, and what carrying you would do to her, and still, she loved you more than anything."

I let out a quiet, bitter laugh. "And look what good it did her."

He pulled me out into the street, where we were met by a disorienting downpour. The wind howled angrily against the cliffs and the merchants' carts around us swayed with the force of the storm. Townspeople were seeking shelter under awnings and crowding into taverns and shops. The angry, rippling lake loomed behind a dock that had all but emptied out, its water thrashing at the half-sunken, driftwood stilts.

"Can you fly in this?" I asked him, my voice lost in the gusting wind.

"I can, but it won't be pleasant for either of us." He squinted up through the rain at the narrow clock tower in the distance, water plastering his dark hair to his forehead and dripping into his eyes. His shirt was soaked. "It's late. We should stay here for the night. Come on."

Kane dragged me through the storm, around carts and boats and scraggly trees with no leaves. The wind chilled my bones through my cloak, but I didn't mind. Sorrow, despair—both had been replaced by a dull headache that made me feel more tired than anything.

Finally, we arrived at the cornflower-blue door of Kane's seaside cottage.

Using a single wisp of obsidian lighte, he opened the home to us and we slipped inside.

Deafening silence enveloped me.

It was dark and icy cold—clearly no one had been here for months. I stood awkwardly, shivering and dripping on the rich hardwood floor.

"I'll just be a moment. Make yourself comfortable." He crossed the room to a round, rustic table, and slung his sword and scabbard off, dropping them atop it beside a small vase that held two wilted orchids, completely dried up and nearly paper-thin.

Pulling his coat and gloves off, he dropped them as well before moving to the iron fireplace. A single match and few logs formed a small but mighty fire, flames blossoming like flowers from the kindling.

Kane motioned for me to sit in front of the hearth as he slipped into the dark kitchen. I heard him rummaging before he came back with a kettle and placed it atop the flames. Then, with one match, he lit all the lanterns in the home and a few dark, dusty candles as well.

Amid the newfound glow, I assessed the cottage in earnest.

It wasn't unlike Kane's bedroom in Shadowhold: masculine, dark, a little cluttered, surprisingly warm and cozy. The bay windows overlooking the lake were as exquisite as he had told me earlier. Soft linen curtains framed them with care, and a low, cushioned bench jutted out from underneath the glass, making for a nook one could sit in and peer out into the abyss from for hours.

"Arwen?"

"Yes?" My voice didn't sound like my own.

"Do you want to come sit down?"

"Sure."

A pause, and then, "You aren't moving, though."

I tried to remember why it was worth doing anything. Worth sitting down, getting warm. I was suddenly sure, with complete confidence, that nothing mattered at all.

When I laughed, Kane's brows pinched together.

Crossing the room to me, Kane unlaced my cloak from my neck, his cold, wet knuckles grazing the sensitive skin at the base of my throat. He pulled it off me cautiously and took my frozen hands in his.

"Can you come take a seat over here with me?" The gentleness in his voice made me itch. I didn't like when he was like this. Soft and kind and pliable. It meant he was worried about me. That something was wrong.

And it was true. Everything was wrong.

"I'm fine," I said, and walked stiffly over to the white couch with its sea-hued pillows and thick, knitted blanket. I sat down in front of the now roaring fire and tucked the blanket around me like a shield.

"You're still shivering," he said, sitting down beside me, the cushions sagging under his weight.

"And you're dripping on your own couch."

Kane looked down at his soaking shirt, wet strands of hair hanging over his brow.

"So I am," he said, and stood, slipping his white shirt off over his head in one fell swoop. His golden skin glowed in the dim firelight, a sheen of rain still coating his lean, muscled torso. Kane walked behind me, into another room, and came out a few moments later in a dry black shirt and soft linen pants as dark as the sky outside. He strode back into the sage-tiled kitchen—much too small for his rippling shoulders and considerable frame—and dug through the cupboards before he found some loose tea and two mugs.

"Here," he said, once he had poured the boiling water into both of them and handed me one. "It'll warm you up."

The warmth from the mug seeped into my chilled hands as promised, and I brought the ceramic to my lips, letting the steam tickle my nose. Jasmine and chamomile. Maybe a bit of vanilla . . . I sipped, willing the tea to mend whatever was shredded inside of me.

Kane sat and watched me until I set the mug down on the low antique table in front of us.

"I was what made my mother ill. All those years, trying so hard to heal her." My stomach turned. "She was only sick because she had me."

"You didn't know, bird. There was nothing you could have done differently."

"I understand that, but . . . I also killed all those men. On the beach—"

"Men who had slaughtered an entire capital. Men who were there to *kill you*."

I shook my head. He didn't get it. "Maybe Powell was right all along. To hate me. To beat me. I was the reason his wife was suffering."

Kane's face was calm, but something solemn simmered behind those eyes.

"I want to tell you a story," he said, placing his mug on the table.

When he didn't continue, I nodded once, kicking off my shoes and tucking my knees underneath me.

"I was about the Fae equivalent of eighteen when I decided to overthrow my father. My older brother, Yale, was the first person I told of my plan. Years earlier, the seer had told our family of the prophecy. My father had hunted every day for the last full-blooded Fae after that. Had his spies and sentries look through every village, every home in Lumera. But the Fae was nowhere to be found." He paused, his eyes lifting to mine. "So I told my older brother it was time we did something. Before he found this Fae girl, had her killed, and lived forever, slowly draining our realm of lighte, building up his wall, forcing our people into slavery.

"It wasn't right, the way he ruled. Not just for the people, but for the realm itself. Our seas were running dry, our green fields shriveling into land so barren it cracked. My brother and I knew what the prophecy said. That only the last full-blooded Fae could kill him, but I thought prophecies had loopholes, and semantics that could be worked around. I had the Blade of the Sun—it was a prized possession of my father's, and he kept it in his throne room beside his crown—and I had . . ." He looked down at his hands ruefully. "A lot of passion. I was young, angry, ready to fight—I wanted to do something worthwhile to help my people.

"So I went to every powerful person I thought I could convince to join me. Briar and her husband, Perry, took little convincing. Griffin was even easier, of course. Dagan was our kingsguard and the best swordsman I knew. He was the only mortal that fought beside us. With the help of the very seer who spelled my father's fate, I even convinced Aleksander Hale to join us, the leader of a peculiarly savage race of Fae called Hemolichs. There were others, too. Nobles, spies, generals."

"How?" I asked. "How did you convince them all to risk everything?"

His answering laugh was bitter. "Sheer will and a deep well of rage. I think they knew I was going to do something with or without them. Some of them probably joined out of fear. Others out of the same naive hope I had. Hope for change."

I gave a shallow nod and brought the steaming mug to my lips, the room suddenly chilly again despite the roaring hearth.

"I went back to Yale months later with my plan. We had everything we needed, but I wouldn't do it without him. I couldn't. He was my older brother, my closest friend." Kane sighed. "I worshipped him."

My heart might have been bleeding. "What was he like?"

"Brilliant. Funny. Agreeable. He hated conflict and never had a cross word to say about anyone. He was stronger than me," Kane admitted with no shame or arrogance. "And calmer. I had always been ruled by my emotions. They often say the dragon child is controlled by whatever is in their heart."

"That's what your father called you that day at Siren's Bay. 'The dragon child.'"

"He used to say we were the same. The only two dragon-shifting Fae in our family. In all the realms, now. Every time he says it, it makes me sick," Kane said, staring up at the ceiling.

"What did your brother say when you went back to him?"

Kane laughed, bleak and unfeeling. "'You're going to get us all killed.'" He finally turned to face me, eyes piercing. "And he was right. As always. It was exactly what happened."

I knew how the story ended, but still, his words pulled the air from my lungs.

"Aleksander turned on us. Told my father everything in return for freedom for his people, enslaved as one of my father's many armies. I, too, had promised them freedom, but we were the riskier bet. So my father knew we were coming." Kane's voice had grown quiet. "I only landed one single blow on him with the blade. Down his back, along his spine. In that moment, harnessing the Blade of the Sun, I thought I had vanquished the greatest evil to ever live. But all he did was laugh."

Lazarus and his punishing gray eyes, knowing in that moment he had won. As horrible an image as any I could fathom.

"He said it was the only chance I would ever get, and that I had failed. And then, he annihilated us. Days later we were brought out to the gallows to watch those we loved executed in front of his entire court."

I couldn't stop my sharp intake of breath. My trembling legs. I didn't want to hear any more. I didn't want—

"Dagan's wife and infant child, Griffin's parents—his father was Lazarus's own general. Briar's husband. Each of them, hanged one by one. I can still hear the creak of the wood beneath their feet as they walked . . . The snaps of their necks. I dream of it nearly every night.

"It was a vicious show of power and mercilessness. He made sure every single Fae and mortal in the realm knew never to cross him again," Kane said, his hands shaking. "And then he brought up my mother."

My stomach sank so quickly I was sure I would vomit. I gripped my mug until my fingertips grew white.

"His own wife, Arwen, his own queen." Kane's eyes were shining. "He had her killed because he knew it would devastate me and Yale more than it could ever hurt him. I can still remember the look of shock on her face. They hadn't had a happy marriage by any means, but still. She had never seen it coming.

"Before I could move a single muscle, Yale . . . He tried to save her. Got about four feet before my father took him out himself. He killed him instantly. A spear of ice to the base of his skull.

"They hanged her moments later, while she was still weeping over her son's body. I lost them both. Because of my stupid, fearless righteousness." He wiped brusquely at his eyes before taking another sip of his tea. The rain continued to slam against the cottage roof.

Hot tears coated my cheeks. "Kane, I . . ."

"My biggest regret isn't trying to overthrow him. It isn't even that I failed. It's that I didn't die protecting them."

"How can you say that? They *chose* to fight beside you."

"That's why it should only have been me up there," he bit out. "They died because of my failure. I have to live with that, every day."

He leaned back and released a long, slow breath. "After, my father assumed we would be so scarred, so beaten into submission that we would return to our rightful places in his court. He even offered Griffin his father's post as general.

"Some considered that generous. Many felt it was better to be with Lazarus and alive than against him and dead. Or worse. But we couldn't stay another minute in Lumera under his rule. So Griffin and I fled to Evendell, with as many in tow as we could manage."

Kane was quiet a moment, before adding, "I spent the next fifty years blaming myself for what happened—hating myself because of it. There was no end in sight to my self-loathing, to my need for revenge—it was the only thing that could justify their sacrifice. Could make my life worth living. It was all that mattered to me." His eyes lifted to mine with a look I had never seen in them before. "Until I met you."

Too many emotions were welling up inside of me. Ones I had been fighting to keep buried for weeks and weeks—

"You are not to blame for your mother's suffering, Arwen. You are pure good, pure light. I'm sure that's why your mother lived as long as she did. Not in spite of you, but *because* of you."

More tears ran down my cheeks, swift and heavy. "I'm so very sorry," I whispered. "I can't even imagine—"

"We all have to live with our choices. But you didn't make any to hurt the ones you love. These things happened *to* you, Arwen." He took the mug from my stiff hands and placed it on the table with his own, before threading my fingers through his. "You are not to blame. For any of this. You have to forgive yourself."

I wanted to say *I'll try*, but all I could manage was a nod.

He sighed once, releasing my fingers, and drew his hand across his still-wet eyes. "And I'll always be here for you, to help."

And I don't know if it was the pain—the raw vulnerability in his voice—or the revelations of the day, or the brutal past week, or simply the rhythmic pounding of rain against glass and stone, but a surge of emotion I had been stifling down, pressing into the farthest, most buried recesses of my very soul came barreling out with the force of a tidal wave.

"But I won't," I whispered. "I won't be here."

My chest and neck felt hot and sticky, and I realized I was well and truly crying. "I don't want this," I admitted through the tears, the truth spilling from my lips after all this time. "I never wanted to sacrifice myself. I want to end Lazarus, I swear that I do. I want to save all the suffering people, kill him for what he did to you, and Dagan, and Griffin, but . . ." The words were barreling out too fast to catch, to cram back inside. "I want a chance at a real life, too. I want to watch Leigh grow up, to have a family of my own, maybe.

There's too much I've never seen, too much I'll never do. And I'm so scared . . . of what it will feel like. If there will be anything after. Of how much it will hurt." I choked on the word. The pain I imagined would devour me as the life was drained from my heart.

"I don't want to be the full-blooded Fae. I don't want to save the realms. I don't want to be brave." All the thoughts that I had buried so deep within myself were finally free. It was the most agonizing relief I had ever felt. "I don't want to die, Kane."

"I know," he said. "I know you don't."

He wrapped me in his arms and I wept into his chest. I cried for my short, lonely life, which was going to be snuffed out right when I might have finally found the things worth living for. I cried for Leigh and Ryder losing another family member. For Mari. For Dagan.

And I cried for Kane. For the horrendous things he had seen. For those he had lost. His guilt, his suffering. His mother. His brother. His too-large, passionate heart that only ever meant to do good. And for the fact that even if I succeeded in killing his greatest enemy, Lazarus would still win. He'd still take someone else Kane loved with him when he went.

I cried and cried and cried—fat ugly tears, deep heaving sobs. I couldn't breathe. I didn't want to. I wanted to suffocate in my grief and leave the weight of the world on someone else's shoulders. And all the while, Kane held me, rubbing slow circles into my back. Tucking my hair away from my wet face. Murmuring soothing words against the top of my head.

Until finally, there was nothing left to expel.

No more grief. No more truths. No more tears.

I was free.

# 36

ARWEN

I PEELED MY FACE FROM KANE'S NOW SOGGY SHIRT AND looked up at him.

"Feel a bit better?"

I sighed in affirmation, long and heavy.

"Accepting this fate with ease, estranging yourself from everyone to spare them the pain of losing you . . . It's been killing you, Arwen. It's the antithesis of who you are. You are hope incarnate."

Despite everything, my blood sang at his words. "I didn't want to be that weak, vulnerable little girl anymore. The person I was when we first met—I couldn't to go back to that."

"You told me once that emotions aren't weaknesses. Take some of your own advice. Admitting you don't want to die isn't cowardice. In fact, it's the opposite."

It reminded me of something Dagan had said months ago. *"There is only true courage in facing what frightens you."* And in Azurine, how vulnerability was what made us human. Gave us something to fight for.

Kane's expression was softer than I'd ever seen it. He wiped the tears away from under my eyes but didn't release my face. Instead, he brushed his calloused thumb over my cheek with such gentleness my face began to heat.

"We will find a way out of this," he murmured.

There was no other way. Not if we wanted to conquer Lazarus, and we both knew it. I opened my mouth to protest, but he continued.

"I told you I used to dream each night of their deaths. Now, I dream of something else, too. I dream of losing you to him the same way. I wake up dripping sweat, heart pounding through my chest, sheets torn around me with your name still lodged in my throat."

I stilled at his words.

"I said it before, on the ship to Citrine all those weeks ago—I will not let anything happen to you. Nothing, not even the good of all the realms combined, is worth the loss of *you*. We will find another way."

I stared at Kane—his still-wet cheeks, his simmering silver eyes lit with nothing but adamant, unbending will. Such determination, and still so calm, so assured . . .

"I want to believe you, but I'm so, so scared to have hope."

He released my face. "I'll do it with you."

Then he rose and took both our mugs to the kitchen.

I stood on wobbly legs, blanket still draped around me, and gazed out at the bay windows that overlooked the staggering lake. The black water churned in the storm that had yet to yield, and I wrapped the thick wool tighter around my body.

I felt Kane's presence behind me as we watched the rain splatter the glass.

"Will it lose its potency if I give you the same speech?" I turned to face him, remembering once again how thoroughly he towered over me. "That you are not to blame for the loss of your mother and brother? For any of them? They chose to fight beside you for a cause they believed in. Their deaths are solely on Lazarus's conscience."

Kane's gaze lingered on the tortured waves behind me. "I think I know that now. It's the things I've done since . . . what my revenge has driven me to . . . that I'm not sure I can recover from."

"You can. You have."

Kane's eyes dropped to mine, pupils flaring. "I planned to use you. To murder my father. Knowing it would . . ."

"We were different people then."

"I'll regret it as long as I live."

I didn't have it in me to argue with him. So I only said, "I'm so tired."

"Let's get you to bed."

Kane took my hand in his and led me past the living room and through a narrow hallway adorned with paintings and candles and leathery books before opening the door at the end.

His bedroom was decorated similarly to the rest of the cottage. Rich and intimate, comfortable, soft. Dark wooden beams crossed the lofted pale ceiling, white and cream candles peppered the space. A simple milky-white bed with a carved driftwood headboard was piled high with too many fluffed pillows. Two glass-encased oil lamps had been placed on either wicker bedside table, and a warm, woven blue rug flattened beneath my toes.

While I ogled his private room with little dignity, Kane lit one glass oil lamp and opened a broad walnut wardrobe to pull out a cotton shirt that matched his eyes. He held it toward me. "You can sleep in this if you'd like."

A bookcase stuffed with crinkling spines and tattered pages stood in one corner beside large windows that looked out upon the obsidian lake. Beneath them sat a chaise with a worn gray pillow and a thick fur slung across it. An ideal spot for reading and watching the boats and waves below. There was a hearth in here, too, and Kane retrieved two logs from a seagrass basket and crouched to light another warming, crackling fire.

The rain pattered against the shingled roof. When the hearth was good and roaring, he stood, and we stared at each other, the single oil lamp dancing shadows across both of our faces. Close enough to touch, neither of us moving to do so.

The mere inches between us twitched and quivered with energy.

"I'm going to sleep on the couch, out there," he said, while at the same time, I said, "Will you stay with me?"

I swallowed awkwardly. "Never mind." I balled the shirt up in my hands and looked anywhere but his eyes.

"Sure," he said, before raising a hand overhead, grasping his shirt from the back of his neck and yanking it off in one fluid movement to reveal his toned chest. He crawled into the side of the bed without the lit lamp and turned his eyes away.

I knew he wouldn't look, but for some reason, my heart raced as I dropped the thick blanket to the floor and lifted my flowing blouse up and over my head. I shimmied from my leather pants, placing them on the chaise and leaving me standing in my undergarments.

Blood pumping wildly in my veins, I tucked my hands behind my back, along my spine, to unclasp the shallow bodice, lifted it off my body, and threw on the gray shirt before crawling into the other side of the bed and snuffing out the oil lamp.

The sheets were cool and thick but warmed by Kane's body heat across from me. I turned to face the window, rain still dribbling down in rivulets, and the mattress shifted as Kane positioned a pillow to his comfort.

We lay in silence save for the storm and that crackling hearth, which emitted a soft glow and a bleary warmth through the room.

"Comfortable?" Kane asked quietly.

"Yes. You?"

"Mhm."

"You don't have to stay in here with me."

"I'd never leave you alone, bird."

*"Don't you know I love you, Arwen?"*

Tears I couldn't quite explain pricked at my eyes, and I hoped he couldn't hear them slip down my cheeks.

# 37

## ARWEN

I WOKE UP FEELING MORE LIKE MYSELF THAN I HAD IN A long, long while.

The stark daylight seeping in through the windows of Kane's bedroom was so bright it took my eyes a minute to adjust. But when they did, I could see the clear haze of morning fog over Lake Stygian. Sparkling, black as night, and tempestuous as ever, but somehow more striking, clearer than it had been yesterday before the rain. The lake stretched on and on seemingly forever, only interrupted by the jutting, ashy stone cliffs that surrounded it, and that one imposing mountainous shape of Hemlock Isle that sprouted from its center.

I rolled out of the absurdly comfortable bed—a bed fit for a king, something I forgot Kane was from time to time—and a resounding *pop* snapped my eyes over to the fireplace. It was alight with heavy logs, roaring and crackling. Kane must have made a fresh fire this morning while I slept.

He had been . . . more than kind, more than patient with me last night. Had held my hand through such enormous revelations. One after another after another.

My mother, my role in her illness . . . My father, a being I hadn't even understood conceptually until mere days ago, let alone knew existed.

The enormity of my parentage made me feel small and powerless, so I pushed it from my mind for the time being and searched the room for my clothes. They weren't on the chaise where I had left them last night, but in their place was a folded blue dress with cap sleeves and scalloped collar and . . . a pair of new, clean leather boots.

My heart swelled.

I took the gifts and changed swiftly, folding Kane's shirt and placing it on top of the down duvet.

Then, either out of gratitude or stalling, I made his bed, folding the sheets back and fluffing the pillows. And then I combed my hair with my fingers in the mirror for another ten minutes at least to look less like a crazed banshee.

I was definitely stalling.

I steeled myself and opened the door.

It was as if I had stepped into a dream I once had. One in which Kane was no longer the king of Onyx, son of Lazarus, prince of Lumera . . . but rather, just a man. One who loved dense history books with cramped, too-small script and a thick slice of cloverbread slathered in honeyed butter. Who maybe worked in the local fish market of Crag's Hollow. Who had a wife that liked to wake up and take a brisk run along the tops of the cliffsides before her day began in the apothecary.

Like in my dreams, Kane was sitting at that round table, facing the windows to the lake below, warm coffee puffing steam into the room. His mussed, raven bedhead disheveled around his face, and a large, weathered book in his hands. On the table beside him were two plates, each with that dark, spiced bread I loved so much, some smoked fish, and two bright yolky eggs.

He was a vision.

Not just his painful beauty—the exceptional features that rivaled the finest portraits I'd seen in all of Onyx—nor his body, chiseled as if built painstakingly by the Stones themselves, visible under his thin cotton shirt. But his . . . soul. He was resilient, powerful, passionate. Unafraid to do whatever he believed was right. But also sensitive, thoughtful, wise. Selfish at times, and yet so, so selfless when it came to those he loved.

When it came to me.

My heart thumped wildly in my chest as I stared at his back.

I swallowed. Then I swallowed again.

*Oh, Stones.*

I had been so unbelievably naive. My own stupidity clanged through me like a bell chiming midnight in an empty town square.

Before, it had been enough to accept my fate, to prepare for death, as long as I didn't still feel anything for him. As long as that thread wasn't tethering me to this world. To this life.

But now that I could admit my fears—now that I was willing to *hope* again—

Now it was so clear, I didn't know how I had ever convinced myself otherwise.

I was still completely, eternally, devastatingly in lo—

"You're staring." Kane's voice resonated through the room, though he didn't look up from his book.

I shuffled forward, despite the knot twisting inside me. "Thank you for the food. I'm starving."

He set the book down and took me in as I sat, watching with interest when I ripped a piece of bread and let the sweet, light flavor melt in my mouth. I couldn't meet his eyes. His beautiful eyes, like glittering, moonlit water kissed by the stars.

When his silence became unbearable, and my chewing too loud in my ears, I looked down at bluebell-colored fabric and said, "Thank you for the dress, too. It's lovely. And the boots. You didn't have to do all that."

Kane shrugged, sipping his coffee. "Your clothes were still damp this morning. And you haven't had boots since Azurine. I wanted some fresh air anyway . . ."

"You woke up and made two fires, went shopping, marketing, and cooked breakfast . . ." I glanced around. The fog outside made it hard to tell what hour it was. "Did I sleep very late?"

"No, no." If I didn't know him better, I'd say he looked . . . bashful. "It's only six."

"Six!"

Kane shrugged. "I woke early."

I shook my head. He was another breed, this man.

"That's why the bread is so fresh. It was made an hour ago."

I nodded, eating another mouthful.

And another.

Adrenaline sliding along my bones, I reached for his hand, only to think better of it and bring my fingers down to the skirt of my new dress, twisting the soft material. "Thank you."

"You keep saying that."

I blushed. "I keep feeling it. I'm grateful for everything. For you staying with me. For helping me admit—" I swallowed hard. "Well, just for helping me."

He only nodded, eyes sliding over mine, across my face, along my neck.

I shivered.

"Arwen," he said, and my breath hitched. "A raven came from Shadowhold this morning."

Nerves seized my heart. "Is Mari all right?"

"Everyone is fine. They're all there, actually."

"Griffin, Mari, and Fedrik?"

"And your siblings, Amelia, Dagan . . ."

"What? Why?"

"Broderick and Isolde feared being aligned with us in the eyes of our enemies. The letter from Eardley said they sent anyone with meaningful ties to Onyx back days ago. Their ship arrived late last night."

"Why didn't they tell us when they made the decision to do so?"

"Perhaps Isolde realized I killed her repugnant friend. Knowing her, she'd still not want to risk our wrath. Better to ask for forgiveness than permission."

"And the other refugees? From Peridot and Onyx?"

Kane's answering nod was grim. "Everyone. They feared 'symbolic association.'" Kane muttered under his breath, "Cowards."

All those people staying in Shadowland. All that effort to get them somewhere safer—

"There's no way Citrine will help us now . . ." I sank back into my seat a little, pushing the still-warm cloverbread away from me.

Queen Isolde and King Broderick were quick to take care of their own, everyone else be damned. Fedrik alone couldn't change their minds. Who knew if he'd even attempt to after I told him I wouldn't be returning to Citrine with him? At least, not without Kane.

"How unsafe is Shadowhold for everyone?"

Kane's jaw went tight, weighing. "The forest functions like another wall around the fortress. Almost my entire army is stationed there. Most of our weaponry, cannons, beasts. But once my father knows we're there . . . he could attack any day. Eardley is sending the majority to smaller Onyx towns. The rest of us will just have to be ready."

So we'd have to regroup quickly and get back on the road for the blade. Maybe take Leigh and Ryder and Mari with us . . .

"And about what Beth revealed . . . about your parentage."

"Ah, yes," I said, swallowing my fear. "That my father is a Fae God?"

"If what Beth said is true, we'll need to consult priests and scholars to learn more. If that's what you want to do."

The time for sulking and hiding from the truth was over. It felt better to be honest. To be vulnerable, as Dagan and Kane had both encouraged. "I'm a little afraid of what I'll learn. How is it possible that a Fae God and a human woman created a full-blooded Fae?"

"I'm not sure."

"Well, I do want to know more eventually. Once we find the blade and ready our armies to fight Lazarus. I'd like to know who my father was before I die."

Kane stiffened, his eyes flashing with protest. "You're not going to die, Arwen."

But I could tell even he didn't believe his words. I gave him an honest smile that felt truer on my face than any smile had in weeks.

"If anyone can find a way around this prophecy, you can. But still, I'd like to learn more about him before I lose the chance."

Kane's face was resigned as he said, "Then I will make it so," before standing and placing his empty plate in the kitchen.

"Come now, bird, we have a lot to do today."

I followed him out the front door. For the first time I allowed myself to hope that I would be back here again one day. Leigh would love this town. Maybe I'd take her to the sweetshop. Get her a candied apple or a salted taffy. I didn't want to think this would be the last time I'd step foot in Kane's cottage, so I didn't.

"Do you think any of them will be able to pull something useful from what Beth told us?"

Kane raised his eyes to the sky. "I'm not sure. But my coin is on Mari."

Despite the morning's news and realizations, I couldn't help the smile that pinched my cheeks at the thought of seeing her awake. "Mine, too."

"I MISSED YOU," I MURMURED INTO MARI'S CURLED HAIR. IT smelled like cinnamon and cloves and the lilac soap that they used in Shadowhold.

"I feel like I just saw you yesterday," she said back, muffled by my shoulder.

I had raced off Kane's dragon form, through the gates of Shadowhold, not stopping for a single soldier, guard, or citizen until I had reached the throne room, where Kane told me everyone would be convened.

My eyes had landed on Mari before anyone else, and I swallowed her into a hug so embarrassing I was sure she had turned beet red. But I didn't care. My knees shook with the feeling of having her in my arms, healthy and alive.

Finally, I pulled back and looked at her. She was thinner, face a little pale and gaunt, but that didn't worry me.

It was her eyes that were concerning.

Not anger or fatigue swimming in them, but something much worse. Grief. A chasm of grief hidden in the flowers of her irises. "Are you not feeling well?"

She shrugged, a little self-consciously. That, too, was odd of her. "I feel fine. As if we were in the jungle a day ago." She swallowed hard. "Arguing."

"Every single thing you said to me was true," I said. "I was selfish, and cold, and had built up a lot of walls that were doing just as good a job keeping away pain as all the people I cared about. You were honest with me and I didn't want to hear it. I'm really and truly sorry."

Mari dipped her head in a nod. "I'm sorry, too. You were right all along about the amulet being unhealthy for me. I don't think I'll be doing magic for a while, though." She tried for a smile but looked like she might cry.

My heart stumbled over a beat at the sight. Mari wasn't a quitter. She didn't back off something when it went wrong—she pushed and prodded and argued until it was right again. She was bullish. Fearless. Stubborn.

Something was terribly wrong.

# 38

## ARWEN

THE THRONE ROOM WAS SO SWAMPED WITH SOLDIERS AND generals, so packed with commotion as they awaited the return of their king, I could hardly hear over the din. I gripped Mari by her elbow and tugged her into a shadowed alcove. The wrought-iron candelabra above us cast her curled hair and soft freckles in quiet illumination.

"What's going on?"

"I don't want to talk about it really."

"That's very disturbing, coming from you."

Mari didn't smile—also alarming—but took a shuddering inhale. "I can't seem to do magic anymore."

The chatter and clanging of armor that bloated the throne room fell away to the single pinprick of Mari's words. "What do you mean?"

"What do you think I mean?" The fiery retort relaxed me some. That was the Mari I was used to. "I haven't been able to since I woke up."

"Did you tell Briar?"

She shook her head. I should have known. Mari was not one to ask for help readily.

"Mari, do you think—"

"That I was right? That the amulet was the only reason I could do anything and now I'm back to being a magicless witch like I was before we stole it from Kane's study? Yes, I do."

"You knew it was helping you all along." I shook my head. "I never should have doubted you."

Mari offered me a begrudging smile. "So you believe me now . . . What changed?"

"Briar said you rigged the amulet magically to bolster your power. I knew you hadn't, though. Which means the only way it could have given you power, and made you ill, was if you were from her lineage, and able to use it because *she* crafted it. Kane said her coven hasn't been seen or heard from in hundreds of years, but maybe . . . somehow . . ."

"My mother . . ."

"Did you tell anyone else?"

Mari made a face. "No, but . . ."

"But what?"

"You're going to laugh."

"For some reason I doubt that."

"I was going to tell Griffin. I thought that he might be able to help. Or just listen, I don't know."

"But?"

"*But* he has been such a prick to me since I awoke. Ignoring me, walking away mid-sentence when I ask him to please put his pack next to the other ones in order of weight and not height because clearly that makes no sense, how does ordering them by *height* make *anything* easier—"

"Mari."

"Sorry." She sighed. "I just thought, back in Peridot, that we were becoming friends. Good friends. Or maybe even something more than that . . . And that's hard for me. I never had a lot of luck in that arena growing up in Shadowhold. Mostly, the boys here were really cruel. But Griffin . . . Well, it's pointless now, isn't it? I guess helping me walk down a single flight of stairs at Briar's was enough to make him hate me all over again. Stones forbid he do one damned thing for someone else." She folded her arms across her chest. "Arwen, he practically dropped me like a lit match as soon as he could."

"Griffin sat by your bedside for days on end without eating or drinking. He read to you. *Slept* beside you. He let Kane travel to Crag's Hollow without him so he could stay with you."

"So he's loyal, like a good dog."

I missed her so much and also I was going to strangle her. "He couldn't bear to leave your side! He couldn't hold you as you walked down some stairs probably because he was *this* close to vomiting out the words *I love you, please order me around for the rest of eternity.* And it scares him almost as much as it scares you."

Mari's eyes widened. "I do not order people around!"

I glared at her, but couldn't help a half smile. "First things first." I sighed. "You need to tell Briar about your magic. If anyone can help you get it back, it's her."

"Maybe this is a blessing. I was all right before magic. I'll be all right again. Maybe there's something in my lineage that shouldn't be touched." The look in her eyes told me there was more to that theory, but she moved past it. "Please tell me you've been faring even a little better?"

I exhaled with an audible *whoosh*. "I have a lot to catch you up on."

"I feel like this happens to us far too often."

"Maybe one day our lives will be boring."

Her brows rose quickly before lowering as she schooled her face. But I knew what surprised her. It had been a long while since I'd spoken about the future as if I might still have one.

"Go find Leigh and Ryder, and we can show them Shadowhold together. Last night I told Leigh about Kane's art collection and promised I'd show her my favorite paintings in the castle. Did you know she can really draw?"

"Yes." I smiled at the colorful memories. "Our house back in Abbington was full of her art."

"After, you and I can go to the great hall, drink too much birch-wine, and tackle everything I missed." Her eyes had brightened a bit, and my heart was starting to re-form from the mangled shape it had contorted into at her confession. She would survive this. I would help her to. "Starting with you and Fedrik. He's been asking about you nonstop."

Bleeding Stones, *Fedrik*. I had almost forgotten.

"And speaking of, look who it is."

I whirled to see Fedrik walk into the throne room, followed by Griffin, Kane, and a handful of Onyx generals. I waved brightly at Barney and Dagan among them, which earned only a nod from Dagan—an obvious sign of his deep and steadfast love—and a full, ear-to-ear grin from Barney, welcoming me home.

*Home.*

I had barely luxuriated in how good it felt to refer to Shadow-hold as such when Fedrik cut away from the group and directly toward me. He looked radiant, as if filled with sunbeams, despite the dark, rich stone walls and obsidian thorns of Kane's throne behind him.

"Arwen," he said brightly. "How was your trip?"

"It was . . . informative."

"Kane tells me you found the seer but her clues on the blade were a bit ambiguous."

"Yes, but at least we have a lead now. It's here in Onyx. And we got a few other helpful pieces of information we can hopefully tie together, too."

"Good to hear. Mari, do you mind giving us a moment?"

Mari couldn't hide her sly smile as her eyes locked on mine. "Not at all. I'm going to go find the other two Valondales and teach them a bit about fine art. It's been a while since I felt like a snob."

Fedrik drew closer once Mari had left us. "I'm sorry I left Briar's abruptly. Griffin said you'd be back last night."

"We got caught in a storm."

His blue eyes flared. "I'm sure you did. Have you made a decision regarding my offer? I'm sailing back to Azurine today."

"Fedrik—"

"What offer?" Kane asked behind me, his voice like lightning across a desolate sky.

I spun to face him, my eyes pleading. *Not now.*

Fedrik only smiled. "Well, you were going to find out eventually." He stood a bit taller, still at least half a foot beneath Kane. "I asked Arwen to come back to Azurine with me. At least until you've found the blade and prepared for battle. It'll be safer for her, and frankly"—he looked around at the dark drapery and flickering, wrought-iron candelabras—"a little more scenic."

"A generous offer," Kane said, his voice dry, "if Arwen wasn't our key to finding the weapon."

"She already told me it's here in your own kingdom. For all we know you've had it all along and are just delaying the inevitable."

Kane stepped toward him with intent. "Mind your tongue, or I'll sever it from your mouth."

"Kane." I leveled a glare at him.

"And there he goes," Fedrik drawled. "Hostile and threatening once again."

Griffin strode over to stand beside his king. "I don't think I've ever seen you so aggressive, Fedrik. Didn't get your beauty sleep?"

But it was Kane who loosed a dark and venomous chuckle. "He's angry. He wants her and knows she'll never be his."

There was that predictable Kane cruelty. And to the very person we needed to vouch for him to Citrine. "Don't talk about me like I'm not here." I pulled Fedrik away from the prying eyes of the throne room by the arm. "Come on."

Kane called to our backs, "Enjoy the soaked kingdom."

"Is that the kind of brute you always imagined yourself with?" Fedrik asked as we passed Kane's sentries and roamed out into the hall.

"Not particularly," I admitted once we were alone.

"Let me show you a better life. Maybe not with me, but surely not with him."

"Fedrik, I can't come with you."

"I'm not trying to sweep you off your feet, Arwen. But you haven't even—"

"I'm in love with him."

The quiet hall was already a reprieve from the teeming throne room, but there was a peaceful calm in my mind as well as soon as I spoke the words aloud.

A serene, steadfast resolve solidifying around that singular truth.

Of course I loved him.

I had been falling in love with Kane since the day we raced in the woods. Maybe even since he had given me his fox fur when I'd been so close to breaking. He never let me, though. Not then, not after Siren's Bay, and not now.

Denying it for so long—it had been a cruelty to both him and myself. Saying the words—even to Fedrik—felt like walking through those enormous ornate doors to Shadowhold. It felt like coming home.

Fedrik's brows knit inward. "I can't say I'm happy for you two."

"You don't have to. I don't think it would be fair to him to be together."

"That's a load. He's utterly devoted to you."

I said nothing. I understood his anger.

"If he made you think . . . He is such a fool." Fedrik shook his head. "Always has been."

I smiled weakly as a handful of soldiers with masks like skulls and sleek leather armor passed by us and into the bustling throne room. "What will you tell your parents?"

"Some version of the truth."

"Which is?"

Fedrik's face gave nothing away. "I'm not sure yet. Look, if you change your mind, I'm just a sea away."

I nodded, and once he had strolled back into the throne room, I sagged against the cool stone wall.

Maybe Fedrik was right. Maybe we were both fools.

Was it not foolish to know we loved each other and not act on it? Not try to be together, in whatever way we could?

Or was it foolish to confess my love to Kane knowing I might be ripped from his grasp any day now? Knowing how many he'd already lost. Remembering how pained he looked when he'd admitted his love . . .

I wasn't hiding from what might tether me to this life anymore. I wasn't concealing my feelings for my own benefit—I was doing it for his.

Was that foolish? Or a mercy?

I stared across the bustling castle, gloomy and shadowed as ever—Stones, I had missed this place. The candles flickering in the summer wind that slipped through wide-open stained-glass windows. The fireflies drifting around in drowsy late-afternoon air. I knew fall would be here soon, and all the trees would turn the maple color of my childhood.

I wondered if I'd be here to see it. What it might feel like to blend my old home and my new. What I might look like, wrapped in my familiar fox fur, my new boots stomping through the crisp, fallen leaves all over the courtyard. The children I might treat in the apothecary, knees scraped from hay and hands blistered from carving gourds.

Did Kane love the rusted red and sunflower yellow of the leaves when they grew here in his bountiful keep? Or still loathe them as much as he did back in Amber? If he did, I would have to convince him otherwise. If we were both still here then, I would drag him, grumbling and rolling his eyes, into the gloomy woods and force him to jump in the leaves with me like schoolchildren. To brew cider with me, as rich as the one from Mariner's Pub—mulled and sweet and spiced. I'd show him all the reasons autumn was spellbinding and gorgeously melancholy. Why even as a citizen of Onyx, it would always be a part of me.

"Arwen?" Mari rounded out of the throne room with Ryder and Leigh in tow, shaking me from my hopes.

*Hope.*

That's what that felt like.

Leigh flew into me with racehorse speed. The stone floor of the hallway was cold on my knees as I sank to the ground and held her, blonde hair filling my vision. Ryder joined us on the floor, making the hug smell of tobacco.

"You've been smoking," I whispered into them.

"I would never," Leigh swore against my back.

"Not you." I grinned, pulling on one of her curls. "How are you both?"

Leigh withdrew and spoke first. "You're in love with Kane?"

My eyes widened. "Eavesdropping?"

Ryder blanched. "I wasn't, just her."

"You love him, but you're not going to tell him?" Leigh's face was grave.

"Leigh, this has nothing to do with you."

"When will you stop treating me like a kid?"

My heart sank. We were already fighting. "Why are you so angry with me these days?"

"I'll let you two talk," Ryder offered. Torchlight glinted along his hair as he ambled down the stone hallway back toward Mari.

"I'm not angry with you," Leigh said.

"Yes, you are. You've been furious with me since the day we left for Citrine, and I cannot for the life of me figure out why."

"I'm not angry," she conceded, and with more maturity than I had seen from her before, said, "I'm afraid."

For a moment, I couldn't fathom an adequate response. Of course she was afraid. How had I been so blind?

"Me, too," I admitted, taking her hand in my own. "Of Lazarus, of this war. But what do your fears have to do with me and Kane?"

"No, that's the problem," she said, yanking her hand from mine. "You can't be scared, too. One of us has to be brave."

"Leigh . . ." I started, her words a vise around my heart. "I wish I knew what to say to make everything feel safe again."

"I know there isn't anything."

"Maybe not. But you know what? When I was most scared, there was one thing that helped me."

"Running?"

"No." I grinned. "Even better."

Her eyes lit with curiosity.

"Dagan taught me here in this very keep how to protect myself with a sword. It made me feel strong and powerful. Like I could face things bigger and more frightening than me. Like maybe one day *I* could be the frightening one. I'd like to teach you, too."

Leigh held my eyes as she considered the offer. "I'll never be as strong as you, though. I'm not Fae."

It was shocking to see myself, however briefly, through Leigh's eyes. As the brave one, the resilient one, her full-blooded Fae sister. No wonder my childish avoidance of Kane had upset her so. She was looking to me all along to be strong. For us. For her.

In the place of our mother.

"You don't need to be Fae. You can harness power only *you* have. Bravery comes from in here." I pointed to her heart.

Her eyes stayed fixed on me as I stood. "So, what are you going to do?"

"Help Kane track down the blade. Find a way to save the realms and my own life. And figure out the love story if we make it that far?"

Leigh's lips cut a flat line. "I hate that plan."

I slumped against the stone wall behind me once more. "Yeah, me, too."

"You two ready to explore?" Mari called from around the corner, Ryder behind her like an eager pet.

"Let's do it." I grinned back at them. I'd help Mari with her magic block later tonight. Figure out what in the world to do about Kane later, too. For now, it was enough to spend the afternoon with the people I had missed so much. I'd tell them what I'd learned about my mother, about Powell. I'd share with them my fears, and my hopes, my faith in the future.

What I should have done weeks ago I could do now. And that would have to be enough.

"I found the painter you were looking for," Mari said to Leigh as we started down the hall. "His abstract work is in the north wing gallery below the vault and above the . . ." She trailed off, cringing.

Leigh swallowed. "Above the what?"

"The . . . torture chamber." Mari grimaced. "But! This place really isn't as scary as you might think. Most castles have a torture chamber, it's not just us!"

Leigh did not look pleased.

"It's actually pretty interesting, Leigh," Ryder added. "One of the most prolific thieves of all time was held in there. I read all about it last night in the library."

I might have made a comment about Ryder suddenly being interested in books now that they had been given to him by Mari, but the words dried up on my tongue.

"Who?" I asked.

"Drake Alcott," Ryder said, barely able to contain his pride in knowing the answer.

The vault that had housed the blade for forty-five years was only two floors above the torture annex. Where notorious, world-renowned thief and con man Drake Alcott had been kept. Hadn't

Niclas said he had been sent away five years ago? The same time the blade went missing . . . And to Hemlock Isle. An island here, *in Onyx.*

I stilled. "Ryder . . . you're a genius."

"Stones, don't sound so surprised."

But I was already moving. Ignoring their calls as I ran back into the throne room, past those sentries once more, searching for Kane—but he was nowhere to be found. I turned to Griffin and Barney and the herd of Onyx soldiers that surrounded them.

"Where's Kane?"

"Not sure," Griffin said coolly. "But he thinks you're leaving for Citrine with Fedrik."

*Bleeding Stones.*

"I need to find him. Right this moment."

"I think he's in the gardens, Lady Arwen," Barney supplied.

"Thank you."

I raced for the castle garden as fast as a bird in flight.

# 39

## KANE

Maybe she'd like the pansies. I reached for their long stems but retracted my hand. Too boring. The spider orchids were more joyful, more unique. Like her.

I plucked a handful and added them to the growing bouquet. Spindly bat flower, cerulean daisies, and pitch-black lilies, of course—her namesake and the flower that populated my dreams most nights.

I trudged back through the castle doors and up the winding staircase to my room.

I had given Eardley Beth's father's description. Griffin would walk him through where Halden and his men had last been stationed in Peridot, and we'd hope the man was still being kept there, alive.

Dagan would get ravens to our spies, as he had when the blade first went missing. If the blade was in Onyx, someone had to have quite the network to have kept it a secret for the last five years. Dagan would start with Briar and go from there. Beth had said it was *"thrown beneath heaps of other weapons. Tied to another master, but yearning to be paired with its mate.*" He'd search every weapons cache, every hoarder, every high-ranking criminal boss in every city. Again. We'd do it all again.

And I would track down the White Crow.

Arwen was leaving with Fedrik. I wasn't bitter. I wasn't angry. Or, if I was, it wasn't the emotion I was leading with.

I wanted her to be protected, to live, and to enjoy doing so. I'd never free my mind from the sound of her sobs last night. Thousands of years I'd live if I failed to take her place. And that memory would stay with me through each and every one.

I had to do *something*.

And have hope something could be done.

Stepping into my bedroom in Shadowhold after all these weeks away felt like bathing after a hot day spent in mud. I sighed, deep and even, and walked toward my desk to twine Arwen's flowers, but my eyes lingered on my bed.

A memory, so potent it was as if I had stepped backward in time, shot through my mind at the sight. One of Arwen, in that very bed, two days after her battle with the wolfbeast. She was wearing my shirt, eating breakfast, laughing as she bit into an apple.

"Kane," Arwen said, breathless.

*Oh Gods.* I had finally lost it. I was hallucinating now.

"Kane?" she said again, this time a murmur of worry twined with the urgency.

I whirled.

There she was. Hand clutched to her sternum, breathing rushed, lit by a pool of fading sunlight in the foyer of my room.

"Are you all right?"

She stepped inside, olive eyes wild. "You weren't in the gardens."

"I was—"

"I have to . . . I have to tell you something."

I quirked a brow. "Go on."

"I'm in love with you."

My heart stilled.

"Also, I think Drake Alcott stole the Blade of the Sun and took it with him to Hemlock Isle, and it's still there now, five years later. Are those for me?" She pointed at the flowers in my hand.

My mind roared with utter silence, and I leaned onto the desk behind me. "You . . . love me?"

She strode forward, stopping just close enough for me to smell the orange blossom of her swaying hair. "I'm sorry I didn't say it sooner. Back in Azurine, that night we kissed. Or at Briar's. Or in your cottage earlier today . . . *Stones*, Kane. I had so many opportunities to be brave." She stepped even closer. "But it would've made what I have to do impossible. And at the time—" She looked up as she searched for the right words. "At the time it felt like the only way to make it through was to not . . . want things. But I'm not afraid of hoping now, because of you." She stopped to take a shaky inhale, left breathless by her own confession.

Relief soared through me like a bird on a tailwind. Light and smooth and—

And then fire thundered through my blood.

I dropped the flowers and captured her soft, full lips in mine, sighing at the taste of her on my tongue. Arwen's startled eyes closed a heartbeat later, and she tilted her head, allowing me to press myself even closer to her. My tongue to lick over hers. I nearly groaned.

Such an uncanny feeling, to experience something I had fantasized about more times than I could count. The sincerity of it all. Of her feelings. Of *her*.

I would consume her. Slowly. For days. Years. Hundreds of years.

She sighed into me, and my cock swelled with the need to be inside of her.

"Wait." She pulled away, chest rising and falling. "What about the blade?"

*Fuck the fucking blade.*

"Right." I stepped back, clearing my throat. "How did you put that together?"

"Mari mentioned something about the vault being close to the dungeons. Which made me think back to Halden's explosion. That night, when your guards interrupted the forum, they said he had been trying to access Shadowhold's vault. That got me thinking—had any other prisoners ever tried the same thing given the layout? The proximity? Back in the caverns Niclas told me Drake Alcott was sent to Hemlock Isle five years ago. It didn't mean anything to me then. But now I know Hemlock Isle is a prison, and he went there around the same time you said the blade was stolen. And he was a great thief . . ." She shook her head. "When Ryder said Alcott had been imprisoned here in Shadowhold, I realized it was never in the Cavern or anywhere else. It went from your vault to Hemlock Isle, and it's been there ever since."

It made sense—when we sent Drake to Hemlock, I hadn't even known the blade was missing.

"I'll go retrieve it first thing in the morning," I said, bringing my lips down to her neck. Her earlobe. She was so petite, I had to hunch almost comically. That was how few times we had kissed. How little I knew the shape of us together.

Not anymore. I'd memorize the way our bodies fit together. Sear it into my skin.

"You're not going alone. I'm coming *with*—" Her voice hitched as my tongue slid down her neck toward her collarbone and my hands found her ass. "You," she hummed.

I chuckled into her skin, but she pushed me back and straightened. "I'm serious, Kane. Wherever you go, whatever you face, that's what I'll face, too. All right?"

"Yeah." I grinned. "All right."

"Good. Because that's what I want. For as long as we have together."

"We will have a lifetime. There is no other way this ends."

She wrapped her hands around my shoulders. Olive eyes—whip-smart, fierce, fearless eyes—stared up at me. That gorgeous skin glowing in the light of the fading sun.

Her open, trusting, warm expression.

An expression of love.

I claimed her mouth with mine once more, cradling her head in my hands as I pushed her into the post of the bed behind us. Twining my lips with hers, fisting my hand in her silken hair, and trying wildly to align our mismatched hips—

Messy and eager and fumbling. Like a hormone-ravaged boy. Trying to get as close as I possibly could to her. To close every gap between us. But there was too much fabric in the way. I needed to feel her skin. I regretted every single decision in my life that led me to purchase the dress this morning. I abhorred the thing.

But I didn't immediately detach from her to remove it. I couldn't quite think straight—I couldn't concentrate properly around her when she *wasn't* palming at my cock over my pants with her perfect little hands. Now it was a challenge in itself to string two coherent thoughts together.

My mouth moved down her neck, her skin tasting like cream

stirred with sweet honey. Or the purest vanilla from a far-off land. I pressed my tongue against the sensitive skin under her ear and felt her shiver. Licked her collarbone indulgently until I was sucking her breasts over the fabric of her dress, my hands slinking up her back.

And she was *moaning*. Mewling as I worked her nipple, the dress growing damp but neither of us able to detangle.

I wanted to fuck her with my fingers. To plunge them in between the folds I knew would be plump and ready for me. Finding some semblance of discipline, I released her just long enough to yank the dress over her lithe shoulders, over her head, letting it fall to the floor in a heap. And then I stared at her, gawking shamefully like I had never seen a woman in her undergarments before.

Lurid thoughts danced in my mind.

Lifting my hand to cup her heavy breast through the chemise, I ran my thumb across her pointed nipple, and the simple act made my cock throb so hard I winced.

Arwen's eyes nearly rolled back in her head as I flicked my finger across the pebbled point a second time, eliciting a choked moan.

"There you go," I encouraged.

Arwen reached up and wrapped her hands around my neck to pull me into her, her lips finding mine again, before reaching frantically for the laces of my pants and yanking at them. I was happy to help, ripping the laces off faster than I had ever done anything in my life and sliding the trousers to the floor. I tore my shirt over my head and tossed it, nearly catching a lit candle on the mantel behind me and setting the room ablaze.

Neither of us would have even noticed.

Arwen's eyes went wide as she stepped back to drink me in before she ran a single finger along my lower abdomen above my breeches. I jerked with the contact and my balls tightened. I needed to—

Before I could finish that thought, or act on it, she raised her lips to me, reaching on pointed toes to kiss my chest. When her tongue licked down my ribs, my eyes rolled back in my head. She hummed in satisfaction, pleased with herself, and dipped her head lower. And then those lips were on my hip. And brushing along the line of my waistband. Only cotton separating my length from her mouth.

I must have made some effort to stop her, to make sure she knew she didn't have to do anything she didn't want to, but—

Her lips on my bare thigh. On the thin skin between my navel and cock.

Too heady, too euphoric—it was beyond anything I could resist. Possibly beyond anything I could handle.

My hand sought clumsily for something to grasp, and settled on the beam of the four-poster bed. I might've fisted my hands in her long, chocolate hair, pulled it tight as she sucked me off, guided her mouth around me, but I'd wait. Let her figure out first how she liked it.

Her hot, wet mouth continued a trail of indulgent, luxuriating kisses along my waistband, her fingers roaming up my thighs, her nose tickling the fine hairs of my low stomach . . . When she ran one warm hand over my length, I grasped the bedpost so violently the wood splintered beneath my fingers.

I needed her mouth on me.

She was torturing me. Teasing, taunting—

Cruel, wild, vixen bird.

Until . . . a tremble.

A pause, a barely audible gulp—

Without realizing they had been closed, my eyes shot open and down to her. "What's wrong?"

Arwen shook her head, on her knees as she ran her hands up my legs, and they were—shaking. Her hands were *shaking*.

I fought against the all-consuming urge to split the bedpost creaking under my palm in two.

A deep breath. I needed to take a deep breath.

I looked down at her again. So delicate from this angle. Her entire hand only half the width of my muscled thigh.

"Arwen," I tried, burying the fury and disgust I felt at myself for not saying it sooner. "You don't have to do this."

Her eyes were soft under those full lashes. Not reluctant. Just nervous, perhaps. "I *want* to. I just—" Her breath came out in a whoosh. "Haven't before. And I'd like it to be good for you."

"Anything you do will feel . . . unbelievable."

"Just tell me if I hurt you or bite you or something." Slowly, with precision, she took off my breeches and pulled the base of my cock into her hand. The head was already sticky, and my cock twitched with her warm breath.

I grunted. And breathed. Slowly.

Resisted the urge to thrust into her closed fist.

*Debased. That's what you are. She's already hesitant and you want to fuck her shaking hands?*

After a few teasing strokes, she wrapped her mouth around me.

Stars sprang into my vision and all the blood in my body rushed downward.

I bowed, palm outstretched against the bedpost once more, as she swirled her tongue and pumped her fist. If Arwen's tongue sweeping up my shaft, her hand lightly wrapped around my balls, her soft lips exploring the head of my cock—

If it was a dream, I'd stay here for eternity and never wake up.

She lifted those eyes—filled with nothing but passionate, primal desire—to mine, her mouth full of me, lips wrapped obscenely around my—

I had to stop her.

The base of my spine was tingling, that swell of pressure building low in my abdomen—

Gently wrapping my hands around her shoulders, I moved to bring her up from the floor. But she didn't budge, continuing to suck me thoroughly, deeper into her, and I snarled as a plea formed at my lips.

"Arwen," I nearly slurred, desperate and tensing. "Fuck."

"You want me to stop?"

"No. But I need you to." The words fell out with a half laugh, and before she could protest further, I pulled her to her feet. Her lips were red and glossy, her eyes slightly wet from exertion, her cheeks flushed—I kissed her, humming as our tongues twined, as I sucked her full lower lip into my mouth.

Stripping the chemise and undergarments off her, I laid her down atop the dark sheets. Slick and blushing, chocolate hair fanned across velvet pillows, she looked like a blossoming dark lily from my garden.

And she knew what she did to me. Her pleased expression told me as much. "Come here," she whispered.

And I obliged, caging my arms around her, tangling my legs between hers. On my thigh I could feel how soaking wet she was, nearly dripping with need that had pooled at her center.

Knowing that was a response to having my cock lodged in her mouth was almost enough to bring me back to the brink of release.

In an effort to calm down, I conjured dusty books and history lessons in my mind.

Anything but Arwen's full, heaving breasts, which were bouncing below me as she squirmed and writhed on my thigh, panting and clawing at my back.

"Hurry," she said faintly, running her fingers through my hair and along my neck. I brought a hand down to spread her legs and trace her glistening, wet lips. To drag my thumb up the center of her until I reached the top and pressed down. Until I felt her contract beneath me with a little whine, and that pressure returned to my cock.

Shit. *Shit—*

"We can slow down. There's no rush." I sounded like a man starved.

She only angled herself closer, canting those hips, her tongue licking against my own. "There is," she said. When she tugged my hair, just this side of forceful, my eyes rolled back in my head.

*Fuck.*

I reached down and positioned myself at her slick, tight entrance and barely slid in before I blacked out from ecstasy.

# 40

ARWEN

Kane's first thrust was slow and cautious, and I couldn't help the shameless mewl that tore through me as he slowed. *More*. I needed so, so much more.

"Is this all right?" He sounded like he'd punctured a lung.

I couldn't even answer. I was in shambles.

From the sheer onslaught of emotion—being with him, held by him, loved by him after all this time—breathless just from the beauty of his forehead pressed gently against my own.

That, and the sting. I knew he was large. Had seen him handle himself when he made me come with his mouth. I hadn't been able to look away that night—his cock was perfect. Not that I had seen so many in my life, but there was no denying the symmetry of it, the heft, the thickness.

But I hadn't been prepared for *this*—heavy and hard and long— I felt like my entire body was stretching to accommodate him. The stretch was painful, and yet the most pleasurable sensation I'd felt in my life. I needed more friction, more movement, just *more*, but Kane hadn't moved since pushing into me—

Why hadn't he moved?

"More," I begged, rocking against him. The need was near ruinous. Liquefying my core and making me lightheaded.

His silver eyes were raised up to the gossamer canopy of the bed as if he were praying to those Fae Gods. Pools of sunset light highlighted his furrowed brow and taut cheekbones. His jaw tight, teeth clenched. I lifted a hand to his face to ease the tension.

"I'm fine, Kane," I whispered. Was that what he was worried about? "You don't have to be so gentle with me."

"Please, stop," he ground out. "Just for— I just need a moment."

"Stop?"

"Talking, moving, breathing . . ." he said between clenched teeth.

I laughed a bit and dragged my hands down his long back until I felt him shiver. "I thought you were the great Kane Ravenwood, king of sex, stamina of a racehorse, unwavering will of a dragon—"

"Look who's being cruel now," he said, eyes finally meeting mine with a tilted grin that told me how much he liked it. "I can't help it. You unravel me."

He pushed into me just a little more, and I clenched around him. Clawed at him. This was—

It was too—

*Oh, Stones.*

"Again," I begged him, breathless.

His impressive length sank even deeper inside of me than I thought possible, and a delicious, satisfying ache spread from my core across my limbs. I stifled a moan. And that spot at the apex of my thighs, throbbing, *pulsing* with need—

My breath hitched in my chest and he edged into me until I was sealed tight around him and I knew he couldn't thrust any deeper. Until a moment later he did just that, and an absurd moan split from me. I slapped a hand over my mouth to cover the mortifying noise.

But Kane pried my fingers from my lips. "Never do that again," he warned, eyes lit with something primal. "I want to hear every sound you make when I am inside you."

I held his gaze as he shifted my legs to open me up wider, to accommodate just a bit more of his length. My eyes rolled back as the angle pressed him into my innermost wall, and I squirmed from the chaos it released across my body.

And the noises. The sound of our joining, of him rutting inside of me. Filthy, obscene, soaking wet—

Kane pulled out almost fully, and I nearly clawed at his chest to bring him back, to sheath him inside me once again, but he did just that. He thrust into me nearly to the hilt. Pleasure built. Low in my stomach, and pinching at my nipples—

"Does that feel good?" he asked with no cockiness, no pride.

"So, so good," I babbled. "Kane—"

It was so good I wasn't sure I'd be able to stand it, but he didn't relent, pushing into me at a steady rhythm, and nudging that spot deep inside me that wound me tighter and tighter and *tighter*—

"Say it—" A slow pumping. A stifled groan. "Say it again."

I knew what he was asking for. "I love you," I said. And repeated it, over and over, lifting my lips to his, sighing into his mouth as he thrust, too dazed by explicit splendor to really kiss, but still shivering from the feeling of his tongue against my parted lips.

He lifted my knee a little, and I was already so close, so lewdly, shamefully wet, our friction had soaked my thighs and the silky sheets beneath us, and I needed—*needed*—that release and—

I cried out with the new fullness of him as he sank in again. He groaned once, looking down at that spot where our joined bodies met. At me, so full of *him*.

I didn't ever want it to be over. I wanted to stay in this moment with him. To continue to be one.

As if he could feel me holding on, his lips curved and he wrapped an arm underneath me, rolling us so I was on top of him.

I groaned at the sensation of our shift, and he swore in unison. I wouldn't be able to handle it—

"Use me," he growled.

I did as I was told, sinking down deeper onto him, my own body sucking him in. Bracing my hands on his muscled chest. He felt like hot, slick marble. Carved and cut and strong.

If my movements were too jerky or disjointed, he didn't seem to mind. His glazed eyes, that rigid jaw, those guttural grunts from the back of his throat—all told me he, too, was struggling to hold on much longer. I ground myself against him, the friction bringing me closer and closer, while beneath me, Kane bucked his hips in smooth, pulsing thrusts, winding me tauter, until I felt myself falling over the edge.

Ripples of pleasure tore through me—

My vision blurred and shattered. My hands shook and I sobbed through the sensation, the contractions, the *rapture* of being with Kane.

Satiated and still swimming in the heady fog of my climax, I noticed Kane moving to draw out of me.

"No," I cried out. "Do not stop."

"We shouldn't—" He sounded like he was barely breathing. "I don't want to impregnate you."

I adjusted my hips to sink him in deeper. "I'll brew something for that."

Kane looked as if he had never heard better news in his life. "Are you sure?"

"Please," I begged. I wanted to feel him.

It was all the encouragement he needed. Kane proceeded to pound into me, grasping my hips hard enough to bruise and slamming himself upward with stifled groans. The friction was too good . . . Knowing that he was spilling himself inside me only wound me tighter, and I rode him until I came again.

Exhausted, weary, and limp, I collapsed onto his slick chest, sucking in lungfuls of air. For a moment, I could only hear our twin, ragged breaths. That, and the faraway hoot of a single owl in the early night. The soft rustle of leaves through the open balcony window.

"How do you feel?"

I peered up at him, only to find that satisfied male grin I loved so dearly. But more than that, there was a quiet joy in his eyes. A peace there that I'd never seen before. "Wonderful. You?"

"There is no word for what I feel right now."

I crawled off him, despite his yowl of protest, and snuggled into the crease between his neck and shoulder. It smelled like sweat and fir and leather.

"I live here now," I said into his neck.

"In Shadowhold?" he mumbled, already half-asleep.

"In this nook. The nook of your neck." I was babbling. Satiated and sleepy and silly with happiness.

"You can live in my nook forever, bird."

"I love you."

"I have always loved you."

Then a blissful, heavy slumber overtook me.

~✧~

MY EYES SHOT OPEN, PULSE RACING, BROW CLAMMY, AND hands fisted in Kane's luxurious dark sheets. As my eyes adjusted to the pitch-blackness of his room, I tried to remember what dream had shaken me so violently from my sleep . . .

I rolled over and a pleasurable soreness pinched between my legs. I was still sticky with Kane's come, but my own wetness had gathered there, too, and the restless, unchecked need that coursed through me told me plainly what had awoken me.

My eyes fell to Kane, breathing evenly on his back beside me.

Desire spread through my body like ink in water. The single shining lock of hair that had fallen in front of his eyes, his cheekbones jutting in the filtered bars of moonlight, those full masculine lips . . .

Feeling the mattress sink underneath my careful movements, I snuggled into him and inhaled cedar and the heady sweat of a deep sleep. Kane shifted, nuzzling me slightly, but his eyes remained closed as his chest rose and fell.

Still lying on my side as I faced him, I brought my hand down his chest in lazy caresses. More admiring than anything—the taut golden skin, his defined muscles, a few varied scars here and there. I pressed one kiss into his neck, inhaling like he was fresh air after a storm, then lingered another kiss along his jaw.

"Something I can help you with, bird?" Kane murmured through a fog of sleep, his eyes still closed.

I fought the blush that rose to my cheeks. "I was hoping I could help *you*," I whispered into his shoulder before I dragged my teeth across the skin there and listened as he groaned softly.

"By all means," he purred, widening his legs as if to say, *have at it*.

A little thrill hummed through my veins as I let my hand travel down his stomach and under the sheets, where Kane was still bare. He was velvet soft and impossibly hard by the time I wrapped my hand around him. I whimpered and dropped my forehead to his shoulder, already feeling swollen and damp. My nipples tight and sensitive against Kane's arm, my breasts heavy and full. I stroked him slowly, addicted to the low sounds that fell from him, and his involuntary upward bucks into my hand.

Pumping faster, I moved to crawl on top of him and use my mouth, some absolutely base and filthy part of me dying to feel him spill against my tongue, to taste his release, but Kane sat up in one fluid push and pressed a broad palm to my collarbone, pinning me against the pillows.

"Not this time," he said, fully awake now.

"Why not?"

He grinned that wolflike smile at me through the darkness. I could have caught fire from the raw lust alone. "I can't come too quickly again. You'll never let me hear the end of it."

I wanted to tell him I had just been teasing earlier, that I was actually flattered by how attracted he was to me, but he silenced my thoughts when he covered my lips with his own.

He tasted of sleep and warmth and fresh mint, and I groaned into the kiss, releasing his now-twitching cock and wrapping my arms around his neck. I could kiss him for ages. Forever.

His calloused hands drifted along my naked body as he ran his nose over my neck, my collarbone, my sternum. He brought his mouth to my nipple and sucked the bud indulgently, bringing a hum to my lips.

"Can I have you from behind?" he asked roughly around my breast.

I nodded, body tightly coiled and mind clouded with desire. He could do whatever he wanted to me, but I wasn't able to form words right now, and he knew it.

"Arwen?" he asked, his voice a little like silk as he flicked his tongue over my breast and rubbed my other nipple between his thumb and forefinger.

"Anything," I groaned, not sounding at all like myself. "You can do anything."

Kane gently flipped me over so I was on my stomach and moved behind me, lifting my hips up and nudging my legs apart with his knee until I was spread open for him.

He swore, pulling my thighs up and nearer to him. But he didn't touch me further, and I could feel the cool air dance across where I was already pooling for him—my own need and his from earlier leaking from me.

But I wouldn't ask again.

If this was a game between us, I was determined to win at least *once.*

I arched my back, and—feeling some kind of boldness I never had before—reached a hand behind me to part myself even wider for him. I wondered if he could see the mess he had made inside of me. If he liked that.

Kane grunted at the sight, a deep rumble, and I could have purred. He rubbed a huge hand across my ass and thighs, grazing my already wet center. My answering gasp made him hum with satisfaction and he brought his mouth down to that aching spot between my legs and ran his tongue across me.

I cried out, louder than I expected to, and squirmed as he licked up and down, teasing me with open-mouthed kisses at the apex of my thighs, and from such an obscene, vulnerable angle.

I waited for the shame to come, but it never did. I trusted Kane. Implicitly so. I would have let him do anything to me. From any angle.

The thought only made me hotter for him.

Finally he ran a single finger through my plump folds—my own need and his spit and come dripping from me, nearly down my thighs. He plunged the finger inside as he continued to work that spot with his lips and tongue and teeth. And the noises, wet, rhythmic— Oh, *Stones* . . .

"Kane," I groaned, burying my face in the mattress below me. "Oh, *oh*, I can't—"

"Relax," Kane whispered, still surging that finger in and out of me. "I've got you."

I tried to take a calming inhale but the pleasure—

It was too much.

I was going to come apart. I *needed* to.

But he was slowing his finger, pulling it out . . .

Rather than bring his mouth back to where I craved it, he placed soft kisses along my thighs and up to the base of my spine, caressing the sensitive skin, grasping my backside as roughly as he seemed to let himself. And then he moved those lips to my hip bone, his fingers still rubbing between my legs lazily, the other hand massaging my back, my shoulder, my thigh, as if he was soothing me through the delicious torture he was inflicting.

*Sadist* . . . I loved it.

I bucked and keened and wrang myself out begging for more. His mouth. I needed his mouth. I squeezed my eyes shut as my hands twisted in the nearest pillow.

"Kane," I pleaded. "Let me come." I nearly ripped off a silk tassel.

"I can't stop," he purred between my legs. "I'm too greedy."

I was beside myself with a need so indecent it was teetering on agony. "Please, please," I whimpered.

"Fine, fine. No need to yell," he drawled casually, his voice husky and low.

Relief flooded me.

Finally, finally, *finally*—

Kane lifted up to his knees and nudged inside.

# 41

KANE

I GRASPED ARWEN'S SLENDER HIPS, MY THUMBS NEARLY touching at her spine, and rocked into her. I could do this—take my time with her. Nice and slow and agonizing. Just a hair shy of painful.

Arwen bucked and rolled her hips, her slick core contracting. I ground my teeth with the force of keeping my cock in check. Her tense whimpers were so sweet. Desperate little sounds that brought me closer and closer to the edge.

But this time felt different than before. Different from the frenetic, frenzied declaration of love—that hurried, near-haphazard rush to join, to become one. And different, too, from Briar's—that first real night together cautious and tangled in misunderstood feelings. Now there was . . . time. Time and promises and hope all unfurling generously between us.

"Harder," she breathed. Then, a whimpered afterthought. "Please."

There was nothing in this world, no torture, no suffering, that could keep me from obliging her request. I unleashed whatever part of myself I had just barely been succeeding in holding back and drove into her, over and over, mumbling how *tight* she was, how *perfect* and *wet* and *good.*

The moonlight fell in pale beams over the rumpled bedsheets, painting Arwen's long, silky brown hair, her back, and the faded scars striped across it. My heart squeezed as we moved together.

I wanted to be closer to her.

Leaning forward, I pulled her up by her shoulders until she was kneeling between my legs, her back flush against my chest. Her scars pressed to my heart.

"I missed you," I breathed against her ear, kissing her temple, her brow, wrapping my arms around her collarbone and stomach as I continued to thrust. We panted, messy, slick, and sweating. Arwen letting out one choked moan after another as my hands ran down her arms and thighs. Flushed and misted in sweat as we grasped and groped—her breasts bouncing with our rhythm. The sight was so erotic it was nearly excruciating. Some base, possessive, wholly male part of me wanted to come all over them.

She was *mine.*

But there would be another time for that.

The thought that this wouldn't be the last time I was with Arwen in this way was almost as euphoric as the sex itself.

At the sound of Arwen's groans and the weight of the back of her head against my chest, I picked up the pace, bringing my hand down to the apex of her thighs and stroking her until she squirmed.

She clenched and shuddered with her release, sobbing as she arched against me. It was my name on her lips that pulled me over the edge with her. A savage combustion of pleasure, white-hot and pulsing through my entire body.

Arwen collapsed onto the bed beneath us and I lay down next to her, careful not to crush her under my weight, both of us winded as if we had been running for miles.

"Is it always like that?" Arwen rolled onto her back, eyes fluttering open to stare at the sheer canopy above us.

"It never has been for me."

She raised a brow in silent question. "But you . . ."

"Have had a lot of meaningless, disconnected sex with a lot of women. None of whom I loved. None of whom were *you*."

Arwen nodded, but she didn't seem concerned either way. Perhaps she had taken our conversation in Mariner's Pub to heart and was comparing herself less to others.

"I'm not ashamed of my lack of experience," she said, her eyes bright on mine. "Or your surplus of it. I just want to be enough for you."

A laugh rumbled out of me, and Arwen laughed, too, even as her brows knit together in confusion. "You really have no idea what you do to me."

Arwen rolled her eyes.

"I'm serious. Here, I'll show you. Make the pinched face you do when you're mad."

Her eyes filled with mock insult. "What pinched face?"

"When you're angry with me, your brow furrows and you get a little pinch between them, right here." I touched the spot in the center of her forehead. "And down your nose. It means you're about to lay into me, which for some masochistic reason I find wildly attractive. So much so, it gets me hard."

The look on her face told me how little she believed me.

"A bit like a bull," I said, placing a hand behind my head in disinterest.

"Hey," she snapped, brow furrowing and nose scrunching up.

My cock twitched and I grabbed for her hand, placing it under the sheets so she could feel the proof for herself. "See?"

Arwen let out a surprised laugh. "You're sick."

"Yes," I admitted. "Completely lovesick for you. I have been for months."

Her eyes fell to my lips and she leaned in to kiss me, long and slow and soft.

"My beautiful bird."

"My king," she purred in response.

I groaned, laying my head back into the pillows. "Talk about things that really do it for me."

"You love when I call you *my king*?" She scoffed. "So drunk on power."

"I love when you call me your anything."

It was still night, but now that my eyes had adjusted, I could just barely make out a silver outline on the trees that surrounded the keep. The sun would be rising soon.

I traced my hand lightly across Arwen's shoulder, closing my eyes to the gentle sounds of her breathing. She grasped my hand in both of hers. "This ring is my favorite of yours," she said, touching the onyx signet I wore on my pinky.

"It was my mother's."

"She had great taste," Arwen said softly.

"She did. She would have loved you."

"You think so?"

"Definitely. You would have gotten along like old friends. She wasn't necessarily funny, but she had a great sense of humor. She laughed hard and often, like you."

"I wish I could have known her."

"I would have been instantly excluded."

A laugh breezed out of her. "Like you and my mother at that dinner in Siren's Cove. She adored you." Arwen tucked her chin into my chest. "I wish she could have seen us figure it out. Could have known that I was happy."

"She knew you. Perhaps better than anyone else. She knew you would be happy, Arwen."

We sat in a content quiet, and I began to doze off before Arwen squirmed beside me.

"I can't sleep now."

I smiled. "Breakfast?"

She sat up to peer out at the balcony windows. "It's not even morning."

"Exactly." I eased out of bed and threw on my breeches. "I'll send for some food and we can eat as we watch the sun rise."

"That sounds blissful," she said, falling back into the plush pillows behind her. My bed was so large, the sheets and pillows nearly engulfed her.

"One thing," I added as I headed for the door to my study, guilt already creeping in that it had taken me this long to remember. "Can I let Acorn in? He hates to sleep alone, and I haven't seen him yet after being gone for months . . ."

"You're kidding," Arwen said, eyes wide. "The strix really is your pet?"

"Of course." I frowned. "What do you think I keep him around for? His conversation skills?"

Arwen's mouth lifted in a smile, but fear still flickered in her eyes.

"You said you trust me always. I would never let something happen to you. Especially not at the claws of my own strix." I didn't blame her entirely. Acorn's glowing yellow eyes and owl wings paired with his goblin-like features and torso had the same effect on most people: terror. It was one of the many, many things I loved about him.

As soon as the door popped open, Acorn bounded inside like a tornado, long wings nearly slapping me in the face, claws scrambling to find a grip on the hardwood floor.

"Hello to you, too," I cooed. But he flew past me and prowled onto the bed, sending Arwen wriggling away. Acorn only curled up beside her, screeching happily and rubbing his front claws together.

"See, he loves you."

"He tried to eat me!"

"Now, how can I blame him for that?"

"Kane," she said, still twined in blankets she must have believed would protect her. "He really did almost kill us."

"If I recall correctly, *you* almost killed *him*. When you *broke into my study*. To *steal* from me."

"Well, that was after you kept me in a dungeon."

She said it with nothing but humor, but I felt my smile fall. I pulled the door open and asked the guards down the hall to fetch us breakfast before striding back into the room and opening the balcony windows.

A pleasant, chilly breeze caressed my face as I looked down on my keep. The barely peeking sunrise beyond the treetops had brought out the stablehands and landscapers, a young man washing the masonry, and various soldiers just waking up or shuffling through the barracks to take a piss.

All people whom we needed to protect.

As badly as I desired it, we couldn't hide in this room forever.

When I turned back to face Arwen, the first rays of dawn light had just feathered across her face, highlighting that delicate nose and those full lips. She was tentatively petting Acorn—*very* tentatively—but he was thrilled, eyes half-closed and burrowing deeper into the duvet.

Her beauty made my heart twist.

No wonder she was the daughter of a God. That kind of regal, arresting splendor could never be found in a mere Fae. Even a full-blooded one. I crawled into bed beside her, tucking her warm body into mine. Acorn scooted to nestle at our feet.

"I was only joking about the dungeon," she said after a while. "You can't carry that with us the rest of our relationship."

"I know." She was right. It was no way to begin a life together. "When you do me the honor of becoming my—"

She pushed a finger to my lips. "Don't."

"All right," I said, muffled.

"I mean—" She shook her head. "Do, eventually. Do ask me. I want to be wed. I want to be with you, but first . . ."

*First let's make sure she has a life to spend with me at all.*

Arwen's hand splayed across my chest as we listened to the rhythmic sounds of Acorn's snores twined with the wind rustling between the balcony drapes. Arwen dragged a finger across my forearm. All its small raised lines and pale white marks. "Why do you have so many scars? Are these from being in your dragon form?"

"Some." I scanned my own biceps and torso. "I wish I had more valiant stories to tell you. Most of them are from a pretty standard Fae childhood."

Her brows met in confusion.

"Fae heal very quickly. Growing up, Fae children tend to find themselves in precarious situations because they know they can survive almost anything."

I could hear the pieces clicking together in her mind. "So, when I heal quickly . . . that's not due to my healing abilities, that's just part of being Fae?"

I dipped my chin in confirmation.

"Would I also age very slowly? Would I have lived thousands of years?"

"Yes, bird."

"Longer than Mari, and Ryder, and Leigh . . . longer than you?"

I tucked a finger under her chin and brought her eyes to mine. "Yes. You *will* outlive us all. Even me. I'm not full-blooded. But I've got at least another thousand years in me, so don't get too excited."

Arwen continued her lazy strokes, this time across my abdomen, and I shut my eyes against all that stood against us as soon as we left this room. Hemlock wouldn't be easy, but hopefully we could get in and out, as long as—

"Why are you so . . . fit?"

I choked on a laugh. "What do you mean?"

She sat up and stared at my abdomen. "You're practically carved out of stone. Do you exercise a lot or something?"

I shrugged. "I suppose I do. In my free time. I don't have a lot of . . ."

"Hobbies?" she supplied.

"I was going to say friends." The truth sounded fairly depressing. "Other than Griffin. And Acorn. So I train whenever I can. Sometimes out of boredom."

"I know you didn't appreciate my offer of friendship in the caverns, but you are probably my closest friend. Don't tell Mari."

I chuckled. "I'd say don't tell Griffin, but I'm sure he wouldn't give a shit."

"Oh, yes, he would. He loves you."

"I haven't the faintest idea why."

She pushed back to put space between us and held my eyes in hers. "Don't kid yourself. You're a good man, Kane."

If I had any hope of that being true, I owed her one final truth. "I have to tell you something."

"I swear to the Stones, Kane, if you have kept one more horrible secret from me, I will castrate you."

"I doubt castration will be necessary, but I don't want anything else between us, either. Last night when you came to my bedroom, I was preparing to leave for the Pearl Mountains."

Arwen paled. "Why?"

"Remember what Beth said about the way of the Crow? Long before we found you, I heard rumors of a sorcerer who lived there in isolation. Someone who might be able to make me a full-blooded. I hoped to take the place of the Fae from the prophecy. I'm not even sure if it can be done, but apparently this *White Crow* is our best chance. I have to go see him, Arwen. I want to find a way for us both to survive. But if for some reason that's not possible . . . if there's a way I can take your place—"

"Absolutely not," she said, sitting up straighter. Acorn jolted awake with Arwen's movement before realizing nothing was wrong and closing his eyes once more.

"Arwen—"

"That is not a price I am willing to pay for my life. You'd be dooming me to an existence of grief. That's not a noble sacrifice; that's you taking the easy way out."

*"Arwen—"*

"You told me—*promised* me—that we would find a way out of this, and I am choosing to finally have some hope, and now you tell me your brilliant plan was to kill yourself?"

"No," I said calmly, attempting to ease her hysterics. "I won't go. If that's what you want, I won't go see him."

"Thank you." She exhaled.

"We'll find another way."

"We have to," she said. "We just have to."

⁓⟡⁓

WE CALLED A MEETING TO CONVERGE IN THE WAR TENT AT six. Inside, noblemen and soldiers crowded the space, sharpening weapons, poring over maps, and discussing strategy over piping-hot mugs of coffee and tea. At the sound of our entrance, over two dozen eyes landed on us like moths pulled to a flame, focusing on our hands, twined together.

"Holy Stones." Mari clutched her collarbone, looking up from the spell book in Dagan's grasp. "Did you two finally—"

"*Definitely*, they did," Amelia said, lounging in a leather love seat next to Ryder, who peered up from a desk stacked high with diagrams.

"You two are so foul," Ryder said.

Mari rolled her eyes at him, but it was Amelia's reaction to Ryder that caught my eye.

She blushed. Actually *blushed*.

And not secretly, privately, hiding her face from him, like some schoolgirl with a crush on Arwen's brother.

No—this was the flush of a shared secret. A private joke between two people who had shared something intimate. Thinking nobody was watching them, Ryder and Amelia made the briefest eye contact, so fleeting, so quick that I was sure I had made the whole thing up.

Until he brushed his hand against her folded arm and they both fought a smirk.

Maybe something had happened between them while stuck in Citrine together. Ryder surely had the blind arrogance needed to get within a foot of the impenetrable Amelia.

But what on earth did she see in *him*?

I wanted her to be happy—to find someone she cared about, and not just for the benefit of her father—but *Ryder*?

The kid was a weasel. A thief, a coward who paraded around as brave but seemed to always protect himself first and everyone else second, if at all. He was a self-serving, boastful creep who likely knew of Arwen's suffering at the hands of his father her whole damn childhood and did nothing about it.

As if Arwen could sense my tension, she gave my hand a squeeze. When I caught her curious expression, I shook my head as if to say *it's nothing*. I'd fill her in on what I saw later, once we had returned safely to Shadowhold with the blade.

Right now, we had more important matters at stake than who may or may not have been sleeping with whom.

# 42

ARWEN

KANE AND I CHOSE NOT TO TELL ANYONE SAVE FOR
Griffin about our trip to Hemlock Isle. When I asked why we
shouldn't bring more men with us than those already stationed on
the prison island, Kane had explained that Hemlock was a precarious ecosystem that functioned almost as if it were its own sepa-
rate kingdom. To bring an army might disrupt the island's fragile
order. Or worse, incite war. Griffin was the only one we trusted
not to fight us on the decision to go alone. And the fewer people
who knew where the blade was at any given moment, the better for
us all.

Kane and I approached Griffin and Eardley, who were wound
into some kind of tense debate. Eardley had rich dark skin and a
strong jaw. He looked a bit too pretty to be a lieutenant, but when
he spoke, the entire room went silent straining to listen, nearly as
much as when Griffin did. They both fell quiet at our arrival.

"Morning," Kane said. "Has the battalion left yet to track down
the seer's father?"

"Yes." Griffin nodded. "Late last night."

"Good."

"We're discussing who should travel back to Citrine to appeal to Isolde and Broderick," Eardley said. "See if that changes anything for them regarding their armies."

"My father should go," Amelia suggested from her seat, feet propped leisurely atop a trunk of swords. "He's the closest with King Broderick. They won't work with the lot of you."

"My daughter is right," Eryx said. "King Broderick was only hostile because of your history, Kane. He'll listen to reason when it comes from me alone. We're old friends."

"Are you?" Kane asked, mocking. "I so wish you'd tell us more often."

Before a reddening, blustery Eryx could respond, Lieutenant Eardley said, "I fear they may refuse even King Eryx asylum in Azurine."

"Send him with Prince Fedrik," Kane instructed. "Lazarus will never know of one extra passenger aboard his ship, and Queen Isolde and King Broderick only fear the optics."

Griffin folded his arms across his chest. "Where is the prince?"

"He left with a convoy to Sandstone," Eardley said. Sandstone was a port town on the coast where an Onyx ship would surely bring him back to Citrine. "If we move very quickly, King Eryx just might make it in time to travel with Prince Fedrik's vessel."

"Go, then," Kane said.

A small thrill of admiration ran along my spine and up my neck. I loved seeing Kane in his element. He was good at this—strong and effective, inspiring both fear and hope in equal measure.

Eardley dipped his head and pulled his skull-like helmet from the cluttered table before departing. Eryx, too, bid us farewell, but not before adding, "Amelia, do as you are told while I'm away. I do not want to hear that you were difficult." The expression on Amelia's face at her father's final words turned my stomach sour. I looked away.

"That just leaves Mari," Kane said.

"Me?" She cowered slightly, which even Ryder cocked his head at.

"I'd like you to return to Briar's manor and study under her. It's been a long while since I've had a talented witch by my side in battle, and we'll need just that if we are to defeat Lazarus."

Mari paled so severely she looked like she might collapse again, but before I could rush over to her, she said, "Of course."

"Good. Commander Griffin, see to it that she arrives before nightfall."

"I'll come visit," I said to her.

Mari looked anything but reassured. But Griffin had already homed in on Mari like a hawk. Protective, concerned—studying her as she chewed her lip. I knew he would ensure Mari was cared for.

"Arwen and I are chasing down one final lead on the blade. We'll communicate through ravens and spies." Kane faced me and took my hand once more. "Ready?"

But I spied my brother, his brow furrowed as he inspected something alongside Amelia.

Kane had been right. And Mari, too. I had let my own insecurities foster jealousy and resentment toward him for too long. I didn't want to be that person anymore. "I just need to do one thing first."

"I'll meet you at the gate."

I released Kane's hand and slipped over to Ryder. "What's going on here?"

"None of these little boys know what a boomerang is." Amelia showed off the curved weapon to me.

"Neither do I. Should I be terribly ashamed?"

"No, you aren't a soldier. Nor did you say you *knew every weapon in existence or you'd give me twenty coin* and then fail to produce said coin."

Amelia's light eyes cut to Ryder harshly and he grinned. "I told you I'm good for it."

I smiled a bit. "Don't hold your breath."

Ryder frowned at me.

"You throw it," Amelia explained, "and it returns to you, without any magic. So you can reach enemies without the close proximity of swordplay."

"It seems too dull to hurt anyone," a gap-toothed soldier said, reaching for the wooden weapon.

"Not when it's going faster than a mare." Amelia stole the boomerang back from his grubby hands. Then she turned to me, cool as a layer of frost.

"I'm happy for you and Kane. It was about time."

"Thank you," I said, before taking Ryder's arm in mine. "Can I speak with you for a moment?"

I weaved us through the frenetic energy of the tent until we made it outside. My eyes fell to an unimpressive patch of baby-fine grass between two soldiers' tents. Growing again after its seedlings had been ripped from the earth in a struggle months and months ago. Reborn after a gruesome death, newer, stronger, and taller than before. Just there, right outside this war tent, Kane had saved me from a horrific fate at the hands of Lieutenant Bert.

I had been so afraid then. So weak. Just a pawn in the larger game at hand. I didn't even recognize that girl anymore.

Wind rustling my hair, I faced Ryder. "I have something I need to get off my chest." I kept my voice low, but there weren't any soldiers around. "Something I should have said a long time ago."

"Is it that you and Kane are in love?" Ryder said, amused. "Because I put that one together all by myself."

"No." I studied my brother. I had let this plague me, and him, for far too long. "It's that I'm sorry."

Ryder's brows pulled inward. "For what?"

"For being so jealous of you, for so much of my life. My whole life, actually."

"*You* were jealous of *me*?"

I winced from the shame. From his incredulousness. "I think I told myself a story in which everyone wanted to be your friend before mine, or Powell and Mother loved you more, and . . . I don't know. One day it was true because I had made it true. Does that make sense?"

"Not really," he admitted.

"Everyone in Abbington adored you. And they weren't wrong to. You were more social than me, happier, braver—"

Ryder's sigh cut me off. "Braver? I'm a deserter, Arwen. That day I stole the Onyx coin? The day I sealed your fate? I *ran*. Ran and left all my men to be killed."

I shook my head even as I knew the words to be true. Hadn't he told us as much? That all his men had died, and he had only made it out scot-free by hiding? Why hadn't I heard it then? That he was not a hero from a folktale as I had once told him, but as scared as the rest of us.

"You," he said, studying my face, "are actually brave. What you have to do, it's . . . horrible. I couldn't go through with it."

The all-too-familiar swell of tears built behind my eyes. "I'm not sure if I can, either," I admitted.

"You're the bravest person I know, Arwen. You suffered my father's beatings for so many years while none of us knew. You were always glad to put yourself second to Leigh or me or Mother. I'm sorry you ever thought otherwise about yourself."

I hadn't known how much I needed to hear those words until he said them. "It's all right. Everything that happened . . . it led me here. I know we'll find the blade on Hemlock Isle. It's the only place that makes sense. And then we'll defeat Lazarus together."

"I don't know if—" He shifted on his feet. "I don't think I'm strong enough to lose you."

"You were fine with it once." My own words surprised me.

"How can you say that? You're my sister."

"You let me go. You let me run back toward certain death in Abbington. I don't think I knew it then but . . . it broke something in me."

There was such freedom in the words, I didn't know how I had gone so long without saying them.

Ryder paled. But to his credit, didn't argue. Didn't falter. "I never should have let you go that day." He shook his head. "I didn't want to be the one to do it. I told you I was a coward. Probably still am. I'm sorry, Arwen. It should go without saying—and it's my fault that it doesn't—but I don't want you to die."

And I didn't want to fail him. Any of them. "We're going to try to find another way to defeat Lazarus."

"Why am I not surprised? Optimistic as always," Ryder said with a rueful smile.

I wanted to tell him how wrong he was. How I'd been suffocated by clouds of misery for weeks before I allowed a single ray of hope to peek through. But at some point, without realizing it, I had made peace with the fact that Ryder and I just didn't know each other so well. Maybe, if we did in fact find a way out of this, I could try to change that. Maybe today, this moment, was the start.

I wrapped my arms around my brother and held him to me. "I'll see you when I'm back. Keep an eye on Leigh?"

"I will. Travel safe. And good luck."

I hurried through the barracks, the morning bright and filled with sunshine, even though I could feel the air turning crisp with early fall. I would never tire of seasons. If Kane and I were lucky enough to have a real life together, I would only live here in Onyx. Or anywhere like this, where I could experience all the seasons every few months. A sweltering summer full of dips in the pond, a colorful spring of blooms and chirping birds, a frigid winter— maybe even with a sprinkling of snow, another sight I had never seen—and a chilly autumn that would always remind me of Amber. Of my mother.

For better or for worse, that ray of hope had blossomed into a blinding sunrise. I wanted to live. I wanted to see everything. Experience everything. With Kane, with Mari, with Leigh, and even Ryder—for as long as I could.

I felt a massive presence at my side, long strides matching mine, and looked up to see Griffin accompanying me to the gates of the keep.

"Something I can help you with, Commander?"

Griffin stopped short and I stumbled to do the same. He stared at me pointedly, as if debating something.

"Out with it. I have a dragon to catch."

But he didn't smile. *Color me shocked.*

"I need to know you'll take care of him."

My brain stalled at his words. "Kane?"

He nodded once.

"I'd never hurt him, Griffin. I love—"

"Forget that. I'm not talking about your *will-they-won't-they* relationship."

I narrowed my eyes at him. "Did Mari teach you that term?"

"I'm serious."

"Aren't you always?"

"Hemlock Isle is a lawless wasteland. Despite it being Onyx territory, Kane doesn't have as much power there as he'd like to think. I understand why he can't bring an army with him. It's not part of the island's code. But it's a dangerous place, and if I'm not there, you must protect him."

My heart swelled against my ribs.

"You're more powerful than him, Arwen. The last full-blooded Fae. Tell me you will do what you did at Siren's Bay again if you have to. To protect Kane, but also to protect the Onyx king. The champion of Evendell. He must live, for the sake of the realms."

"I swear to you. I will protect him with my life."

Griffin lifted his chin in acceptance and turned to leave, but I caught him by the sleeve of his tunic.

"Thank you. For looking out for him now, and always. Even protecting him from me, when that was what he needed. He's lucky to have you."

Griffin nodded, then removed my hand from his tunic carefully, and I fought the urge to grin. "And you," I said, before he could walk away. "Help her? The amulet was a crutch, but I know she doesn't need it to do magic. Help remind her what she's capable of?"

"I'll do what I can. But know this: she's worth as much to me now as she is harnessing all the magic in Evendell."

I felt my throat bob. Mari had shared her loss with him. "You should tell her that."

He only grunted.

I gave him a shallow nod before hurrying over to Kane, who was leaning on the gates, waiting for me.

"What were you two talking about?"

I grinned and kissed his cheek. "You."

———✦———

I DIDN'T THINK I'D EVER TIRE OF SEEING THE WORLD FROM the back of Kane's dragon form. Every tree, cottage, and wheelbarrow reduced to a tiny, fuzzy blotch of green or brown and then filtered through a haze of clouds passed by in flight. It was easier to remember how simple things were up here. How finite. Somehow the stark enormity of our continent contrasted with our small, blurry lives brought me a great, curious kind of peace. For those fleeting hours, among soft, pale rays of fading sunlight and soaring eagles that flew at Kane's side, I didn't feel the crushing pressure of all that lay ahead.

And then, in the distance, I made out the singular, volcano-like island past Crag's Hollow, where Lake Stygian became the shimmering Ocean of Ore.

Erupting from the churning, murky water, Hemlock Isle almost resembled a mountain, if the point had collapsed in on itself and left sharp shards of rock and mineral in its wake. Angry whitecaps of foam smashed against the stone where the land protruded from the sea, and before I saw what awaited us inside, Kane hurtled us down through the narrow mouth of the island, as if we were a thread moving through the eye of a needle.

Sea salt was quickly replaced by damp earth and decomposing wood. A wet, green forest stretched beneath us, not too unlike the Shadow Woods. But this forest was not tangled, knotted, and dark, a harrowing moat of branches around the jewel that was Shadowhold. No, this was something entirely different.

As we swooped and weaved through trees, I could make out doors and windows built into the trunks and bark around us. Wooden roofs and rope ladders connected lantern-lit rooms to one another. An entire city built not on top of the woodland or in its stead, but rather within the trees themselves.

We were moving too fast to discern any people, but there must have been thousands of prisoners exiled here over the years to have built a city such as this one into the mouth of the island.

Finally, Kane landed on a grainy wood platform suspended between three trees with mossy rope and dotted with glowing golden lanterns. Amid the cacophony of birdsong and the thick, earthy smell of the forest, I dismounted Kane, my eyes searching to confirm we were alone, and I felt him shift back to himself, the sharp taste of lighte in the air and heavy on my tongue.

"What *is* this place?"

A metropolis stretched above and below us. Homes, armories, blacksmith tables, shops for produce—all carved from the trees, dotted with torches, and tied together by a web of interconnected walkways, ladders, bridges, and ramps.

"Hemlock Isle is quite the feat of human will, isn't it, bird?"

I merely nodded, my eyes still glued to the suspended passageways and unfamiliar pulley systems.

"When I took the throne from King Oberon, he told me very

little about the prison land. Just that there were men and women in Evendell that were too dangerous, too cunning, to be kept in dungeons alone. Witches and sorcerers especially could escape almost any cell, as evidenced by the jailbreak we had back in Shadowhold."

I shook away the memory of my aiding Halden and his magic friend in their escape from Kane's keep.

"Oberon's grandfather found the island first—a mountain protruding from the sea, hollowed out, with a forest growing inside, the cliffs that make up the walls of the island, both internal and external, too smooth to be climbed—there was no way in or out, unless you could fly."

"What about other Fae? Or those who can use spells to fly?"

"There are no Fae in Evendell with enough lighte to shift other than Griffin and me. And in all my years, I've never heard of, let alone *known*, magic powerful enough to allow for flight. Still, I've had guards stationed at the lighthouse in Crag's Hollow for the last five decades, in case anyone flew in or out." Kane shrugged. "They've never seen a thing."

"So, you and Griffin bring prisoners here in your shifted forms—"

"Or we send them on one of my other trained, flying creatures."

I gave Kane a look of dismay, but he merely shrugged. "You think you've seen all the winged tricks I have up my sleeve?" He shook his head in mock disappointment. "Come on, bird. Give me some credit."

Now was not the time, but later, without a doubt, I would be asking for a rundown on all the other grotesque creatures Kane kept in his castles.

"So, King Oberon flew prisoners here, left them to their own devices, and one day he found they had built all of this?"

"Indeed. The island has no hills or fields for farmland, and the lower down you go"—Kane peered over the platform into the dense, darkened treetops below us—"the less sunlight you get. So, with few tools to work with, the prisoners built into the trees that were already growing. Up and up and up."

My eyes swept over the pathways that twined and twisted ahead of us, shrouded in shadow from the steep cliffs of the mountain that surrounded the island on all sides. Like being inside a giant vase, the bottom littered with trees. And the forest that grew upward—it was as if the branches were trying, straining, to reach the sun that evaded them.

Within the maze of rickety bridges, mismatched stairs, and torchlit homes were dirt-caked men and women milling about. The bony spine of a shirtless boy reflected the light of a dim lantern and snagged my eye in the distance. The child couldn't have been more than Leigh's age, and he was climbing a ladder with some kind of skinned animal leg wedged between his teeth.

My stomach turned thinking about life in these conditions. Even for prisoners—thieves, murderers, enemies of the kingdom—it didn't seem just. I hadn't thought enough about the ramifications of being with Kane. That if I were to survive Lazarus, and save this kingdom, that I might truly . . . rule it by his side. I waited for the racing heart, clammy palms, tightness in my chest—the panic I knew would come at the thought of such an undertaking.

But no such feeling came.

In fact, I realized I might be decent at helping Kane rule Onyx. I had skills that he lacked: patience, positivity—I didn't have his temper nor the cynicism that sometimes crept into his worldview.

Something bright and hopeful settled in me at the thought of the good I could do for the people of Onyx. Maybe for the people of Evendell altogether. Maybe I would even start with this place.

I opened my mouth to ask about children born on the island, and thus undeserving of this fate, but Kane cut me off. "I adore your beautiful brain, and all the questions and thoughts I know are percolating inside of it. But don't let the elflike tree houses fool you. This entire island is inhabited by the most menacing criminals born to our continent. I'd like to get you out of here as quickly as possible. Then you can ask me anything you wish."

"Agreed. Where to?"

"The guard station first. They'll escort us to the city's leader. The last time I had spies sent here, they said the island was ruled by a warlord named Killoran Grim. We'll find him up there." Kane pointed to a well-lit wooden platform tented in dark patchwork canvas. "I wish I didn't need you for this. But when we examine his weaponry, the blade will call to you. We'll be home in time to have rabbit stew for dinner, and something even better for dessert." Kane pressed a kiss to the top of my head, and I tried to nod brightly.

I wasn't scared.

How could I be with him beside me?

# 43

## ARWEN

I FOLLOWED KANE DOWN A ROPE BRIDGE AND THROUGH THE remarkable wooden city. It might have felt whimsical—magical, even—if I hadn't known it was populated entirely by violent criminals. The sun had slipped behind a cloud, bathing every textured slat and mossy stretch of rope in flickering shadow.

I clung to Kane as we climbed past burly men without teeth hacking into cured meat and women washing dingy linens, pouring the dirty water directly off the platforms and into the foggy depths below.

When we reached a decayed turret with a thatched roof, Kane peered inside and I did the same. It was empty save for two dusty mugs and a blue sparrow picking at a fetid apple.

"Is this where your guards are stationed?"

Kane lifted the empty mug to his nose and sniffed.

"Where are they?"

He didn't answer but the worry on his brow was clear. "Perhaps we should return tomorrow, with soldiers."

I shook my head, emboldened by his earlier confidence. "We're already here. Lazarus could come for Shadowhold any minute, and now that everyone who was evicted from Citrine is there . . ." I didn't want to finish the thought.

Kane released a deep sigh, taking my hand as we walked down the rope bridge and farther into the heart of the city. We wove through throngs of uninviting, grimy faces. Up ladders and down ramps and back up winding stairs with sections of rotted wood carved by mold and termites. I watched my feet out of an abundance of caution not to trip and fall right through.

A snapping sound had my eyes off my leather boots and up on a handful of rocks tumbling toward my head. I brought my hands over my face in cover, but the boulders hovered in midair, buoyed by a dark satchel of mist, before flying unnaturally to the right and toppling down into the trees and branches beneath us.

I caught my breath. "What was that?"

Kane shrugged, but concern played across his eyes. "Something shaken loose above us. Perhaps some children trying to give their new guests a head injury."

I peered up at him. "You used lighte. You never do that."

"Your face is too pretty. It would be a great shame to see it caved in."

I didn't laugh. "Don't deflect."

"Don't pry." Kane offered a crooked smile and kept walking.

"I will never stop prying, and you know it," I said, following after him. "Why did you do that?"

"To protect you."

"You could have moved me out of the way. Why did you use your lighte? And out in the open like that?"

Kane stopped walking and turned to face me. There was

nobody else on the canopied ramp. A single firefly whizzed past his brow. "Fae can harness lighte from various elements. Air, earth, metal, wind, water, fire, ether—the list goes on and on. My lighte comes from the depths of the earth. So I'm strongest, or the lighte flows out of me easiest, in places much like this. Surrounded by dirt, soil, wood. Sometimes the rotting leaves, the decay of the forest itself."

"But you weren't as strong in Reaper's Cavern."

He lowered a brow playfully. "Ouch." When I blushed, he said, "That was stone, not earth."

"That's why you love Shadowhold. Why you prefer it over your palace in the city. It's surrounded by dark woods."

Kane continued to walk. "Come on."

"And what about mine? It comes from the air?"

"You're full-blooded, so it might be even wider. Air, sun, fire."

"How did Dagan know that?"

"He's always been good at determining a Fae's lighte source. Perhaps it was your bright and sunny soul." He was walking ahead of me, but I could see the smile curving at his lips.

"I wasn't very bright and sunny with Dagan in the beginning."

"A light like yours cannot be dampened by circumstance."

We hiked up another set of stairs under a tangled mesh of vines and long, pointed pine needles. I wiped a spiderweb from my face. "What's the rarest element a Fae can pull lighte from?"

Kane didn't turn back to me as he said, "Blood," but looked behind his shoulder at my audible gasp. "They are a very rare breed, the Hemolichs. Aleksander's men. The one who betrayed us. Hemolichs draw power from corpses, wounds, even their own injuries, making them unmatched warriors. Some drink the blood of animals, mortals, or other Fae to keep their lighte strong. In Lumera, common slang for them is 'vipers.' But it's a nasty slur."

Before I asked one of a hundred follow-up questions, we pushed through a curtain of hanging willow and came face-to-face with two grim guards. One was missing an eye but hadn't bothered with a patch of any kind.

"King Ravenwood of Onyx Kingdom. I'm here to see Killoran."

Without another word, the one-eyed man lifted a stained fabric partition and we stepped into the covered fortress.

Lounged across a makeshift throne of knotted wood was a man who looked like he ate nails for breakfast. Leathered skin, cropped hair, and a stiff, mercenary mustache. Somehow bulky and lean, nearly all muscle, and presiding over a grotesque, dimly lit chamber.

Three topless women in beaded necklaces and skirts of gossamer were sitting around him like house cats. Haggard and hungry, each woman was chained to his throne with thin, crudely cut metal chainwork.

Men clad in rusted metal armor crowded the lair, each with their own unsophisticated weaponry—axes, clubs, and bludgeons. They packed the room like cramped teeth, all eyes focused on their leader.

Killoran's throne sat before a wide, white marble table. Cluttered with weapons, chalices—

White marble . . . What kind of white marble could they—

*Bone.*

Femurs and sternums I'd worked on my whole life—my stomach heaved as I realized I was regarding a table crafted of *human bone.*

But my stomach—it wasn't a pit of nausea. No, it swirled and turned with something . . . different.

A tender, troubling pleasure. Like pressing on a bruise.

And my head—

Images were jumping into my mind that had no business being there: lips and ice, glass shattering and expanding, the echoing drops of blood on a silent, marble floor—

"King Kane Ravenwood," Killoran roared heartily. "To what do we owe the pleasure?"

I shook my head violently to dispel the uncanny feeling.

"Killoran." Kane dipped his head in greeting. "Just some swift business."

"Don't be daft. Let me offer you a drink. Or one of my wives?"

My blood boiled as I took in the glee in which Killoran dipped his head toward the brunette behind him. "Gisal here has a tongue that will—"

*"No,"* Kane cut in, voice savage, before straightening himself. "That won't be necessary. We are looking for a sword that was mistakenly brought here five years ago. My armorer needs a look through your weapon cache. Should only take her only a few minutes to find."

"Even a pretty young king like yourself must know—nothing is given for free here."

Kane's lip curled upward and it sent a shiver down my spine. "What can I offer you? A great weapon hewn in your name? Enough meat and bread to last a year? More spirit than all your men can drink ten times over? Name your price."

Kane seemed so calm, so at ease—almost as if he was having *fun* with Killoran.

Killoran grinned up at the bald man to his right before turning back toward us. "Do you know what it's like here in the winters?"

Kane's face remained bored. "Can't say that I do."

Killoran grinned again, but this time his eyes had grown cold. A foreboding feeling dropped into my stomach.

"In the wintertime, just a few months from now, the sun will fall behind the cliffs' edge before noon every day. All of Hemlock, plunged into unforgiving darkness for hours and hours before night even begins. Can you imagine how pale we all become? How thin when it is too dark to hunt well? How bored we get? Do you know what boredom does to those like us with demons in our heads?"

Kane's eyes narrowed.

"And you must know what it's like in the heat of summer. When this asshole of an island begins to cook and boil like the depths of a valley? When our wells run dry and bodies—men, women, children—begin to pile up? Can you imagine the stench? Do you know what cooked, rotting human flesh smells like?"

I swallowed hard against the nausea that twisted, greasy and bitter in my stomach. I knew his words were a threat. Kane must have felt similarly, because he stepped in front of me, ever so slightly, his hands resting casually at his sides, though I swore black thorns danced around his knuckles.

Kane bared his gleaming white teeth. "I'll flay the skin from your muscles before I grant you freedom."

But Killoran only laughed. "Freedom? Is that what you call your world out there? Free? No, pretty king," Killoran drawled. "Your world is not my freedom. Despite Hemlock's fickle isle, I have everything I could possibly want here. Out there, in your world, I am a nobody. A murderer, a rapist—" I flinched at the word, and Killoran's eyes lit with delight. "Just a scummy piece of human grime. But here—" Killoran gestured to the stacks of rusted swords and spears lined against the walls, the abhorrent table before him, covered in dented steel goblets. The gaunt, chained women at his feet, and the men who would lay their lives down for him without a single beat of hesitation. "Here, I am a *king*. Just like you."

Kane's jaw went stiff, and I swore I could feel the rage radiating off him. Rage at this man, dangling our safety like a rat above a python's open jaws. Rage at the comparison between the two of them. On his worst days I knew this was how Kane saw himself. Ruthless, cruel, self-serving.

"There's nothing we can offer you?" I asked, surprising both myself and Kane.

Killoran leaned forward with interest, giving me a broad, hateful smile. "So, the armorer girl can speak."

I bit the inside of my cheek, that peculiar, distant aching in my stomach back once more. "So she can."

"I never said you have nothing to offer me. In fact, you can offer me the one thing I need most."

"Well, get on with it. I have dinner plans," Kane said, running a hand through his hair, the picture of disinterest. "And even more important ones for dessert."

Killoran sat back in his throne and the wood groaned behind him as he lifted his legs. The thin blond girl who had been next to his feet moved without hesitation underneath them, contorting herself into a human footstool.

I swallowed pure bile but didn't give Killoran the satisfaction of looking away.

"When I came here, I was only seventeen. An orphan with few

options, I had joined a crew of men in the Blade Moors, done things that would pull the breakfast from green eyes over here"— Killoran pointed a blunt finger at me—"and was given a one-way ticket to Hemlock with the very man who had taught me all I knew.

"I had thought *we* were bad, but the men and women in this place . . ." Killoran huffed a rueful laugh. "I had no idea of *bad*. But it turned out I didn't have to be the baddest, or the meanest, or the toughest." Killoran ran a hand over his mustache. "I just had to be the *smartest*.

"Night three, I killed the man who had raised me—who had taken knives and lashings for me. I plunged an axe into his esophagus in front of thirty other men." Killoran chuckled as if it was a fond, silly recollection.

"The next day, the entirety of Hemlock followed me. My own band of merry warriors." Killoran grinned wide, all too pleased with himself. "It took me years to grind my way to where I am now. Years, and lives, and more sacrifice and hard work than you've ever known in your life, pretty king."

Kane's jaw tensed. "My patience is waning. What is it you want, Grim?"

I wished I could speak directly into Kane's mind. *He's playing with us. Let's go. We'll come back with your army.* The bizarre feeling that hadn't left since I entered the room was spinning wildly into spiked fear and carving at my insides. I wanted to leave. Now, now, *now*—

"You haven't even heard the end of the story! So young, so impatient." Killoran clucked his tongue. "I've ruled the island for two decades now. The longest anyone has ever held on to this throne. And now, after all I've done for the people of this island, all the factions I have aligned, I hear there's a *mutiny* brewing?" Killoran's eyes had narrowed into slits. "I don't need your weapons, your finery, your provisions. What I *need* is to prove my power. My smarts."

I didn't know who moved first.

Kane's night-black lighte wrecked and thrummed through the room, against the walls, punishingly loud and metallic on my tongue. It spun around us—out of his hands like sable crows' wings, sailing through the lair, slicing Killoran's men with the razor edges of dragon scales, talons, and poison fangs. Ropes of that guttering power flew from Kane's spine, his hackles raised, and strangled a snarling man I hadn't even seen coming.

And the *blood*—

So much seeping, oozing blood—

The men, dropping one after another, some sliced at the throat, gore pouring into the threads of their clothes, others carved through the skull or cracked down the chest like ripe, halved fruit.

But one of Killoran's men was already grasping me around my middle and hauling me backward. I cried out, unable to yank free—

But I drove my elbow into his nose, a satisfying *crack* reverberating in my ears alongside the feel of more blood—warm, wet blood—seeping into the fabric of my blouse. The man behind me barely flinched.

I screamed again as he wrenched me away from Kane—

*Kane.*

Kane, who would decimate all of them. All these humans. They would—

Where was he?

I struggled to crane my head down, fought the man who held me, my spit flying, teeth gnashing, and finally, *finally*, when I was able to look beyond the ceiling—

All the blood in my body turned to rigid ice.

Kane was on the ground, face crushed into splintered wood, near unconscious. His arms were pulled behind him by one lone thug, a knee denting into his back. The guard had wrapped a chain—lighter in color than iron, but appearing heavier than steel—around Kane's wrists.

Kane groaned and struggled against the man until he tied a leather gag around his mouth.

"What's wrong with him?" I shrieked. "Why can't he move?"

"Lilium chains," Killoran said, stepping around a river of dark blood from one of his slain men. "The only alloy that can suppress a Fae's power. A prisoner or two have been brought to the island still in them over the years. They're near impossible to get off. Had to slice through my fair share of wrists to collect the metal. Neat trick, huh?"

Killoran feasted on the shock that spread over my face, a body still twitching by his feet. "Oh, you thought I didn't know your king was Fae? After all my years here, all the men delivered from the Onyx Kingdom? Men who spoke of a king that never ages, who is never seen alongside his prized dragon, who has, on rare account, been seen using darker magic than any sorcerer or witch?"

I shook my head. I had no *words*. None, save for "Please—"

"The Fae king of Onyx has power that I need. Power that will allow me to stay in control."

What kind of power could he take from Kane? He couldn't have his kingdom, and Kane would never serve another king, let alone a despicable monster such as—

Harvesting.

That's what he meant. He'd harvest Kane's lighte.

The thought was more sickening than the thug's arms wrapped around my middle.

"And you," Killoran said, stepping around a bound Kane as if he were a heap of garbage. "The king's pretty armorer will make a perfect meal for the beast. Did I neglect to mention the creatures that we share the island with? Who crawl up from the depths below when they're hungry?" Killoran shook his head, laughing to himself, and that woozy, swirling pit in my stomach doubled. I cringed as the sensation crawled through my body like vermin. "I'll be honest with you. I make it sound a lot worse than it is. Their dinner is but our meager entertainment."

Tears pooled in my eyes. I couldn't move. I couldn't think.

I needed to use my lighte.

But all I had mastered was healing and forming a protective bubble around myself and others. Aside from that, I had only ever produced destructive rays of energy that set anyone near me aflame or turned them into red mist.

I couldn't risk hurting Kane. Not when he couldn't protect himself.

"Onyx Kingdom will have your head," I vowed. "King Raven-wood's army would go to the ends of the continent for their king."

"Oh, dear! A mass of men already weakened from fighting two other kingdoms. However will my army of violent, depraved prisoners beat them? An army of men and women who had to be the strongest, the most vicious, to survive."

I didn't exhale.

The warlord raised a single brow. "If Onyx Kingdom tries to invade *my* island, where I know the landscape better than my own ass cheeks, they deserve to be slaughtered."

Kane, near unconscious, groaned from the ground.

"Relax, pretty king." Killoran shook his head. "I'm not going to hurt your men unless they come for me first. You two really have the wrong idea about me."

Killoran was out of his Stones-damned mind. I struggled against the man who held me, his nose still dripping blood down the back of my shirt. "You have no idea what you're do—"

A blow to my temple sent my head swimming with pain, and a swift darkness overtook me, alongside the sound of Kane's muffled roar.

# 44

❦

## ARWEN

*K*ANE'S BROWS KNIT INWARD. HIS HEAD COCKED TO THE side. *"Don't you love me?"*

*"Of course I do." Of course, of course, of course . . .*

*"Then let me take your place. Let me die for you."*

*I opened my mouth to tell him no—please, please no—but only embers fell out. Little embers, each with wings. Tiny winged embers falling from my tongue, like ash in wind. Lighting me up from the inside. Setting me ablaze.*

My eyes flew open and I gasped wildly, drawing damp forest air into my lungs. I thrashed—

My arms.

They were tied behind me. Wrapped in something. My legs, too, and across my middle. Oh, *Stones*, my lungs. They were seizing. I needed air. I needed to move. And something smelled like rot. Like carrion. Like death—

The howls and shouts of Hemlock's inhabitants shook the fog of panic from my mind, and I fought to breathe through my pounding headache, my eyes adjusting to the darkness. All I could make out were wooden bridges and wicker structures lit by lanterns and torches overhead. I was suspended somehow, across a long, thin net that webbed between all the trees and posts and branches supporting the city.

Above me, in the houses and along the interlaced bridges, stood men and women, some husky with tattoos, others thin and under-fed, street urchin children weaving in and out of legs to get a better look. Killoran had mentioned *entertainment*, and the slowly gath-ering crowd told me all I needed to know about their show of choice.

My shackles weren't leather or metal or even lilium. But rather stiff, translucent silk. It looped around my wrists, my stomach, my legs, and spread between the trees, the two platforms, forming the netting that held me between the branches and pines.

Not netting. It wasn't net at all.

It was a *web*.

A thin yet impenetrable web laced around the lower trees of Hemlock's city. And strewn throughout—

Bodies. *Carcasses*. Half-eaten, rotting, and decomposing all along the tangled silk.

Despite the churning in my stomach, I didn't dare look away—I couldn't. Not until I figured out what had killed them. Their state of decay was the only clue I had to decipher whatever was coming to kill me. I squinted at the torn limbs and open wounds.

No, not torn. Burned. Boiled and bubbled as if—

*Acid.*

Whatever trapped and hunted these less-fortunate prisoners devoured them with acidic venom. I wasn't an idiot. I knew from the webbing what was possible. Had heard stories from Halden and

Ryder over the years of widows: spiders the size of lions, with the upper bodies and heads of women. The venom in their fangs so toxic, one touch to the bloodstream could boil you alive.

I struggled against my thin, corded restraints. Bouncing myself on the net, I dug at the threads I could reach with my fingertips, but the tangled silk was stronger than chain. Unmovable.

*Bleeding Stones.*

I needed to do whatever I did that day with Halden. I had disintegrated rope somehow. How had I done that?

My lighte buzzed and tingled at my fingertips and in my palms. I clenched my jaw and gnashed my teeth.

I could sense it bubbling up.

*Thank the Stones.*

Feeling the heat, seeing it illuminating the dark—

I cast my eyes down over my shoulder and nearly hurled my entire stomach into the depths, swallowing any lighte back into my body in a flash.

The thin web under my bound body was all that kept me from the endless, knotted pit of trees and cliffs below. If I escaped from this impenetrable silk net and freed myself, I'd likely slip right through the gaps and plunge, screaming, to an instant death.

A violent noise dragged my eyes upward. Killoran stood atop a rickety balcony like a king surveying his subjects. Beside him was a still bound and gagged Kane, who was shouting something. Hoarse, as if he had been yelling for hours.

It was my name.

He was trying to shout my name. To wake me.

I moved my head vigorously until I saw his shoulders slump, his fears momentarily assuaged.

What I needed wasn't a way out of these restraints, but a way to reach the bridge or platforms surrounding me without slipping through the silk so that I could climb up to them. But the howls of the crowd were growing louder. Riotous. Roaring. They knew what was coming. They wanted a show.

*Come on, Arwen. Think, think, think—*

Beneath me, the leaves began to rustle.

And then she appeared. At first, just her eyes. Beady, yellow, whirling in different directions—all eight of them peering over the netting, glowing like embers. And obscuring them were delicate, dark lashes as fine as her silk trap. She tilted her elegant head up, revealing two flat nostrils bare of a nose and lips as red as rubies, too dainty to contain her spiked fangs.

The widow's long legs, dusted in black hair, protruded out and onto the web until she stood before me. The torso of a slender woman, claws—pincers—where her arms should be, all of her covered in the grotesque membranes of a near-translucent black spider. Straight sable hair hung from her head, so long it trailed across the fibers of her net as she prowled forward, and my dread turned heavy and leaden in my stomach.

She could walk across her web just fine. Either that otherworldly grace, or those sticky, membranous legs—whatever it was, she wasn't slipping through.

"Hemlock," Killoran bellowed to his people, "tonight we sacrifice another to the creature that lurks beneath. A beast I caught and imprisoned with my bare hands, lest you forget." The faces above me, mottled by firelight and shifting shadows from the sun still shining somewhere far, far up above, cheered and roared at his words.

"And not just any sacrifice. The prized armorer of King Kane Ravenwood of Onyx Kingdom!"

*Oohs* and *aahs* reverberated through the crowd as more people—haggard women and slick, scrawny men—peered out of their windows and left their posts, following the cries of an audience entertained.

"And how did I manage to steal her from him?" Killoran roared. "Well, why don't you ask the king himself?"

My stomach turned on itself at the horror, the humiliation, as he jerked Kane up by the tunic at his shoulders, and presented him, gagged, beaten, and chained, to his followers. Louder now than I had yet heard them, the crowd screamed and hollered, swarming on top of one another, disorderly in their delight.

It was almost enough to steal my attention from the creature stalking toward me and her ravenous intent. But the torchlight glinting off something around her neck stilled my racing thoughts.

A collar.

A thick iron collar, tethering her to the depths below. One she strained against, halting repeatedly to stretch her long, graceful neck from, but the chain was too taut, and each time she drew closer, or retreated, it retracted with her movements, never leaving her any slack.

But that collar was made of solid chain. And I was weaponless—

My eyes flitted frantically to the other bodies.

But none of them had what I was looking for, and she was prowling closer. One slender bent leg after another, moving with such eerie grace as her pincers snapped once, twice—

And the crowd, the prisoners, roaring with glee, cheering her on.

*Focus. One of them has to have—*

I just needed to know it was possible. That her venom could do what I needed it to.

Leather belt, suede pouch, wooden club, no, no, no . . .

*There—*

A metal shield.

Strapped to the back of a decomposing body was an iron shield, boiled by the widow's acidic poison, liquefied as if it were butter.

Melted.

Her venom *melted* metal.

Those pincers, too close now. The sound like a knife being sharpened before it cut into fresh meat. Slicing, snapping, clicking. The silk shook as the creature hovered above me, and I—

I didn't squirm. I didn't cry. I sucked in a great lungful of air and braced myself. The widow crouched low, and the fine hairs of her legs tickled my shoulders and nose. Slowly, she cut through my restraints with those gleaming pincers, taking her time as she freed my arms, my torso. Her hypnotic yellow eyes shone, her lips parting to reveal the shining white fangs inside.

Her nostrils twitched, pupils rolling together to follow my involuntary jerks and spasms every time a fine hair touched my skin. She cocked her head to one side, and then the other . . . waiting.

Waiting for my struggle, for the hunt—

But I lay still, despite the audience's groans and bellows for me to scramble away. I shuddered through the horror, the smell of earth and musk, as the creature opened her gruesome arachnid mouth, let out a hungry, fevered hiss, and tore her venomous fangs through my thigh.

My vision tunneled to a single pinprick.

It was worse than agony.

The closest I had come to feeling even a whisper of this kind of pain had been the night Kane's healers purged wolfbeast venom from me. And that—that had been a splinter, a papercut, a *stubbed toe* compared to this.

I shrieked.

*Sobbed—*

Bellowed as acid ripped through muscle, flesh, my very bones, until I could feel my blood bubbling, *sputtering* under my skin.

Another wave of relentless anguish hauled me under and I screeched, my voice like a banshee in my own ears—

*Do not faint. Do not faint.*

All the while the crowd cheered for my death. For my evisceration. Some faraway part of my brain remembered what needed to be done. My only chance at survival.

I reached with arms that didn't feel like my own for the metal chain connected to the widow's collar. Tugged and wrenched it looser, longer, until I had enough slack to bring the chain down to where the creature's fang was still impaled in my leg and ran the metal through my own bubbling, sizzling flesh.

Moaning through clenched, gritted teeth, I nearly vomited from the splintering, nerve-shredding torture. One more minute—

One more second—

Until finally, *finally*—the widow's chain snapped, liquefied by its own acid, with a wonderful *crack*.

I had to move very, very quickly now, lest the widow realize she was free and take off, leaving me to plummet through the gaping holes of her web. I pushed one hand into my thigh and felt the lighte eagerly pour through me, sealing up the wound, purging the acid, cooling the burning, ripping venom.

I exhaled with the fleeting relief, and with my other hand I clawed for her collar, dodging as she lurched toward me, her toxic fangs just narrowly missing my neck.

The crowd booed their displeasure as I ducked to the side, the silken lattice swaying and bouncing with my every movement. The widow crawled around me, pouncing to pierce me with her fangs once more.

I rolled, skirting another blow, the web dipping uneasily and my foot slipping through a gaping hole.

More cheering, more rabid joy—

My hands wrapped around the thin strands of silk, the fibers too slight, too dainty to hold me—

My stomach plummeting as I reached, and reached and *reached*.

And finally grasped her collar.

My fingers twined around the metal chains, pulling myself upright and, despite the pain, over the creature until I was seated atop her like a horse. She screeched out a wicked sound, and I wrapped my hands in her hair to hold myself steady. Her bony exoskeleton was thin, and bowed under my weight, the reedy, prickly hairs grazing my arms. While the crowd thundered with glee as I tried to hold on, the widow's flexible body writhed and shrugged, trying to buck me off. I yanked the chain around her neck harder, rearing her up like a steed on its hind legs.

"Come on," I said, grunting. "I freed you, *come on*—"

Suddenly she took off, and I was thrown backward as we skittered toward a large oak platform bursting with spectators. Their shouts of elation quickly bled into gasps of terror as the widow's legs scurried over vines and stairs and bodies. I held on for my life, tugging at her silky hair as she hissed and shrieked, fangs snapping.

I just needed to get closer, higher, over to where Killoran and his men were beginning to panic, scrambling for their weapons, crawling over one another to aim their crossbows at us.

The widow lunged for a cowering, dirtied child and I yanked her back with all my strength until the tendons in my arms were straining, sweat beading and pooling on my brow—

Back, Stones-damn it, *back*—

She screeched again, so close to my ear it sent my teeth gnashing.

"That's not the one you want," I bit out. "How about the man that chained you?"

The widow retracted from the boy and cocked her elegant head in my direction. Long, silken black hair spilled over my knee and I wriggled from the sensation.

"He's up there." I tugged the chain toward Killoran's war room. "And I'm going to kill him."

The widow took off, climbing vertically over the unpolished posts, pails of water, a butcher's hut—one long, elegant leg plunging through a cut of beef as patrons ran for the bridges and dove off the platform, away from her still-dripping fangs.

Higher still she climbed as arrows rained down on both of us. But if I had practiced one single skill with my lighte in the weeks since Siren's Bay, it was the iridescent golden shield I flowered around me, which protected us both from the weapons that sailed overhead.

We climbed high enough that I could see Killoran, dragging Kane by his lilium chains away from the balcony and into his throne room. The widow would keep climbing, keep feasting through the city. This was my shot—

Without even steeling myself, I released her hair and leapt.

I landed hard, halfway onto the knotted beams of Killoran's balcony, hands scrambling to grip the ledge. I hoisted myself up and over the mismatched wooden planks and slumped down onto the floor to catch my rough, ragged breaths.

I was mere feet from Kane, who was too pale and drenched in sweat, trying to call to me through the leather gag.

But I couldn't hear him. I couldn't hear anything except the roaring in my ears and the racing of my heart and that pulsing, unfathomable pain in my mind, back again. I tried to push myself up but my sight had blurred—

Killoran's men had me in their grip within seconds.

Exhaustion consumed me and I sagged against their steadfast hold.

"No matter," Killoran muttered from across the room. "I'll dispose of her myself," he roared to the crowd outside. But all I could hear were their screams as the widow prowled through their city, plunging her spiked legs through their canvas roofs and tearing her fangs into anyone in sight.

Served them all right.

I hoped she went to bed very full tonight.

Killoran stalked toward me, unsheathing his sword.

And suddenly that mind-altering sensation, that crippling, gooseflesh-inducing twist . . .

It was replaced by an onslaught of sea wind and cackling, white-hot coals and the unflinching stare of death and a cold morning filled with dazzling sunbeams and—

I strained against the assault and squeezed my eyes shut.

An assault of sequences I hadn't ever seen—a child inside a womb, a decaying fox in a wood, a chorus of bells, ashes and embers and flames—I sucked in air as I tried to grasp one image, one sensation, and make sense of it before another invaded my mind. I strained against my captors as the power battered me.

Unrelenting madness and ecstasy and power.

Pure, persistent *power*—

Beckoning to me—

To its master.

Reunited, though we had never met.

I was not afraid.

I knew what it was.

I knew why it belonged to me.

The only thing on this continent that could cause such sickness and euphoria and turmoil in the same heartbeat.

Killoran was wielding the Blade of the Sun.

# 45

## KANE

*A*GONY.

Not my lighte, drained through the lilium, taken from my body against my will like a relentless bloodletting for the last few hours on end—

Nor my throat, raw and shredded from roaring for Arwen. For her life, for her to wake, for her to fight, to run. Powerless and unable to help her.

No, the agony racked through me as I watched Killoran stride toward us, debased and menacing, blade raised, ready to cleave Arwen in two.

A rage I didn't know existed within me—hadn't known of for two hundred years—sloshed and jerked in my heart like a torrential storm. Until I couldn't think, couldn't see, couldn't bark through my gag anymore at Killoran to stop, to leave her be, to take me in her place.

When the warlord stepped around the corpses that littered his floor toward Arwen, who had sagged in the arms of his thugs, I saw nothing but the pulsing, throbbing vein of his jugular.

His life force.

The only thing standing between him and the woman who could save our world.

Every realm.

Every human.

Every Fae.

I didn't think as I lunged for him.

It was uncanny, feeling my dragon fangs pierce through my gums, through the leather gag, while my lighte was still suppressed by the chains. A feeling that my entire existence would say should not have been possible to experience. No Fae had ever used lighte while bound by lilium.

The pain was excruciating. As it often was, for the brief moment in which my body recomposed itself when I shifted. Only now the lilium chains kept me in a suspended state of anguish, unable to fully shift, and that rage, caged like a beast inside of me, shot free in the only way it could.

Through my very mouth.

I heard Arwen's gasp of horror before any of the others in the room.

But by then Killoran was already dead on the floor at my feet, his gurgling scream as I shredded through his throat the last sound he'd ever make. Below me, that throat torn clean out, tendons and flesh peeled back and ripped apart in a gory, wet mass where his neck once was. I would've smiled.

But in my mouth—

I spat the bastard's remains onto the ground before sinking to my knees. The sharp enamel of my dragon fangs retracted back into my gums and at last offered some reprieve from the pain.

But then, the pain was elsewhere.

Burning, rippling, in my side.

I knew the feeling of steel lodged between my ribs. I sucked in a lungful of air.

*Fuck.*

Killoran must have landed one final blow in my side as I ripped his throat out. I just needed to maneuver my hands free of the lilium so I could dislodge Killoran's blade before any of his men could finish what their leader had started.

My eyes snapped up as the two men holding Arwen staggered back like they had been burned. As if her skin had singed them, curiosity freckling the ugliness in their eyes.

Arwen rushed me. "Hold still. I'm going to pull it out—"

"Whatever you say, bird," I grunted. "But hurry."

Arwen wrapped her hands around the sword, and I squinted against the bright light.

*Bright light?*

I started at the sight before me—Arwen by my side, Killoran's sword wrapped in both her hands, both her and the blade *glowing* brighter than any fire, any star ever could. Its hilt adorned with all nine stones, like a bejeweled kaleidoscope, iridescent and luminous, brilliant and blinding like the sun itself.

The blade. It had been Killoran's weapon.

But the men were upon us, bludgeons and clubs drawn, faces wet with fury and lust for our deaths.

I couldn't even stand—

With one move, Arwen yanked the sword from my torso.

I clenched my teeth against the discomfort, unable to tear my eyes away as Arwen swung a clean half circle. The force of wielding the weapon nearly shot her into the air, and explosive light blasted from the steel, bisecting every vicious thug in the room. Killoran's wives screeched their terror, ducking, as their gags of disgust twined with the sound of crunching bone and burning flesh.

Arwen barely took in the gore and shed limbs around her. The six or seven men severed in half as if they were simple loaves of bread. The blade that shone like it contained every star in the sky.

I stood gradually, arms still locked behind my back, dull pain splintering through my abdomen as she placed one hand against my split flesh. "Stay still."

"There's no time. The rest of Killoran's men—"

"We'll go when you're healed."

"I'm fine, I've been stabbed a few dozen times. Barely hurts."

I gave her a relaxed grin as a bead of sweat slipped down my brow. She huffed and I felt the lighte seep from her fingers into my wound.

She only needed a minute before we headed for the curtain, but something stopped her cold. Arwen pivoted and ran back through the blood-drenched war room. Diving over body parts and pools of gore and viscera, Arwen reached Killoran's empty throne, where the three topless women were cowering in a huddle.

"Run," she warned, slicing the Blade of the Sun through their chains—fluid arcs of Arwen's light sending sparks and wisps of metal into the air. "And to the east, away from the widow."

The women moved swiftly, muttering their thanks.

"The Blade of the Sun," Arwen murmured. "Inside my heart. *Stones*, I hate prophecies."

I raised a brow in question as we followed the women toward the exit.

"*You*, Kane," she said, turning back to me. "You are my heart. I found the blade inside you. Literally."

I might have rolled my eyes if I felt I could afford to exert a single extra ounce of energy. I sagged toward the nearest wall to avoid planting face-first into some crook's entrails.

"How do we get the lilium off you?" She looked to the chains still pinning my arms behind my back.

I gestured toward the blade in her hand. "What's your aim like?"

Arwen's face blanched and I almost found it in me to laugh.

"There has to be another way."

"None that I can think of." My voice was hoarse and I could still taste slick, human blood on my tongue. "Now, bird." I knelt before her on the suspended wood and turned my wrists to face her blade.

"I have no idea how to control this. What if it slices through your arms like it did those men?"

Voices were beginning to echo through the pathways and winding rope bridges. Calls for our heads.

"Who needs arms? Just *do it*."

"Stones help me," she muttered, and brought the shining blade down swiftly on the lilium chains with a *crack*.

*Thank the Gods.*

I twisted my wrists around and rubbed at the singed flesh. Just a scratch.

No time for basking in the comfort of mobility or the lighte returning to my body. We had to get out of here. "Come on."

Arwen and I barreled past the curtain and down the crooked

stairs toward the heart of the suspended city. We hurtled through bridges and shops, the crowds that had cheered so callously for Arwen's death long gone, hiding from the monster she'd freed. We raced until we reached the roof we had first arrived on, the one closest to the eastern edge of the island.

Below us stretched the endless pit of rotting, sunless trees that grew from the bottom of the island. Above us, the open mouth of the volcano-like island, and the sky.

I readied myself to shift, widening my stance, making sure I was far enough away from Arwen.

But nothing happened.

"What's wrong?" I hated the fear in her voice.

I tried again. Nothing. And the voices were getting louder.

"Kane?"

"I can't shift."

"Why not?"

I fought the urge to roar until the entire island shook. "I'm too drained. From the lilium. I need— *Fuck*. I just need time."

"Fine," Arwen allowed, wrapping her hand around my shoulder. "We'll climb down and hide until—" Her voice drifted off into a gasp.

"Until what?" I turned to face her. But my eyes landed on the same blood-chilling sight that stole the words from her lips.

A wretched gray wyvern, circling below us, and the blurry form of a soldier with hair as white as snow saddled on its back.

Lazarus, in his dragon form. And Halden. Alive. And kneeling at the base of my father's neck, a speck in his mighty wingspan, head tilted to search the forest below.

For us.

Arwen's words were barely audible. "How did they know we would be here?"

Dread ripped through me. "Griffin was the only one who knew. And he would never—"

"Of course not."

A silent wind swept her chestnut hair around her face. More shouts and roars from the trees below. More bridges swaying and crunching with the stomping of boots. A few errant shrieks from the western edge. The widow, I was sure.

I dragged us under a swath of large pines, and we crouched beneath a gnarled tree root. The wind pounded us both, and before Arwen could tuck her wayward strands behind her ear as she so often did when deep in thought, her eyes shot to mine, guilt flooding them like the swell before a wave crashes onto the shore.

"What is it?" I bit out.

"Ryder," she whispered. Barely audible. "I told him where we were going. I never thought he would—"

"I'm sure he didn't."

Arwen looked over at the gray-scaled wyvern circling around through the trees and soaring up over the edge of the cliffs. Searching. Then her eyes found the blade in her hand, the sun dripping off its steely face in glossy rays.

Horror blurred my vision. "Do not even think about it."

"Kane—"

"I said *do not*. We'll stay here until they're gone."

Arwen's face was hardening. Along with her resolve. "He knows we're here. He won't stop until he finds us. Until he finds me."

My heart was pounding too loudly to think straight. This couldn't happen. I would never let this happen. I had told her as much. "We'll bide our time until I regain my strength and then weaken him just enough to make it back to Shadowhold. Rally the army."

Arwen stood, now in plain sight of any prisoners who were hunting us down, and moved backward for the edge of the platform. "We'll never beat him."

I stood, too, reaching for her. "It's the only—"

"Kane." Arwen took my hand in hers, her thumb brushing my knuckle slowly. Soothingly.

I could hardly breathe. "Arwen, I will not let you—"

"I don't want to run anymore. Buy time so that tens of thousands can lose their lives in a war? Citrine won't fight alongside us. Peridot's been pillaged. It's not a war we can win. But I'm here now. With the blade. Lazarus is flying below us, and for once, somehow, we have the advantage. I can end this *right now*." Arwen held my hand firmly and I already knew what her next words would be. "And I'm going to."

Grief, incomprehensible *grief* ripped my heart in two. "What about the White Crow? I can still take your place."

Arwen's face nearly crumpled, the first ounce of emotion slipping through her mask of still, unwavering strength.

"Your sacrifice would be worse than death for me. Condemning me to live without you? Knowing you had died in my place? Don't do that to me. Please, don't do that to me."

Beth's words rang in my head. *"It's possible, but the cost will be greater to her than her own life."* I gripped her arm. "I cannot live without you."

"You'll survive. I know you will." Arwen took my face in her hands. Her eyes held nothing but uncompromising will, though they brimmed with tears. "I wouldn't have changed a single thing."

"No," I roared. I didn't care if the entire island heard me. I wrapped my hands around her arms.

"Kane—"

My chest. I couldn't *breathe*. "No." I held her tighter. "You need to *listen* to me." It could not end like this. "Listen to me, *please*, Arwen—"

"I love you," she said, hands soft against my jaw. "This is how it has to be. I could never outrun my fate. And I don't want to anymore. But you have to live. Be brave. Forgive yourself. Do that for me. *Live*, for me."

And before I could say another word, stronger than she had ever been—stronger *than me*—she jerked free from my grasp and leapt off the platform, graceful as a dove.

# 46

ARWEN

THE WIND WHIPPED MY HAIR INTO MY FACE, STINGING MY eyelids and cheekbones and the skin of my lips. The blade's power thrummed through me, rising in my heart and pounding in my head. Igniting my lighte, which seeped through my blood, and sang in my soul like a songbird.

Salty tears ran up my face as I fell, but I was . . . calm.

This was right.

The blade and I were one. And everyone's pain, everyone's suffering, would all be over soon.

My final moments were with Kane. That was a luxury. A blessing. I only hoped—I only *prayed*—that he could find some happiness when of all this was finished. That one day he would wake in the mornings without blaming himself for my death or anyone else's.

As I fell past leaves and branches and dark trunks of wood, it was the last thought in my mind.

And then I landed with a grunt on the sharp, scaled back of Lazarus.

He jolted with surprise, a roar ripping from his reptilian maw—

His elongated, elegant neck swiveling to find me crouched along his spine.

Dry, punishing wind stung my face. I scrambled for purchase with my free hand and swung the blade into the air before plunging it down into his back.

Another ear-splitting, bone-rattling roar—

And a ricochet of glaring, golden lighte streaming out from the fine point of my blade and into Lazarus's reflective, glasslike scales.

I strained to keep my eyes open against the brightness, shook with the force of my lighte leaving my body in huge, penetrating bursts, funneling through the blade—

Shook with the fear, with the raw *power* coursing through my muscles and limbs—

Why . . . why was nothing happening?

I swung the blade into the air to bring it down again, harder— *much* harder—this time, but it never made contact.

I was shoved forward, grunting with the force as my face was thrust into the piercing ridges of Lazarus's scarred spine, my mouth tasting ash and wind and ice.

Halden propelled his body into mine again, attempting to use the angle to pry the blade from my hands. I drew my knees up, knotting myself until I had leverage to stand, and hefted the blade with all its might—a mere extension of my hand—out of his grasp and directly toward his head.

Halden ducked, barely catching his footing on Lazarus's craggy back. We breathed heavily in unison, uneven pants drowned out by a wind that howled like it was in agony.

And Lazarus, beneath us, only sailed higher. Before I could discern why, Halden lifted his sword and it whined through the air toward me.

The blow missed by a mountain-sized margin as I feinted right and drove my own blade forward, narrowly nicking his rib cage.

I was better than him.

Stronger.

More confident in my footing as Lazarus ebbed and bowed through air currents.

The Blade of the Sun—*my* blade—hissed pleasurably against my palm.

"You don't want to do this," I yelled into the wind as Lazarus swooped to the side, nearly knocking Halden off and sending him plummeting toward a dark green death.

"I don't have a choice!" Halden spat back as we sailed up, up, *up* into the sky, the bright sun now blinding over the ledge and harsh wind making it impossible to see what was up and what was down.

Halden heaved his sword again, sloppy and haphazard, and I deflected the blow with my blade. My muscles throbbed sweetly, and I drew in a breath as I thrust once more, this time clipping his sword and sending metal splinters like ribbons into the air.

Lazarus was still moving. Heading for the lip of the island. Escaping, with us. With *me*—

One tentative foot after another, I maneuvered until I could grasp an outstretched wing with one hand, my blade firmly clutched in the other. I kicked Halden in the chest with all my strength, quads straining, pushing myself dangerously close to Lazarus's narrow neck.

His neck . . .

His soft, penetrable neck—

Halden caught himself against Lazarus's tail, sword dangling from his left hand. It was only then I noticed two things: the crudely healed burns that covered one side of his face in splotches from where I had lit his tent aflame back in Peridot, and his right hand.

Or rather, lack thereof.

A mottled stump was all that remained where his hand had once been. A hand that he had bitten the nails of in worry and irritation. A hand that had helped my mother wash vegetables for dinner. A hand that had caressed my face. Had seared hot iron into my flesh.

Now, gone.

"Halden," I heaved, air funneling erratically in and out of my lungs. "Your hand."

But he stayed silent, sucking in a lungful of air himself, his scowl both defensive and ashamed. Halden turned his sword on me.

"He did that to you? Punished you by . . . by amputation?"

"I deserved it," he ground out. "I let you escape."

I shook my head. I didn't want to kill him. Somehow, after everything, still I didn't. But I couldn't fail now. Lazarus continued to beat his powerful wings, carrying us farther from Hemlock Isle. I had to move—

"I'm Fae, Halden. You can't win. Please."

"I picked my side. Perhaps it was the losing one. Either way, it's the one I chose."

"Anyone can be redeemed. You can join us."

"You never changed, did you?" As if answering his own question, he shook his head. "Not anyone, no. Not me."

Fat tears dripped down my face as the wind pummeled us. "I don't want to kill you. But I will if I have to."

I thought of Kane. Of how I had always assumed it was easy for him to take a human life. The bodies of all the men I had killed back in Siren's Bay flooded my mind, their blood soaking the sand and rocks of the beach. And Killoran's men, corpses bisected like meat in a butcher's shop by the very blade in my hand—their bodies filled my vision, too.

And suddenly we weren't so different, Kane and I.

And I knew there was no other way.

Swallowing a ragged, heaving sob, I moved forward against the force of the wind and swung. Halden's steel met mine in midair, but it was no match. His blade turned to liquid silver in his palm the moment it touched mine, raining down in droplets on Lazarus's back. Shards of steel like hail, littering my hair, my hands—Halden's eyes widened as he beheld nothing but a pommel in his hand.

This time, I didn't hesitate.

I drove my blade into Halden's heart. Through his flesh, his blood, his muscle, the blade sank. He screamed as pure white flames poured from the blade—a conduit for my lighte—and erupted from his chest. That itching, scorching sensation twisted again at my shoulder blades, and I felt it ratchet up my spine as the fire consumed Halden's body whole in mere seconds, his last expression one of awe as he looked past my head toward my back.

When the flames cleared, there was no blood. Only the charred remains of my oldest friend turned enemy, as Lazarus abruptly tilted and the ashes fell unceremoniously down into the forgotten depths of Hemlock Isle.

And then I couldn't help the tears as I wept for all that had become of him.

Of me.

And for what had to happen now.

I reached for Lazarus's membranous, veined wing. Not polished and sleek like Kane's. There was no beauty to the thick sinew under my palm, like the hide of a bull, tipped by a horned peak the color of stale blood. That talon alone was longer than my forearm, and I choked my grip higher up on his wing, reaching for it. I needed the stability. I only had one chance.

I climbed higher, lurching for his neck.

The underside, with its thin scales covering more fragile skin. That's where I would sink my blade.

The air shrieked in my ears as we ascended, Lazarus still sailing for that lip of Hemlock. Soon we'd be soaring over the depths of Lake Stygian. Did he realize Halden was dead? That nobody stood in my way now? Would he deposit me in the deadly waters? Miles from shore, left to drown agonizingly slowly?

Faster then. I had to be faster.

Wrapping my knees around Lazarus's back, holding on to him with every fiber of strength I had, no matter how he dropped and weaved, I raised the blade high into the air and moved to slice it along his throat.

But the edge never punctured the skin—

Lazarus spun violently, a near barrel roll, sending me and the blade flying down, down, *down*—

My hands clutched wildly at nothing, slipping through air as I plummeted after Halden's ashes, the blade flying from my grasp—

No, no, *no*—

And again, that sensation in my shoulder blades, like points trying to break through my flesh, to hold me up in the air somehow—

But I couldn't focus on it, couldn't feel my lighte—

All I could hear was my own screaming echoing in my ears as my stomach flipped over and over on itself. Plunging, tumbling, I was *free-falling*—

Until I could see below me the gray wyvern with bloodred eyes dive past and extend one scaled palm open, waiting to catch me as I fell.

*No*—

Not to catch me—

His claw, sharper than any dagger, than any blade, positioned directly under my tumbling body.

To *impale* me—

I thrashed at the air, shooting my power out to call the still-falling sword toward me.

Tears ripped at my face with the effort.

Reaching for it. For anything, please *anything*—

I heard Kane's roar. Not a plea but a howl of pure agony. Of devastation. Of loss. Of boundless, unending sorrow—

The last thing I felt was searing pain as Lazarus's open, outstretched claw pierced through my stomach with a wet *squelch*.

# 47

KANE

THE BONES OF MY KNEECAPS CRUNCHED AGAINST THE hard, dry wood below.

I couldn't move.

I simply knelt on the edge of the platform, roaring. *Roaring* until my throat bled.

She was just hanging there . . . Limp, broken, impaled on a single jagged claw—suspended in air, speared through the center like a bowed ribbon. Elegant somehow, as if dipped in a seductive waltz by Death himself.

Dead.

She was dead.

Like the snuffing of a candle that plunges an entire room into pitch-blackness. And with it, the extinguishing of my soul.

I retched onto the knotted wood beneath me.

Over and over and over.

No, *please, no*—

I shook, panting while my mind went hollow—save for the

deafening blare of her final words: *"Live, for me..."* Her words and the thrumming of my heart. My wrecked, annihilated, *decimated* heart.

And the crushing emptiness—

When everything in my gut had been purged onto the ground beneath me and I was panting on my hands and knees like a rabid animal, my eyes blurred with tears, my teeth gnashing, I forced myself to stand.

But Lazarus was gone from the sky.

Claws landed behind me and I braced myself with steadying, brisk breaths for whatever mercenary of his had come to kill me, too.

*Please,* I thought. *Kill me.*

*I want to be with her.*

*Please.*

But it was Griffin's hand on my shoulder as he turned me to face him, eyes harsh, expression grim, as he said, "We have to go."

Ryder stepped out from behind the commander and took in my expression. I must have looked wrecked. Ravaged. Because he uttered a single, appalled *"No."*

Griffin's eyes shot from me to Ryder and back. "Now."

"No, no, no—" Ryder pleaded. "This is all my fault. I did this. It's my fault—"

"Ryder," Griffin cautioned, his voice sharper than a knife's edge.

But Ryder didn't stop. "I told her. I knew the minute I did that I shouldn't have. How could Amelia have done this? How could—"

"What did you do?" The words flew from me, the rage a brief and welcome respite from the pain. I hadn't even realized I was moving. Hadn't realized I had Ryder's throat in my hand, hadn't realized his face was turning a shade of ghastly, satisfying blue. I tightened my grip.

"Kane," Griffin snapped, ripping at my arm. "Kane, control yourself. It was a mistake. He made a mistake—you're going to kill him!"

Ryder choked and sputtered.

*Good.* I squeezed harder, feeling his airway close under my hand. "Why should you get to live?"

Ryder's purple face strained back at me, sniveling and wide-eyed. Enduring the pain. Accepting it.

*"Why?"* I bellowed.

Griffin shook me. "This is not what Arwen would have wanted!"

I released Ryder. Bit my cheek until I tasted blood.

"No," Ryder croaked, rubbing at his neck. "He should kill me. I told Amelia where you'd be. And she told Lazarus. Why would she do that?"

"She must have cut a deal." Griffin's voice was hollow.

"For what?" Ryder asked.

"Her people, I'm sure."

Ryder shook his head. "When I couldn't find her, I had a bad feeling, but I never thought . . ."

I couldn't listen to him anymore. Couldn't hear anything but my heart. Beating too slow. Barely beating at all. I knew I was moving toward the edge of the platform, but I couldn't feel my legs. I would be with her. Had to—

"Kane, stop, they're gone."

I shoved around Griffin, his lumbering chest in my fucking *way*, but he put himself in front of me again. Firm. Stern. "Kane, *she's gone.*"

Sobs racked from my chest. I didn't sound like myself. I didn't sound like anything. I knew my face had crumpled, that tears were blurring my sight, and no matter how they purged from me, they wouldn't soothe the emptiness, ease the unendurable agony—

I moved again for the edge of the platform. For that bottomless, depthless, blackened forest. For the peace I'd find at its base. But Griffin pulled me into him.

Awkward at first. Stiff.

Not as much an embrace as a steel grip to prevent me from my own—

I wrenched from him, from his resolute warmth, his support—but he held vehemently firm.

"I'm sorry, brother," he said.

Resonant silence whirred in my head. The sun had fallen behind the lip of the isle's mouth. It was cold now. Not frigid, but crisp enough to raise the hairs on the back of my neck and my forearms limp at my sides. The smell of burning—perhaps a lantern or torch knocked aside in the widow's destruction—crested the air in my nostrils. Voices wailed and the stomping of heavy boots sounded below us.

"We need to leave," Griffin said. "There are men coming for you . . ."

I jerked my chin in agreement as he released me. Guided us both away from the ledge.

"I have to ask," Griffin said. "The blade?"

"He took it. With her . . ." I couldn't say the word.

*Her body.*

She was just a body now. Just a shell.

When Griffin shifted, I climbed atop his feathered wingspan, Ryder after me, his face flushed and splotchy from a deluge of tears.

My mind was silent as we took to the skies.

Utterly silent, as we sailed over the depths of the fathomless forest below.

As we moved through the clouds.

Until later—

Hours later—

Lifetimes later—

In the suffocatingly dark, foreboding silence of my study. With no one else around, more than inebriated with drink.

My thoughts crawled to the surface, where I was forced at knife-point to face them.

It was so obvious now. Painfully, punishingly obvious. It had always been his plan. To let me live. To let us both live. So we could find the blade for him before he killed her.

We had been played.

And now, there were only three things left to do:

I would locate the White Crow. Endure whatever necessary to become full-blooded.

Hunt down Amelia, and make her suffer in unimaginable ways for her betrayal.

And then, when I'd torn the world to shreds, when there wasn't a man or woman still breathing who could be faulted for her death, I'd complete the prophecy in Arwen's place. Vanquish my father, drive the Blade of the Sun into his heart, and join her wherever she was now.

With the Gods. In the ground. Nowhere. I didn't care.

I had lived centuries without Arwen. I couldn't do it again.

Until then, I knew only one cure for such grotesque, intolerable pain:

*Revenge.*

# Epilogue

## ARWEN

THE STITCHES WERE HEALING SLOWER THAN I EXPECTED. It was the worst injury I'd ever sustained, but still. My lighte was diminished for some reason. I searched the room with my eyes for the hundredth time for any clue as to who had saved me or where I was.

Dark, bloodred tiles stretched out across the floor. I examined them, noticing the slight sparkle from the sliver of sunlight that slipped between the drawn brocade curtains. If I didn't know better, I'd say the tiles were made of rubies.

My eyes trailed upward, flitting across the jet-black marble armoire lit with at least thirty white candles that never seemed to drip an ounce of wax, let alone snuff out. And next to that, the fireplace of the same obsidian marble, rectangular and covered by a thin layer of glass. I had glared at that roaring fireplace for hours now, trying to figure out how the logs were placed inside, or where the chimney was. I would have thought it some kind of illusion or sorcery if I couldn't feel the licks of woody heat wafting over my face.

And above me, a pearl-covered chandelier. Glittering and elegant and seemingly floating in midair with no rope, chains, or cord. Another mystery that had occupied my mind when I grew tired of wondering how I survived the fall into Lazarus's claw, who saved me, why I was tethered to this bed, and where in the world I was.

That was, of course, in between full emotional breakdowns not very fitting of the savior of the realms, or *the chosen one*, as Beth had called me. Breakdowns during which I tried so hard to loose myself from my impossible restraints that I either panicked until I fell asleep from sheer exhaustion or sobbed until my eyes were swollen shut.

Or breakdowns during which I thought only of Kane.

Of how I had failed him. Failed Evendell, in killing Lazarus.

Of how, most likely, he believed I was dead. And that I had died in vain.

The thought echoed such misery through my body, I could hardly avoid convulsing against it. It didn't help that I had no idea what time it was due to the closed curtains and lack of any clocks. My guess was that it had been at least fifteen hours, and when I thought about how long I might be kept like this, panic sluiced through my chest all over again.

I took a long, filtered breath through my nose and out of my mouth, waiting for my chest to untighten. The room smelled of rich sandalwood and apricot syrup and the medicinal scent of various antiseptics, balms, and salves from the marble bedside table.

Trying to find comfort despite the stitches that nearly bisected me, I tossed in the sheets, as fluid and rich as the fine red wine they shared their color with. Atop them, a dense scarlet duvet interwoven with glittering gold thread painting a pattern of flowers and leaves and little bees. The pillows I had been lying on for hours now were filled with heavy down, and I had enough around me for seven other people to fit beside me comfortably.

But despite the richness of the room, the undeniable beauty, the comfort of the lavish bed, there was something . . . sinister about it all.

Though, maybe that was just the restraints.

I tugged once again on the fabric. Despite its soft feel, the ribbon could not be torn, chewed through, or set on fire with the candle on my bedside—I had tried all three at least a dozen times.

Rather, they were deceptively thick and strong, and I wasn't able to use any of my lighte no matter how—

Oh, Stones.

I was an idiot.

*Lilium.*

The ribbon must have been woven with lilium somehow. It would explain why I was healing so slowly, why I couldn't summon my lighte, why I felt so weak and tired.

It wasn't just the sewn-up wound across my stomach.

I was being drained.

Whoever was healing me must have somehow known I was Fae. But who—

The slick marble doors opened and two women in identical black uniforms and nursing hats strolled in. Neither spoke a word to me as one brought in a tray with more surgical tools and the other began to make the bed around me.

"Who are you?"

Nothing.

"Where am I?"

Nothing.

"Why are you healing me? Why aren't I—"

"Dead?"

I whipped my head to the doorway. The breath whirled from my lungs.

In a rich, rosy robe, holding a steaming bronze mug, stood Lazarus.

The picture of a cozy king on a frigid morning. And yet my heart was racing as if I beheld a monster.

*Because I did.*

"That's not very kind," he tutted as he walked toward my bedside.

I had forgotten that Lazarus could hear my thoughts, and I scrambled to move away from him as he sat casually on the edge of the mattress. Maybe he had done all of this to kill me in his own home. His own bed.

It was despicable. Twisted. Perverse. It was—

"Now, Arwen, why would I wish to kill you?"

I swallowed hard as he feasted his silver eyes on me. I had been wrong before, when I met him the first time on the beach of Siren's Bay. They were nothing like Kane's. *Nothing.*

"Maybe because I'm the only person in this world that can end your life?"

"Yes," he said, sipping from his mug. "A valid point. You are also the only thing in this world that can *create* life. At least, the only life I'm interested in creating."

I blinked.

Once.

Twice.

I wasn't following. And my mind was pounding and spinning.

It was just dawning on me that I was likely in the Fae Realm of Lumera. I wasn't mere days or weeks away from Kane. I wasn't even in the same *realm* as him.

"I'm sure my son will show up here soon enough." Lazarus smiled. "Won't that be a nice surprise for him—the woman he loves, betrothed to his own father. A little perverse for my liking, but—" He shrugged. "What can you do?"

*"Betrothed?"*

Lazarus patted my thigh through the duvet and I recoiled. "I would never kill you, dear Arwen. In fact, I *need* you. For you shall give me the one thing I have desired for over two thousand years. The one thing I have never been able to succeed in giving myself. Full-blooded Fae *heirs*."

Revulsion crawled through my veins like beetles and ants.

"Now that the blade has been destroyed, neither you nor any of our true Fae children can harm me. And why would you wish to? Together, we will repopulate this once-flourishing land with true, pure Fae."

"I will never, ever be your queen," I breathed. "I'd rather die."

"After you've given me my heirs, I'd be glad to oblige you." His lips curled back from his teeth as he beheld what must have been defeat or horror—or both—in my eyes. Then he stood from my bedside and swept through the ornate entry, closing the door behind him with a sickening *click*.

# Acknowledgments

I owe my eternal gratitude to Taylor and Sam, my incredible, fearless agents who took a chance on a genre-blending New Adult series born from TikTok. Thank you for making my wildest dreams a reality.

To my spectacular editor, Kristine—working with you has been the dream come true mentioned above. Thank you for your inspired, brilliant feedback, and for making revisions fun. (It's possible!) Thank you also to Kristin, Anika, Mary, and the entire, wonderful Berkley team. Every time I have an email from one of you in my inbox, it brightens my whole day.

To my first developmental editor, Natalie, thank you for all of your time, our endless Zooms, and for helping to make this an actual book and not just a collection of words splattered onto hundreds of pages.

To my dear friend first and media rights agent second, Olivia, thank you for pushing me to publish this series and showing me how to do so.

To my wonderful beta and ARC readers, thank you all for your commitment to this series, your prompt reads, and your gleeful promotion. I am tremendously grateful.

To my mom, thank you for being my biggest fan. For loving this story so much that I have an actual text from you asking, "Are Arwen and Kane going to have sex in the next book? They really need to." As a child, every time I presented you with a piece of art, you said, with complete seriousness, "We have to save this, it's going to be worth millions one day." And even better, you really believed it, hence the mountains of Container Store bins in storage filled with tea-stained maps from fictional far-off lands. You made me believe in myself, and that I could do something as wild as write a book. And then another book. Thank you.

And to my dad—thank you for showing me how cathartic writing could be when you gave me my first journal at nine. And thank you for reading the PG-rated versions of my books. (Yes, I give my father redacted copies and I stand by that 100 percent.)

To my sisters, Lily, Finley, and Isla—I love you guys so much. I make the TikToks for you. To Susie, Chris, Val, Echo, Aidan, Brookie, Eni, Scott, Alec, and Carly—thank you for celebrating me at every milestone. I am beyond lucky to have each of you in my life.

To my dog, Milo, you are my everything. Thank you for letting me snuggle you as I type by your side into the wee hours.

And lastly, to my thoughtful, imaginative, brilliant husband, Jack—thank you for your support, creative problem solving, and overwhelming kindness, love, and patience. I have an enormous crush on you.

Keep reading for a sneak peek of

# A Reign of Rose

the next book in the Sacred Stones trilogy.

# KANE

I KNEW THIS TIME IT WAS MY RIB THAT HAD CRACKED.

Each inhale sent the mismatched shards straining from one another, and pain radiated into the pummeled muscles of my back. Sitting up was marginally less painful, and I sucked in a slow, bracing breath.

The scent of pine and blood filled my nostrils.

When I blinked my eyes open, they raked down the cascading wall of solid, glinting ice that I had plunged from—its peak still hidden behind thick white clouds, the smooth face marred only by the cracks and dents where I had jammed my fists and feet, unsuccessfully attempting an ascent.

*First you failed them. Then you failed her. And now you're failing again.*

Anguish pierced my heart anew. Fresher, every fucking day.

Wasn't grief supposed to dull with time?

I stood, chest still contracting under two very different kinds of pain, and brushed snow and dirt from my backside. The motion aggravated deep scrapes across my palms. Whatever protective ward the White Crow had cast around his home at the top of that glacial mountain was inhibiting all aspects of my lighte, barring me from shifting into my dragon form, halting my accelerated Fae healing . . .

I trudged through near-blinding white back in the direction of the settlement at the base of the mountain. I'd only made it a few feet when the bruises, scrapes, and blisters across my body disappeared. My toe cut across the snow, demarking where the ward appeared to end.

I winced with the movement. The rib was going to take longer.

If I were smart, or patient, I'd retreat down to that town, get a room at the unsavory, sleet-coated inn, and lie still in devastating silence until I was recovered.

But I wasn't smart.

I wasn't patient.

And I didn't mind the pain.

I was so cold these days it was almost pleasurable, feeling something ache inside my bones.

Pressing my palm to the radiating volleys of pain in my side, I appraised the ice-cold mountain range for the hundredth time. Beyond bare ponderosa branches thick with hoarfrost, and snow prints from hares and caribou, that towering rise of jagged hunches rose and rose and rose, gobbling up the skyline.

"You going to become a dragon and fly at it again?" a nosy voice called from behind me. "That almost worked."

Gods *damn it.*

"No," I growled. And that hadn't almost worked. It had only gotten me high enough into the air to spy the tiny stone cottage that topped the peak, observe the elderly sorcerer tending to a flourishing root vegetable garden, and then, as soon as I flew for him and through the wards, shift against my will in midair and plummet to the ground.

That fall had yielded me one crushed kneecap, a concussion, and two dislocated shoulders. None of which had rivaled the experience of waiting days for my knocked-out teeth to grow back—nothing humbles a man quite like teething in adulthood.

My body shattering against packed snow had been welcome, actually. It allowed me to feel what Arwen had felt—that same gruesome powerlessness. Sailing through the air, instincts screaming at me to fly despite my brain roaring that I *couldn't*—

*"You're not going to die."* That's what I had told her.

A grimace twisted my face.

So I'd tried again the next day. And the next.

The second time I fell out of my dragon form, I had broken my back in two places and lost the use of my legs. I'd lain there for half a day, inside the White Crow's wards, unable to heal, unable to move, until *this* mouth breather had stumbled across my prone form and, upon my very clear instructions, dragged me back toward town and a tingling in my calves told me I'd begun to heal.

I appraised Len through the haze of memories. The wrinkled, crumpled do-gooder had a long face and thin lips that he used to smile far more often than necessary. A dishwasher in the town's only tavern, Len climbed up the hill for fresh water from the well each morning, and had told me that day as I waited for mobility to return that he was all too used to seeing sorry assholes like myself try and fail to reach the White Crow.

"Don't beat yourself up," Len had said, eyes crinkling. "It's a feat when someone can even track the old nutter down."

I cut a glance at him again now, palm pressed against my aching, splintered rib, and cringed. "On your way now, Len."

The older man raised his hands in mock surrender. "Come down to the tavern if you need to refuel."

"Will do."

But I wouldn't.

———— ❧ ————

"FUCK," I GRUNTED, SLIDING DOWN THE FACE OF THE mountain, hands clawing for purchase against the rocks I'd driven into the smooth, biting ice. My chest slammed into one and I spasmed for air, landing hard against the snow. Through my blurred vision, several brown rabbits scattered for the powdery brush.

"You're going to kill yourself before you do whatever you came here to do."

"Why are you always here?" I croaked to Len through a mouthful of ice.

"This is where the damn well is!"

I craned my neck. Len gestured at the water source, yoke balanced across his back, twin pails spilling water from either shoulder. "Help me bring these down the mountain and I'll buy you a pint."

"There isn't time," I said, cheek growing numb in the slush.

It had been months. If Lazarus had destroyed the blade already . . . then I'd have nothing but time. A miserable, aching eternity.

I swallowed a dry heave at the thought and sucked in more frigid air, rolling onto my back with a groan.

*Don't think like that.*

My chest shimmered with that sick, wounded yearning. Her voice in my head. Like bells. Like sweet music.

Arwen would tell me that I couldn't know anything for sure

until I made it to Lumera and found out for myself. And I couldn't confront my father until I, too, was full-blooded and had any chance at destroying him.

Which was why I had to get up *the fucking mountain.*

Up there, where the impenetrable clouds met an icy summit. If there had been a sun to see, it would have sunk behind those peaks hours ago. I could tell by the dim, cerulean light dulling the snow, and the cold seeping into my bones.

In the first few days of my journey to the Vorst region, a few residents of the elevated kingdom told me I had just missed the bright, clear-skied summer. It was cold year-round in the Pearl Mountains—something about the altitude, or the magic that kept the city floating among the clouds—but it was especially brutal in both fall and winter months, when there were fewer than eight hours of daylight and near-nonstop snowfall.

Shadowhold was probably just reaching the tail end of autumn, the Shadow Woods likely replete with toadstools and blackberries.

Another swift kick to the gut. That's what thinking of my keep felt like these days. Not because of how much I missed my people, or Griffin, or Acorn. Not because I longed for the comforts of lilac soap or whiskey or cloverbread.

But because even if this miserable, frost-bitten climb was possible, even if I reached the White Crow, convinced him to turn me full-blooded, stomached whatever anguish that might entail, and somehow still arrived in one piece back to my shadowed, familiar castle . . .

Arwen wouldn't be there.

Her books, filled with flattened petals, unopened. The swath of my bed I'd so foolishly hoped would be hers, eternally cold. I'd never hear that peal of laughter or smell her orange blossom skin.

And I'd watch my home become a crypt.

I rolled over, burying my face in snow, and roared until flames ran through my lungs. Until tears burned at my eyes and my chest rippled against the ground, the agony shredding me, the guilt, the untenable sorrow—

"*Stones alive,*" Len breathed. "You need a break."

"No," I grumbled, spitting ice and pushing myself up. "It helps. I'm fine."

"It's almost nightfall. You can't scale a mountain of ice in the dark with a broken rib and a punctured lung. Are you trying to die, boy?"

I'd asked myself that same question so many times I'd lost count. "Depends on the day."

"One pint, a hot meal, and you'll be back to falling off the mountain again by sunrise."

Perhaps he was right. I was slinking dangerously close to that tipping point. The one where my own death was looking just a bit too attractive. Where I'd either join her or stop having to live each despicable day without her. But then her sacrifice would have been for nothing, and that—that I couldn't allow. In life, or in death.

Dry wind bit at my skin as I grunted and limped toward Len. Alarm erupted on his face as I drew near, but I only lifted the pails from his shoulders and moved past him, prowling down the mountainside. Len's sigh of relief was audible as he stomped through the snow after me.

Vorst was barely a town. It was barely a village. That aforementioned seedy inn, a nearly bare general store, a temple, and Len's quiet stone tavern made up the entire region. Inhabited only by those passing through, solitary lifelong merchants like Len, or the rare scholar or priest who sought remote corners of Pearl to study or serve the Stones in peace.

Len's tavern—which he made clear to me three different times on our trudge over was not *his* tavern, but his cousin Faulk's—was a frrostbitten slate-gray hovel in the outskirts. I had to duck to enter, and, due to the low, slanted ceiling, hunch once inside, which sent currents of pain through my still-bruised abdomen. With few options—the grim space had only a handful of mismatched stools and one bench with a man snoring beneath it—I sat down in a back corner beside the tavern's hearth, at a table built from an over-turned pig trough. A single pillar candle melted atop it, stuffed into an empty wine bottle and flickering for its life.

"What can I do you for?" Len asked, prodding the crackling fire.

The heat permeated through my stiff, wet clothes. Remnants of ice and snow were melting beneath the layers, and I removed my gloves, flexing my hands closer to the flames. "I'll take that pint. And whatever you have to eat."

Len nodded once, returning minutes later with a foamy ale and a lukewarm meat pie. One bite told me it was mostly gristle, but I ate the entire thing regardless and then asked for a second. Being this far from the White Crow's wards helped with my injuries. I twisted to loosen my rigid spine.

"Want to know what Faulk tried to name the tavern?" Len asked, sitting down on a low stool across from me and pulling some animal's hide over his knobby legs.

Irritation pricked at my neck. I couldn't tell the elderly man to scram when he had offered me the first hot meal I'd had in days. But I really, *really* would have liked to.

When I remained silent, he said, undeterred, "The Frozen Yak."

"Yeah . . . That's terrible."

"I told him every patron will think of rock-hard vomit when they eat."

My eyes found the soupy pie before me, and I lowered my fork.

"You're obviously not from here, but in Vorst, yaks—"

"No offense Len, but I'd prefer a bit of—"

"Solitude?"

I let my silence answer his question.

Len only leaned forward. His cracked lips spread wide with a curious grin. "What do you want with the old Crow anyway?"

The fire popped beside me, and the snoring man bathed in shadow rolled to his side. I sighed like an ox. "Is it even him up there?"

Len sniffed, the wrinkles on his face creasing with ease, as if he did that all too often. A chronic dripping nose from chronic winter. "It's him, all right. He's come down once or twice. Bought seeds for his garden."

"Does anyone in Vorst speak to him? Any way to send word?"

Len shook his head.

"Not even for—"

"The king of Onyx?"

I choked on a piece of lard-laden crust.

"People talk," Len said, leaning back. "Even in towns as small as these. Your kingdom's been missing a king for the last two months. And not so many men can turn into dragons. Only two, by my last count."

Suspicion ground my jaw shut. Was this some kind of . . . "What do you know of my father?"

Len made a face. "This whole kingdom is mostly scholars. He's a Faerie, right?"

I said nothing, back rigid, reedy fork mangled in my grasp.

"Why'd you abandon your kingdom?" Len asked, plucking the knife from beside me and twirling it across his knobby fingers. "Aren't you at war?"

The rage that spiraled through me nearly blew out my fingers and tore through the thin man. He was only spared by the equal rage directed back at myself—the truth in his words, all my mistakes, being forced to travel here and leave them all behind. And so soon after . . .

"I didn't abandon them," I growled. "My men are preparing for battle. I'm here to retrieve something we need in order to win."

"And what's that?"

Len's curiosity had graduated from mildly irritating to deserving of a fork through the throat.

"Come on," he drawled. "Who am I going to tell? The rodents?"

I took a breath. "The man I seek to destroy can only be killed by a certain type of Fae. I need the White Crow to make me . . . able to beat him." I said the next words very slowly, as if to infiltrate Len's feeble mind. "Can you help me reach him?"

Len's eyes softened, and for a moment, I thought he might actually answer me. "Why are you just doing that now? When you've been at war for years?"

I stabbed my warped fork into the soft center of the pie, ignoring him. Two more bites and I'd head back up—

"If you answer me, I might be able to help you reach the wizard. I have lived beneath him for sixty years."

I didn't want to talk about her with this toad. I didn't want to talk about her with anyone.

But Len's eyes held my glare like he hadn't a fear in the world. And if I left now, I'd never know if a single ounce of kindness to this man might have made all the difference. It's what she would have encouraged me to do.

"We had someone else," I finally said. "Someone very dear to me. She died."

"My condolences, boy. I recently lost a woman I cared for myself. Hadn't seen her in many years." Len sniffed again. "Still hurts."

The unmistakable scuttle of rats' claws tinkered against the low slate roof, and drew a grunt from the man still sleeping under the rot-holed, whitewashed bench beside us.

Len leaned back again, even closer to the hearth. "What would you give to bring her back?"

*Anything.*

I only finished my ale.

"What would you give?" Len pushed.

This dishwasher's hunt for companionship was shredding my last nerve. "Why ask such a thing?"

"Why not?"

"I don't dwell on hypotheticals."

Len chuckled, toying with the knife still in his hands. Then he reached for my supper, and broke off a piece of crust, crumbling it in his hands and scattering it across the floor.

The fat, wiry rat crawled out of the floor tentatively at first. Drawn to the scraps, but no fool. The rodent waited with practiced patience until Len scooted in closer to the makeshift table and turned his back on the scene.

"What are you doing?"

"I don't want you to dwell, boy." Len faced me, but his eyes were on that rat, grasping at greasy crumbs with thin pink hands. Before I could stop him, Len lashed at the creature with his knife and speared the thing clean through in a gory *crunch*.

"For Gods' sake, Len . . ." The man was senile. And all alone in this icy, lonesome town. I stood to leave, wondering if there even was a Faulk.

"Sit," he commanded, laying the impaled rat on the table, its meager blood pooling around my half-eaten pie.

Mists of shadow twined around my fists. I had no desire to hurt Len, but this was—

"And none of that," the old man said, jerking his chin at my hands. Len removed the knife, placed it on the table, and waited. I had no reason to stay, but some curiosity, perhaps some long-buried loneliness of my own, kept my feet from moving, and I watched as Len drew one wrinkled hand across the rat's plump corpse.

With no incantation, no lighte, no otherworldly glow, the rat twitched. And twitched again. Len hadn't said a single word when the rodent's curved spine reattached with an audible *crack*. The long-tailed vermin released a disturbing, harrowing squeak before rising and scampering across the table. It crawled to the ground and back through the gap in the floorboards from which it came.

My heart rattled my broken rib cage.

It was more than Briar Creighton herself could do.

Necromancy.

My eyes shot up to Len once more. That crinkle at the corner of his eyes. The smirk playing at his lips.

"It's you. You're . . ."

"Now answer me, boy."

Knees loose, I dropped back down into my seat.

The White Crow had been with me all evening long.

I was a fucking fool.

And now I knew his question for what it was.

A test. One which I didn't have the right answer to. I knew the truth—that I'd give anything, any limb, any life, any realm, to bring Arwen back. That I would shear the skin from my own bones, tear the world to pulp to hold her in my arms even just one last time—

But I had no idea if it was the response the White Crow sought.

"I'd give more . . ." I managed on a breath. "More to bring her back than you could ever know."

"What if it spelled your own death?"

"In a heartbeat."

"Yes, that's an easy one, isn't it? What about an innocent's? What if her resurrection demanded an equal debt paid—"

Suddenly I was back on a ship in the heart of the Mineral Seas, reaching for a tear-stained, blood-soaked Arwen. *"I knew I couldn't go through with it. Not even for the good of all of Evendell . . . Do you hear me? I was willing to sacrifice the entire world to keep you alive!"*

"Yes," I admitted. Shame thick on my tongue, eyes down on the drying river of rat blood, tacky and black on the tabletop. "I'd kill for her. A thousand times over."

"And if I raised your lover from the soil, brushed her off and made her new, and gave you the full blood that you seek? If I said neither of you had to die, then what would you do?" The White Crow's teeth flashed in the fading light, breath swirling in a room now icy cold. I hadn't realized my bones were chattering.

"Would you still take your new skin," he continued when I remained silent, "reborn as full-blooded just as the prophecy required, and slay your father? Knowing you were fated to die, as she once was? *Knowing* you could have lived a near eternity beside her? Would you still sacrifice yourself for the good of the realm?"

*No.* If the Gods were that cruel, and somehow this wily, wicked sorcerer could turn me full-blooded Fae *and* resurrect Arwen . . . Then, no. There was no use lying to myself. Pretending to be some noble man that I wasn't, and would never be, especially now. I wouldn't be strong enough.

"A great disappointment."

"No." The breath shot from my lungs. "I didn't say—"

Another swipe of that wrinkled hand and the old, nameless tavern of Vorst transformed.

When the spots cleared from my vision, my hands were braced on a rich maple dining table. Clean, polished, *sparkling* in gentle candlelight. The room glowed with dozens of the lit pillars.

Not a tavern anymore, but a bachelor's den: plush periwinkle settees, layers of mismatched cream rugs and exotic, overflowing bottles of wine and crystal decanters filled with spirit. Wood and leather and the spiced aroma of incense: frankincense and bergamot.

I hadn't even noticed how earsplitting the endless howl of wind against the mountains and whistling through the mighty trees had been until it was gone. Until that roar was replaced by indulgent silence.

And the veil of frigid cold. Despite the elevation and season here in Vorst, Len's magic had doused the entire hideaway in temperate air. A light breeze rustled the loose, patterned curtains. It felt like honey in my lungs.

And still, my blood chilled as my mind stuttered to a halt.

Not magic.

And before me . . . not Len. Or, still Len, but perhaps as he'd looked thirty years ago. Virile, wise, angular. The kind of man you'd trust with your life, but perhaps not your woman.

Len, the White Crow . . . whoever he was, was no mere sorcerer.

"What *are* you?"

# ABOUT THE AUTHOR

**Kate Golden** is the bestselling author of viral sensation and debut novel *A Dawn of Onyx*. She lives in Los Angeles, where she works in the film industry developing movies with screenwriters and filmmakers. When she isn't telling stories, Kate is an avid book reader, film and TV fanatic, and functioning puzzle addict. She and her husband can be found hosting cozy game nights and taking hikes with their sweet pup, Milo. You can keep up with her on Instagram at Kate GoldenAuthor and on TikTok at Kate_Golden_Author, where she is known to post both spicy and heartbreaking teasers for her upcoming books.

Ready to find
your next great read?

Let us help.

**Visit prh.com/nextread**

Penguin
Random
House